SISTERS OF SORCERY

Mindless Ones couldn't talk, and they didn't dance.

What they did do was smash things that got in their way or fry them with deadly optic blasts.

"Ardina! Watch out!"

But it was too late. The Mindless One had been gathering its power for a blast strong enough to stun a being made of pure cosmic energy.

The ray caught Ardina full in the face, rendering her senseless. To Patsy's horror, the golden woman plummeted out of the sky, the impact of her body forming a grave-deep crater in the sand and causing tremors to ripple through the island's bedrock. As the Mindless One turned its attention to Patsy, the legion's remnants scooped up Ardina and ran for the portal.

Everyone knows cats have nine lives. Patsy had already used one up, so she supposed she only had eight. She was pretty sure she was about to cash in one of those now as the Mindless One's second optic blast sent her flying face-first into the surf. It was all Patsy could do to watch helplessly as the portal irised out of existence.

Then blackness did the same to her vision, and she welcomed the release.

MARVEL UNTOLD

Sisters of Sorcery

MARSHEILA ROCKWELL

ACONYTE

FOR MARVEL PUBLISHING

VP Production & Special Projects: Jeff Youngquist
Associate Editors, Special Projects: Caitlin O'Connell and Sarah Singer
Manager, Licensed Publishing: Jeremy West
VP, Licensed Publishing: Sven Larsen
SVP Print, Sales & Marketing: David Gabriel
Editor in Chief: C B Cebulski

Special thanks to Darren Shan

First published by Aconyte Books in 2022

ISBN 978 1 83908 165 1

Ebook ISBN 978 1 83908 166 8

Cover art by Fabio Listrani

Distributed in North America by Simon & Schuster Inc, New York, USA
Printed in the United States of America
9 8 7 6 5 4 3 2 1

ACONYTE BOOKS

An imprint of Asmodee Entertainment Ltd
Mercury House, Shipstones Business Centre
North Gate, Nottingham NG7 7FN, UK
aconytebooks.com // twitter.com/aconytebooks

For Jeff, Arthur, Frances, Max, Holly,
and David. You're why I do this.

And for the "witches" they burned, and
the ones who have since risen from
those ashes, sisters of sorcery, all.

PROLOGUE
Sky-Island, Somewhere
Above the Atlantic Ocean

"Umar and Hecate, Demeter, Jord." Clea spoke the words of Papa Hagg's spell with authority, one hand raised to the sky and wreathed in power, the other clutching the mystic knife she had just driven into the Silver Surfer's side.

"Blazing Apalla, guide my reach forward.
On the edge of a knife blade, at the crest of a storm,
By moontide and lifesblood, come forth and take form!"

As she spoke the final words of the incantation, Clea tore the knife from the Surfer's side and a blinding light erupted from the wound, as though the cosmic being were bleeding radiance.

Then that radiance began to coalesce and take form. Light flowed like liquid gold as the Power Cosmic shaped itself into sinuous curves, then hardened muscles, and finally, a wild mane of hair. A golden woman now stood before them, the feminine reflection of the Silver Surfer. Even though Clea had known intellectually that the spell would create another being from the Power Cosmic the Surfer had bled, she hadn't expected… this. Nor the rush of mingled satisfaction and guilt that accompanied the breathtaking woman's magical birth.

And then the woman spoke.

"I… *am*. Ardina. I am called Ardina."

She was also the fourth and final female counterpart needed to cure the corrupted Defenders – or the Order, as they were now calling themselves – before they destroyed not only themselves, but the entire Earth.

Ardina had been created to counterbalance the Surfer's power. Jennifer Walters, aka She-Hulk, was there to subdue her cousin, the incredible Hulk. Namorita was there to handle her own cousin, Prince Namor of Atlantis. And Clea herself had been recruited to deal with her husband, Dr Stephen Strange. Together, the women would free the Defenders from the curse their old enemy, Yandroth the Foul, had placed upon them with his dying breath.

If they failed, they wouldn't live to see the consequences.

Clea smiled grimly. Things were about to get interesting.

An untold distance away in the Dark Dimension, Umar the Unrelenting lounged on the Azure Throne watching the scene unfold as the Flames of Regency cavorted about her head. Those who worshiped her as goddess were rare outside of the Splinter Realms, so when her name was invoked from afar, her curiosity was piqued. Seeing that it had been the ever-rebellious Clea who had called upon her power had only deepened Umar's interest.

The profound pleasure she had experienced in handing her brother Dormammu such a resounding defeat to reclaim her throne had begun to wane, and she was becoming bored and restless. Her thoughts had lately turned toward the other dimensions that made up the Archipelago of Anguish and Redemption. After all, if she could best the dread Dormammu, sucking away his power in the process, what couldn't she do? Maybe it was time to reunite the Splinter Realms – under *her* rule. With the mystical golden battery Clea had just created for her combined with Umar's own nearly limitless strength, interdimensional conquest was well within her grasp.

Umar smiled hungrily. Things were about to get interesting.

PART ONE

CHAPTER ONE
A Private Beach Somewhere in the South Pacific

"Cheese and crackers!" Patsy Walker – aka, the super hero Hellcat – exclaimed as she stretched on her beach blanket in languorous imitation of her namesake. "Isn't this the life?"

Her companion, Ardina, a golden woman formed of the Power Cosmic with no need of stretching, languorous or otherwise, merely shrugged. Unlike Patsy, she sat well back from the lapping waves, under the shade of a large striped umbrella. This was not out of concern for her complexion, but because tropical sunlight reflecting off her metallic skin tended to blind everyone in her immediate vicinity. Patsy had taken to wearing dark glasses around her since their vacation had started, even indoors.

"If you say so, Patsy Walker. Though I am not sure I understand what snack food has to do with the quality of human life."

"Only *everything,*" Patsy laughed as she turned on to her stomach and propped herself up on her elbows to peer through oversized brown lenses at her friend. Ardina sat ill at ease on her lounge chair, still very much the newborn despite having been alive for several months, and not yet having mastered the concepts of either relaxation *or* snack food in that time. "But that's beside the point. Samantha's parents have given us the run of their private beach, along with the use of their palatial beach house and its staff, for as long as we need. It's a quality of life that few humans are afforded, even me with my so-called America's Sweetheart mercantile empire. We should enjoy it while we can."

"Yes, it was kind of your friend's parents to allow us to stay here. To allow me to stay here," Ardina replied.

"Valkyrie is your friend, too," Patsy insisted. Ardina only repeated both her earlier shrug and her words.

"If you say so, Patsy Walker."

Patsy was about to remind the golden woman that saving the world from the Order had garnered her quite a lot of friends when the fine hairs on the nape of her neck stiffened and the sweat on her skin cooled to goosebumps, though there had been no accompanying salt-laden ocean breeze.

She sat up, her blue and yellow Hellcat costume manifesting on her body without conscious thought, an instinctive response to a threat she sensed but could not see. She scanned the tree line for movement, but there was nothing.

Then her demonsight flared.

"Look alive," Patsy said, all trace of humor gone from her voice. "We're about to have company."

No sooner had she finished her warning than a portal opened above the bright cerulean of the ocean. For the barest of moments, all it yielded was a glimpse of a twisting darkness that made Patsy's stomach churn. Then it began spewing demons.

Patsy had spent a fair amount of time around demons. She had married a half-demon, Daimon Hellstrom, died and gone to Hell, been rescued and returned to life, and even brokered an alliance between Mephisto, Hela, Pluto, and her now ex-husband Daimon, to save Hell from falling under Dormammu's control.

So, yeah, she knew a thing or two about demons.

She knew they came in all shapes and sizes. Some were human-sized flies that walked upright and carried big sticks. Some looked like they'd just stepped off the set of a low-budget lagoon-monster movie. Many of them had multiple sets of something – arms, mouths, eyes. Some had horns, or tusks, or claws, or all those things, and more. And some defied description in human terms, with unrecognizable body parts arranged in unfathomable patterns.

And she knew they had all sorts of different abilities. Some could breathe fire, or spit poison, or cast spells. Some flew, some burrowed, some oozed. Most were just dumb brutes, but some were diabolically clever, able to reason, calculate, and execute plans of their master's or even their own devising.

Patsy knew one thing more about demons.

If you were a Hellcat who could not only sense demonic energy auras, but also track them across great distances, then for you, demons had something akin to a mystical scent that was unique either to them, or to their particular hell dimension and its particular ruler.

And these demons gave off a mystic stench like a hunk of skunk-sprayed limburger that had been fished out of a restaurant dumpster and left to sit in the hot sun for a day or two. They didn't smell all that great in the physical sense, either.

Patsy was pretty sure she recognized that foul odor, and then a giant, crudely formed humanoid figure with a single glowing red slit of an eye shambled through the spinning portal, and she was certain.

A Mindless One. An unthinking denizen of the Dark Dimension whose sole purpose for existence was to destroy whatever happened to be in front of it. These were Dormammu's minions.

But what the hell were they doing here? Was ole Dormouse trying to conquer Earth *again*?

Why here, though? The island held nothing of value to an invading force, unless you were in some bizarre need of sand or palm trees. Knowing him, he'd picked this spot specifically to annoy her.

It was working.

Well, she supposed she could beat the reason out of one of his minions after she'd dispatched a few and brought the odds down to something a little more reasonable than twenty to two.

Patsy knew she couldn't go toe-to-toe with the Mindless One, so she didn't even bother with it at first. She launched herself at the first demon within range of a cartwheel and a roundhouse kick, one of the lagoon-monster variety, with weird fins protruding from its bulbous green head. Her foot connected with the vertical slits she assumed served as its nose, and the creature collapsed into a Christmas-colored heap, pawing ineffectually at its face with webbed claws and burbling its pain to the impassive sky.

But Patsy didn't have time to appreciate her handiwork, or even to wonder what an aquatic-seeming demon was doing henching for the guy with a fireball for a head. She was already slicing past another pair of demons that looked like minotaurs, with tusks covered in either drool or venom, or maybe both.

Didn't matter – a single swipe left them on the sand and she was on to the next one.

Well, the one after that. A golden blast from somewhere above and behind Patsy's right shoulder drilled into the pig-nosed demon she'd targeted and sent it slamming back into one of its axe-wielding buddies. A quick follow-up blast sent that duo through the portal opening, and it didn't look like either of them would be in any shape to make a return trip.

Fifteen to two. That was a bit better.

Patsy focused on the gaggle of demons to her left, since Ardina had gone airborne and seemed to have the right flank covered. Wait, was it a gaggle? She knew there was a collective noun for a group of demons – she'd used it in her autobiography *Gidget Goes to Hell* – but the word escaped her at the moment.

Unlike the demons themselves.

Another pig-nose went down beneath her front claws, while a bat-winged one harrying her from the air caught her back claws across its abdomen, grounding its flight. A big one in the rear of the group – no, legion, that was it – was barking orders while a mismatched pair in front of him dropped to what Patsy assumed were their knees and began firing short red bursts at her from weird rifles she'd never seen before. Not that it mattered. She had long since learned how to shift just…
so, causing mystical energy to glance off her aura, twisting and sliding out of magic's grip like the proverbial greased hog. Or, in this case, cat.

*Hell*cat.

She danced a deadly ballet with the barrage of energy pulses, every sandy ciseaux and pirouette twirling her closer to both the weapons and their wielders. A quick feint to the left took her out of the line of sight of one of the demons, his unfortunate partner becoming a momentary obstruction between him and his target.

A fact that didn't seem to bother the creature in the slightest as he simply shot *through* his counterpart, the hellish red beam exploding out of the other demon's gut, leaving a gaping hole and sizzling innards in its wake.

Patsy wasn't quite fast enough to dodge the unexpected bolt, and it cut and cauterized a stinging path across her thigh as she somersaulted away, berating herself for getting hit. All this lovely lazing around had slowed her reflexes. At least she wouldn't have to worry about the wound becoming infected.

Another of Ardina's golden blasts of cosmic power finished off the remaining shooter, taking off two of the order barker's six arms in the process, and then there were ten. Approximately.

So, five to one. Patsy grinned. She'd take those odds in Vegas.

Well, if it weren't for that pesky Mindless One.

She had almost allowed herself to forget about the lumbering hulk, mostly because it hadn't actually done anything yet. It had popped out of the portal, waded slowly through the churning, pink-tinged water and up on to the beach, then shuffled through the sand like Exhibit A from a hardcore slow-vs-fast-zombie debate. Then it had just stopped and stood there, a win for the dark horse team backing stationary zombies.

Patsy had almost allowed herself to be lulled into a false sense of security, to think that she would have time to deal with the Mindless One after the demons that were actually in motion had been taken care of. As if it were just going to stand there patiently and wait for her to finish ripping through the ranks of its fellows before politely inquiring to see if she had any room left on her dance card.

Almost.

She knew better.

Mindless Ones couldn't talk, and they didn't dance.

What they did do was smash things that got in their way or fry them with deadly optic blasts. And since this one wasn't doing a Hulk imitation, that could only mean…

"Ardina! Watch out!"

But it was too late. While Patsy had been waltzing her way across the beach, leaving destruction in her wake, the Mindless One had been gathering its power for a blast strong enough to stun a being made of pure cosmic energy.

The ray caught Ardina full in the face, rendering her senseless. To Patsy's horror, the golden woman plummeted out of the sky, the impact of her body forming a grave-deep crater in the sand and causing tremors to ripple through the island's bedrock. As the Mindless One turned its attention to Patsy, the legion's remnants scooped up Ardina and ran for the portal.

Patsy launched her cable claws at the rearmost of the demons as she raced to beat its comrades to the spinning black aperture that led, she was certain, to the mind-bending landscape of the Dark Dimension. But this one was an oozer, and the thick cords of steel alloy sailed right through its jelly-like form.

Cursing, Patsy vaulted over the demon Ardina had maimed, grabbing up its sundered limbs and using them as throwing sticks. She hit one of the less ephemeral demons square in the back of its third head, knocking it off balance. Unfortunately, it was one that held Ardina's arms and its momentum carried it, the golden woman, and three other demons through the portal with a high-pitched, truncated scream.

Everyone knows cats have nine lives. Patsy had already used one up, so she supposed she only had eight.

And she was pretty sure she was about to cash in one of those now as the Mindless One's second optic blast caught her full in the back, sending her flying face-first into the surf. Stunned and hurting like she hadn't since maybe before she'd donned Greer Nelson's cast-off catsuit, it was all Patsy could do to roll over far enough to keep her nose and mouth above the water. She could only watch helplessly as the Mindless One trundled after the demons and the portal irised out of existence behind it.

Then blackness did the same to her vision, and she welcomed the release.

Patsy woke, spluttering and choking on a mouthful of salty water. She scrambled to her feet, grimacing in pain as the warm sand shifted unhelpfully beneath her. She was momentarily relieved to see from the tide's minimal progression inland that she hadn't been out of it for too long.

Long enough, though.

Ardina had been kidnapped, and she'd done nothing to stop it. Worse, she'd practically abetted the perps by being so caught up in taking out the cannon fodder that she hadn't understood what was really happening until it was too late.

Whoever had organized Ardina's abduction had studied Patsy and had figured out that one of her greatest weaknesses was thinking she didn't have any. Granted, she'd survived the torments of Hell and come out stronger and scrappier than ever, but she was hardly invulnerable. The spasming muscles and protesting nerves all along her spine were a humbling reminder of that fact.

Patsy limped through the tugging whitecaps until she was near where the portal from the Dark Dimension had materialized. Normally, she was able to detect and use dimensional wormholes. She called them her cat flaps, like the pet doors that let domestic cats come and go as they pleased. But much to her frustration, she sensed nothing where the portal had been, and no others close to it that she could use to follow Ardina and her captors.

Not that Patsy was in any condition to mount a one-cat rescue operation. An argument could be made that she might need rescuing herself, if the nerves currently screaming at her from the vicinity of her lower back were any indication.

A low groan from near where Ardina had taken her swan dive caught Patsy's attention. She had thought all the legion members who could leave had done so before the portal closed, but it looked like they didn't believe in "No Demon Left Behind."

Carefully moving closer, Patsy saw the formerly six-armed demon sitting in a pool of greenish blood, looking dazed. Apparently, Ardina's blasts weren't quite as good at cauterizing the wounds they created as some of the demon weaponry was. The demon was at the tail end of bleeding out.

Better make its last moments count.

Employing her cable claws once more, she sent them flying, like steel extensions of her will, to wrap around the demon's throat, cutting off its pitiful moaning.

"I know you can speak; I heard you playing general earlier. So, here's the deal. You're dying, and I don't have the skill or, honestly, the inclination to do much about that. What I *can* do is make it quick. *If* you tell me why your hell bros took my friend. That work for you?" She didn't need to ask who had sent them, considering where they'd come from.

The demon considered for a moment, then nodded.

Patsy let the cables loosen just enough for it to speak.

"Kill the cat. Bring the battery."

"Battery?" Patsy repeated, nonplussed. "Battery for what?"

The demon shrugged and shook its head. Apparently that information was above its paygrade.

Patsy sighed. She didn't particularly relish what she had to do next, even if it was ultimately a kindness, something the demon hardly deserved.

Tightening the grip of her cable claws again, Patsy took a deep breath and was about to put the pitiable creature out of its misery when it took a great heaving sigh, shuddered, and went limp. The cables went slack. Patsy gently lowered the demon's body to the sand before extracting her claws, glad that this was one death not being added to her tally.

She didn't know what Dormammu needed Ardina's cosmic energies to power, but whatever it was, there was no chance in any hell that it was good. And no chance that she could handle it alone; Hellcat might be a creature of magic, but she had no aptitude for its use.

Luckily, Patsy knew someone who did. A sometime Defender and the Sorceress Supreme of the Dark Dimension who, if Patsy remembered correctly, also happened to be Dormammu's niece.

Clea Strange.

CHAPTER TWO
The Dark Dimension

Clea sat alone in the rebel headquarters, staring at the magical map spread out before her on the roughhewn table. She had long since dismissed her council of generals and lieutenants and now she shared the quiet war room with only dust and doubt.

Her eyes passed over the constantly shifting landscape of the map section that depicted the Never Hills, its random undulations still able to make her nauseous if she spent too much time contemplating them. Luckily, they weren't her focus tonight. Umar's forces didn't like fighting there any more than her own did, so it had yet to become a battleground of any significance, but she knew that might not last. Nothing about the Hills ever did.

She spent a few brief moments studying the shining barrier that separated the most populated areas of the Dark Dimension from the territory of the Mindless Ones. The sinuous golden line was as bright and strong as ever, with no visible areas of thinning. She breathed out a quick sigh of relief before moving on.

Her attention this evening was centered on Umar's palace, the seat of the Azure Throne. It had proved nigh impregnable during the many times it had changed hands over the millennia, from Dormammu to Umar and back again, a constant tug-of-war on a scale that made mortal sibling rivalry look like ants fighting over crumbs.

The palace remained the one obstacle to the rebellion's success. It had never been taken by force, only by magic and treachery – the magic Dormammu's and the treachery Umar's. But now that Dormammu had been defeated, perhaps for good, and Umar had absorbed his power, it did not look like there was much chance of the royal residency falling to those means, either.

Clea almost wished she could reach out to Stephen for guidance, as she used to… but no. It was at least partially Doctor Strange's fault that Umar had been able to defeat her brother Dormammu in the first place, as Earth's Sorcerer Supreme had thrown in with the power-hungry Faltine goddess to protect his world from the Dread One. He hadn't appeared to give much thought to the fact that doing so would subject Clea's own world to Umar's reign once again, and Umar was easily the more malicious of the two despots. That Stephen could so casually and callously put his own world's needs above hers was perhaps understandable.

It was not necessarily forgivable.

As she contemplated the palace-in-miniature, chin on her fist, Clea gradually became aware of a buzzing sensation in her ears. Irritated and thinking it a swarm of the small insects that plagued the underground hideout, she brushed at the sides of her head, yet came away with nothing but strands of silvery-white hair for her trouble.

Realizing it was not bugs bedeviling her, Clea sat up straighter and tilted her head to the side, concentrating on the sound. It wasn't a drone so much as white noise, a pattern of static like what came over the radio during her and Stephen's car rides when they passed through a tunnel. After a moment, she thought she could make out words.

Clea… need you… hurry…

A moment further, and she recognized the voice.

Patsy Walker. Hellcat.

Clea hesitated for the space of a breath, recalling that the last time she had left her rebels and their battle to free the Dark Dimension from the Dread Siblings and come to the Defender's aid, she had been promised assistance in return. Assistance that had yet to materialize.

But ultimately that didn't matter.

Patsy wouldn't be calling out to her unless she was in dire straits and truly needed her. Clea had no choice but to answer her old friend's call.

Patsy needed caffeine, acetaminophen, an ice pack, and the darkest, quietest room in the Parringtons' beach house. Some anti-nausea medication couldn't hurt, either.

Using her psionic powers had often left her with killer migraines in the past. Then the Titanian priestess Moondragon, who had fostered those abilities within Patsy and trained her in their use, had seemingly taken the powers away again in a fit of pique.

Telepathy had never really been in her bag of psionic tricks even before Moondragon's temper tantrum had emptied it out, but Patsy had always been able to sense when her loved ones were in danger. She supposed it wasn't telepathy so much as empathy, but the connection was the important thing, not the words used to try and define it.

Clea was someone Patsy loved; she'd been a dear friend since Hellcat's earliest days with the Defenders, and a source of great comfort when Patsy's mother had died. Though their paths had diverged greatly since their attempt to start that team anew with Valkyrie, she still knew Clea would do anything for her, just as she would do anything for the purple-loving Sorceress Supreme.

And that they would both do the same for Ardina, who wouldn't even be here if not for them.

Unlike telepathy, empathy wasn't just a one-way street controlled by the mind reader, not when both parties shared in the emotional bond. It went both ways, and it was that two-way connection that she hoped would allow her to reach Clea across whatever vast distances that separated them.

So, she concentrated on those ties of love and friendship, remembering past battles against the likes of Mandrill and his Fem-Force, the Order, even Satan himself, calling to mind images of Clea and the feelings of warmth and affection those memories evoked.

There.

Patsy didn't know where "there" was, exactly – probably the Dark Dimension – but distance was meaningless where love was involved, and her questing mind had brushed up against the bright silver and violet beacon that was Clea's essence, like a moth seeking flame, minus the whole burning to death part.

She homed in on that lodestar and, focusing every ounce of psychic ability still left to her, began sending the same message toward it over and over.

Clea… need you… hurry…

She only stopped when the pain in her head threatened to split her skull in two, not knowing whether her call had been heard or not, but too exhausted from the effort to attempt anything else for now.

Patsy supposed if this didn't work and Clea didn't show, she would have to enlist the help of Doctor Strange. Not an appealing thought; she knew how strained his and Clea's relationship had been of late. Long distance romances were hard. They were even harder when they spanned dimensions instead of globes.

Add in one party's rampant womanizing, and, well… maybe she should try contacting the Surfer instead? He could travel between dimensions, and he did sort of have a vested interest in Ardina, her having been the Eve created from his cosmic Adam's rib, so to speak. Though he hadn't exactly forgiven any of them for that little stunt yet…

Yeah. This better work.

As she lay back on the world's most comfortable sectional couch, which had probably cost as much as the annual royalties she made on all her books combined, Patsy's back twinged painfully again. That Mindless One had really done a number on her, but she knew she'd been lucky. It could easily have killed her, especially catching her unawares like that. As it was, she was definitely going to need some downtime to get back into fighting trim.

Which in turn meant it was unlikely that she'd be able to accompany whoever she ultimately did wind up getting to go after Ardina.

All the more reason for it to be Clea.

Patsy went back to trying to send her message across dimensions through her tenuous empathic link with her friend, doing her best to ignore both the pain in her head and in her lower back.

Clea… need you… hurry…

"By the Vishanti, Patsy, there's no need to shout."

Chapter Three

Clea sat on a chair matching the much-vaunted sectional, waiting for the Parringtons' doctor to finish his examination of Patsy. It had always been a source of secret ironic amusement to her that Stephen Strange, at one time a celebrated neuro-surgeon who had kept the moniker of "Doctor" when he began his study of the mystic arts, had taught her few healing spells beyond those lending temporary strength to an ally so they could continue to fight. What curative charms she knew she had learned herself, but neither those nor the basic first aid training she'd received at Stephen's insistence would be enough if her friend had some type of spinal-cord injury.

Patsy had suggested summoning a healer from amongst the Defenders or Avengers, but the only other individual Clea knew for certain could both heal with any ability and get here quickly was Norrin Radd, and the Silver Surfer was not taking her calls these days. He had still not forgiven her for plunging a knife into him to create Ardina, even though he acknowledged the necessity of it afterward. Clea supposed she couldn't blame him – she *had* literally stabbed him in the back.

"What about Doc Strange?" Patsy had asked, and Clea's answering snort had been both derisive and incredulous.

"Stephen? No. His focus is on putting broken universes and timelines back together these days. Not so much people."

Or hearts, she'd thought, but hadn't said.

So, they had called the non-superpowered doctor and now she sat looking around the well-appointed room while the doctor poked and prodded Patsy's back, hips, and legs, eliciting several quickly suppressed gasps of pain. Bowls of fresh purple asters adorned every table, blooms that weren't indigenous to this tropical climate, but which Clea knew were common to the Centerville, California area where Patsy had grown up. Stephen had never cared much about money, conjuring it as needed, but Clea imagined it must cost a lot of it to have flowers flown in every day just to make Patsy feel more at home.

Finally, the doctor stood and turned so he was facing both Patsy and Clea.

"Nothing is certain without imaging, but from my physical examination, I'd say it's more likely muscular than nerve-related, probably a strain. The symptoms should fade on their own, especially if you're not particularly active." He looked pointedly at the formfitting Hellcat suit Patsy still wore. "For now, I'm going to prescribe some muscle relaxers, painkillers, and partial bedrest. It won't do your back any good to stay on the couch for a week watching your favorite soap operas, but you do need to take it easy for a while. No gallivanting off saving the world. Doctor's orders."

"Thanks, doc," Patsy said, sitting up slowly to shake his hand, obviously trying not to wince as she did so. "Sort of figured that's what you'd say."

At Clea's raised eyebrow, she shrugged.

"Not my first rodeo," Patsy said, which clarified absolutely nothing.

The doctor gave a perfunctory chuckle as he scribbled something illegible on his prescription pad. Then he handed the slip to Patty and showed himself out.

As soon as she heard the door close, Clea turned back to Patsy. "Alright. Now that I've been reassured that you will not, in fact, be permanently paralyzed if I don't rush you off to the nearest operating table or summon any Defender or Avenger with even a smattering of healing ability within a hundred-mile radius of us, I will 'chill out' as you suggest and you can tell me the story again. And don't leave out a single detail. Anything can wind up being important information once placed in its proper context."

"…and that's all I could get out of Dormammu's goon before he went to whatever afterlife demons get sent to," Patsy finished up, taking a drink from one of the sweating glasses of lemonade currently leaving wet rings on the Parringtons' glass-topped coffee table. A uniformed member of the house staff had, unbidden, brought out a tray holding a pitcher and glasses before disappearing back into the woodwork. "I don't know what he wants Ardina for, but it can't be good, for her *or* you."

"A reasonable enough conclusion to draw," Clea agreed, eschewing her own glass of the too-sweet, too-tart drink after one sip. "But an incorrect one."

Patsy had swapped out her catsuit for a more comfortable graphic tee and sweats after the doctor left, so Clea could clearly see her brow furrow beneath wisps of red hair as the other woman frowned at her.

"How do you mean?"

"Though I don't recognize any of the demons you described, I can tell you that they were not Dormammu's minions."

"But, the Mindless–"

"I didn't say they weren't from the Dark Dimension. Clearly they were. But they didn't take Ardina on Dormammu's orders. They couldn't have, because Dormammu is no longer ruler there. Umar is." Clea couldn't keep her mouth from twisting around the name, even more sour on her lips than the lemonade had been. She hoped her explanation would be enough to get Patsy to drop the subject. Umar was – and likely always would be – a touchy subject for Clea.

"Ah," Patsy replied, nodding. But her frown didn't dissipate entirely. "I met her once, when ole Dormouse had kidnapped me so I couldn't rat him out to Mephisto. She was suspended upside down in a magic bubble trap at the time. Still cool as a pickle and twice as spicy, though. Tried to manipulate me into letting her out. Didn't work, of course.

"Well, at least not on me," Patsy amended. "Obviously someone let her out at some point if she's the one running the show now."

"Indeed," Clea responded, trying vainly to steer the conversation elsewhere before–

"Say," Patsy said suddenly, her demeanor brightening. "You're Dormammu's niece, right? So doesn't that make Umar your…?" She trailed off in sudden embarrassment. "Oh. Right."

Clea's smile was tight as she willed her cheeks not to flush.

"Yes. Dormammu is my uncle. Which makes Umar… my mother."

It was still hard to force her mouth around those words, all these years after learning the truth. She'd grown up worshipping Umar and Dormammu, just like everyone else in the Dark Dimension. Then Stephen had come along and revealed the siblings' true natures, how they cared nothing for the people, instead manipulating and using them as mere props in their constant tug-of-war for the throne. Fueled by that knowledge, Clea had joined the rebellion against Umar and become its leader, determined to depose the evil tyrant once and for all.

And then she had discovered that evil tyrant was her own flesh and blood. That the tyrant had, in fact, given birth to her. Clea's whole world had turned upside down, and she'd been haunted by a burning question ever since: If she came from such evil roots, how could she herself be good?

"Hey, I'm really sorry–" Patsy began contritely, but Clea waved her words off with an impatient gesture.

"My lineage is hardly your fault, Patsy," she replied, determinedly tamping down both the nagging question and her worries about its answer. Whatever else she might be, she wasn't her mother, or her uncle, and that would have to be good enough for now. "Whether it's of relevance to this situation remains to be seen. But one thing is clear: if my mother plans to use Ardina as a battery, then she most likely has one of two goals. Either she's decided to stamp the rebellion out for good, or…"

"Or what?"

"Or she's decided ruling the Dark Dimension isn't enough for her anymore and has set her sights higher. Which means the entire Archipelago of Anguish and Redemption could be in danger."

"That… sounds bad," Patsy replied, her face squinching into an exaggerated look of dismay.

Clea laughed, appreciating her friend's attempt to lighten the mood.

"You have a rare gift for understatement," she replied, her smile sitting easier on her lips this time. Still, it quickly faded.

If Umar was indeed planning a campaign against the entire Archipelago, it was more than Clea and her rebels could handle alone. Umar's power had already swelled to god-like levels with her absorption of Dormammu's magic. If she also had the Power Cosmic to draw upon – a thought that was almost too horrifying to contemplate – Clea wasn't sure who would be able to stop her.

But she had to try. Her lineage wasn't any more Clea's fault than it was Patsy's, but it *was* her responsibility. Not to mention Ardina's wellbeing. The woman wouldn't even exist if it weren't for her.

"If we …" she began, then stopped herself as Patsy shifted her weight on the couch and tried to hide a wince. "If I am to stop her, I am going to need help. Very powerful help."

"Doc?" Patsy ventured again, her tone not particularly hopeful.

"Not a chance," Clea replied flatly. "Umar wouldn't be in a position to conquer anything if Stephen hadn't aided her in overthrowing Dormammu. Whether it was under duress or not, he is literally the last person on Earth I would ask for help right now."

"OK, then. No Doc. Then who?"

"I have just the person in mind."

That person was the Scarlet Witch. Doctor Strange himself might well have trouble besting her when it came to magical power these days. Clea had worked with her once long ago when they were both less accomplished and more naive. They had bargained with Hela, the Norse goddess of death, traveled to Niflheim, and battled frostlings and fire-trolls, all to try and reassemble the shards of Eric Masterson, who had been a stand-in for the thunder god Thor at that time. Wanda Maximoff had been the one who, in the end, had figured out exactly how to do that, though she had doubted herself every step of the way.

Clea knew that Wanda's power and confidence had only continued to grow from that point, and her hexes could alter the fabric of reality itself. She imagined that even with Ardina's power bolstering her own, Umar would have a hard time combating that.

She hoped so, anyway.

Closing her eyes, Clea prepared a quick incantation to summon Wanda. It wasn't exactly polite to pluck a fellow magic-user out of her daily life and transport her suddenly from there to here without getting her permission first, but dire times sometimes called for ill-mannered actions. She'd already spent more time than she could spare making sure Patsy was in no immediate danger of death or permanent injury.

"From whence the Scarlet Witch doth abide,
Winds of Watoomb bring her now to my side!"

"Oh, no, Clea!" Patsy exclaimed in alarm, her face losing all color. "You do *not* want to do—"

It was, of course, too late.

With a sound like a strong wind scattering autumn leaves and a rising chill to match, Clea's call was answered.

But to her surprise and Patsy's evident relief, it was not Wanda Maximoff who answered her summons, but Wanda's old teacher, Agatha Harkness.

Or, rather, Agatha Harkness's ghost.

"Hello, Clea, my dear. So nice to see you again after all this time. Wanda is currently… indisposed. Is there something I can help you with?"

If not for the fact that she was translucent and floating in midair, Agatha could be an older version of Clea herself, summoned from some far-distant, far more conservative future. The older sorceress sported the same silver hair as Clea, but whereas Clea's was long and flowing, Agatha's was short and more severe, parted in the middle and brushed back in lofty wings that accentuated her aristocratic features and haughty eyebrows. Like Clea, Agatha favored shades of purple. But while Clea's own clothing tended to be more formfitting for ease of movement, like the magenta and lilac leotard she now wore, Agatha's long, prim dress, with white lace at collar and wrists, was considerably more demure. A cameo depicting the Three Graces at Agatha's neck and a shawl the color of fine wine about her shoulders finished off the picture of a frail old woman holding onto the past.

Of course, Agatha was hardly frail. Far from it. She was rumored to be older than Atlantis, and her knowledge of magic surely rivaled if not surpassed Stephen's, though she practiced witchcraft as opposed to the mystic arts. A trivial distinction, since their disparate methods still yielded the same results.

"I don't understand," Clea said, a bit nonplussed by the appearance of the witch's shade. She hadn't seen Agatha since Dormammu had kidnapped the old woman and her then-student, Wanda, in one of his many unfruitful bids for revenge in response to one of his many earlier defeats. The old woman had been decidedly more corporeal at the time. "I summoned Wanda. Why did you… manifest? Also, are you… *dead*?"

"To answer your first question, let's just say that all of Wanda's calls are being forwarded to me for the time being and leave it at that, shall we? To answer your second, for the moment, yes. But you of all people should know that dead hardly means powerless." Agatha's rigid smile invited no further interrogation.

That didn't stop Patsy.

"Why don't you tell her the whole story, old woman?" the redhead asked, her tone accusing and inexplicably angry. "That Wanda lost it, killed you, and practically destroyed the Avengers before they could get her under control? All because you wiped her memory so she'd forget her kids, who never actually existed in the first place?"

Agatha's smile widened, though probably not as much as Clea's eyes.

Clea had no idea what Patsy was talking about, but it sounded as delightfully intricate as the plot of one of the daytime serials she and Wong sometimes enjoyed back at the brownstone when Stephen wasn't at home. She'd been largely unaware of Wanda's unfolding drama, so caught up had she been in her own.

But now Clea understood Patsy's earlier alarm. The sorceress had seen the damage Wanda could do when she lost control of her powers; if the Scarlet Witch had been so far gone as to kill her beloved mentor, it was frankly amazing there was still an Earth for any of them to be standing here having this conversation on.

"If Clea had time for that tale, I imagine she would have used a telephone rather than a summoning spell." Agatha turned her attention to Clea, effectively dismissing Patsy. "Isn't that right, dear?"

"Actually, I would *love* to hear that story. Sadly, you are correct, and time is of the essence. The Days of Wanda's Life will have to wait for an occasion when Umar isn't planning on using our friend to facilitate interdimensional conquest."

"And what is it that you were hoping Wanda would do for you, had she been able to answer your summons?" Agatha was all business.

"Join me in standing against Umar. She has absorbed her brother Dormammu's powers and is more puissant than she has ever been. And she's kidnapped Ardina, who is formed of the Power Cosmic, seeking to augment her power even further. I created Ardina using a spell and knife given to me by Papa Hagg when we were facing off against the Order." Again, Clea felt guilt well up inside her at the memory. What right had they to bring Ardina forth from the Power Cosmic solely for Earth's need, as though the golden woman were merely a tool to be used and not a sentient being with thoughts and feelings of her own, just as the Surfer was?

"Yes," Agatha responded, interrupting Clea's spiral of self-reproach. "The four corrupt Defenders needed four pure counterparts to return themselves and the world to balance, I remember. Go on."

"Wanda has bested the Dread Siblings in the past, and she's the only one I can think of strong enough to help me stop a supercharged Umar."

"And Stephen–?"

"–is not an option," Clea finished firmly.

Agatha's eyebrows rose an inch or two.

"Hmmm. Seems I missed more being dead than I had realized," she said musingly, as if to herself. Then her gaze sharpened, and her smile took on a calculating quality.

"Well, no matter. I have more than one student, and Earth has more than one Sorcerer Supreme."

CHAPTER FOUR

Stunned silence greeted the ghost witch's words.

"Whatever do you mean?" Clea finally asked, wondering if death had addled the old woman's mind. It would be perfectly understandable, especially if that death had come at the hands of a witch who could rewrite reality. A witch who had been both a beloved student and a cherished friend. "There can only be one Sorcerer Supreme at a time."

"Oh?" Agatha asked, one of her eyebrows arching so high it almost reached her hair. "I should think that if Wanda's episode has taught the magical community nothing else, it at least exposed the lie that any edict governing the use of magic is truly immutable. Laws, as they say, were made to be broken."

Clea had no response to that. Luckily, Agatha didn't seem to expect one. She continued as if she'd merely delivered her opinion on the state of women's fashion these days rather than having undercut the foundations of all magical learning. Then again, Clea supposed it hadn't actually been Agatha who had done that. It had been Wanda.

"That being the case, the idea of multiple Sorcerer Supremes existing at the same time is hardly a scandalous suggestion. However, I am speaking of a woman who wore the Eye of

Agamotto before Stephen. Her name is Margali Szardos of the Winding Way. As you can imagine, she's very skilled and wields a great deal of power. And the student I mentioned is Holly LaDonna. She was originally Wanda's pupil, back before the children… happened. Then she became my student. She's both adept and eager and I believe she'd be an asset to your mission. I'd be happy to make introductions. Though of course we'd go to them, as opposed to summoning them here. Manners, you know."

Clea ignored Agatha's implied reproach. To be fair, it wasn't as if she'd pulled the old woman away from her life, since she technically didn't have one at the moment. One would think she might actually be grateful for the company, considering.

A former Sorceress Supreme and, reading between the lines, an untested apprentice. And Agatha had pointedly not volunteered herself. Dead might not mean powerless, but it did generally mean less powerful, so the ghost's reticence came as no real surprise.

Still, this was not the sort of aid Clea had been hoping for. Not even close.

But they had a saying on Earth that beggars couldn't be choosers. She would have to take what she could get.

"That would be lovely, Agatha, thank you."

"Excellent. Is there any business you need to finish here before we depart?" She pointedly did not look at Patsy. Clea got the feeling that the redhead had annoyed her, and that she was not one to brook annoyances.

Patsy didn't wait for Clea to speak.

"Go. Save the world. Dimension. All the dimensions. Whatever," she ordered, making a shooing motion. "I texted Val, and her mom is on the way here to look after me even as we speak, so chances are high I will need rescuing next. The sooner you leave, the sooner you'll get back."

Clea couldn't help but smile at her often hotheaded, always bighearted friend.

"You're sure?"

"Does cheese go with crackers?"

"...yes?" Clea hazarded, not at all certain. Stephen hadn't been one for keeping snack food on hand. If it weren't for Wong, he probably wouldn't bother with a refrigerator or pantry at all.

"Darn tootin'. Now, get! You're blocking my view of that overcompensating TV screen, and my favorite show is about to start," Patsy said, forced cheerfulness evident in her voice. She made no move toward the several remote controls lined up like soldiers on the coffee table near the lemonade tray.

"Oh, and Clea," she added softly, "don't get dead."

Before Clea could open her mouth to respond or say goodbye to her friend, Agatha uttered a string of words she couldn't quite hear. The world blurred and spun, then quickly righted itself.

Clea was used to teleporting via various means, so she wasn't particularly disoriented. Still, it was customary to give your passengers warning before hurtling them through space-time. And Agatha had the gall to scold *her* about manners?

They were in a clearing next to an old-fashioned carnival wagon, though there was no matching carnival in sight. The sun had just cleared the tops of the eastern mountain range and shone brightly in the crystal blue sky, warming her skin and fading Agatha's spirit to little more than an outline. Birds chattered and sang as they flitted amongst the trees. The smells of pine, wet grass, flowers, and rotting wood mingled together like a perfumer's Frankensteinian experiment, but it somehow managed to be a delicate, ephemeral scent instead of the olfactory assault it should have been.

It was beautiful. Charming, like something out of one of Stephen's books of fairy tales and folklore.

But the fairy tales Clea had read were usually about witches, and they were seldom the good kind.

"Welcome to Germany," Agatha said.

"Bavaria, to be exact," a woman spoke from behind Clea, her words oddly accented and her tone cold. Almost as cold as the knife blade Clea felt pressing into her throat. Clea hadn't heard her approach, which meant the woman was one of three things: incredibly stealthy, a magic-user, or both.

"But don't get comfortable," the sneaky, knife-wielding sorceress added. "You won't be staying."

Clea didn't get comfortable.

Instead, using the martial arts and self-defense lessons both Stephen and his manservant Wong had drilled into her during her time on Earth, Clea kicked one foot back until she met her attacker's shin, then scraped it down the length of the woman's leg as hard as she could, finishing the maneuver off by stomping on her attacker's unprotected instep.

Even as her leg was moving, her elbow was also in motion, as Clea took advantage of the woman's slackening grip to swing it up and behind her, planting it somewhere in the general vicinity of her attacker's cheek. She thought she heard a crunching sound – broken teeth? – but couldn't be sure because she was already spinning away, preparing to call upon the Flames of Faltine.

The incantation died on her lips at the sight of the woman who'd spoken.

Before her stood a woman with sun-kissed skin and wavy brownish-red hair, much of it hidden beneath a red kerchief tied around the crown of her head. She wore large golden hoops in her ears, a peasant blouse, and a bright blue skirt. She was barefoot, and unsmiling. Blood trickled from the corner of her mouth, smearing onto the back of one hand as she reached up to wipe it away.

What momentarily stayed Clea's tongue was not the bloody evidence of her handiwork, but the translucent image of another woman superimposed over the kerchiefed one. She wore the same features and unwelcoming expression, sans the fat lip, but seemed to stand taller. Her skin was that odd shade of green people here called chartreuse, and she wore a golden cap with spiraling ram's horns on either side, covering green hair several shades darker than her skin. Her flowing white dress billowed slightly in a wind Clea could not feel. Ornate knee-high boots completed her ensemble.

So, this was Margali Szardos? But which woman? The one who seemed to be human or the one who seemed to be something else entirely?

Clea thought she knew.

"That will be enough of that, ladies," Agatha admonished.

When the woman replied, both mouths moved.

"Agatha Harkness. It's been a long time. Though not long enough, apparently, if you're bringing attack dogs to my door." Clea bristled inwardly at that, but she refused to give the abrasive woman the satisfaction of a visible reaction. "I don't think we've seen each other since that whole debacle with the 'Alakazam Squad' and Ego the Living Planet, or whatever it was His Hubris insisted upon being called," Margali said, shuddering in delicate distaste.

Agatha made a noise that might have been disgust or accord. Possibly both. Clea didn't know the old witch well enough to be sure.

Margali gave Agatha's ghost a critical onceover. "You're looking rather insubstantial these days."

"I could say the same for you, Margali," Agatha replied tartly, gesturing toward the green wraith. "Why don't you drop the illusion? It's not as if it's fooling either one of us."

Margali shrugged.

"You never know who might show up at your doorstep, what they might be peddling, or who they might have been sent to kill. Better safe than sorry, no?" She gestured meaningfully at her lip.

After a moment, the woman in the kerchief began to fade and the one with the horns became more solid until soon only one stood there. Her eyes blazed yellow, with no irises and no whites. The hostile expression both women had worn remained on her face, though the blood was gone.

"But if you're going to criticize me for using illusions, Agatha, perhaps you might explain why a witch of your ability, who could take on any guise she likes, chooses to look like an old hag? And why you keep up that facade even in death?"

Agatha's shade laughed at that.

"I'd hardly go so far as 'hag', thank you kindly," Agatha replied. Again, Clea wasn't sure if the affront in her tone was real or sarcastic. "I choose to present myself as an old woman because I *am* an old woman, Margali. Older than Atlantis, they say. I've lived a long life, and I'm not ashamed to display the toll of those years on this human flesh. We all pay it eventually, even those of us whose lives are magically extended.

"But more to your point, surely you've noticed that

women past a certain age become invisible here? Once your childbearing and rearing days are done, they think you have nothing more to offer. This is a Western mindset, of course. Other cultures tend to revere their elders. As should we all.

"But there are advantages to being invisible, underestimated. Because when you do finally choose to show your claws, they sink that much deeper."

"Now, that's a philosophy I can appreciate," Margali declared, smiling in dark amusement. Clea found that she preferred the hostile expression. "Well, we might as well get on with it. Come join me for morning tea in my wagon. You can tell me what favor you've come to ask, I can demur, and we can all get on with our day. Though I might be willing to read the future for you before you go... Clea, isn't it? Seems like a peek through time's veil might make your trip worthwhile, after all."

She shooed Clea before her toward the rickety steps at the back of the wagon, telling Agatha to be polite and use the door like a living person when the ghost witch would simply have phased through the wagon wall.

Clea was a bit nervous having the woman behind her and out of her sight, but she did as she was bidden. She reached out for the door handle, but it turned before she could touch it and the door swung inward. Clea took a deep breath, then crossed over the threshold and into Margali Szardos's Sanctum Sanctorum.

She didn't know exactly what she had been expecting, but it wasn't this.

Stephen's Sanctorum held magical tomes with provenances stretching back millennia, many not even from this planet, or this dimension. Likewise with the many artifacts and working items he kept there. And, of course, there was the plush, high-backed chair where he liked to think and meditate, and that Clea had had to pull him out of, spent and world-weary, more times than she could count.

Margali's wagon was nothing like Stephen's inner sanctum. For one thing, it was cramped; if Agatha weren't incorporeal, there might not actually be room for all three of them to stand with any regard to personal space.

A small, round table took up the bulk of that space, with a chair on the door side and another chair opposite. A long, black cloth embroidered with moons and stars covered the table. At its center sat a crystal ball. To one side of the ball was a tarot deck, to the other, a teapot with two cups and saucers. Clea could see steaming tendrils rising from the teapot's spout, though there was no hotplate nearby on which it might have been heated.

One wall bore a framed carnival poster depicting two trapeze artists swinging toward one another over an audience that seemed an impossible distance below, with no net separating them. One a blonde woman, and one a blue demon, complete with a pointed tail. Clea recognized him as Nightcrawler, one of the X-Men, but she didn't think she knew he'd ever been in a circus, nor what his connection to Margali might be. Curious. Beneath the audience, in gold lettering, read the words "Herr Getmann's Traveling Menagerie."

The other wall bore a small window, its curtains drawn. Colorful, mismatched rugs overlaid the floor and one another with no discernable eye for pattern or design.

Behind the table was a waterfall of silver beads. Clea assumed Margali's sleeping quarters lay on the other side. Or perhaps her torture chamber. As Patsy would say, the jury was still out on that.

The entire place stank of patchouli, and Clea had to suppress a sneeze.

Margali brushed brusquely past her to take her place in the far chair, gesturing for Clea to take the other. With a sidelong glance at Agatha, Clea did so.

"So, what favor have you come to ask from Margali Szardos of the Winding Way, hmm? I assume if you needed someone hexed that Agatha still has enough power as a specter to accomplish that easily enough. And you are no mean sorceress yourself, from what I understand."

Margali leaned forward, placing her green chin on her green fist and gazing at Clea with those unnerving, unblinking yellow eyes. Clea found it impossible to tear her own gaze away, or to blink herself, and her eyes soon began to burn and water under Margali's scrutiny. Finally, the other sorceress broke eye contact and sat back in her chair, which creaked beneath her in mild protest.

"No, you would only be here if what you want is something only Margali Szardos can provide, yes? Now, I wonder, what could that be?"

"Stop playing games, Margali," Agatha snapped, what little patience she was known for having apparently been exhausted. "You know as well as I that there's only one thing you have better access to than I do. At least in my current state."

"And that is … ?"

"Amanda Sefton. Or should I say, Jimaine Szardos?"

Margali froze at the name, and it only took Clea a moment to work out why. Amanda Sefton was the young woman who ruled Limbo. If her real name was Szardos, then she was related to Margali. Closely, given the woman's reaction. Hadn't she heard somewhere that Margali had a daughter?

Marvel Untold

Margali's eyes became slivers of blazing balefire. Clea tensed, inwardly cursing both Agatha's bluntness and her temper. Of course the witch didn't have to worry about angering Margali – she was already dead. Clea quickly ran through a series of incantations in her mind, settling on the Crimson Bands of Cyttorak. Sometimes, as Stephen liked to say, defense was the best offense, and the bands would keep Margali from being able to attack. Hopefully long enough for the other two women to talk some sense into her, though Clea was beginning to think the heat death of Earth's universe might happen first.

"What do you want with my daughter, you old–"

"Oh, for pity's sake, woman. Just stop. I'd hardly have come to you if I wanted to harm her. Quite the opposite, in fact."

The slits widened, becoming matched marquis-cut citrines. "Go on."

"I think Clea is better equipped to explain than I," Agatha replied, and two sets of eyes, one murdered and one still slightly murderous, turned toward her.

"As the Winding Way is part of the Archipelago of Anguish and Redemption, you will no doubt be familiar with the Dark Dimension, another 'island' in the chain, and the never-ending struggle between Dormammu and his sister Umar for its control."

"Of course I am," Margali snapped, eyes narrowing again. "What has that to do with Amanda? Or me?"

"Umar recently defeated Dormammu, and in the process was able to absorb his power, increasing her own to deific proportions. And she has apparently tired of ruling only the Dark Dimension. She has set her sights a little higher this time, and has captured a woman formed from the Power Cosmic to ensure that her own supply of power is more than up to the task."

"'Higher' meaning…?"

"The entire Archipelago. The Winding Way and your daughter Amanda's realm of Limbo included."

"Ah."

Margali said nothing more, but her blank eyes clouded over, taking on a faraway cast as her thoughts appeared to turn inward. She was silent for so long that Clea feared she might have astral projected to the Dark Dimension herself to ascertain the truth of Clea's words.

In the ensuing silence, Clea heard her own breathing, and Margali's. She heard the birds outside the wagon go quiet as the wind rose, the silver beaded curtain tinkling and the china teacups clinking together in response. The small wagon shook with some of the stronger gusts, and Clea had to wonder if the wind was natural or magical in origin. Margali made no sign of hearing it either way.

Finally, the green-skinned sorceress's eyes cleared. She looked first at Clea, and then at Agatha, her face expressionless. Clea knew what her answer was going to be even before she spoke, though, and her heart sank.

"While I do appreciate your warning, ladies, Amanda can take care of herself. And the Winding Way cannot be ruled, per se, as it is much more than just a physical place. Nothing Umar could do to it would keep it from my reach, so I see no reason to put myself in jeopardy pointlessly by trying to defend it." Her next words were directed at Clea. "Agatha's already dead. Are you so eager to join her? Because this mission *will* result in your death."

"You saw that in your crystal ball, did you?" Clea retorted, angry at the other woman's lack of compassion, her own heart breaking for all those an unstopped, unstoppable Umar would leave decimated in her wake if Clea couldn't find help.

"No, child. I didn't need to consult the spirits for that. Any fool with an ounce of common sense or self-preservation could deduce the same. But I'd be happy to read your fortune for you before you leave, regardless. Margali Szardos does not break her promises."

She gestured to the table.

"Pick your poison, hmm? Tarot, tea, or the much-maligned All-Seeing Sphere?"

"Why don't you try reading Amanda's future instead?" Agatha suggested.

"I told you, old woman–"

"If she's truly in no danger, then what's the harm?"

Margali glared saffron daggers at the ghost witch and Clea was suddenly glad she wasn't sitting between the two of them.

"Perhaps you're not quite as convinced of her ability to take care of herself as you claim?"

"Are you suggesting Margali Szardos is a liar?"

Agatha laughed. For the first time, Clea was struck by how substantial a sound the old woman's derision could make coming from incorporeal lungs.

"Oh, I am more than suggesting. Show me a magic-user who doesn't traffic as much in deceit as in arcane mysteries, and I will show you a charlatan. But you're deflecting. You're not at all sure, are you?"

Margali's lips thinned.

"Or prove me wrong. Please. It happens so rarely and is so refreshing when it does." Agatha's tone hardened, and it was clear she was done with suggestions. She expected to be obeyed. "Draw… a… card."

If possible, Margali's face paled to an even lighter shade of green and her lips compressed until they were almost nonexistent. Clea could tell she was afraid of Agatha, even in death. But she lifted her chin proudly, picked up the deck of cards, and shuffled three times in quick succession. Then she drew the top card and laid it on the black tablecloth.

The card depicted a pregnant woman on a plush throne in the middle of a fertile field, trees and a river at her back, a crown of twelve stars upon her head, a wand in her hand, her gown dotted with lush pomegranates. The card was upright facing Clea and Agatha, which meant it was upside down facing Margali.

"The Empress, reversed," Agatha said. "A bad mother – you, obviously. News to no one. Draw another. For Amanda."

Glowering, Margali did so.

Another woman, this one in profile, a sword held tall and straight in one hand, the other outstretched as if waiting to receive something. Butterflies crowned her head, and dark storm clouds gathered at her feet.

"The Queen of Swords, upright. The bearer of the Soulsword rules Limbo. Normally that would be Illyana Rasputin, the former Magik. Perhaps it will be again. But for now, it is Amanda. The cards are being very literal today. One last card. What happens to Amanda if you don't help stand against Umar?"

Margali flipped the final card over.

A tower in flames, its domed top being struck by lightning. Two figures fell from its height, one a woman wearing the same sky blue as the Queen of Swords. Fire was shown raining from a black sky.

"The Tower, upright. Total chaos and destruction. It doesn't get much clearer than that, Margali. Without your aid, Limbo will fall, and Amanda with it."

Margali's skin was such a pale shade of green that it was hard to tell, but Clea thought she had gone ashen at the sight of the card. Clea wasn't very familiar with the tarot, but it seemed to her that tools of divination seldom spoke with such clarity. She wondered if Agatha was somehow manipulating the cards. She *had* basically just said trickery was a magic-user's greatest weapon.

But Clea didn't want to trick Margali. She wanted the other sorceress's help freely given.

Still, she couldn't afford to anger Agatha's ghost, either.

Margali was about to gather the three cards back into the deck when, on a hunch, Clea stopped her.

"Wait! Draw one more card. They've shown you what happens if you don't help. Ask them what happens if you do."

Clea thought she could feel two needles of fire drilling into her from where Agatha hovered, but she didn't dare look that way. She kept her attention on Margali, and on the cards. If Agatha had been manipulating them, hopefully Clea's addition of a question would throw her off enough that the answer could actually be trusted.

Margali looked suspiciously at Agatha, as if she was beginning to share Clea's doubts, and drew a fourth card.

Two figures crowned with flowers faced each other, large goblets in their hands, which they looked to be in the middle of swapping with one another. One figure wore the sky blue of the Queen of Swords. The other figure wore a tunic dotted with what might be pomegranates, if you squinted hard enough. They stood beneath a caduceus and a lion's head flanked by wings.

"The Two of Cups, upright. Harmony and balance," Agatha announced, though the card's positive meaning was not reflected in the witch's dour expression. "In your and Amanda's case, I suppose, it would mean… reconciliation? Unless there are some impending nuptials of which I am unaware?"

In an aside to Clea, Agatha said, "What an insightful idea, dear!" Her tone was not complimentary in the slightest. There were regions of empty space that were warmer.

Some of the tension went out of Margali at the sight of the fourth and last tarot card. Clea didn't know if it was fight or fear, but either way, it seemed promising, so she pressed the small advantage she'd won.

"Mother-daughter relationships are always fraught, even under the best of circumstances. But unless either mother or daughter is beyond redemption, I think keeping a connection open between them is worth whatever it takes," she said, aware that she was being a complete hypocrite in doing so. She hadn't spoken to her own mother in years, and what few words they did exchange were inevitably on a battlefield. "After all, you only ever really get one chance to be a mother to your daughter, or a daughter to your mother, even in a world full of magic where death is not always an end."

Margali laughed sardonically, a sound that took Clea by surprise and almost made her jump. "Spoken like a daughter who has cut off her mother, or a mother who has done so to her daughter. But true for all that."

Then she pushed her chair back and stood.

"Very well then, ladies. You have convinced me. Margali Szardos will join your effort!"

"Three cheers," Agatha muttered, but Margali had ducked beneath her silver beads, letting them drop behind her with a clatter, and Clea doubted that she heard.

She returned in her more human-seeming guise, carrying a

long wooden staff that was easily as tall as she was, capped with a glowing yellow stone suspended in a gilded cage. Clea fancied it a third eye.

"I am ready," she announced, unnecessarily.

"Where to now?" Clea asked Agatha.

"We need to collect Holly."

"And where is she?"

The world was already blurring, and the witch's response seemed to stretch along with reality, the words drawn out and mired in the muck of magical transit. But Clea had no trouble understanding them.

"Whisper Hill."

CHAPTER FIVE
Whisper Hill, Upstate New York

Agatha let out a long-suffering sigh.

"It's simply impossible to get good help these days."

It was the middle of the night here, and they stood before the ruins of a large manor house, illuminated by a low-hanging gibbous moon. Blackened and scattered timbers gave mute testimony to a violent explosion in the not-too-distant past. Just visible beyond the mounds of rubble was a small cemetery, its headstones jutting up like crooked teeth, gray and dying. It seemed undisturbed by the nearby cataclysm.

"I'm so very sorry, Agatha," came a contrite feminine voice from behind them. "It was Nicholas Scratch, pretending to be you. Ebony and I knew him for a fraudster right away, and he imprisoned us in the basement. But the others were fooled, and he lured them here – the Salem's Seven and the Fantastic Four – intending to sacrifice them to Shuma-Gorath, He Who Sleeps But Shall Awaken, in exchange for his resurrection. His plan was foiled, but…"

Clea and the others turned to see a short young woman with neon pink hair standing there in an oversized gray sweatshirt emblazoned with the words "This Witch Don't Burn," ripped blue jeans, and nondescript sneakers, all stained with soot. She gestured to what remained of the once-grand structure.

"…well, as you can see, there was considerable collateral damage. Ebony and I barely managed to escape. We've been living in the caretaker's shed, trying to salvage what we can from the ruins and waiting for your return."

As she spoke, a black cat – presumably the aforementioned Ebony – appeared out of the midnight mists and wound itself about her legs, purring. She picked it up, stroking its fur as it nestled against her, its yellow eyes staring hard at Clea and Margali. It did not acknowledge Agatha's presence.

"I'm really sorry, Agatha," the young woman repeated. "I know this place meant a lot to you."

"Don't trouble yourself, Holly, dear. One of these days, I will be forced to tear Nicholas limb from limb," she replied cheerily, "just as he did to my lovely home. But Whisper Hill isn't just my home, it is a part of me, and so can no more truly be destroyed than I can."

"You're not actually indestructible, Agatha," Margali reminded her with a sidelong look.

"No, but I do appear to be very hard to get rid of, don't I?"

Margali snorted in apparent disgust, but she didn't argue the point.

During their exchange, Holly's eyes had grown wide, and her mouth had formed a silent, shocked "O". At first, Clea thought it was because of the older witches' verbal sparring, but then she realized the girl, who was facing them, was also facing the ruins of Whisper Hill behind them, and that's where her gaze was focused.

Turning, Clea was astounded to see the manor pulling itself

back together, timbers flying from their scattered landing places to align, damage-free, into their proper places as joists and trusses, beams and studs. As if time were rewinding in this one spot only, the manor was framed out, walled, and roofed in a matter of minutes. Then lights blazed on in every window of the stately three-story home and its high, Gothic tower.

Agatha smiled.

"There. That's better."

She floated over to the steps leading up to the front veranda, then gestured theatrically to the house. The front door swung open.

"Welcome to Whisper Hill."

Once inside the grand abode, Agatha led them into a stuffy parlor and bade them sit on the velvet-covered couches that faced a roaring fireplace. Above the mantle was a portrait of Agatha holding Ebony. It could have been painted yesterday. Or three hundred years ago.

"The house is spelled, of course," Agatha said, apropos of nothing, except perhaps Holly's still-huge eyes as she tried to take everything in, her astonished gaze roaming over every inch of the room.

"It's a perfect replica. Just as it was the last time you were here with me," she said to her mentor in an awed whisper.

"Exactly, my dear," Agatha replied, and Clea was surprised that the old witch's sarcasm was even thinly veiled. She must be fond of Holly. Or fonder of her than she was of Clea and Margali at any rate, which was perhaps not a particularly high bar to clear. "That's rather the point. Unfortunately, when one jaunts about with super heroes, one can expect a certain measure of destruction to follow, and this is hardly the first time Whisper Hill has been demolished. I'm sure it won't be the last. So, the house has been spelled to rebuild itself whenever it senses my presence. It took some sticktoitiveness, to be sure – that sort of spell requires rare components and takes days to cast properly – but the results are well worth the effort, don't you think?"

"Yes, Agatha, you should definitely look into a job on one of those home improvement shows if someone ever bothers to resurrect you. You can call it 'Restoring Relics' or some other such nonsense. But here and now, I fail to see how you patting yourself on the back for some parlor trick furthers our goals. If we're to recruit the girl, recruit her already!" Even though she still wore her human form, Margali's eyes blazed yellow and Clea thought she could detect the faint scent of sulfur. She wondered if the two sorceresses might yet come to blows, though how much harm they could cause one another, with Agatha being dead, so both less powerful and less vulnerable, was anyone's guess.

Clea decided to keep it a guess.

"This is Holly LaDonna, is it not, Agatha?" she asked, turning her smile on the pink-haired woman who sat on the couch with her. Margali had, unsurprisingly, chosen to sit on a separate divan, alone. They both looked completely out of place in this stuffy, formal setting.

"Forgive my rudeness. Being dead tends to strip one of one's bondage to social conventions after a while."

Clea gave Margali a warning look. Now was not the time to debate what Agatha's rudeness quotient had been when she was alive. Margali, who had leaned forward, taking a breath to presumably do just that, blew it out instead in a frustrated sigh and sat back on the couch, arms crossed and glowering.

"Holly, allow me to introduce you to Clea Str–" Agatha caught herself quickly, then continued on smoothly, the lapse barely noticeable. Unless you were expecting it. "Clea, Sorceress Supreme of the Dark Dimension, and Margali Szardos of the Winding Way, the once and perhaps future Sorceress Supreme of Earth. Ladies, I present to you my apprentice, Holly LaDonna."

Clea was beginning to think Holly's eyes would never shrink back to their normal size. Surely, as Agatha's pupil, she'd seen her fair share of magical wonders? And hadn't she first been Wanda's student? She'd been there when Wanda and the Vision's impossible children had been born, the same children whose erased nonexistence had caused one of the most powerful witches in Earth's history to lose her grasp on accepted reality. And now she was doing the bidding of the spirit of one of the casualties of that incident. Truly, nothing should surprise the girl by now.

Holly reached out and excitedly clasped Clea's hands in her own, startling the sorceress.

"It's such an honor to meet you! To meet you both," she said, smiling at Margali to make sure she knew she was included. Margali's glower deepened. "Clea, the way you used that mystic gemstone to transmit your fight with Umar to all the people of the Dark Dimension, so they could see her true nature for themselves and stop believing in her, weakening her enough to defeat her… simply masterful! And you, Margali, swapping bodies with your daughter to trick and defeat Belasco… genius! Truly!

"Agatha has had me study all the most powerful magic-users on Earth and elsewhere, especially the women. There really are so few who aren't considered just straight-up villains; it's *so* stereotypical. The world is so afraid of women having power, but what have the men done with it? Constant wars, widespread poverty and famine, global warming? They know they've bungled it all, and they're afraid we'll show them up if they give us an inch. It's infuriating!"

Margali laughed, seemingly genuinely amused.

"Down with the patriarchy?" she asked sardonically.

"Oh, you'd better believe it," Holly replied, raising an enthusiastic fist.

Margali looked at Clea and at Agatha's ghost hovering over Holly's shoulder. Her smile was feral. "Oh, I *like* this one."

"As long as she understands we're not going to smash the patriarchy," Clea cautioned, trying to rein in the girl's enthusiasm a bit. She appreciated it, of course – who wouldn't be pleased to be included in Agatha Harkness's list of powerful sorceresses? But this wasn't about her. "We're going to smash Umar."

"Umar?" Holly fangirled excitedly. "She's amazing, isn't she? How many times has she defeated her brother Dormammu and given Doctor Strange a run for his money? I–"

Margali snorted. "We're not joining her fan club."

"Well, no, of course not, but 'If you know the enemy and know yourself, you need not fear the result of a hundred battles.'" Holly shrugged. "*The Art of War*. Hard to argue with a master."

Margali burst out laughing. "A Sun Tzu-spouting feminist for an apprentice? Leave it to Agatha Harkness!"

As Margali's laughter continued, Clea supposed that Holly's demeanor, no doubt heavily influenced by Agatha, made a certain amount of sense. The old witch had been through the trials at Salem, and Clea knew she'd aided several war efforts over the years. Agatha was no stranger to the cruelties of either warfare or oppression, so it was only natural that she would teach Holly to take what was useful from one to combat the other.

"I don't know where you found this one, Agatha," Margali said, wiping tears from the corners of her eyes in the wake of her mirth, "but she is a, what is it you say? A peach? She is a peach. I would hold on to her."

Agatha, who had been silent throughout their exchange, just smiled.

"Well, Holly, before you agree to anything, you should know exactly what you'll be getting yourself into," Clea said, preparing to give the exuberant young witch a quick summary of their mission and its many dangers.

"Do *you* know?"

Clea frowned.

"Know what?"

"Exactly what we'll be getting into? I mean, beyond the obvious – going to the Dark Dimension and fighting Umar, who I'm assuming has gained some allies or some other RPG buff, if you need a Smash Squad to help take her out."

"Well, no, but–"

"OK, then," Holly said, grinning and holding her hand out to shake Clea's. "You need me? That's all I need to know. I'm in."

Clea found the young woman's blind faith more than a little disconcerting. She was used to leading, but not as an authoritarian – she asked for and appreciated the input of her rebels, and she had been called out on bad decisions more than once. To have someone who knew her only by reputation buy into her plan and join her cause so willingly, without question… well, if it were anyone else besides the guileless Holly LaDonna, Clea might be suspicious of their true intent. But Holly wore her intent on her sleeve.

Clea took her hand and returned her smile.

"Well, then. Welcome to the Smash Squad, Holly."

Holly was upstairs in her room packing a few essentials for interdimensional travel, whatever that meant. Margali had laughed again when she said it and asked if she were packing *The Art of War*, to which Holly had replied that she didn't need to; she had it memorized.

Clea took the opportunity to ask Agatha some questions about their newest recruit.

"She's very passionate, and seems intelligent and quick on her feet. But has she ever actually been outside this dimension?"

Agatha, who'd been petting Ebony with a ghostly hand as the cat lay on the back of the couch, looked up. Clea hadn't realized until now how piercing her blue eyes were. And was she becoming more substantial? Perhaps being here in her home, a source of power, strengthened the tether that held her to her old life.

"No, but I believe there are other benefits to including her that outweigh her interdimensional inexperience. Umar is not likely to be very familiar with the type of magic Holly wields, for one thing, which gives you a much-needed advantage. She's also an... unconventional thinker. And this will be a good test of her abilities."

"Test?"

"Yes. To determine her readiness to continue down the Witches' Road." Agatha was very matter of fact about her designs on Holly's life and her haughty expression dared Clea to challenge her.

Clea dared.

"So, we're to act as your... exam proctors?" Clea asked,

affronted and truly angry for the first time. She rose from the couch, both to better give vent to her growing fury and to better prepare herself for possible retaliation. Agatha was not one who brooked challenge lightly. "Do you think this is a game? This is my home we're talking about. My home, and Ardina's life. It's not some situation for you to manipulate for your own benefit. I came to you – to Wanda – for help, not to be used in some scheme to determine your apprentice's fitness for duty. Going up against Umar won't be some trial by fire for her if she isn't already fit for this mission. It will be a death sentence."

Margali was following the exchange with interest, leaning forward with her elbows on her knees and her face cupped in her hands, but she made no move to intervene. Clea noted that she seemed to be enjoying the spectacle of someone besides herself sparring with Agatha. Well, perhaps Clea could give the other sorceress some pointers in that regard.

"Calm yourself, child." Agatha radiated boredom, but her tone was dangerous. Clea did not think the Crimson Bands of Cyttorak would hold a spirit, but the Winds of Watoomb had brought her here, so they must have some effect on the old witch's ghost, surely? "She has skills that will be an asset to you, and she has agreed to go, knowing the dangers as well as any of us can hope to know them. If I choose to use her performance during this mission as a means of judging her readiness for advancing her studies, who are you to object?"

Before Clea could respond, Agatha, grinning ferally, went for the kill.

"Remember, *I* will only be observing from afar. *You* are the one placing her in danger."

Clea wanted to argue, to point out that the girl would never enter this undertaking if she didn't have Agatha's blessing, but the old witch was right. And Holly was clearly an adult who could make her own decisions. Who was Clea to gainsay either one of them?

"She's got you there," Margali opined, with obvious relish.

"Yes," Clea replied with a defeated sigh. "Yes, she does."

Holly chose that moment to reappear wearing a small backpack in the shape of a teddy bear, and she, Clea, and Margali took their leave of Agatha, Ebony, and the almost sentient Whisper Hill.

Or at least, they tried to.

Clea grasped the hands of her companions, readying herself for the journey to the Dark Dimension. Her ability to travel there easily from Earth was sometimes hampered, perhaps because she, like Umar, drew some strength from the people and the dimension itself. And while she knew there were spells that could teleport multiple people across dimensions, she seldom had cause to attempt them.

Perhaps it was the adrenaline still running through her system from her argument with Agatha. Perhaps it was her own self-doubt. Or perhaps her connection to her home truly was too weak. Whatever the reason, when Clea closed her eyes to center herself, concentrated, and then cast the teleportation spell, she felt an electric shock run through her, like the time she'd accidentally touched part of the exposed prong of a plug that hadn't been pushed all the way into its socket. Other than that, nothing happened.

Holly, who had closed her own eyes on Clea's advice and had not yet reopened them, asked innocently, "Are we there yet?"

"Not yet."

Puzzled and annoyed, Clea tried the spell again, with the same shocking but otherwise underwhelming results.

Frowning, she tried another spell. Usually, she didn't have to use an incantation to journey from one dimension to the next, but perhaps with the added cargo, she needed a more potent vehicle.

"My will reverses the Conjurer's Cone,
And the Winds of Watoomb carry us home!"

No sooner had she uttered the last word than she and the other two women were thrown violently backward, their hands coming unclasped as Holly fetched up against the couch in front of Agatha, Margali took out an antique side table with its Tiffany lamp, and Clea herself slammed against the stones of the hearth, narrowly avoiding the fireplace's hungry flames. Dazed, she pulled herself into a sitting position, noticing as she did that there were scorch marks on her palms. A quick perusal showed that the other women bore them as well.

Not only had Clea's spell failed, it had somehow bounced back on the three women, its energy arcing through them and exploding outward instead of creating a portal and pushing them through it. Something was very wrong here. Clea didn't think it was her magic, but she couldn't be sure, and that bothered her more than she cared to admit.

"Are we there now?" Holly asked timidly. She somehow had still not opened her eyes, and now she seemed afraid to.

Clea's answer was grim. "No. And we may not be able to get there."

Holly's eyes shot open and she stared at Clea, obviously shaken. Apparently, the thought that one of her female magic-using heroines might not be able to do something they set out to do had never occurred to her.

Margali climbed to her feet, frowning.

"Are you saying *you* can't get us there or that getting there isn't possible?"

"I'm not sure," Clea said, answering honestly. This was no time to be prideful about her abilities not always being as strong on Earth as they were in her home dimension, no matter how much the thought stung. "Why don't you try?"

The other sorceress side-eyed her doubtfully, her lips twisting in what Clea interpreted as scorn. She gave a nonchalant shrug and climbed to her feet, pausing for a moment to resume her horned, green-skinned appearance, much to Holly's delight. Margali waited for the other two women to link hands and for Clea to take hers, and then slammed the end of her staff onto the parlor floor. The light from the yellow gem exploded soundlessly, enveloping the three women in flames that burned without heat and left no mark, flashing so brightly that Clea and Holly had to let go of each other to cover their eyes.

When the light faded, they were still in Whisper Hill.

Margali's frown deepened. And while Clea was secretly glad to know she wasn't the only one having trouble teleporting to the Dark Dimension, she was also growing increasingly alarmed.

There had to be a way in. There just had to.

"Let me try returning to the Winding Way."

She banged the staff against the floor again, once more blinding her companions and searing their souls.

When Clea was able to blink away the bright spots crowding her vision, she saw a corporeal Agatha holding Ebony, staring down at her with eyes that judged and found her wanting. For a moment, she thought they'd traveled through time, rather than dimensions. Then she realized she was looking at the portrait over the fireplace in Agatha's parlor.

They hadn't moved.

"Limbo, then," Margali snapped, her ire rising.

Clea and Holly were ready this time and closed their eyes, Holly wincing in anticipation of the staff's fiery ablution.

When they opened them again, nothing had changed.

"Agatha?" Clea's voice wasn't yet frantic, but it was getting there.

"Yes?" the ghost asked, eyebrows shooting up in surprise. No doubt she thought her role in this drama ended, her last lines spoken putting Clea in her place. She was most likely right, but Clea had to try.

"Can you get us there?"

She willed the other woman to say "yes."

Agatha shook her head.

"I'm sorry, dear. Bouncing around the globe does take its toll, you know, and I don't have the energy reserves I used to. I am not up for dimension-hopping right now. Don't forget, I *am* dead."

"Of course," Clea replied. She couldn't hide the disappointment in her voice, though she was more than just disappointed. She was crestfallen. Devastated. She didn't know what to do now.

"I can't get through, no matter what I try," Margali said. She'd been trying other spells, while Clea and Agatha talked, to no avail. The sorceress bared her teeth in frustration. Clea was honestly surprised to see she wasn't fanged. "I think Umar has somehow managed to block off the Splinter Realms, barring all entry. Probably all exit, as well."

She looked at Clea with something resembling pity.

"Perhaps we will have to enlist the aid of Doctor Strange after all," she said, and Clea hated to admit that she was probably right.

Clea couldn't get back to the Dark Dimension. Which meant she couldn't rescue Ardina or stop Umar from using the golden woman in her grand scheme of interdimensional conquest. Clea's people would suffer. Ardina would most likely die. Other dimensions would be decimated.

And all because Clea wasn't strong enough to do what must be done.

Her own lips twisted, and she thought she might be sick all over Agatha's expensive rug.

"Well, we needn't go so far as all that, I think," Agatha said.

"What do you mean?" Clea asked. She didn't dare to hope the old witch might have a solution to this conundrum. She wasn't sure she could handle the heartbreak if Agatha turned out to be wrong.

"There is another way into the Splinter Realms."

At Clea's questioning look, Agatha's ghost smiled mischievously.

"Well, out with it, witch," Margali snapped. "My patience is wearing thin."

"Margali, dear, I don't believe you ever had any patience to begin with," Agatha retorted. "Be that as it may, you could still try using the Crossroads."

The green-skinned sorceress blinked her yellow eyes at that, apparently at a loss for words. Whether it was because of Agatha's insult or her suggestion, Clea couldn't tell, but she figured she'd better fill the silence, just in case.

"The Crossroads? Truly, Agatha?" Clea was surprised at the suggestion. The Crossroads was a nexus of dimensions, allowing access to virtually every universe in existence. But it was also a veritable death trap to the uninitiated. "You must know as well as any that if one doesn't know how to properly navigate the Crossroads, then going there is practically a death sentence, because there is very little chance of ever leaving. And I certainly don't know how to travel those roads. Do you, Margali?"

The other sorceress shook her head. Clea didn't even bother to ask Holly.

"Well, it will require a bit more globe-bouncing, and probably a great deal of convincing, but I know someone who does know how to navigate through the Crossroads; she's actually very skilled at it."

Clea pursed her lips in annoyance at the old witch's dramatic pause and Margali started tapping her foot. They had neither the time nor the patience for Agatha's theatrics, but that didn't seem to faze her. Not much did.

"Elizabeth Twoyoungmen of the Tsuut'ina Nation. You might know of her as the Talisman."

Chapter Six
Tsuut'ina Nation Reserve, Canada

The world shifted, and none of them were prepared for the sudden cold that cut through them, slicing through thin fabric and bare skin to the bone, causing first an incongruous burning, and then a deep, unyielding ache. Snow was falling from the night sky in apocalyptic amounts, driven by a vengeful wind. Clea couldn't see Agatha through the blinding white, and Margali and Holly were blurs of green and pink, respectively.

"Agatha!" she yelled. "We've got to get out of this storm! Can't you take us somewhere—"

Suddenly the wind slackened and stopped. Its roar quieted. What snow had been in the air swirled to join the heaped mounds on the ground, but more did not fall. They were still encompassed by the raging blizzard, but its fury could no longer touch them. A shining pink bubble surrounded the three living women, and Agatha floated into its confines to join them.

"About time, old woman," Margali snapped, angrily brushing snow off her horned helm and out of her hair. They were all still wet and shivering. The bubble did not protect them from the sensation of cold, only from the dangers it held. Still, it was a powerful conjuration, given the strength of the storm it sought to buffer.

"Oh, it's not my doing," Agatha replied, unperturbed. "You have Holly to thank for not freezing to death. Yet."

Clea looked over at the pink-haired woman in surprise, and sure enough, she stood with her hands cupped as if around an invisible orb and her lips moving in an inaudible incantation. She smiled at Clea and winked.

"Wonderful," Margali said, her tone indicating that it was anything but. "But, Agatha, you deposited us into the middle of a violent storm, itself apparently in the middle of nowhere."

Clea realized that the other woman was right. Wild places had a certain stillness to them that populated areas lacked, and even in the middle of a blizzard, all she could sense here was the peace of uninhabited earth. She shivered, though not from the cold, suddenly feeling very small and lonely.

"Why are we here?" Margali continued, oblivious. "Where is this Elizabeth, this Talisman, you spoke of?"

Clea thought now would be the perfect time for Twoyoungmen to make an appearance. She was almost expecting it, in fact, given Agatha's flair for theatrics.

But no such dramatic entrance seemed to be forthcoming.

And Holly's smile was becoming strained. Clea wasn't sure how much longer the young witch could keep her spell up. She conjured a winter coat like the one she'd worn in New York with Stephen and some gloves and Uggs for herself, then did the same for Holly, though she was sure to make the other witch's jacket pink instead of purple like hers. She didn't bother with Margali; if the green-skinned sorceress wanted that skin covered, Clea imagined she'd already have conjured warmer clothes for herself.

"I can't be entirely certain," Agatha answered after a moment, slowly. "The Tsuut'ina reserve covers almost three hundred square kilometers of land, and Elizabeth could be virtually anywhere within those borders. I had hoped bringing us somewhere near the eastern border of the reserve and the adjacent city of Calgary would give us a starting point in locating her, as I believe there is currently some conflict over a proposed roadway alignment between the two, on reserve land. That's the sort of thing Elizabeth would be involved with these days, so even if she wasn't around, the people there would know how to find her. Obviously, it wasn't my intent to set us down in the middle of the storm of the century."

There were furrows in Agatha's forehead above her aristocratic eyebrows. Clea didn't know if they were caused by worry, weariness, or anger over being challenged, but this was the first time she had seen the old witch display anything other than confidence, if not outright arrogance. And while she had carefully used qualifiers like "believe" and "hope" in her explanation, she seemed to have studiously avoided using the word "know". Clea thought this might be the first time the crafty shade had ever been completely honest with them. She couldn't help but wonder why.

"So… you don't know where we are, and you don't know where she is?" Margali said, her tone morphing quickly from disbelieving to enraged. "What in the uncountable hells were you *thinking*?"

"Umm… Agatha? Margali?" Holly was trying to break into their conversation, to no avail. Clea realized that her bubble had already shrunk to half its original size. Holly was sweating now, despite the cold, and no longer grinning.

"I believe I have made my thought processes in that regard

quite clear," Agatha replied, the temperature of her tone dropping almost as swiftly as that inside the shrinking bubble. A few snowflakes floated down through Agatha's head, but the ghost seemed not to notice. "I may have overshot my target a bit, which would likely place us in a Canadian military artillery range. I have no idea if it is still active or not."

"You... have... no... idea..." Margali's words trailed off into a thunderstruck silence.

Agatha made the mistake of trying to fill it.

"I *did* tell you I was tired."

Margali's eyes blazed yellow and the sorceress grabbed her staff with both hands, opening her mouth to utter something irrevocable.

"Margali, don't!" Clea shouted at the same instant, preparing a quick Shield of the Seraphim to cast between the sorceress and the ghost.

Neither woman got the chance.

"Will you all kindly just *shut up!*" Holly had fallen to her knees in the snow, back bowed with the effort of keeping her protective bubble active. It continued to shrink as they watched. If Margali hadn't been so angry and focused on Agatha, she probably would have noticed the snow beginning to coat her hair and horns before now, or the wind whistling around them, stirring the skirts of her dress.

If Clea hadn't been so preoccupied with keeping the peace so her mission would not be impeded, she might have noticed the creeping cold beginning to slice at her unprotected skin again. Or Holly weakening and needing help Clea was too preoccupied to give.

If Agatha hadn't been a ghost, and therefore unaffected, she might have thought to warn them their protection was failing.

But probably not.

Clea hurried over to Holly's side, kneeling beside her in the snow.

"Let it go," she said as she put one arm around the young woman's shoulders. "You've done enough. Save your strength."

As the bubble collapsed completely and the wind came howling in with a vengeance, intent on punishing them for having defied it, Clea heard Holly laugh.

"Save it for what?" she asked. "We're not making it out of here. Except maybe as popsicles."

"Of course we are," Clea assured her, trying ineffectually to brush the gathering snow from Holly's pink head. But she wondered if she was lying to the young woman. Or to herself.

Her hands were freezing despite her gloves; she couldn't feel her fingertips. It was the same with her toes. She had started shivering uncontrollably and was having trouble thinking. Could she even cast a spell in this state? Could Margali? It seemed both Agatha and Holly were, as Stephen might say, tapped out.

No, Clea thought. They would prevail.

They *must*.

And that's when the shooting started.

CHAPTER SEVEN

Clea instinctively pushed Holly down, covering the girl's form with her own. The sound of gunfire was something she did not miss from her time in New York; it was unpredictable, jarring, and always accompanied by a brief thrill of fear. She hated it.

Holly's body was stiff and unyielding beneath Clea's, not because she was resisting, but because the temperature had plummeted, and she was that cold. Like a corpse, Clea thought, before shoving that image violently away. She didn't know much about how Earth temperature was measured, but she did know below zero was generally not good. She had a feeling they were long past that.

She could feel her brain starting to shut down, her own body no longer responding to its commands, her thoughts becoming sluggish and confused. She had one chance to save them. If she didn't get this spell out and get it right, she wouldn't get another, and they really might all die.

Then, with every ounce of strength that hadn't yet frozen solid, she forced her icy lips open and called out the only spell she could think of, trying to tweak it to apply to these dire circumstances. She'd seldom attempted twisting the intent of a spell to cover a situation it was not truly meant for. She didn't know if it would work.

But she knew what would happen if it didn't.

"For us under assail, with cold become harm,
Rise Shield of the Seraphim, to protect and to warm!"

Instantly, a glowing dome of yellow appeared over the women, arcane glyphs pulsating across its surface. The wind still blew, and the snow still fell, but the deadly seeping cold began to abate and Clea could hear whatever ammunition was being fired at them pinging off the shield's mystic surface.

Shaking with relief and adrenaline, she pushed herself up into a kneeling position, and Holly rolled out from under her, flopping onto her back.

"You're going to have to teach me that one," she said weakly, and Clea laughed painfully.

"I only just learned it myself."

But Margali seemed to be in better shape than either of them, or else the spell had allowed her to recover her wits faster, for she responded almost immediately by climbing to her feet, planting her staff, and doing the most Margali thing possible.

She attacked.

White hot bolts of bedevilment shot from the stone of her staff, arcing out through Clea's shield like mystic missiles and alighting upon any weapon that had discharged in their general direction.

"Margali, no! Those are soldiers! Peop–!" Clea shouted, but to no avail. Though she was sure Margali heard her, her words had no effect. Instead, a series of explosions, small and large, lit up the falling snow in an undulating line, like an earthbound display of the aurora borealis. But seldom had the famed northern lights been so deadly.

Much to Clea's relief, however, Agatha had landed them in a portion of the artillery range where the soldiers were, in fact, not people. The weapons that had fired at them were unmanned, probably automatically triggered by their mere presence once Holly's shield dropped. Though how they could tell the three women from the piles of drifting snow, Clea wasn't sure. If the weapons system relied on pressure plates, wouldn't the weight of the snow have activated them long before now? Stephen had once called this place the Frozen North. It had to snow like this on a fairly regular basis for the land to have gained such a moniker. And Agatha's exaggerations notwithstanding, Clea very much doubted this was the "storm of the century". No, it didn't make sense for weight to be the trigger, or the weapons would be firing constantly.

But if weight didn't set off the weapons, what would?

Probably anything that *wasn't* frozen. Heat signatures. Which meant…

Too late. Heat was rolling off Margali's staff in shimmering waves as she fired bolt after angry bolt, intent on destroying whomever or whatever had had the temerity to attack her. That heat was far greater than the meager warmth generated by three women. Any artillery batteries that had not yet been triggered would perceive it as an incoming army.

Holly, who was sitting up now herself, had figured it out too. The color of her face was indistinguishable from the snow swirling around it.

"Oh, gods, she's going to get us all killed, isn't she?"

Gunfire erupted around them from all sides, so much coming so quickly that the dome created by Clea's shield seemed to be ringed with fire. Even if she had been at full strength and not half-frozen when she had cast it, her spell might have weakened

Marvel Untold

under such a barrage. And Clea had been nowhere near full strength.

Where bullets had been pinging off its surface before, now they were lodging in the shield. To Clea's dismay, some of the larger ones were slowly forcing their way through, technology versus magic.

It wasn't long before the battle turned in favor of technology.

Clea and Holly yelled at Margali to stop, but the green-skinned sorceress was lost in her fury. It was only when a smaller caliber bullet grazed her arm, leaving a thin red trail, that she seemed to comprehend what was happening. Her staff went dark so abruptly that it was as if all the lights in the world had shut off simultaneously, and Clea was momentarily blind. When she blinked the scene back into focus, her shield had disintegrated. She and Holly threw themselves back to the ground as bullets whizzed over them.

The barrage continued for several more eternally long moments before the firing guns registered that the large heat source had been extinguished. Their mission accomplished, the dutiful artillery returned to standby mode.

When she deemed it safe again, Clea raised her head, then climbed to her feet, helping Holly in turn climb to hers. Margali stood where she had before, several holes torn through the skirts of her dress and the tip of one of her golden ram's horns missing, but otherwise unharmed.

"We need to find someplace safer where we can regroup and figure out what to do next," Clea said. Holly nodded in vigorous agreement.

"I concur," Margali replied grimly. "But I already know what we need to do next. We need to track down and kill a certain ghost."

It was then that Clea realized that the spirit of Agatha Harkness was nowhere to be seen.

Had the old witch brought them all this way, only to abandon them in a fight where she could not be harmed? Was she truly such a rank coward? Clea had a hard time believing it, but Agatha, like Margali, kept her own counsel, and her idea of the greater good did not always match everyone else's.

"We're currently more likely to be killed than kill someone else," Holly piped up suddenly, "so I'd suggest we focus on the 'regroup' part of Clea's plan." She pointed into the storm. "When Margali's own personal war was lighting this place up like the Fourth of July, and Clea and I were playing duck and cover, I saw a building illuminated over that way. I can't imagine they'd have an inhabitable structure out here that didn't have at least a space heater – one that won't trigger a firing squad. Maybe other supplies, as well. I say we head for it."

"That sounds like an eminently practical idea," Clea said, and Margali didn't argue, so they began walking in the direction Holly had indicated. The going was slow, their progress hampered by seeping exhaustion, the triumphant return of grave-numbing cold that bit even through conjured attire, and a stiff headwind. Still, the dark shape of the building Holly had spotted finally came into view.

The young witch had taken the lead once they got that far, eager to show them to her prize, when she took a step forward, then suddenly shifted oddly. Almost as though the ground she had expected to be solid beneath her foot… wasn't.

"Don't move!" an unfamiliar woman's voice shouted from the direction of the building. "Not unless you want to learn the definition of 'unexploded ordnance' up close and personal."

Holly obeyed instantly, which Clea decided could either

be a testament to her intelligence or her gullibility. Clea and Margali also froze, not knowing if their next steps might trigger other "unexploded ordnance" in the area, or even what that meant.

A shape appeared out of the calming storm, resolving itself into the form of a scowling woman with deeply tanned skin and long black braids that swung loose from beneath her fur-trimmed parka hood. Black gloves, jeans, and high, laced boots sporting the same fur trim completed the picture.

"It's a good thing Agatha came to fetch me from camp when she did. Though I'd have come soon enough, regardless. You didn't really think you could stage the equivalent of a magical OK Corral on my peoples' land and not get my attention, did you?"

"Agatha's with you?" Holly asked. There was no disguising the relief in her voice.

"I am, child," Agatha replied, floating into view behind the Tsuut'ina woman. Clea couldn't be sure, but she seemed more translucent than usual, almost as if she were starting to fade. That didn't bode well. "Now, be still and do exactly as Elizabeth says."

Holly became a veritable statue, with only regular white breaths pluming out from her nose and mouth and then quickly dissipating in the cold night air to show she was even still alive.

Clea was impressed by the girl's discipline until she noticed how wide and frightened her eyes were. She exchanged a glance with Margali, who seemed to have come to the same realization as Clea: Holly wasn't doing this of her own accord.

Turning her attention back to Agatha and the Tsuut'ina woman – Elizabeth – she saw that the latter wore a circlet on her brow that shone almost as brightly as her now-glowing eyes. She had her arms out in front of her, one gloved palm pointing skyward and the other facing the ground. With a look of concentration on her face, she slowly raised the upward-facing hand higher while keeping the other hand firmly in place. Holly rose in the air, like some priceless artifact being moved from its museum pedestal by invisible ropes and the world's slowest, most careful crane.

Finally, though, Holly was deposited in the snow next to Clea and Margali. Clea caught her as Elizabeth released whatever immobilization spell she had used, and Holly stumbled forward, her original momentum still governing her movement, even though she was no longer walking, and hadn't been for many minutes.

Then Elizabeth began raising her other hand, just as deliberately as she had raised the first. The other four women, three living and one dead, watched as a metal object was teased slowly from the ground, clumps of frozen dirt and snow falling off it as it rose to a spot about six feet in the air. There it rotated slowly, the only thing moving now that the snow and wind had finally stopped. Clea realized that Elizabeth wanted them to get a good look at it.

The object appeared to be an oversized bullet, with a set of fins circling the primer end. And that's when Clea understood exactly what the Tsuut'ina woman had meant by "ordnance".

What Holly had stepped on was a bomb. One that had sat dormant until the young witch's foot had landed in just the right place, with just the right weight, to activate it. Clea chose not to dwell on just how close a call that had been.

"The rest of you can relax," Elizabeth said. "That was the only one. Here, anyway."

Clea didn't find her words particularly comforting, though

she was glad to be able to move again without being worried about being reduced to flesh fragments, or burned to death, or whatever it was this particular weapon of mankind's wars did. It was probably better not to speculate.

"This is the legacy that the Canadian government has left my people. First they took our land from us, then they desecrated it, and now they 'give' it back – as if you can give away something that you do not and have never possessed. As if anyone can own the land, or the water, or the air.

"This land was supposed to be returned to us 'clean'. Cleared of all the remnants of their occupation, even in this small part we still allow them to use. And this is what they give us. Ground littered with unexploded ordnance just waiting for some innocent soul to stumble across…"

As Elizabeth had spoken, the bomb had been rising in the air, still slowly spinning as if on display. When it was little more than a black dot against the steel-colored sky, it stopped. But Elizabeth didn't.

"…and be blown to Creator."

At those words, she released her hold on the bomb and it exploded, a flash of bright gold and copper-colored light, then a corona of white smoke, and seconds later a loud "crack" sound followed almost immediately by a concussive wave that rocked the women where they stood.

The blast was large enough that it would have killed Holly instantly and left a maimed Clea and Margali to bleed out in the snow. Elizabeth had saved all their lives.

As if reading Clea's mind, Elizabeth spoke. Clea noted that her coronet was no longer glowing, and neither were her eyes.

"So, now that I've saved your sorry behinds, does someone who is *not* Agatha want to tell me why you're here trespassing on a military training facility dressed like you *want* to die of hypothermia? The CliffsNotes version, please."

"I... don't know what that means, but we need your help," Clea said.

Elizabeth snorted.

"Tell me something I don't know, Captain Obvious."

Surprisingly, it was Holly who spoke up.

"OK. I'm Holly, this is Clea and the demonic-looking one over there is Margali."

"CliffsNotes," Elizabeth repeated.

"Fine," Holly replied. "Umar – Big Bad of the Dark Dimension, megalomaniac, etc. – got a hold of the Power Cosmic in female form and plans to use it to help her conquer all the Splinter Realms. We're trying to stop her, but she's barred entry to those dimensions. So, we need to use the back door, and you're apparently the only one who has a key."

The scowl that had never left Elizabeth's face deepened.

"Let's get inside the guard shack, and you can start from the beginning. I'm still going to say 'no', but at least then it will be an informed decision." She turned and began walking toward the building they'd been trying to reach before Holly's close encounter with death.

"Oh," Holly piped up as they followed Elizabeth to the shack. "I left out the juiciest part."

"And what's that?" Elizabeth asked without looking over her shoulder.

"Clea is Umar's daughter."

Chapter Eight

Inside the shack, Elizabeth flipped on the lights and the heat while Clea and Margali settled around a square table and Holly checked the small kitchenette for something to eat. She came back with bottled ice, an unopened box of Breton crackers, and a few ancient paper napkins that looked to have been collected from various fast-food restaurants. When Margali wrinkled her nose, Holly shrugged.

"Sorry. I just deliver the news."

Clea, however, smiled and reached for one of the bottles, opening it and taking a drink of what little melted water was actually in the bottle before pulling the cracker box over and opening that. Her rebels would consider this a feast. Umar had put blighting spells on most food-bearing plants in the Dark Dimension, save for those near her castle that she and her minions could more easily control. It was part of the way she made the people dependent on her. A population that needed their ruler to survive was less likely to revolt.

Less likely.

The other women followed Clea's example while she explained the situation in the Splinter Realms to Elizabeth in more detail, along with their need for a guide through the

Crossroads. If she squinted just right, Clea could almost imagine they were having high tea back at Stephen's brownstone on Bleecker Street. Except for the tea, the cakes, and the pleasant conversation parts.

And the freezing cold part. The guard building was heated by a small furnace, but apparently it took a while to get going, because if Clea's shivering and Holly's chattering teeth were any indication, it was only marginally warmer inside than it had been outside. The only real difference seemed to be the decided lack of bombs.

Elizabeth had chosen not to join them at the table. She was the only one not sitting or eating. She stood leaning against the wall that faced the door, arms crossed. It didn't look like she planned on staying.

There was a long silence after Clea had finished her tale, broken only by metal gripes and groans from the furnace as it finally deigned to force out some heated air. The silence went on long enough to become awkward, and Clea felt the need to say something, anything, to fill it. But what? She had already laid out their dire need. What more was left to say? She hadn't begged, but she would, if it came to that.

And as the silence stretched on, it seemed like it might, indeed, be coming to that.

Then Agatha spoke.

"Elizabeth has heard your story, but I don't think any of you know hers."

If looks could kill and Agatha weren't already dead, the glare Elizabeth sent her way would have been seriously concerning. Then again, since Clea didn't really know what the source of Elizabeth's magic was or the extent of what she could do with it, maybe she should still be concerned for Agatha, dead or not.

"As I understand it, Elizabeth's father, Michael Two-youngmen, was the spiritual leader for the Tsuut'ina tribe, and a member of the Canadian super team, Alpha Flight."

"Old woman, I'm warning you," Elizabeth began, frowning, "in my culture we respect our elders, but..." She trailed off dangerously. Agatha paid her no heed.

"He and Elizabeth were estranged for much of Elizabeth's life, until an encounter with one of the Great Beasts forced a reunion neither had planned and only one of them wanted. That encounter unleashed Elizabeth's latent hereditary mystical abilities, whereupon her father tricked her into putting on the Coronet of Power – or Enchantment, if you like – and becoming the Talisman, a figure out of legend. All Elizabeth wanted was to return to being a college student with a normal life, but her father's duplicity took that from her, just as his past lies had taken away any chance they had at a normal family life. Am I getting it right so far, dear? This *is* the CliffsNotes version, after all."

Elizabeth's face was a mask of fury and she actually growled.

"Then, he sent you into and allowed you to become lost inside the void contained within his medicine pouch, choosing to save... Snowbird, was it? – instead of you. Always so ready to set aside the role of father for the role of the super hero, Shaman. Adding insult to injury, after forcing the powers of the coronet on you, when you didn't use them the way *he* wanted, he stripped them away from you again, causing you tremendous physical and psychic pain. Ironically, it was only the interference of the demoness Dreamqueen that convinced him to return the coronet to you, the one for whom it was forged. And it was his shortcomings that forced you to take the drastic, heroic steps that left you braindead as you saved a multitude of innocents.

"Where was he while you recovered, hmm? While you learned how to walk and talk again? By your side? Or playing super hero? Yet even so, here you are, after his death, shouldering his burden, carrying on his legacy as spiritual leader to your people. You're remarkably forgiving."

"*Enough!*" Clea did not shout, but she was no stranger to command, and her voice carried force even without volume. She didn't know what Agatha was playing at, but it was clearly infuriating Elizabeth, which wasn't going to help their cause any, and Clea wasn't going to stand idly by and watch another woman be attacked out of seeming spite. "Agatha, stop this instant with… whatever it is you think you're doing here." As Clea spoke, Elizabeth pushed away from the wall without a word and stormed out of the shack. "It's vicious and mean-spirited and I won't have it. If this is the price of your help, you can consider your services no longer needed."

Both Holly and Margali looked at her in surprise, Holly's astoundment suffused with fear and Margali's tinged with admiration. Agatha was unperturbed.

Clea hurried after Elizabeth, conjuring new clothing around her, a purple parka and boots modeled after what the other woman wore. They were much warmer than the coat and Uggs she'd conjured upon their arrival here. Apparently, New York City winters tended to be a bit less severe than Canadian snowstorms.

Elizabeth had not gone far; she was standing outside the shack with her head tilted back, looking up. The clouds had begun to clear, and Clea saw a trail of stars stretching across the sky like sprinkled diamonds. The sight was breathtaking.

"It's beautiful," Clea said as she walked over to stand beside Elizabeth. "Like a river of jewels."

"The Cherokee have a legend about how the Milky Way came to be. They say there were some people in the south who pounded corn into meal every day, and every night some of the cornmeal went missing. They investigated and found dog tracks leading north, so they hid themselves, and lo and behold, that night, a dog came out of the north and began eating the cornmeal. They jumped up and chased him away, and as he ran, cornmeal fell from his mouth, leaving the trail we now see as stars. So they call it 'Where the dog ran.'"

"I like that," Clea said, "though one would think they would choose something more glamorous than cornmeal to make the comparison."

"Why? Because you consider gems more valuable than food staples? To Indigenous people, corn *is* precious. There was no more reverent comparison they could make. To understand the story, you must change your perspective, and see it through their eyes. Most settlers don't bother." Elizabeth side-eyed her. "Although I guess you're more like a tourist."

The women stood silent for some time as Clea considered Elizabeth's words, Agatha's story, and her own urgent need. She didn't know what thoughts occupied Elizabeth's mind during those brief moments of companionable quiet, but she imagined some of them might be focused on how to resurrect Agatha so she could kill her again. The old witch brought that desire out in people. Perhaps Wanda was less at fault in that regard than Clea had been led to believe.

Finally, she gathered the disparate threads of her own thoughts into a last, desperate plea, and broke the silence.

"I may be just a tourist here, but I am also the daughter of a … difficult parent. Two, actually, though my father is dead now. But he was dead to me long before that. And my mother denied my existence until she was forced to acknowledge it in front of the entire Dark Dimension when I first stripped the Flames of Regency away from her. While I imagine she would be more like rat poison than cornmeal, just as your father might be more like glass than diamonds, they have both left trails behind them that we, as their children, must reckon with. Like it or not, we are the ones who must decide what happens to those trails. Do we clean up their poison and expose their faults? End and erase their trails? Or do we remake them into something that embodies the life and truth our parents eschewed, for the good of our people? We cannot change who we are, or who they are, or were. But we can make the decision to either carry on their legacies, or to end them."

She turned to face Elizabeth. Clea wasn't used to being so open about the morass of feelings that defined her relationship with her family – not even with herself, let alone anyone else – and she didn't much like it. She finally understood the Earth idiom "spilling your guts", because it felt like she had spewed hers out all over the ground. She could only hope it would be enough.

"I don't know what your choice is, Elizabeth, or if you've even truly made it yet, but I know what mine is. What it has to be. I have to end Umar's legacy. I must obliterate her trail and create a new one for my people. And I can't do it without your help."

Clea grabbed Elizabeth's hands up in her own, heart in her throat, willing the other woman to sense her sincerity and grasp the gravity of her words. She searched the Tsuut'ina woman's brown eyes for any sign that she understood the depth of Clea's need, her people's need. Finally, she uttered the words that she had hoped would not be needed.

"Please, Elizabeth. I'm begging you."

"No."

Clea blinked. She couldn't have heard that right.

"What?"

"I said, 'no,'" Elizabeth repeated matter-of-factly.

"But why? I'm not asking you to fight Umar. I'm just asking for you to guide us through the Crossroads." It took everything she had to keep the pleading tone out of her voice. She had already begged once. She didn't want to do it again.

"You're asking me to become the Talisman again, against my will. You're no better than my father in that regard."

"I understand," Clea said, her anger beginning to grow. "Having the option to use or not use the power available to you in service of your people must be freeing."

"I'm still serving my people."

"Of course. As your father would have wanted, I'm sure." Even as she said it, Clea heard the echo of Agatha's words in her mouth, and they tasted like bile.

Elizabeth turned her scowl on Clea.

"That's not why I do it."

"Isn't it? And... does it truly matter?"

Clea could see Elizabeth cycling through and discarding responses in her head. Clea wasn't particularly proud of manipulating the other woman in this fashion, especially after she'd just scolded Agatha for doing essentially the same thing. But if that's what it took to get the Talisman's help, she would do it, and worse.

And what could Elizabeth say, really? Even if she hadn't taken over the mantle of spiritual leader because of her father, she was still walking in his footsteps, performing the role he had written for her. One of them, anyway. The freedom she so prized was a carefully constructed illusion.

And if she said she was doing it because her people needed her, then how could she justify refusing to help Clea, whose people also needed her?

She could continue to refuse, Clea knew, but not without seeming churlish, even childish. And perhaps even that would not sway her – Elizabeth did not seem to be the type of woman who cared much what others thought of her, after all – but the call to serve was hard to ignore. Clea had seen it with Stephen, with the Defenders and Avengers, even with her own rebels. And once that bell was rung, there was no unringing it, or unhearing it. No hiding from it forever. There was only heeding it.

"I think I hate you," Elizabeth said finally, her scowl fading a bit as her mouth twisted into a rueful smile.

"That's fair," Clea replied with a smile of her own. She hoped it didn't look as relieved as she felt. She hadn't really been sure that would work. She supposed she should thank Agatha for teeing this one up for her, as Patsy might say. If the old witch hadn't torn the scab off the wound that was Elizabeth's relationship with her father, Clea wouldn't have been able to pour salt in it so effectively.

"We should get back to the shack before the others send a search party."

"You really think Agatha would do that?" Clea asked, only half-joking.

Elizabeth laughed.

"You're right," she said. "We'd better get back before they leave us for dead."

In the guard shack, Elizabeth made her announcement.

"The fair Lady Clea has convinced me to guide you through the Crossroads to the Dark Dimension. But you're on your own after that. Colonialism never dies, it just comes back wearing a different mask, and I have my own battles to fight here against it. Mostly of the sort that the Talisman's powers aren't much use in."

"Now that that's settled," Agatha said, her voice betraying the slightest tremor, "I think it's best if you ladies get on your way. Contrary to the rumors I started, I am not actually omnipotent, and yours is not the only adventure I am shepherding. A spirit needs her beauty rest."

Clea saw then that Agatha had indeed faded during their time together, her purple dress and shawl now the color of wilting lilac, her silver hair become a muted pewter. Her flesh – if it could be called that – had taken on the cloudy, yellowish cast of ancient vellum.

She looked exhausted. Worse, she looked weak, and that was a state Clea imagined she allowed few people to ever see her in.

"Go back to your coffin and rest, Agatha," Elizabeth said, and not kindly. "I'll take it from here."

"Those are vampires, dear."

"Bloodsuckers, soulsuckers, what's the difference?"

Agatha considered a moment. "Better tailors." She didn't elaborate on which group her words applied to.

"Ah."

Luckily, Holly chose that moment to interrupt the exchange, which was quickly going south, as Stephen was wont to say. Agatha had a penchant for driving conversations straight to Earth's less festive pole. "I'm sorry, Agatha. I didn't realize it was that bad."

"It's quite alright, dear. It's my job to look after you, not the other way round," Agatha assured her, though Holly did not look much comforted. Then she addressed all of them. "I'll be taking my leave of you all now. I wish you good luck and godspeed. Knock on wood, fingers crossed, and whatever other gestures your philosophical or religious practice of choice employs."

"That's very egalitarian of you," Elizabeth muttered, rolling her eyes. Agatha ignored her.

"And Holly, my child, if you should need me – truly need me – call out and I will find a way to answer."

"Thank you, Agatha," Holly said tearfully. Margali handed her a napkin from the table. Clea noticed that she didn't check first to see if it had already been used. Still, it was more concern than the sorceress usually showed.

"Think nothing of it, dear. It's no more than I would do for any of my charges. You're all like children to me."

And with that, Agatha Harkness was gone, and it was as if she'd only ever existed in their imaginations. Clea could almost believe that to be true if it weren't for Holly's quiet sniffling.

"Are you alright?" she asked, putting an arm around the young witch. Holly had an odd look on her face, less grief and more misgiving.

"I guess? I mean, Agatha isn't one to show affection," she replied, a comment Clea thought was a colossal understatement. "Especially not to me – I'm the low apprentice on the totem pole, no offense to Elizabeth. So... Agatha admitting to a soft spot? Yeah, it got to me. Obviously, I idolize her and want to impress her. But I've also come to really care about her over the years, and it's... gratifying? – to know she might feel the same about me.

"All the same, it's kind of hard to appreciate the sentiment, considering."

Clea was puzzled. "Considering what?"

"You remember that guy I mentioned, Nicholas Scratch? Scumbag who trashed Whisper Hill?" At Clea's perplexed nod, Holly continued, "He killed Agatha once, you know. Years ago, right before she met Wanda. He wouldn't hesitate to do so again, given the opportunity. And you heard her say she'd be happy to return the favor."

The information did little to alleviate Clea's confusion.

"I don't understand how that relates…?"

"Nicholas Scratch is Agatha's son."

Clea thought her eyes might just have gone as big around as Holly's, and they only widened more at the pink-haired witch's next words.

"Agatha looking on you as one of her children isn't necessarily a blessing. It just might be a curse. A fatal one."

CHAPTER NINE
The Crossroads

"This is so cool! It's like the web a spider makes when you give it caffeine!"

Clea and the other women looked at Holly with varying degrees of surprise and confusion.

"This place," she explained, gesturing to the chaotic network of paths between dimensional portals that Elizabeth had transported them to. There was no rhyme or reason to the layout of the pathways, nor did gravity play a factor in their alignments, as some curved up and over or under their neighbors, the portals they led to flipped on their axes, as were the images of the worlds beyond. "It's like when NASA gave those spiders all those different drugs and then recorded the kind of webs they wove. The ones who got LSD made webs even more geometrically regular than a normal one. The ones on marijuana and sleeping pills just gave up halfway through and wandered off. But the ones they gave caffeine to spun bizarre webs that abandoned the 'hub and spoke' model altogether and were filled with random, disorganized cells. That's what this place reminds me of."

"Great," Elizabeth said. "Someone remind me to lay off my morning joe when I get back home."

Clea was glad Elizabeth could follow what Holly was saying. She herself was still trying to wrap her head around the idea of a space program giving arachnids drugs just to see what would happen.

Meanwhile, Margali chimed in with, "Why is she here, again?"

Clea answered her with a silencing glare. Apparently, no one had ever told the green-skinned sorceress not every thought that went through her head needed to come out of her mouth.

"Well, we might as well get this show on the road," Elizabeth said, the Coronet of Power shining on her brow once more, an outfit of low-cut, curve-hugging red buckskin complete with fringes replacing her parka and jeans. A fur-lined cape now flowed from her shoulders and sandals adorned her feet. A necklace of bones graced her throat and a worn-looking bag hung from one hip. Her long black hair, now unbound, fell past her waist. In response to the other women's looks, not all of them complimentary, she shrugged. "Hey, you wanted the Talisman. You got her."

"I'm guessing the Talisman doesn't see much action in wintertime," Holly said brightly, attempting to lighten the mood.

"The Talisman wouldn't see any action at all anymore if it were up to me."

With that, Elizabeth turned and led them a short distance along the road on which they'd appeared, ignoring the many branches they passed that led off to portals or to their own multi-branched pathways.

Soon they came to a hub where several of the roads met.

There, an improbable tree grew, with a thick gray trunk from which hundreds of arms sprouted, their hands all pointing in different directions. Holly made a disgusted face and Margali wrinkled her nose in distaste, though Clea knew the Sorceress Supreme of the Winding Way would have seen many equally strange things during the course of her magical career, just as Clea herself had.

"This," Elizabeth announced, "is the Crossroads."

"The… weird, gross tree?" asked Holly, somewhat timidly after Elizabeth's earlier rebuff.

"The whole place. The tree is just the… anchor, I guess you'd call it? Those who wander here without a navigator will always find themselves circling back to the tree, no matter how far or long they've walked. It's the alpha and omega of the Crossroads – the first thing you see when you get here and the last thing you see when you die here. You see all those hands?"

Clea looked to where Elizabeth had gestured, as did the other women. The hands were not all human. Some were furred and clawed, some bore talons, some more than five fingers, some fewer. There were webbed hands, and scaled ones, and paddle- and spoon-like appendages which looked unlike any hand Clea had ever seen. They seemed to multiply as she tried to count them, the tree growing taller to accommodate the increasing number. She wondered if that was an optical illusion, or a premonition.

"They say each hand belonged to someone who came to the Crossroads and never left. We want to make sure none of our hands become ornaments on the universe's ugliest holiday tree."

"But what is the Crossroads, exactly?" Holly asked. "I know it's a dimension that leads to all other dimensions, but… how?"

"You practice magic and you're asking how a place like the Crossroads can exist?" Elizabeth asked, quirking a brow.

"Magic has rules," Holly retorted.

Elizabeth gave a half-nod, half-shrug, conceding the point. "The Crossroads probably does too – it's just that no one's been able to figure them all out yet. But basically, the Crossroads is 'a nexus of worlds, a realm of overlapping realities, a convergence of choices'. Although, for those trapped here, it's just another hell."

"Let's not get trapped here, then," Holly said, and Margali, who'd been silent up until now, tapped her staff twice lightly on the roadway to signal her agreement.

"Hear, hear."

"That also means staying on the path and keeping away from the portals. Though you won't necessarily get hurt if you step off a path. You might just fall forever. There's more than one way to be snared by the Crossroads." Elizabeth was looking pointedly at Holly as she said it.

"Yeah, of course," Holly replied, her tone implying that it was the most obvious thing in the world and the other woman was a bit dense for even bringing it up. "Stay on the path. Fairy Tale 101." Clea noted that Holly waited until Elizabeth turned away before rolling her eyes, though.

Elizabeth spent some time considering each of the pathways that branched out from the Crossroads tree, her eyes closed and her head cocked as though she was listening to something the other women couldn't hear.

Which would be anything other than their own footfalls, voices, and breathing, for the Crossroads were eerily quiet otherwise. Clea wondered if it would be different the closer one got to a portal, but here at the tree, silence reigned. Straining to listen for noises in the distance only resulted in the onset of a low-pitched ringing in her ears.

"I guess it's more like the spider on ADHD meds," Holly said, mostly to herself. "Or maybe both."

"I'm sorry?" Clea asked, unsure if she had heard correctly.

"This place. I said it was like the web a spider hopped up on caffeine would make, but that was before I saw that there actually is a hub and spoke of sorts. Namely, the hand-tree. The only other web that had a hub and spoke but was still super disorganized was the one the spider on Benzedrine made. So I guess this place would be what a cosmic spider god who'd consumed too much stardust and moon cheese would shoot out of its butt."

"Speak English," Margali demanded, frowning.

Holly shrugged. "I thought I was."

Just then, Elizabeth turned her attention back to her companions. "This way."

Having no reason to doubt her, and glad to let all discussion of spiders fall by the wayside, the others followed when she began walking down one of the twisting pathways. Clea noticed as she passed the Crossroads tree that the hand pointing down this road had an eye on the end of its fingertip. As she walked by, it winked at her. Clea looked away quickly, shivering.

Following pathways in the Crossroads was like hiking in an Escher painting or traipsing along a Möbius loop. When roads curved above Clea's head, she couldn't be sure if the roadway was upside down, or if she was. The thought made her nauseous, so she did her best to keep her eyes on the path ahead of her, focusing on Holly's heels.

Holly, who was following Elizabeth, didn't share either Clea's reservations or her dubious stomach, apparently. She craned her neck, trying to see down every branch and into every portal they passed. Some of the portals were so far away, they were just open mouths, glowing orange or green or purple like a carnival ride. But others were closer. So close, in fact, that the worlds inside could be seen, and if one were still enough, heard.

Holly stopped several times to do just that, which in turn caused Clea to stop abruptly, which then angered Margali, who was bringing up the rear. And then Elizabeth would turn around to see why they weren't following and glare at them all.

But none of that deterred Holly, and Clea supposed she couldn't blame the young witch. This was the first time she'd ever been in any dimension outside her own, and to see so many worlds that weren't Earth would naturally pique both her sense of wonder and of curiosity.

Of course, they had a saying on Earth that curiosity killed the cat. Clea imagined it killed a lot of other things, too. Relationships, for one. It certainly had for her. If she hadn't wanted to see what Stephen was up to while she was away…

Lost in her own dark thoughts, Clea didn't immediately notice when the heels in front of her disappeared. She didn't notice anything amiss, in fact, until the screaming began.

CHAPTER TEN

Clea's head snapped up just in time to see a third tentacle reaching out from the portal nearest her, a watery world that had caught Holly's interest. And then caught Holly herself.

The pink-haired witch was wrapped up like an aquatic mummy, only her head and feet showing. There were far more than three tentacles by now, and as another coil covered Holly's mouth, the screaming stopped. Clea thought the sudden silence was far more unnerving than the screams had been.

Its prey sufficiently immobilized, the owner of the appendages began to pull Holly back through the dimensional portal from which they had issued.

Margali readied her staff, shooting out a bolt of bedevilment at the creature before Clea could warn her against it. As the silver-haired woman expected, the bolt – which missed Holly's head by an inch at most – did little damage to the thing, only causing it to squeeze Holly tighter and draw her in more quickly.

"Margali, don't!" Clea shouted, as the green-skinned sorceress readied herself for another attack. "You'll either make it crush Holly, or you'll hit her yourself and save it the effort. Sometimes offense isn't the best offense."

She knew that was sufficiently cryptic to make the other woman pause for a moment, and that was all she needed.

"O Demon Claws of Denak,
Free my friend from this attack!"

Stephen would have laughed at her, Clea knew. The spell might not be flashy or eloquent, but it got the job done.

From out of nowhere, a multitude of spectral yellow claws came screaming shrilly past the women, grabbing on to the various tentacles that held Holly and tearing them to bloody bits. Clea, who was the closet to the portal, had to step back to avoid the spatter of brownish ichor and bits of wriggling flesh. Within moments, Holly was free, and what remained of the creature had pulled itself back through its portal, leaving slimy streaks on the pathway that led to it, its only prize the remains of Holly's backpack and whatever had been in it.

Once the last bit of tentacle dropped off Holly, the screaming claws disappeared as if they had never been. Clea rushed over to Holly's side, helping the shaken young woman down the path to the main roadway.

"What were you *thinking*?" Elizabeth snapped, her voice as angry as Clea had ever heard it. She had stomped over to stand in front of Holly and was shaking a tanned finger in the other woman's face, as though she were admonishing a child. "Didn't I *just* say to stay on the path and keep away from the portals? And didn't you *just* reply in the affirmative, that that was rule number one when it came to fairy tales, before rolling your eyes at me behind my back?"

"How did you–?" Holly began, then interrupted herself, "And actually, what I said was–"

"I don't care what you said!" Elizabeth shouted. She grabbed Holly by the shoulders and shook her. "You could have died, you little idiot! And it would have been my fault for letting it happen!"

And then she threw her arms around Holly and hugged her so tightly Clea thought she might have to recall the demon claws. "You scared the life out of me! Don't ever do that again, OK?"

"O-OK?" Holly managed with a hiccup, her eyes wide and shimmering. Clea realized she was crying. When Elizabeth pulled back and released the young witch, Clea saw that the Talisman's eyes were also shining, but she wasn't sure if it was with unshed tears or with unvoiced rage.

"Listen," Elizabeth said more calmly, addressing all the women as she stepped away from Holly. "I know I'm just here to be your guide through the Crossroads. And that's all I want to be, frankly. But while you are here, and I am your guide, you are my responsibility. I don't know how you settlers and sorceress-slash-demons from other dimensions reckon responsibility, but Indigenous people take it very seriously. It's foundational to our worldview. And while I wasn't raised in my culture and am still learning and reconnecting with it and my people, I do know this. There is no hierarchy for us, with man standing at the top looking down at the four-leggeds and the land. We are all equal, all connected. Which makes us all family. So, while I'm here, I'm like your big sis. That means you listen to me, and I keep you safe. Got it?"

"Sure thing, sis," Holly said, with absolutely no trace of sarcasm in her tone or expression. The other two women just nodded. Clea didn't know what Margali's thoughts were on the matter, but she herself found it interesting that Elizabeth could hold this view on family while still despising her own father so much.

Then again, families were complicated, as Clea well knew. And she had heard the saying while on Earth that love and hate were just opposite sides of the same coin. She wasn't sure if that was true, but she did know it was entirely possible to hold conflicting and contradictory views about your family, especially your parents. Part of her still mourned the loss of her relationship with her father, Orini, who had chosen his master Dormammu over her, although that choice had ultimately resulted in his death. And part of her still longed for a relationship with Umar, even after all the pain and destruction her mother had caused, even knowing she was evil to her core.

Even knowing that, while Umar had spared her life once, there was no guarantee she would choose to do so again.

Margali probably felt similarly, Clea decided. She remembered hearing rumors that Margali had once tried to kill her foster son, Nightcrawler, because he had killed her other son, Stephan. And even if that wasn't true, how many times had she betrayed Amanda? Yet she was here in part to protect her daughter, a daughter who might well run her through with the Soulsword the moment she saw her. And Clea didn't even want to think about the dynamics of Holly's codependent relationship with Agatha Harkness.

Families were just complicated. Even found ones and chosen ones. It was the nature of the beast, she supposed.

Having delivered her speech and gotten a satisfactory response from all her little sisters – most of whom were far older than she – Elizabeth turned back to the road and began leading them once more along the pathway to the portal they actually wanted to go through. Margali fell in line after her, leaving Clea and Holly to bring up the rear.

As the two walked, side by side this time, Clea noticed that Holly looked pensive. "What's wrong, Holly?"

Holly looked up at her with those doe eyes, wide and full of worry. "Clea, can you promise me something?"

"Of course," Clea replied, wary but willing. According to Elizabeth, they were sisters now, and she supposed sisters made promises to one another, and kept them. She wouldn't know.

"Can you keep this a secret?"

Clea was confused, but sisters kept secrets as well as promises, didn't they? "What secret?"

"My screwing up and almost getting sucked into another dimension by a rancid octopus thing," Holly replied. "Please make sure Agatha doesn't find out. I'd never hear the end of it."

Clea opened her mouth to promise when Holly continued, "Plus, she'd probably make me eat calamari for, like, a month, just to make sure I'd learned my lesson." Holly's expression was completely serious. "And I *hate* seafood."

Elizabeth led them through the mind-bending pathways of the Crossroads without further incident. Clea kept a close eye on Holly, but the young witch never strayed from the center of the path. She did still walk slowly, rubbernecking as she tried to catch a glimpse of the worlds that lay beyond those portals close enough to see from the road.

And sometimes hear. Everyone paused for a moment when shrill screams tore through the quiet, coming from a nearby portal. Flickers of fire could be glimpsed through its fanged-mouth doorway, and wisps of sulfurous smoke drifted over its threshold.

Clea looked at Elizabeth questioningly. Nightmare's realm was one of those in the Archipelago of Anguish and

Redemption. It was one of the two dimensions next to the Dark Dimension, in fact, with Otherplace, or Limbo, being the other. If this doorway led to Nightmare's domain, perhaps they should use it instead of waiting until they found the portal that led to the Dark Dimension. They would only be a hop, skip, and a ... leap, was it? – away from their goal. It might save them some time.

Elizabeth shook her head, already knowing what Clea's question would be.

"Sorry. Wrong hell."

As they resumed walking, Clea turned her attention back to Holly, whose head was still swiveling this way and that as she tried to take everything in. Clea could understand the girl's excitement. Knowing there were other worlds was not the same as actually seeing them, especially for the first time.

Holly's enthusiasm was mildly contagious, and Clea let herself be caught up in it. She looked where Holly looked, trying to imagine that she had never seen these wonders before, that she was coming to them fresh and unspoiled.

There were many watery dimensions, but Holly understandably did not spare much attention for those. Desert worlds, ice worlds, jungles. Doors that seemed to open to nothingness, while others led to star-spangled space. Then there were the portals that led to worlds like those Clea was more familiar with, but which were brand new and a source of never-ending astonishment to Holly. Kaleidoscope worlds, their colors and features changing according to some unknown schedule. Translucent worlds seemingly made of gelatin. Others that spun and whirled in hues and patterns Holly had no words for, having never encountered them on Earth.

A few doors were closed off. Some of those had clearly

been sealed from the outside, perhaps by survivors of some apocalypse as a warning to those who traveled the Crossroads not to enter. Clea thought it more likely their closures had been at the hands of either enemies or beings wiser and more powerful than those who lived on the other side of the barrier. Or perhaps by conquerors who wanted to control access to their possessions. That thought made Clea shiver; she could only imagine what horrors they might find awaiting them at the doorway to the Dark Dimension.

Some of the locked doors were crisscrossed with enormous chains, some had been bricked over, some pulsed with magical or technological forcefields. Vines bearing black blossoms grew over one; Clea assumed the flowers were either poisonous or carnivorous. Possibly both.

More interesting by far were the doors sealed from the inside.

These presented as doorways with shadowed entrances at first, but if you tried to look closer, you'd find your gaze sliding away of its own volition, and if you were lucky, you'd only be left staring at your feet, or the loops of road above or below you. If you were not so lucky, you might be turned around entirely, staring at the next portal either before or behind you on the pathway and not knowing which it was. These portals did not want to be seen; would not exist at all if the inhabitants of the worlds within them had their way. So, they were spelled to direct curious eyes elsewhere, lest someone from the Crossroads decided they wanted to know what was worth spending such effort to hide.

Clea supposed garden worlds full of riches might lie beyond those portals, but didn't think people generally locked themselves in just to keep out thieves or nosy neighbors. These spells were not "Keep Out" signs. They were more akin to "Quarantine" placards, or ones that read "Condemned".

So, of course, Holly wanted to know everything about them, from how the "nothing to see here" spells on the doors worked to why someone would choose to nail them shut from the inside, as it were.

"It's not like there're any zombies running around out here to hide from, right? Or walking, or shambling, or however it is they're getting around?"

"I wouldn't think so," Clea answered, chewing on the insides of her cheeks to hide her amusement. The girl was just trying to understand things in her own terms. She wasn't trying to be humorous, she was trying to learn. Clea needed to meet her questions in that same spirit.

She did wonder, though, how Agatha might have responded to such a query, or if Holly would have dared ask it at all.

"Why barricade yourself in like that, then? Knowing you won't be able to get out again? I mean, obviously I'm still a novice compared to you all, but I'm actually pretty well-versed in magical theory and energy signatures, and these spells… they're not reversible." Her brow furrowed with concern and her eyes shone with sympathy. She was no doubt trying to put herself in the spellcasters' shoes. Clea doubted that was something she'd learned from Agatha, who struck her as about as empathetic as a cat when its tail had been stepped on.

"No, not usually," Elizabeth replied, having noticed that the two of them had slowed to a stop and come back to see what the problem was. Meanwhile Margali just leaned on her staff, looking bored and impatient. "Sometimes the zombies are on the inside, and the last person bitten realizes there's only one way to stop the spread."

Clea wasn't completely following their conversation. She had, of course, studied magical and supernatural creatures while under Stephen's tutelage, but she didn't recall actual Earth zombies propagating through bite. She was, in fact, rather certain that was vampires. But Holly and Elizabeth seemed to be talking about a type of zombie Clea wasn't familiar with. She might need to refresh her studies at some point, but considering zombies, biting or otherwise, were not a threat in the Dark Dimension, she didn't anticipate that happening any time soon.

"Got it," Holly said, nodding. "Makes sense. It's sad, though."

Elizabeth snorted. "Get used to that, cuz."

"I thought we were sisters?" Holly replied, confused, to which Elizabeth just gave a small laugh and then shrugged.

"Sorry, forgot who I was talking to," Elizabeth said. Then her words took on a lecturing tone. "Most Indigenous peoples don't differentiate much between siblings and cousins, because aunts and uncles are like second mothers and fathers. And in the absence of a female parental figure – mother, auntie, grandmother – then the eldest female sibling often takes on that role. So, sis and cuz are often synonymous. But honestly, the term doesn't matter. It's whether or not your people accept you as one of their own. That's how we measure belonging. Blood degrees and lineages and all that other nonsense are tools settlers created to define us; they were never the ways we used to define ourselves."

When she laughed again, it was tinged with self-deprecation.

"Sorry. I usually save that sort of thing for sternly worded letters to the Premier and the Lieutenant Governor. Anyway, we use cuz for pretty much everyone, no matter the degree of relation, because we *are* all related, one way or another.

Consider it a term of affection. Unless I'm good and mad when I say it. Then you should probably just teleport to safety."

Even Margali laughed at that, and Clea felt a tension she hadn't realized she'd been holding in break loose and begin to flow out of her, freed by the women's combined laughter. From the looks on their faces, Clea suspected they felt much the same. Elizabeth had both revealed an unrealized fracture in their team, and preemptively healed it, all in one fell swoop. Or, rather, one bad joke.

Clea was grateful, if a bit chagrined. She had ruled the entire Dark Dimension, led rebel forces against both Umar and Dormammu, even marshaled a team against and defeated her mentor, Stephen Strange. She was no stranger to leadership, on both small and large stages. But she had missed this potential weakness in her team.

Maybe because she hadn't really been thinking of them as a team, just as a group of powerful sorceresses with aligning goals. But Elizabeth had made her see that, for this to work, they needed to be more than that. They needed not just to present, but to *be* a unified front, a well-oiled spellcasting machine, or they would stand no chance against a super-powered Umar.

They needed to be like sisters.

Sisters in sorcery.

Holly chose that precise moment of profound reflection to voice her familiar, plaintive question. "Are we there yet?"

"As a matter of fact," Elizabeth replied, "we are."

Then she frowned.

"But something's wrong."

"Of course something's wrong," Margali replied, unperturbed. "You didn't really think it would be that easy, did you?"

Margali's words were directed at all of them, but Clea took

them personally. While she had not expected it to be "that easy", she had harbored hope that it might be. Their road thus far had not exactly been free of hurdles; it would be nice if at least one thing went according to plan.

Then again, it would be nice if there were no need for the plan in the first place.

"A girl can dream," she quipped, forcing a smile she didn't feel, to mask the frustration she did. She of all people knew how ineffectual wishing was as a means of changing one's circumstances.

"Best not, in the Splinter Realms," Margali answered. "You never know who might consider it an invitation."

The other sorceress made a fair point.

"Hush!" Elizabeth said, glaring at them as she concentrated on the portal nearest them. "You're feeling too loud!"

It might have been an odd statement to any other group of women, Clea mused, but these women lived and breathed magic, and knew that emotions, even other people's – sometimes especially other people's – could interfere with spell-casting.

They were also a group of passionate women who felt things deeply, and some of them did not make a regular practice of keeping those feelings to themselves. Clea eyed Margali, who, despite her earlier aplomb, had started tapping her foot impatiently. Elizabeth had better hurry.

Clea wondered what the Tsuut'ina woman's concern was. The world within the portal certainly looked strange enough to be a landscape from the Dark Dimension. Floating islands, pink skies, weird bubbles. And if she stared long enough, it would probably change to something else. Stability was a rare commodity there.

Elizabeth frowned, as if in answer to her unspoken question. Perhaps it was an answer; Clea was not conversant with all the abilities the Coronet of Power both granted and unlocked within the other woman. Telepathy was not out of the question.

"This is definitely the way to the Dark Dimension, but for some reason, its… signal, for lack of a better word, feels… weaker than it should."

"Maybe it's you that is weaker," Margali suggested with a saccharine smile, and Clea found herself surprised anew at the absence of fangs.

Elizabeth rolled her eyes and gave a half-shrug.

"Maybe," she replied, her dismissive tone more of a reply than the word itself. "I'll go through with you to make sure I've gotten you safely to your destination, and then, to quote an annoying old lady, 'I'll be taking my leave of you.'"

Then, suiting word to deed, she turned and stepped through the portal, her body disappearing from the Crossroads but not reappearing in the world inside, at least not anywhere within their field of vision.

"Is… that what's supposed to happen?" Holly asked, her voice wavering.

"Let's find out." The words were barely out of Margali's mouth before she was attempting to shoulder her way past Holly to get to the portal. Holly, taken by surprise and standing too close to the doorway as she searched for Elizabeth, never had a chance. Margali's shove sent her over the threshold, the young witch not even having the time to scream.

"Well," Margali said with an exaggerated sigh. She didn't look at all remorseful for essentially pushing the pink-haired girl into another dimension with no warning. "That's one way to quiet her incessant questions. I suppose we'll have to go after her now."

As she turned to do just that, Clea stepped forward and caught her wrist.

"Listen to me, Margali of the Winding Way, and listen well. I am grateful that you have joined me in my mission, though we both know its goals benefit you and yours almost as much as they do me and mine." Clea's voice was cold and hard. She needed to put an end to this now. Margali's antics were one thing on Earth, where Agatha had been able to keep her on a short leash, ensuring her damage could be contained and didn't draw the wrong sorts of attention. Even in the Crossroads, where Elizabeth had things well in hand. But if she tried to pull a stunt like that in the Dark Dimension, it could very well expose them all to Umar's paranoid gaze, if not just kill them outright. And more than just their lives depended on that *not* happening.

"But make no mistake. This is *my* mission, not Agatha's. Do not for one moment think that because my elderly doppelganger is gone that you are either in charge or free to run wild. I have been fighting Umar since before you ever walked the Winding Way. I know the Dark Dimension like a lover's body; the people trust me, and follow me. So, if you want to ensure Amanda's wellbeing, as well as your own continued access to the Winding Way, then it is in your best interest to stop behaving like a sullen teenager and start acting like the smart, powerful, accomplished sorceress you are."

Margali's eyes had become blazing yellow slits as Clea spoke, her grip tightening on her staff. Clea readied the Shield of the Seraphim to counter whatever attack was coming.

Then Margali surprised her by throwing her head back and laughing.

"Did I hear you correctly? Did you just… tell me to grow up?"

Clea smiled wryly. "I suppose I did."

"You were brave to do so. Brave… and perhaps not completely deluded. I will agree to 'behave' myself, inasmuch as such a thing is within my power."

Clea supposed that was the best she was going to get from the other sorceress.

"That's all I ask."

Margali motioned for Clea to precede her through the portal. "Leaders first."

As Clea was stepping through, she heard Margali laughing again.

"…elderly doppelganger…"

Once through the portal, Clea didn't need to see the dawning realization on Elizabeth's face to know that they were not in the Dark Dimension. She was a child of the Splinter Realms. She could feel the wrongness in her bones.

"Are we there yet?" Holly asked, as Elizabeth helped her up from where she'd landed on a small, grassy hillock.

"It's no wonder your parents foisted you off on Agatha," Margali muttered, having come through the doorway right behind Clea. "The only real marvel is that Agatha hasn't killed you yet herself."

As Clea glared at the green-skinned woman, Holly cocked her head to the side and blinked at her, like a little pink bird.

"Well, she *is* dead. That sort of put a damper on a lot of her plans."

"I would imagine," Margali said.

Clea turned away from them to face Elizabeth.

"Where are we?" she asked their guide.

"Wait," Holly interrupted, "you mean this isn't the Dark Dimension?"

"All the pink didn't give it away?" Margali countered, clearly just snarking for her own amusement now.

"No, this isn't the Dark Dimension," Elizabeth answered, her expression settling into one of grim determination. "It's Liveworld."

"What's that?" Holly asked.

"Nowhere special. Just the realm of the Dreamqueen."

CHAPTER ELEVEN
Liveworld

"Nightmare's daughter?" Margali asked, taken aback. Clea couldn't fault her reaction. She and Stephen had clashed with Nightmare on more than one occasion, none of which had been pleasant. "We're in his domain, then?"

"No. This Play Doh paradise is all hers. It's a pocket dimension, I think. Which would explain why I could sense the Dark Dimension on the other side of its Crossroads doorway," Elizabeth replied. "It's Splinter Realms-adjacent."

"Who's the Dreamqueen?" Holly asked, looking vexed. "I've studied all the great female magic-users, including demonesses, and I don't recall learning about her."

"Probably because she's trapped here most of the time," Elizabeth replied, "unless she can trick someone into giving her access to their world, either by following them through a portal, or by planting dreamseeds in their subconsciousness that can pull her into their world once they've fully ripened. Or someone could let her in on purpose, I suppose, if they were either exceedingly stupid or irredeemably evil."

"You seem to know a lot about her," Clea said, curious,

tamping down hard on a sudden suspicion. Agatha had alluded to a previous encounter between Elizabeth and the Dreamqueen when she'd been badgering the Tsuut'ina woman back in Canada, but clearly there was more to that story.

"I've faced her down a time or two," Elizabeth replied, an unpleasant glint in her eye Clea had never seen before. Not anger – she'd seen plenty of that from the Tsuut'ina woman, both before and after her transformation into the Talisman. Contempt, perhaps? Outright hatred?

The suspicion resurfaced, snaking its dark tendrils back into the forefront of her mind no matter how many times she reassured herself of Elizabeth's integrity.

Still… Elizabeth knew the Crossroads. That was the whole reason Agatha had brought them together. Was there truly no door that led directly to the Dark Dimension?

Had she led them here on purpose? But to what end?

The Dreamqueen was obviously an adversary of Elizabeth's, someone she had battled more than once. Was Elizabeth taking advantage of the presence of three other powerful magic-users to rid herself of a longstanding thorn in her side, once and for all?

How was Clea to know, short of simply coming out and asking the question, no doubt creating all manner of ill will if she were wrong?

And even more if she were right.

There were spells, of course, stealthy enchantments that could be cast on a person unawares to make them reveal more than they wanted to, or ought to. Or they could be snared by clever wordplay or well-sprung verbal traps. Agatha had opined more than once that much of magic was often just simple deceit and misdirection, if not outright trickery, and she was far from the only person in the magical community who held that view. But Clea would not stoop to such duplicity when it came to her companions. Friends deserved forthrightness.

And Clea knew well that there were other less subtle methods of interrogation. She had been subject to such means more times than she cared to remember, usually at Umar's behest, sometimes at Dormammu's. And, of course, most recently at Stephen's hands, or at least those of his evil doppelganger. Intellectually, she knew she couldn't blame him for that, but… doppelgangers were not opposites; they were creatures cut from the same cloth. Who could truly say how much the actions of one said about the capabilities of the other?

"You said this place was 'Splinter Realms-adjacent'?" Holly asked, her question pulling Clea away from that dark place. The pink-haired witch was walking through the hip-high grass they had landed in, running her hand along the tops of the golden stalks. Clea could hear a stream flowing somewhere nearby. A blue sun, or full moon perhaps, shone in the sky while fluffy white clouds drifted aimlessly to and fro. A gentle breeze caressed her hair. It seemed a rather peaceful landscape for a demon's lair.

Of course, the Dark Dimension looked much the same in many places, and Umar dwelt there. Looks were often deceiving.

Clea hoped the same wasn't true of her companion.

"Yes," Elizabeth answered, her tone betraying a hint of impatience. Clea didn't share the other woman's annoyance at Holly's constant questioning – how else was she to learn? – but she did share Margali's surprise that Agatha had taken the garrulous girl on as a student, given how little the old witch liked to be interrogated.

"Well, how do you know that? Is there a map somewhere? I mean, I know the basic breakdown: the Inner Planes, the Prime Material Plane, the Crossroads, the Astral Plane, blah, blah, blah," Holly said, spinning in the grass with her arms outstretched as she spoke, moving her head from one side to the other in time with her "blahs". Then she stopped and stared at Elizabeth. "I guess that's a map of sorts. But there's only twenty places on that list, and there are obviously way more than twenty dimensions, as evidenced by the gazillion doorways in the Crossroads. So how can you tell where one is in relation to the other? How do you know this place, Liveworld, is 'Splinter-Realms adjacent', unless there's a map? And you have it, or have access to it?"

It was an excellent line of questioning. Clea wondered if that was why Agatha put up with the young witch's curiosity. Because she asked questions no one else thought to. Probably, in some cases, the questions no one else dared to.

Perhaps Clea should follow her lead.

Abruptly, Elizabeth burst out laughing, startling everyone.

"A map? I wish! If there is one, I sure don't have it."

Then she grew more serious. "'All the dimensions are reachable at any time from anywhere', or so they say. But that's for those who already either know the way or else have the power to make their own. For the rest of us, there are rifts, places in one dimension that open into another. Earth has many – they're the source of everything from some of our oldest fairy tales and folklore to some of the newest portal fantasy on the bookstore shelves.

"The Coronet of Power allows me to sense these rifts, or at least the stronger ones, and often, I can sense what lies beyond them. So, I could sense the Dark Dimension through

Liveworld's doorway because there's a rift here that leads to it, or to another dimension very close to it. It's not a precise art, or GPS, or whatever you might be thinking. In fact, it's less like having a map and more like having a…"

"Bloodhound?" Holly supplied.

"Not where I was going, but that works too."

Clea felt relief wash through her. Elizabeth hadn't tricked them. She had taken them through the doorway that led to the Dark Dimension, as she had promised to do. It just hadn't been a doorway that led *directly* to the Splinter Realms, and she couldn't know that until she went through it.

That did beg another question, though.

Should they travel through this world to the rift Elizabeth spoke of, or go back to the Crossroads and try to find a more direct path?

She was about to ask when the earth suddenly lurched beneath her. Clea stumbled but regained her balance without falling. Holly, however, was thrown to the ground. Margali would have been too, if she hadn't had her staff to steady her. Elizabeth simply adjusted her stance, moving with the earth as if she were a part of it.

Huge swathes of rock burst out of the grassland like impossible knives, slicing the landscape to bloodless ribbons in moments, turning it from a peaceful prairie into a barren hellscape almost instantly. The pink of the sky tinged to red, and the clouds darkened, lit with flashes of blue lightning. What had been a gentle breeze became a harsh, driving wind that turned every bit of airborne grit into a stinging projectile.

"What's happening?" Clea asked Elizabeth, having to yell to be heard over the howls of the wind.

Elizabeth did not yell back, but her words carried, regardless. "The Dreamqueen knows we're here. Best get ready for her welcoming committee."

But Holly was already pointing toward the top of a newly formed ridge.

"Too late!"

A row of blue-armored troops had appeared on the crest of the ridge, bearing some nasty-looking swords. Others carried polearms. A few had rifles. Some did not wear helms, their tusks and horns and jagged-toothed maws not easily accommodated by such.

But while their appearance was varied, their discipline was not. They began marching down the steep slope of the ridge in precise, orderly lines, another row appearing behind them. And another row appearing behind that one. If Patsy were here, she'd say the odds were tilting rapidly in the wrong direction, but Clea wasn't too concerned. She was no stranger to magical warfare, and even though the women were outnumbered, she was willing to bet the arcane firepower on their side far outmatched that of the soldiers.

The wind had died down a little, so Clea was able to hear Margali's words just before the other sorceress released a blast from her staff at the blue warriors.

"I suppose one good welcome deserves another," she said, as a sustained yellow beam cut down the first row of soldiers. Another row quickly replaced them, and more were appearing behind their position on the ridge every moment. T hey marched over their fallen brethren as if they were nothing but uneven ground.

"Don't waste your energy!" Elizabeth called. "Alpha Flight faced these goons in Liveworld before. They're the

Dreamqueen's shock troops, but they are just that – dreams. They are only as real as you believe they are."

As she spoke, some of the riflemen took aim and began shooting with a sound like hail on a tin roof. Clea and Margali conjured personal shielding without thinking, but Holly was a beat slower. And she paid for it.

A bullet tore through her left bicep, leaving behind what looked like a port-wine stain on her gray sweatshirt, and Holly yelped, clutching at her arm with her opposite hand. She obviously still believed in the bullets, if not the soldiers firing them. Clea felt a momentary twinge of guilt for not having protected the younger woman, despite the fact that Holly was a well-educated witch who could presumably fend for herself. But when you were used to being responsible for other people, it was hard not to keep shouldering that burden, even when no one had asked you to.

"*Damn* it!" Elizabeth swore as she hurried over to the pink-haired witch, who looked up at her in shock.

"I tried not believing the wound was real, but it's still there. And it hurts like hell."

"That's because whatever damage they do while you still think they're real *is* real. Your brain assesses the threat before you're even consciously aware of it, begins calculating the trajectory of the bullet the moment you see it fired. Your lizard brain perceived it as a genuine danger, so your monkey brain trying to argue that it's all just an illusion as the bullet bears down on you isn't all that convincing. Hopefully it believes you about the rest of them."

Clea and Margali had yet to lower their shields, but as Clea digested the import of Elizabeth's words, she was gratified to see the bullets that had been bouncing off her seraphic shield with metallic rings became translucent, passing through the magical barrier as if it weren't there before melting away and vanishing, returning back to the realm of phantasm from which they had been conjured.

Then the soldiers that had fired them began to do the same, and then their fellows, randomly dissipating into an intangible mist, their order and discipline as much an illusion as they themselves were.

Which might mean the mind that created them lacked self-control as well. Clea hoped that was something they could use against the Dreamqueen if the need arose.

Satisfied that she was no longer in any immediate danger, real or otherwise, Clea dropped her shield. She saw that Margali had done the same. Holly's shield had fallen when she was shot, and Elizabeth, of course, had never bothered to summon one.

Elizabeth reached into the pouch at her hip and withdrew some sort of poultice, which she was applying to Holly's wound while murmuring words that sounded like a prayer, but not in any language Clea was familiar with. She wondered if it was the language of the Tsuut'ina people.

As they waited for Elizabeth to minister to Holly, Clea and Margali moved away from the other two, both scanning the horizons for any new threats the Dreamqueen might send their way.

"Lizard brain?" Clea asked, her eyes on the ridge opposite where the dream warriors had appeared. Who knew what this realm's ruler might send against them next? Surely she had more weapons at her disposal than phantoms and fear? Although both could be very effective against unwary prey.

"Something to do with evolution, I think," Margali replied with a sniff and a toss of her green hair. Given her current appearance, and her claim to the title of Sorceress Supreme of the Winding Way, Clea wasn't actually sure if Margali Szardos was human herself or not. And even if she had begun life that way, there was no guarantee she was still human now. Trafficking in magic meant giving up many things; Margali would hardly have been the first to count her humanity on that list. "I think Agatha overstated the girl's ability."

"Holly?" Clea asked, not entirely surprised to hear Margali give voice to the thought, considering how incessantly the sorceress had complained about the young woman. Obviously, the idea that Agatha might have misrepresented the facts for her own purposes went without saying. "Or Elizabeth?"

Margali scoffed, as if the answer were obvious.

Clea could understand her fellow sorceress's misgivings. Holly did seem to attract mishap, if nothing else. But she was also smart, and not afraid to step on toes or push boundaries. Whether you found those qualities irritating or not likely depended on whether your toes or boundaries were the ones involved.

Apparently, Margali's toes were feeling a bit bruised. Or perhaps it was her ego.

"Tell me, can you duplicate her protection spell?" Clea asked.

"That silly pink bubble?" Margali sneered. "Why would I need to? I have my own protection spells."

"That wasn't my question. Do you know the spell? Could you duplicate it?"

Margali's eyes narrowed. Clea had decided that was their normal resting state, and every other expression was the oddity.

"No. So?"

"Is it similar to anything you've encountered before, beyond the fact that it provided a protective magical barrier?" Clea pressed.

"Elements of it seemed familiar, and I didn't hear the exact words she used to create it, but on the whole, it was new to me," Margali admitted. "That doesn't mean I couldn't master it, given the incantation and any necessary components, if I ever found myself in the unlikely position of needing to."

"So, it's new to you. It's new to me as well. It could be Agatha has taught her to tap into some source we're unaware of. It could be that she has created her own spells from whole cloth – a feat that would require far more than a neophyte's knowledge and power. Whatever the case, if *we* don't know the specifics of the magic she's using, what are the chances that Umar will? Or be able to easily counter it?"

Margali's nose wrinkled in an expression Clea might have called a pout if she'd seen it on anyone else. It was a little too terrifying on Margali's face for that meek a description.

"Fine. Maybe she is as strong as Agatha said. That doesn't change the fact that she's annoying."

Clea thought back to when Stephen was trying to teach her about figures of speech, particularly idioms. She believed Margali's words would qualify as a stellar example of "the pot calling the kettle black". She also believed it wouldn't be advisable to mention that fact.

Elizabeth and a newly healed Holly walked over to join the two sorceresses. Beneath the blood-crusted hole in Holly's sweatshirt lay a fresh scar.

"Just because those warriors weren't real, doesn't mean the next thing she throws at us won't be," Elizabeth said, all business. "The Dreamqueen can shape Liveworld in any way she desires, at any time–"

"Hence the Play Doh reference," Holly interjected.

"Yes," Elizabeth said, shooting the pink-haired witch an

exasperated look. "Exactly. So we need to be constantly prepared for anything."

"But, hey, no pressure," Holly muttered, loud enough that they all heard. No one bothered to reply.

Clea had a sudden thought. "If everything here can be constantly changing, maybe so subtly that we're not even aware of it, then how are we to find our way through this world to the Dark Dimension? We can't count on any landmarks there might once have been still being the same, so even if we had a map, it would do us no good."

Elizabeth flashed her a smug smile, her brown eyes sparkling. Clea wasn't sure the other woman should be enjoying their predicament quite this much.

"Well, almost. See, there's two things the Dreamqueen *can't* change about Liveworld. One is the location of the dimensional rift."

"And the other?" Clea asked into Elizabeth's pregnant pause. The smile widened.

"My ability to find it."

CHAPTER TWELVE

The Dreamqueen lounged in her high-backed throne, drawing a long-nailed finger lazily through the water of the gazing pool beside it. She watched as the four interlopers to Liveworld dispatched her dream warriors, first with their magic, then with their disbelief. Three of the four were unknown to her, but the fourth she knew well.

The fourth, she hated.

The Talisman.

The one who'd forced her out of the deadworld called Earth when the ripened dreamseeds she'd planted in the sorceress's Alphan teammates had at long last given her a way in.

She'd been ensconced in an Edmonton penthouse, watching its citizens live out their deepest, darkest fantasies like little slave ants below her, all at her behest, with no realization of the damage they were doing to themselves and others. Vandalization, robbery, assault, arson, even murder, all playing out on this gritty urban stage while she watched and laughed with delight. The Dreamqueen had reveled in the chaos and pain she was causing. It was so much more delicious, so much more alive than the emptiness of her own realm, where nothing existed that she did not create and animate.

She had, for the first time, tasted happiness. Or what passed for happiness for a demon, at any rate.

And then the Talisman had shown up, putting an end to her fun, sending her away not only from Earth, but even from her own Liveworld. She had eventually made it back home, of course, but now she could only see Liveworld as a dull and barren realm, a veritable prison, compared to what she had experienced on Earth. What she craved to experience again.

The fact that the Talisman – Elizabeth Twoyoungmen – was Indigenous, just like the very first human the Dreamqueen had tried to use as a doorway out of her Nightmare-created jail cell, was not lost on her. Indigenous peoples had always been guardians of their worlds, land defenders and water protectors, so it was no real surprise that another would rise to face her when the first fell. Still, the irony seemed like a cosmic slap in the face.

And now the woman *dared* step foot here, in *her* domain, after all the grief she had caused the Dreamqueen?

That *was* a slap in the face.

No. She would not have it. It was time the Talisman paid for her sins.

The Dreamqueen smiled, running the tip of her blood-red tongue over teeth as white and sharp as death. Things were about to become fun.

She studied the quartet of women as they made their way across the landscape, molding it and remolding it in their path and gauging their reactions. The Green One with the horns, Margali, was impatient and hotheaded, choosing to blast her way through obstacles even if easier but longer routes presented themselves. The Dreamqueen did not believe the sorceress was truly a demon, despite her apparent desire to be perceived as one, but she certainly had the temperament of one. Perhaps she was a half-breed.

Whatever she was, she appeared to be drawing her power from outside Liveworld. The feel of it seemed naggingly familiar to the Dreamqueen, and she closed her eyes for a moment to mentally rifle through the memories of her mother, the succubus Zilla Char. As was common among succubi, Zilla was destroyed when the Dreamqueen was born, passing the entirety of her memories on to her daughter in that moment, including her knowledge of magic.

Ah, there it was. The Green One was using the Winding Way, which was both a dimension and a source of magic. Interesting.

The Pink One, Holly, was obviously from Earth, given her clothing. Her magic was what the deadworlders called witch-craft, but it might better be called worldcraft, for its power came from a deep attunement to and understanding of the natural world in which the witch found herself. Many were born with that affinity, and it tended to run in families. But if that innate power proved weak, it could be enhanced through study and the use of natural elements and their properties. That was the sort of witch the Pink One seemed to be. Given enough time, she could likely manipulate Liveworld as well as the Dreamqueen herself. She was already finding that she could change it in small ways. The Dreamqueen would have to make sure she never got to the point where she could change it in big ones.

The Purple One with silver hair seemed to be their leader. The Dreamqueen did not have to access her mother's memories to know she was from the Dark Dimension. Even secluded in her pocket dimension prison as she was, still she had heard of the Dread One and his sister, Umar the Unrelenting. This waiflike thing now marching across the Dreamqueen's world, as calm and assured as if she had an army of witches at her back and this was their training ground, was alternately said to be a revolutionary or a relative of the siblings', and sometimes both. The Dreamqueen did not know her name, but she knew enough. The Purple One would undoubtedly be a threat to be reckoned with and would be the first one she killed.

Second.

The first would be the Talisman.

Her lips pulled back in a soundless snarl as she watched the woman she had hated for so long lead her three companions across a carnelian river that began to boil once they were out of reach of either bank. The Pink One quickly soothed the water back to tranquility, a worrying development.

Elizabeth seemed different now than the last time the Dreamqueen had confronted her face to face, and even from the last time she had watched the Talisman from afar, when Alpha Flight had disbanded. She'd helped Elizabeth then, not out of any concern for the Alphan, but because the enemy the team had faced threatened to permanently dull humanity's capacity for imagination and dreams, the very things the Dreamqueen needed in order to someday return to Earth and take her place as its rightful ruler. She had acted out of pure self-preservation, so saving Elizabeth then did not preclude killing her now. Quite the opposite, in fact.

Now, the Dreamqueen did not need the Talisman. She was free to do as she liked with her old enemy, and she was truly her father's daughter when it came to inventive torture techniques.

But she would have to be careful. The Talisman she faced now was older and seemed to have put aside much of the pride and selfishness that had governed her actions when she had first come into her power. The Dreamqueen did not know all that had transpired in the woman's life since Alpha Flight's surviving members had gone their separate ways, but she had looked in on her nemesis a time or two. Given what she had seen then – a woman who'd "hung up her cape" and sought to live in anonymity – it had been that much more of a shock to see her step into Liveworld in the garb of the Talisman, though that costume had changed in the intervening years.

The Coronet of Power had not.

And though she had never truly sought the coronet for herself before, its acquisition being incidental to her plans in the past, a sugary coating on the baked dessert of her prison break, now… now that it was here, already in her realm, it could be the long-sought key to the Dreamqueen's cage.

Hmmm…

The Dreamqueen sat back in her throne, pulling her finger from the gazing bowl and letting its surface still to opaqueness as she tapped a sharp nail against her chin in thought.

She assumed the group was trying to reach the dimensional rift and escape Liveworld, just as the Alphans before them had. A quick dreamscan of their surface thoughts confirmed it.

Perhaps it would be better to let Elizabeth believe her only aim *was* to kill the foursome, or at the very least to simply prevent them from reaching the rift. Then the sorceress would be blindsided, her focus on guarding only one flank, never expecting attack from another.

Yes… yes, that should work.

And she would still kill the women *after* she got the coronet, of course. They were expecting it, after all, and never let it be said that the Dreamqueen was one to leave her enemies dissatisfied.

CHAPTER THIRTEEN

Elizabeth asked Holly to join her in leading their little party after the incident with the boiling river, saying something about canaries and coal mines that neither Clea nor Margali understood. Clea was content to follow where the two led, as Elizabeth was the only one who could sense the dimensional rift that was their goal, and Holly appeared to have an innate understanding of how Liveworld worked that allowed her to counteract some of the Dreamqueen's less pleasant landscaping choices. Margali, of course, was never content.

"She's leading us into a trap," the temperamental sorceress complained as she stomped her way through a field of bubbling yellowish-green potholes that made the bottoms of her boots smoke. Acid, Clea guessed, taking the longer route around the corrosive pits. She doubted her footwear was as sturdy as Margali's.

"Of course it's a trap," Clea replied patiently. "The Dreamqueen knows what our destination is, and she doesn't want us to get there. Every step we take toward it is inviting ambush. But what other alternatives are there?"

"Find the demon in her lair and gut her," Margali suggested

with a feral grin as she stood on a bit of solid ground and shook steaming globs from the bottom of her feet. The smirk belied the irritation writ plain on her face.

"This whole place is her lair," Clea countered. "How do you propose we track her down, other than doing what we are already doing – heading to the one place we know we will all inevitably wind up?"

"Hell?" Margali quipped, and even though Clea didn't share the common Earth worldview regarding an afterlife – she'd seen firsthand how impermanent death could be, so perhaps had less concern about ever reaching the "after" part – she couldn't help but laugh. She wasn't sure how she felt about Margali as a person, but there was no denying the woman had an acerbic wit.

Kicking off the last of the acidic goo from her boots, Margali looked up at her again, all irritation and no grin now.

"And why are we *walking*, by all any of us might hold holy? Why aren't we flying?"

"I'm not sure Holly can," Clea said, lowering her voice out of deference for the pink-haired witch's feelings.

Margali had no such qualms.

"Then conjure her up a broom!" she spat, loudly enough that both Elizabeth and Holly turned around. "For that matter, why haven't we just teleported to the rift? Why are we slogging about like common, magicless mortals?"

Elizabeth frowned and walked back to Margali, standing toe to toe with her. Clea felt the sudden tension in the air like an electric current and readied a quick seraphic shield, though which of the two she would use it to protect, she wasn't sure. Holly gave them a wide berth and came to stand a little behind Clea. The young woman was chanting under her breath, and

Clea wondered if she, too, was preparing a defensive spell. Or something else entirely.

"Nightcrawler's your son, right?" Elizabeth asked Margali. The wattage multiplied exponentially and Clea could actually feel her hair begin to stand on end in response.

"Foster son," Margali growled.

"I worked with him once, did you know that?" Elizabeth asked. "This thing with Loki, a fire fountain, remaking the world, nothing interesting. Anyhoo, funny thing about Kurt's ability to teleport – he *can* teleport further than he usually does, but he typically limits himself to places he's been before or that he knows the layout of, or to places that are within his line of sight. Do you know why?"

"Of course I know…" Margali began in a huff, only to trail off. Clea wondered if it was because she didn't actually know, or because she had guessed where Elizabeth was going.

"Because if he didn't, he could materialize half in and half out of, say, a brick wall, or a steel door. Which, if it didn't kill him outright, would certainly put him out of commission for a good long while. But you knew that, right?"

Margali, as was her wont, just glared. Clea noticed that the knuckles of the hand that held her staff had turned from green to white as the two women bickered, though. She decided her shielding spell should probably surround Elizabeth.

"Now, obviously, Kurt's teleportation power stems from a source other than magic, so different rules apply, but… the Dreamqueen is watching us – and probably laughing – as we stand here arguing. She would know where we were going the moment we disappeared. She knows that we can't teleport directly into the rift, or we would have done so by now. So all she would have to do at that point is create, say, a kilometer-thick dome of rock around the rift, and, well... I don't think 'flies in amber' carries quite the right level of agony, but you're smart. No doubt you get the idea."

The two sorceresses stared at each other for what seemed like an eternity, and Clea could swear the air between them was actually crackling. The tension, and the quiet that accompanied it, were not only palpable, they were laced with razor wire.

Margali was the first to break the silence.

"I don't like you very much."

Elizabeth blinked once and then burst out laughing, so hard that she doubled over, and Margali reached out to grab her arm, apparently mistaking her amusement for some sort of seizure and presumably trying to keep Elizabeth from falling. Clea heard Holly snicker behind her and felt her shoulders relaxing of their own accord. She let her protective spell go, her magic dissipating harmlessly into the ether, accompanied by Elizabeth's laughter.

After letting herself be pulled upright and wiping tears from her eyes, Elizabeth patted Margali's hand where the other woman still held her.

"Back atcha, sis. But you don't have to like me. You just have to listen to me."

Margali wrenched her hand away, stiffened her spine, and looked down her nose at Elizabeth. An impressive feat, considering she was several inches shorter than the other woman.

"That doesn't explain why we can't fly there. I'm getting blisters."

Elizabeth smiled and shook her head. Then she abruptly disappeared, and reappeared in the sky above them, hovering there like some enormous, furred bird.

Within seconds, a huge hand appeared and slapped her out of the air, sending her tumbling to the ground.

The other women exclaimed in various levels of surprise and horror, with perhaps a bit of schadenfreude on Margali's part, but Clea frowned. That insect-swatting had been a little too… convenient. She wasn't sure she should be believing what she was seeing.

Before any of them could move toward their fallen comrade, Elizabeth disappeared again, reappearing beside them, unhurt. At their confused looks, she shrugged.

"Illusion," she said, and Clea felt her shoulders relax as a small sigh of relief escaped her. Agatha's constant attempts to manipulate the members of her team had left her a little gun-shy when it came to the use of deception to make a point. She was glad Elizabeth had immediately owned up to the trick. They needed to be able to trust each other.

"But you get the idea," Elizabeth continued, oblivious to her spell's effects on Clea's stress level. "A little bit of acidic mud or boiling water seems less hazardous than letting the Dreamqueen play handball with us." When only Holly's expression cleared, Elizabeth clarified, "American handball? Wallball? No? Never mind, then. Basically, it's easier to deal with getting slapped around down here than it is up there."

"Fine," Margali said with a sniff. "But I'm floating."

"Knock yourself out."

"Literally," Holly muttered from her spot behind Clea, but not loudly enough for the green-skinned sorceress to hear.

After that, none of them spoke for a long while. They were too busy with the myriad of obstacles the Dreamqueen placed in their way. She pulled the earth out from under them, causing sheer, steep cliffs to appear beneath their feet. She grew thickets of motion-detecting thorns across their path, sharp points shiny with poison whipping out at them like spiked tentacles with their every movement. More caustic mud, though this time it shot up in unpredictable geysers, so Margali's levitation did her little good. A river of maggots and leeches that stank of sulfur and rot, a torrent of magical incandescent fire that Holly turned to flower petals, a swarm of tiny biting insects that turned out to be spores from some unidentified plant. Their "bites" caused painful pus-filled boils to break out on the women's exposed skin. Elizabeth healed those in much the same way she had Holly's bullet wound, but she wasn't happy about it.

"It's like she's not even trying," she complained.

"Isn't that a good thing?" Clea asked, surprised.

"Just means she's saving her energy for something else. One guess what that is."

Clea didn't have to guess.

The dimensional rift.

And then, finally, they were there.

A circle of stone that resembled Stonehenge without the lintels, pulsing with a similar mystic power. It wasn't until they were much closer that Clea realized that the upright features were not, in fact, ancient bluestones or the like, but enormous teeth.

"We're here," Elizabeth announced, unnecessarily.

"So is she," Holly replied, pointing to a wide blue triangle near the base of one of the teeth that Clea had overlooked in her appreciation of the larger tableau of dentition. "And it looks like she brought some friends."

"Impossible," Elizabeth replied. "The Dreamqueen doesn't have friends. At best, she has minions and playthings, most of which she creates and gives life to."

The friendless Dreamqueen was easy to identify. With a low-cut red bodysuit and high-collared cape, green boots that came up to her thighs, a red horned headpiece, flowing green hair, corpse-pale skin, and pointed ears and teeth, she looked very much like someone's deranged idea of a Christmas elf. Or perhaps a relative of Margali's, given the horns and hair and general unpleasant demeanor. It wasn't a particularly charitable thought, Clea knew. Still, there were definite similarities.

She stood between them and the rift, at the point of a squadron of more of the same dream warriors that had accosted the foursome upon their entry into Liveworld. But Clea was skeptical. They had already shown they could defeat those warriors by simply refusing to believe in them. Surely the Dreamqueen didn't think they'd forgotten what they'd learned in that encounter already?

No, there must be something more to her use of these warriors. The soldiers, unmoving, sparkled like sapphire sculptures in bluish sunlight that had shaded into burgundy as the sky itself turned crimson. Were they just pretty illusions, meant to distract the sorceresses from some flank attack?

Clea was about to ask Elizabeth when the warriors at the forefront of the formation suddenly knelt, shouldered their rifles, and opened fire.

"Not this again," Margali said dismissively, then nearly yelped when a very real bullet whizzed past her ear. She was surrounded by one of Holly's pink bubbles before she could do more than splutter in disbelieving rage. Clea called up a seraphic shield in front of her without thinking, though the shift in stratagem didn't surprise her as it had Margali. She had anticipated the Dreamqueen would serve up something different this time around. But Clea hadn't been expecting the demoness to just reheat last night's dinner in a new bowl.

"She appears to have changed tactics," Holly said to Elizabeth, who nodded. "Going the Blue Fairy route, do you think?"

"Yup. Looks like these puppets are real boys."

"Silly boys. Clips are for girls," Holly replied. Clea – as was becoming the norm – had no idea what the two were talking about, but suddenly Holly whispered a phrase in what sounded like Latin, and every azure firearm rose high into the air, surrounded by a pulsating pink nimbus.

Most of the soldiers let their weapons go before they, too, were borne aloft, but a few did not. They regretted it moments later when the clips were yanked from their rifles by unseen hands and then both guns and ammunition were reduced to steaming slag. The warriors' screams as their hands were incinerated and they plummeted to the rocky ground below were definitely not the stuff of dreams. Nightmares, on the other hand…

Interestingly, after the soldiers' bodies hit, twisted and mangled in all sorts of unpleasant configurations, their figures melted slowly into the ground.

Which made sense, Clea supposed, since that must be what they were made from. The "Play Doh" Elizabeth had referenced. Which in turn presented its own problem.

Clea had no doubt the sorceresses could hold their own against the soldiers easily enough. Margali was already gleefully leveling rows of them with her staff, and Holly was turning the warriors' appendages into snakes and cannibalistic vines. But because the source the Dreamqueen was drawing on to create her troops was the very essence of Liveworld itself, her supply of fighters was effectively limitless. And no matter how powerful she or any of her fellow sisters of sorcery might be, they were not omnipotent. They would run out of strength before the Dreamqueen ran out of spell fodder.

So, they would just have to make sure the Dreamqueen ran out of strength first. Because if they couldn't defeat her, they had no hope against Umar, and that wasn't a thought Clea was willing to entertain. Failure was not an option.

Elizabeth seemed to have come to the same conclusion, for she had eschewed both a defensive shield and attacking the soldiers and was instead stalking toward the demoness, bombarding her with flaming white bolts similar to those Margali focused through her staff. Seeing the resolute expression on the Tsuut'ina woman's face, Clea wondered if Elizabeth had even weighed the magical scales to determine it made more sense to focus on the Dreamqueen than the warriors or if she was motivated by a more personal vendetta.

Ultimately, Clea supposed the impetus no longer mattered. Only the result.

To that end, she dissolved the Shield of the Seraphim and called up the Crystals of Cyndriarr in its place, a spell so deadly that she had never seen Stephen employ it in battle, and she herself only knew of it from studying his spell books. She had never attempted to cast it before, but it seemed like the sort of spell she might wind up needing to use against Umar to halt her mother's campaign of conquest, so perhaps a trial run was in order?

A multitude of rectangular yellow crystals appeared before her, swirling as if caught in a vortex she could not feel. The crystals were thin, like playing cards, and the way the sunlight glinted off them suggested that their tapered edges were sharp. Each crystal glowed with an infernal inner light. Stephen had told her that their touch was certain death... at least to some beings. He hadn't known the entirety of the list of those it would kill and those it would only harm grievously, and Clea had no true idea of where the Dreamqueen might fall on that spectrum.

She hesitated. Clea didn't like killing and had never done so outside the heat of battle. Any fatalities she may have caused had been acts of war, or self-defense. She wasn't sure this clash counted as either.

True, they were battling the Dreamqueen and her Play Doh puppets, but were the four of them in any real danger? She had seen nothing yet from the Dreamqueen to indicate that the demoness actually wanted any of them dead. Well, besides Elizabeth.

As she pondered, she felt a mind other than hers begin to take hold of the crystals, forcing the maelstrom back toward her, the sharp amber rectangles spinning crazily as they were pushed first in one direction, then the other.

Well, that answered that question. There were only four other people here who might try to usurp her spell, and three of them were her allies. That left the Dreamqueen, who was apparently engaging in this battle of wills with Clea while also deftly parrying every bolt Elizabeth sent in her direction.

So maybe a mortal spell was warranted, after all. But not this one. This one needed to be aborted, and quickly, before the Dreamqueen hijacked it and Clea found out where on Stephen's list of harm gradation a half-Faltine, half-Mhuruuk might lie.

She concentrated on the outlines of the spell, seeing it in her mind as a bright yellow line that limned the edges of the vortex and the crystals swirling within it. She saw the points where the Dreamqueen had attempted to infiltrate and supplant her mastery of the spell all along that line, like prying, spindly white fingers. Then she envisioned a multitude of small purple fireballs that she hurled at the yellow line, and wherever they hit, they absorbed the yellow, dulling it, turning it to a mundane, magicless brown. The brown spread around the spell's edges, and when it touched the Dreamqueen's invading probes, they shrank away from it and pulled back as if it were poisonous, releasing their grip. And when the spell's outlines were entirely brown, the crystals, too, dulled. The maelstrom slowed and stopped, then dissipated, leaving the crystals to hang in the air, no longer moving, devoid of all magic and harmless now. They burst into a million tiny pieces, and Clea's spellbreaker was completed.

"That was impressive," Holly said from behind her. "One of yours? You're gonna have to teach me."

The pink-haired witch had moved on from levitating and melting weapons to simply levitating and melting soldiers, which seemed like a much more efficient process, especially since the Dreamqueen did not seem to be keeping up with production. Possibly because she was in a full-on magical duel with Elizabeth at this point, the Talisman and the demoness throwing all manner of mystical pyrotechnics at each other.

Definitely a vendetta, Clea thought. She just hoped Elizabeth didn't get so caught up in her personal feud that she forgot why the sorceresses were here. Defeating the Dreamqueen was only the middlegame.

"I'm more interested in the spell you were breaking," Margali said, startling Clea as she came up behind her on the other side. She, too, had found a more efficient means of dealing with the soldiers, having simply set a wall of arcane fire in front of them that they continued to march through mindlessly, effectively destroying themselves, the Dreamqueen too distracted to order them to do otherwise.

Before Clea could answer, there was a flash so bright around Elizabeth and the Dreamqueen that the other three sorceresses had to duck and shield their eyes, Holly muttering something about mushroom clouds.

When they looked up again, the Dreamqueen was enclosed in a cage with bars made of the same bright material that had caused the flash, and she was decidedly unhappy about it.

"Hurry up!" Elizabeth shouted at them without looking over her shoulder, her attention completely focused on maintaining the Dreamqueen's cage. "Get to the rift and go through! I'm not going to be able to hold this much longer!"

The other sorceresses didn't need to be told twice. Running for the rift, Margali extended her wall of fire to encircle both flanks of the Dreamqueen's azure army, allowing Holly to drop her own spell while keeping their path free of armed and armored obstacles. Clea was in the rear, keeping up a precautionary seraphic shield behind them.

Margali reached the ring of teeth first, slipping between two incisors and disappearing. Holly was on her heels, likewise disappearing. As she reached the henge, Clea looked back to see if Elizabeth needed any help.

The Talisman was running toward her, the Dreamqueen in hot pursuit. As Clea watched, the demoness reached out and grabbed the hem of the fur-lined cloak that flowed out behind Elizabeth as she ran, then yanked. Hard.

Elizabeth was stopped in her tracks. Then the Dreamqueen began to pull her inexorably backward, the Tsuut'ina woman's heels leaving grooves of protest in the ground.

Clea began to run back toward the two foes, afraid any spell she sent at the Dreamqueen from this distance would also hit Elizabeth. As she ran, she saw Elizabeth catch one heel on a rock and use that to lever herself around so that she was facing the Dreamqueen, ripping her cloak out of the demoness's claws in the process.

Clea stopped, unsure of what to do. Elizabeth hadn't turned and started running toward the portal again. Instead, she was stalking back toward the Dreamqueen, hands balled into furious fists.

She hesitated, but Elizabeth did not. She stopped directly in front of the Dreamqueen, who seemed taken aback by Elizabeth's approach when she'd no doubt been expecting the woman to retreat.

"I've had just about enough of you," Elizabeth announced loudly before hauling her right arm back and punching the Dreamqueen full in the face.

It would have been an impressive blow even in a purely physical fight between two mundane opponents. But these were not two mundane opponents, and Elizabeth's blow was fueled by both her rage and the Coronet of Power. The Dreamqueen flew backward a good ten feet, landing ignominiously on her rear in one of the boiling mud holes she'd created.

Then Elizabeth turned back toward her, and Clea wasn't sure which image would stick in her head longer – the murderous rage on the Dreamqueen's face or the intense satisfaction on Elizabeth's.

"C'mon," Elizabeth said, taking Clea's hand, "she can't follow us through." She teleported them both to the dimensional rift and they quickly entered it.

They arrived in the next dimension just in time to hear Holly finish her trademark question, "…there yet?" and Margali's more-displeased-than-usual, "No."

And, indeed, they were not in the Dark Dimension. The Talisman had taken them to another "Splinter Realms-adjacent" dimension, and Clea had a pretty good idea which one it was.

She turned to Elizabeth, an exasperated demand for explanation on her lips.

"Yeah, about that…" Elizabeth began before Clea could speak, having the grace to look at least a bit sheepish.

"No, Holly," Margali said, ignoring the Tsuut'ina woman, "this is most definitely *not* the Dark Dimension. It is, in fact, Otherplace. Also known as Limbo. My daughter Amanda's realm."

An amused laugh rang out from the air above them. It was not a welcoming sound.

"Hello, Mother."

CHAPTER FOURTEEN
Limbo

The voice belonged to a woman, and while Clea had seen many astounding sights in her long life, she could think of few that equaled this one.

The woman wore a hooded white cloak from which protruded two enormous, curving horns. She wore a suit of silvery metal that skimmed her curves and exposed a muscled midriff marked with arcane symbols. She stood upon a glowing round disk that floated above them, its blue-white light shining off her armor and giving her the appearance of some avenging angel, if angels in this dimension bore horns instead of halos and concealed themselves in cloaks instead of wings. In her hand, a massive sword rested, its heft and length enough that a being three times her size might find it a burden. She carried it easily.

"Jimaine," Margali said, craning her head to look up at her daughter. Clea thought that might be deliberate on her daughter's part, to remind her mother whose realm this was, and who was in charge.

"I don't use that name any more," Amanda replied, blue eyes

glittering in the darkness beneath her cowl. Clea thought she'd seen warmer ice storms.

"Amanda, then," Margali said, her tone betraying a measure of impatience that was, for her, remarkably subdued.

"I don't use that name, either. Not here. Not in front of my subjects."

"Fine," Margali responded, and now her annoyance was back up nearer the levels Clea was used to. "Magik."

"That's better," Amanda said, sounding pleased. Clea, however, found she couldn't think of Margali's daughter as Magik, for Stephen's tales had ensured that name was forever associated with the tragic Illyana in her mind.

Amanda let the disk beneath her feet dissolve, plunging the area in which they stood into near darkness. The only sources of light here were the fiery mists that swirled inches above the ground, veins of magma running through the ubiquitous black rock, and an orange glow on the far horizon that could have indicated a demonic city, an equally demonic war, or an apocalypse in progress. Clea did not find any of those options particularly comforting.

Amanda floated down to hover before the four women, her feet obscured by luminescent mist. The smell of brimstone hung heavy in the air.

"What are you doing here?" she asked bluntly, pulling back her hood to reveal strawberry blonde hair and a weary expression. "I didn't invite you and I frankly don't have time to deal with 'guests' at the moment, wanted or otherwise."

"Trouble?" Holly asked, innocently enough. Amanda side-eyed her, but didn't respond.

"Funny story–" Elizabeth began, but Margali shook her head sharply.

"We had no intention of coming here," the green-skinned sorceress said to her daughter, her own golden ram's horns looking somehow less impressive in the face of Amanda's longer, sharper ones. "This is the last place I would have wanted to come, as I'm sure you know."

"Then, I'll ask again. Why are you here?" Amanda spat out the words as if they were coated with something vile, each tasting worse than the last. She had placed the tip of her blade – the Soulsword – into the rocky ground and now leaned her weight on its hilt in a falsely casual pose.

Clea decided she'd given Margali enough time to catch up with her daughter. Any more motherly love would likely result in Amanda tossing them in some forgotten Otherplace dungeon, or worse.

"We're trying to get to the Dark Dimension," Clea replied. "Umar has gained a powerful new energy source, and she plans to use that, coupled with what she has already drained from Dormammu, to conquer the entire Archipelago of Anguish and Despair. Including Limbo."

"*Starting* with Limbo," Margali helpfully interjected, though they had no way of actually knowing that. But what was a little disinformation added on to years of betrayal and hard feelings? Hardly a drop in the bucket, Clea supposed. "Then moving on to the Winding Way, no doubt."

Amanda regarded Clea with those icy blue eyes, and it was then that Clea noticed how warm it was. Limbo wasn't technically a hell, and its appearance, she knew, was largely dictated by the power and personal preferences of its ruler. That Amanda chose to portray Otherplace with a hellish landscape said much about the dimension's corrupting influence on even the purest of human souls.

Clea was about to explain further when Margali suddenly growled and slammed the butt of her staff into the ground. Clea looked around quickly, preparing a banishment spell for demons, since that seemed their most likely opponent, here. But she saw nothing.

"Well, if *that's* your answer," Margali said. And then she sent a flurry of bedeviling bolts singing through the air.

Straight at Amanda.

Amanda raised her blade in a quick blur, parrying the spell and deflecting it into a nearby rock outcropping, which exploded in a shower of stone and fire, allowing the magma trapped beneath it to bubble to the surface.

"What the–?" Amanda began, holding her sword at the ready, but not yet returning her mother's unprovoked attack, clearly confused and angry.

"Margali, what are you *doing*?" Clea demanded at the same time, shocked at the other sorceress's actions. She knew there was bad blood between mother and daughter – much as there was between Clea and Umar – but nothing had been said or done here that was worth coming to magical blows over.

"Fighting back, obviously," the green-skinned woman snarled as she fired another bolt. "If she wants to use that damnable sword against her own flesh and blood, she'll find that Mommy Dearest did not pass on all her tricks. Not by half."

"What are you *talking* about?" Amanda said, parrying the bolt with that damnable sword. She had not yet actually used it against her own flesh and blood, but if Margali kept this up, that would change, and quickly.

"It's the Dreamqueen," Elizabeth said suddenly, she and Holly having taken up defensive positions with their own spells at the ready as they tried to assess the bizarre situation unfolding before them. "She's doing this."

Could that be true? Clea wondered. Elizabeth would know, she supposed, given her close personal relationship with the demoness. But the notion that the Dreamqueen could so thoroughly dominate others outside her own dimension was truly frightening. Especially since Margali seemed to have no idea it was happening. Whatever she was experiencing, she thought it was real.

If she could do that to any of them, at any time… but then, why hadn't she? According to Elizabeth, the Dreamqueen was trapped in Liveworld. If she could truly control those outside her pocket dimension like puppets, why hadn't she already done so and freed herself? It made no sense.

"What? That's impossible," Amanda snapped, her anger beginning to overcome her confusion as Margali bombarded her with a hail of glowing green rocks from above and two more simultaneous bolts from opposite directions. "I'd have sensed it if she were here. No one gets in or out of Limbo without my knowledge."

As she spoke, she spun, drawing a protective circle around herself in the air with the tip of her blade. The bolts of bedevilment impacted her barrier seconds later with a loud crash and a shower of sparks, then fizzled out to nothing. Holly, meanwhile, chanted something inaudible and the rocks above Amanda turned to simple raindrops that fell harmlessly on her hair.

"She's not here," Elizabeth said, keeping her eye on Margali. The other sorceress had seen Holly come to Amanda's defense and had backed up to keep them all in her line of sight. Now she was watching them all suspiciously. "But that doesn't mean her influence isn't, especially since we had to pass through her realm to get here."

"Her influence?" Amanda asked, tracing another spell in the air before her. Not being a student of the Winding Way, Clea did not recognize the glowing sigils, but Margali did, and she hastily brought up a protective sphere about herself in answer. "What are you talking about? Answer quickly, or I end this now."

"She can't act directly in other dimensions, but she can alter the perceptions of people in those dimensions to act for her, especially if she's had some sort of direct contact with them beforehand," Elizabeth began, but seeing Amanda raise her blade again and realizing she was taking too long, she blurted out, "Hallucinations! Margali is hallucinating!"

Amanda frowned dubiously, and she wasn't the only one. Clea was having trouble accepting the idea herself, although it would help explain why the Dreamqueen was still a prisoner. If the only people traipsing through Liveworld were super heroes and sorceresses, who presumably had a bit more interior fortitude than most, the demoness would have a hard time finding someone she could control long enough to unlock her cage.

Margali had heard Elizabeth's explanation and was equally unimpressed. Apparently only Amanda's words and actions were part of the scenario playing out in her mind and she could see and hear the others just fine.

"That's ridiculous! I would know if I were under a spell!"

"Not necessarily," Elizabeth answered, "and, anyway, it's not a spell, so much as a psychic suggestion. She likes to dredge up the things we fear and use them against us."

Margali scoffed. "Now I know you're wrong. I'm not afraid of Amanda."

"Nor I you, old woman," Amanda replied with a snarl, and for once Clea could see the family resemblance. With those words, Amanda sent her blazing sigil shooting toward her mother.

Clea didn't know what the spell was, but she knew Margali would not have immediately responded with a shield if it weren't deadly. She had mere breaths to act.

Dropping her banishment spell in favor of her own seraphic shield, Clea threw herself in the path of Amanda's speeding sigil. When it hit her shield, Clea's spell crumpled, and she was driven back several feet. She felt a stinging, spreading pain in her abdomen. A quick glance revealed that the sigil had burned through her clothing and left its imprint branded on her flesh. The skin around its sharp lines was already blistering and beginning to ooze.

A horrified silence fell.

Clea tried to tune out the pain, with limited success. She was abruptly nauseous and light-headed, and even the slightest movement set her midsection on fire. But she couldn't let that stop her. This was her one chance. She had to take it.

"Amanda, you have to stand down. Let me talk to your mother. She thinks it's not a hallucination because she isn't afraid of you, but I don't think that's the fear the Dreamqueen is playing on here." Trying not to wince, Clea turned just enough so that she could see both Margali and Amanda, but still jump in between them to shield one or the other if necessary.

"What fear is it, then?" Amanda asked, her tone subdued. She still held her sword at the ready, but her weight had shifted subtly. She would not attack again, at least not immediately. She looked shaken, and Clea wondered if it was her own intercession or her injury that had disturbed the woman. Or perhaps it was something else entirely. She was far harder to read than her mother.

"Yes, do tell," Margali said sarcastically from Clea's other side, drawing her attention away from Amanda. She was, as Stephen would say, not buying it.

Or pretending not to. But she, too, looked shaken, and since she wasn't the one who'd actually wounded Clea, the silver-haired sorceress could only assume that her distress stemmed from another source. Perhaps from the fact that she had figured out what Clea was going to say, and she didn't want to hear it?

Too bad.

"Simple. Her fear of losing you."

Chapter Fifteen

The silence returned, but it was tenser this time, fraught. But not with menace, Clea thought. With emotions that neither Margali nor Amanda were willing to show, or even admit to. Which might very well end up being more perilous than any spell either woman had the power to cast.

After a long moment, Margali dropped her shield and lowered her staff. She looked at Amanda with something that might have been chagrin, though it was practically indistinguishable from any of her other grimaces. But Amanda seemed better able to interpret the other sorceress's scowls than Clea, for she, too, lowered her protective circle.

"I'm… sorry," Margali said, almost choking on the words. Then, as if she couldn't leave it at that, couldn't just apologize without qualifiers, she added, "for attacking you without actual provocation."

Amanda studied her without speaking for a long time. Then she sighed, wearily and, it seemed to Clea, a bit sadly.

"Forgiven."

Then she straightened and, in a voice that was all business, said to Clea, "That was brave of you, to step between us." She gestured, and Clea felt a tingling in her abdomen. It passed quickly, followed by a tightness and a dull ache that Clea knew heralded the scar she'd be keeping for a while as a souvenir of this meeting. "And it's brave of you to want to fight Umar for the sake of the entire Archipelago, though I'm not sure it deserves such a champion."

"You're brave, too," Holly interjected. "Won't you join us?" Clea suppressed the urge to shake her head. Holly was ever the one to ask the unpolitic questions.

Amanda looked at the young witch and gave her the smallest of smiles.

"I'm afraid not. My duty is to Limbo, and my place is here. And if Umar plans to bring war to our gates, then I must ready our defenses. But I am happy to give you safe passage through Limbo to help you on your way."

"You'll take us to the rift, then?" Elizabeth asked. Unlike the others, she still had a spell at the ready and continued to watch Margali distrustfully, a fact that Clea found worrisome. The Tsuut'ina woman knew the Dreamqueen's tactics far better than the rest of them. If she was concerned that the demoness's perception-altering abilities might still be affecting Margali, perhaps they all should be.

Glowing blue-white disks appeared beneath their feet.

"I will," Amanda said, and then the women disappeared.

They reappeared next to a sheer black cliff face that shone as if Amanda had assigned a cadre of demons to polish it every day. Clea wouldn't be entirely surprised to learn that she had.

Cutting through the middle of that gemlike surface was a thunderous lavafall – a cataract that mimicked the more familiar waterfall, but instead of lifegiving water crashing down into a deep pool, it was molten rock. The steam rising off that pool reeked of sulfur.

"Tell me this isn't the rift," Holly said, her voice plaintive. "I've got lavaphobia."

"It is and you do not," said Elizabeth, giving her a sternly amused look. "That's not even a thing."

"It totally is. Look it up."

Clea didn't share Holly's alleged fear, but she did have misgivings about walking through a flowing curtain of magma. It was hardly her idea of "safe passage". She said as much.

Amanda scoffed, once again reminding Clea of her mother, Margali.

"I said I'd get you through Limbo safely. I never said I'd get you out. That's your job. You're spellcasters. I'm sure you can figure something out. But don't try to teleport through it. The last person who did that ended up a crispy critter."

With that, she turned toward Margali.

"I won't say it was good to see you, Mother – unlike you, I don't like to lie – but I am not entirely unhappy to find that you are still alive and kicking. And causing trouble wherever you go, of course."

"Like mother, like daughter," Margali replied, with a rare sincere smile.

"Could be," Amanda conceded. She lifted her hood back up with one hand, and her face was once more in deep shadow. "I have to go prepare our defenses now. I hope your quest is successful, and my preparations turn out to be unnecessary."

"As do we all," Clea replied. "Thank you for your help."

Amanda inclined her head, then conjured another blue-white stepping disk beneath her feet and vanished.

"So, I guess it's 'Once more unto the rift, dear friends'?" Holly said.

"Shakespeare now?" Margali asked, but for once her tone was more teasing than irritable.

"Agatha believed in a well-rounded education," Holly replied with a pleased smile.

Clea was glad to see the two bantering, especially considering how close their group had just come to an interdimensional incident – if the Sorceress Supreme of the Winding Way and the ruler of Limbo throwing spells at each other had resulted in either of them getting seriously hurt, Umar wouldn't need to start a war. She could just sit back and wait for a winner to be declared, then bring her forces to bear against them.

The fact that the Sorceress Supreme of the Dark Dimension *had* been injured was beside the point. Nobody was going to war on her behalf. Her rebels already had their hands full in one dimension without branching out into more.

Clea turned her attention to the lavafall. With its glowing reds and oranges set against the glossy black of the cliff, it was actually quite beautiful, in that not-so-silent-but-still-deadly way.

"I don't suppose Agatha's schooling included a flame-retarding spell or the like?" she asked Holly. The Shield of the Seraphim would probably suffice, but she didn't really want to trust their safety to "probably." There was another spell that she thought would work, but she was loath to use it if there were other, safer alternatives.

"Sorry. Advanced Elementalism was supposed to start this year, but, you know, that whole dying thing…" Holly replied, trailing off with a shrug. Then a thoughtful expression crossed her face and stayed there. "But you know, I think the four of us together could form an elemental circle."

Clea wasn't following the young witch's train of thought. "What do you mean?"

"I mean, we each represent one of the four elements. Astrologically speaking, anyway."

"How do you know that? Do you even know when my birthday is?" Elizabeth asked, her tone laced with disdain. Clea knew astrology was dismissed by many magical practitioners as superstitious nonsense or wishful thinking, but Holly practiced witchcraft, which required a deep attunement to the earth and a knowledge of how it was affected by the heavens. The positions of the stars might not impact Elizabeth's spells, but they probably held great sway over Holly's. At least on Earth. Clea wasn't so sure about their effect anywhere else.

"I don't need to. It's obvious you're an earth sign; you're all about shouldering responsibility, even if it isn't yours. And Margali is the fieriest of the fire signs I think I've ever run across. Clea's a water sign, focused on the needs of others. And I'm the flighty air sign, of course."

Elizabeth harrumphed, but Clea thought Holly's analysis was rather "on the nose", if she was getting that saying right.

"How does knowing that help us?" she asked.

"I'm not sure… but I think have an idea."

"An idea to get us through the lava to the rift?" Clea clarified.

"Probably."

There was that word again. But she was beginning to think certainty might not be achievable in any part of this endeavor.

"Well, I'm in," Elizabeth said, surprising them all. She shrugged at their expressions. "I don't know about you all, but I am fresh out of ideas, so if Holly has one, I say we go for it. What do we have to lose?"

What did they have to lose?

Only everything.

"I'm in, too," Clea said.

"OK," Holly said, "first we hold hands to form the elemental circle, then we each speak our part of the spell to create a sphere to protect us from all the elements, including mixed cocktails, like fire and rock. Once we have that established around us, we should be able to walk right through the lava unharmed."

Then she paused.

"Well, you all should. I will, of course, be traumatized because of my lavaphobia." She wrinkled her nose at Elizabeth. "Which is a totally real thing."

"Of course," the other woman replied, trying hard not to smile and failing.

"OK, then, let's do this."

Holly strode over to Elizabeth and clasped one of the Tsuut'ina woman's hands in her own, giving it a quick squeeze before she reached out her other hand to Margali. Clea stepped in quickly and took it instead, leaving Margali no choice but to take Elizabeth's hand and her own remaining free hand. Separating Margali from the main source of her constant irritation seemed like the wisest course of action.

Holly shook her head.

"It has to be Margali next, and then you, Clea. Earth, air, fire, water. It's OK, I'm sure Margali won't bite. Too hard, anyway."

The green-skinned sorceress's eyes narrowed, but she did as she was bidden, trading places with Clea, much to both women's discomfiture. Hopefully the spell would be a short one.

"Alright, I'll start. I'm going to say my part of the spell, for air. Then Margali will be next. I'll say the line for fire, and she'll repeat it. Then Clea, then Elizabeth. Then I'll say the final phrase and we'll all repeat it together." She looked around the circle. "And we can't let go of each other's hands until we're all the way through the rift. Everyone got it?"

As the other women nodded, Clea wondered if they felt as

nervous about this endeavor as she did. It wasn't that she didn't trust Holly. She'd seen the young witch's talent and power firsthand, and she was smart enough not to bet against Agatha's instincts when it came to pupils. Still, she couldn't shake off a feeling of foreboding.

"OK, here we go," Holly began:

"Spiritus Aeris, let out your breath,
A shielding veil twixt us and death."

She looked at Margali, who nodded her readiness.

"Spiritus Ignis, bank your fire,
Refuse to fuel our funeral pyre."

Margali made a face, but repeated the line anyway.

"Spiritus Aqua, unleash your wave,
A raging tide to flood the grave."

Clea repeated the words.

"Spiritus Terra, shake the ground,
Break open our destined burial mound."

Elizabeth copied her.

"Spiritus Elementorum, combine your might,
Open the way and ensure our flight."

As the four women repeated the last line in unison, an iridescent sphere formed around them and lifted them off the rocky ground, carrying them toward the flowing curtain of magma.

"Nicely done," Elizabeth said, and Clea thought she saw Holly blush, but it was hard to be sure in the reflected hell-light of the lavafall.

They were over the middle of the pool of magma when Margali frowned.

"Holly?"

"Yes?"

"This sphere… keeps out… all of the elements?" Margali asked, taking deep breaths between the words. It was then that Clea noticed that her own breathing was becoming labored, and the horrific realization dawned.

"Yes?" Holly asked again, not understanding Margali's point. Yet.

"Even air?"

All the blood ran out of Holly's face.

"Oh, *cr*–"

"You cast a spell that created a vacuum around us?" Elizabeth asked in disbelief, interrupting.

"Uh… yes? Technically?" Holly replied, her doe eyes wide and innocent. "I mean, I've never cast it before, but–"

"You've never cast it before?" Elizabeth's voice was devoid of emotion, but Clea thought the expression on her face might generously be called murderous.

"I told you I hadn't got to Advanced Elementalism yet," Holly replied defensively. "Anyway, I don't think the spell is actually meant to last long enough for anyone to be able to suffocate. If that helps at all."

"You don't *think*–?" Margali repeated incredulously, but Elizabeth cut her off, in that same deadpan tone that seemed to promise so much more violence than merely yelling might have.

"Yeah… no. It *really* doesn't."

Clea had heard enough. She hadn't wanted to use her own spell, because it was potentially as dangerous as Holly's and hard to control besides, meant to destroy attacking demons. But it would work just as well on elementals, and therefore on elements, and it seemed like there was no real choice now, anyway. At least it would leave them all still breathing, something she was having a hard time doing herself at the moment.

Her chest had begun to tighten every time she inhaled, and the sensation of not quite being able to catch her breath made the instinctive need to breathe faster and more deeply even stronger. The lizard brain she apparently shared with her earthborn friends clamored desperately for her to gulp down what little air was left. She tried her best to ignore it.

Before the bickering and blaming could continue and use up even more air even faster, Clea spoke the words of the spell.

"I name Raggadorr, Cyttorak, and Watoomb as well!

Let Ikonn join them, thus the spiral doth swell!

Round and about me let it whip,

Gathering matter in its grip!"

A cyclone of hot wind rose, howling around Holly's sphere, drowning out any further talk. It quickly siphoned magma up from the lavafall's pool, until the women were floating in the middle of a whirlwind of liquid fire.

It might have been beautiful if they weren't all starting to gasp for breath.

Struggling to draw in air and hoarsely coughing words back out, Clea managed to finish the spell's last lines.

"Stab out, spiral; lash out, force!

Now shall these energies take... their course!"

With the final couplet spoken, the fire cyclone curved and bent until it formed a horizontal tunnel facing the lavafall. Then, before Clea could prepare anyone, their sphere shot out of the tube of spinning molten rock like a cannonball, piercing the fiery veil of the lavafall and catapulting them through the dimensional rift into complete darkness.

CHAPTER SIXTEEN
The Dark Dimension

Clea came to with a groan, her head throbbing. She had fetched up against a jutting rock atop a grassy hillock, apparently headfirst. She shook her head woozily and tried to look around for her companions, but the movement only made her dizzy and increased the pounding pain tenfold. She touched the spot that hurt the worst and her hand came away bloody.

Gritting her teeth, she used the outcropping to pull herself up slowly, then to steady herself as she tried to survey the area where she had landed. Grass too dull and jaundiced to be called golden stretched out all around her, dotted sporadically with twisted, red-trunked trees that looked like they were trying to claw their way out of the ground and into the starless night sky. In the distance, a shimmering wall undulated, sparking a sense of familiarity, but her thoughts were still too fuzzy to grasp why that might be.

A groan sounded from behind her, and she turned to see Holly lying on the grass with her head pillowed on Elizabeth's lap. Large fragments of wood littered the ground around them, and not far away squatted the remains of one of the twisted red trees, its shattered stump all that had survived Holly's apparent impact intact.

As Clea began to make her painstaking way over to the duo, Holly's eyes fluttered open and she looked dazedly up at Elizabeth, who Clea now saw sported a split lip.

"Are… are we there yet?"

"Idiot," Elizabeth said with an affectionate laugh that belied the insult. "Now shut up, I'm trying to heal you."

"Oh, and here I thought… you were trying to… stake me," the pink-haired witch retorted, though her words trailed off at the end as her eyes closed and she lost consciousness. A small kindness, Clea thought, catching sight of a long piece of red wood protruding from her shoulder, its sharp, ragged end black with the young witch's blood. Whether the grace was bestowed by the girl's own body or by Elizabeth's magic, she couldn't say.

Elizabeth put her hands on Holly's chest. As Clea watched, Elizabeth's coronet began to glow, then her eyes, then the light traveled down to suffuse her hands, spread around the base of the wooden shard and up its length, and then gradually throughout Holly's entire body. Holly's breathing evened and she seemed to be sleeping peacefully.

Elizabeth's nimbus began to pull the giant splinter from Holly's shoulder, like an invisible, equally oversized pair of tweezers removing an errant sliver. New, fresh blood coursed from the wound as the wood was extracted, only to be swiftly cauterized by the energy that glowed all around both women now.

Finally, the wooden fragment was out and Elizabeth, no longer glowing, began applying a poultice and bandage she drew from her pouch. Clea released a breath she didn't realize she'd been holding.

Elizabeth looked up at her.

"We got lucky. If that had been an inch or two lower, I wouldn't have been able to heal her, coronet or not."

"Not that lucky," Margali replied from behind Clea.

Clea turned carefully. Her dizziness did seem to be subsiding, but she was still wary of making any sudden movements. She didn't want to vomit or wind up passed out in the grass again.

She looked the other sorceress over. Of them all, Margali appeared to have been unharmed in the joint culmination of both Clea's and Holly's spells, which, by the looks of it, had been a minorly spectacular explosion. Well, unharmed except perhaps for some grass stains on her dress and leaves in her hair. Somehow that didn't surprise Clea.

"Did you have some specific threat in mind," she asked, "or is this just you getting your doomsaying out of the way early so you can say 'I told you so' later?"

"You wound me," Margali answered, not looking particularly affronted as she tossed her dark green hair, sending a flurry of yellow stems and grass blades floating down around her like confetti. She wrinkled her nose and then sneezed once, loudly. Sniffing, she continued, "Do you know where we are?"

"The Dark Dimension," Clea replied, unsure why the other woman was treating her like a simpleton and not particularly happy about the development.

"Well, yes. But where, specifically?"

"I'm not sure," Clea said, trying to hide her annoyance. They could be literally anywhere. The Dark Dimension was huge, and only a very small portion of it was populated. She began to say as much and then stopped abruptly as it suddenly clicked why the shining wall had seemed so recognizable, even amidst her brain fog.

It was the wall that separated the territory of the Mindless Ones from said very small portion, thereby keeping the population within it safe.

And she had no idea which side of it they were on.

A question that was answered in the next moment as Elizabeth was helping a freshly awakened Holly to her feet. A bright red ray cut through the night, hitting the ground near Elizabeth's feet and setting the grass there on fire. The next one caught the Tsuut'ina woman in the small of her back. She screamed and would have fallen if not for Holly.

Optic blasts. That could only mean…

"Mindless Ones!" Clea yelled. "Run!"

The other sorceresses reacted instantly.

As Holly formed her pink bubble of protection around her and Elizabeth, Margali covered their retreat with return blasts from her staff, aiming for where the optic rays were originating. Clea kept her focus on the path in front of them. She didn't have to see the Mindless Ones to know they would be too many and too singular in purpose to fend off for long; they always were. Having two of the sorceresses at less than full strength only made matters worse.

As Clea ran, the ground dipped below her, and a wave of nausea swept over her as the minor elevation change registered somewhere in the pit of her stomach.

Make that two and a half.

The night sky was beginning to lighten, though not in any predictable way as it did on Earth. There, Clea had learned, dawn was a function of planetary rotation and orbit around stars. On Earth, the sun so reliably rose in the east that it had been the purview of mythology for millennia, for only the gods were believed to have such immutable power. It had only been relatively recently, as such things were measured, that those myths had been borne out as fact by mankind's fledgling science.

But not so here in the Dark Dimension. Perhaps there were no gods here who cared enough to assert dominion over such mundane matters. Certainly, neither Umar nor Dormammu, who considered themselves the dimension's chief – indeed, only – deities, had ever given the synchronization of its skies any thought.

It had not always been thus. The aptly named Dark Dimension had once been a mostly dark and gloomy place, and when Dormammu had ruled, he had fed off the darkness, drawing power from it. So, Umar had ensured that he would never be able to do so again when she usurped him, allowing light to flourish as it would, wherever it would. She did not care about providing light for the sake of the inhabitants of the dimension or the things that grew there; she only wanted to deny her brother a source of power and to differentiate her rule from his. If he had fed off light, she would have covered the dimension in darkness. It made no difference to her, though in the area where she resided, there were alternating periods of light and dark, simply for the utilitarian purpose of maximizing the amount of labor she could squeeze from her subjects.

But in other places, like here in the Mindless Ones' territory, there were no such hard and fast rules. There was light, and there was darkness, but there was no true order to either. Though the skies were shading now from indigo to magenta to the salmon pink it would eventually settle into like an ill-fitting suit, like an Earth sunset in reverse, it did not mean that "sunrise" would continue into day. Here beyond the shimmering wall, things like "morning" and "evening" were far more tenuous concepts than on the side inhabited by Umar and the descendants of the dimension's original people, the diurnal Mhuruuks.

Which meant that the lighter skies might not last, and Clea needed to find shelter for herself and her companions while she could.

She needed to get to higher, more defensible ground, but they were in the middle of a plain. The only thing that even came close to meeting her needs was another slightly larger outcropping off to their left. They would have to take an angle to reach it, while the horde of Mindless Ones chasing them would go straight, and they'd lose that much more of the only advantage they currently had – their head start. And once they got there, it would be a matter of minutes before they were surrounded, a quartet of injured foxes treed by vicious, powerful dogs who would topple an entire forest of trees in their mindless drive for destruction.

But they couldn't keep running, either. Elizabeth would need to rest before she could attempt to heal herself, Holly's scar was still a raw, new pink that looked more delicate than her thinning protection bubble, and she and Margali, Sorceresses Supreme though they were, could not hold off an endless army of Mindless Ones forever.

"Head for those rocks!" she shouted to Holly, who looked where Clea pointed and nodded, not wasting breath to answer. She needed it for running.

"Margali!"

When the other sorceress spared her a quick glance away from her near-constant barrage of bolts of bedevilment and other worse things from her staff, Clea pointed again. Up to the sky this time.

"You go low, I'll go high!"

"Typical," she thought she heard the green-skinned woman comment, but over the hail of rocks and dirt clods being kicked up from errant optic blasts and the fires lit from those blasts beginning to crackle and spit as they grew and joined at worrisome speeds... well, probably not.

Then Clea herself rose into the air, not by virtue of any spell, but simply using the inherent power of flight all Mhuruuks – and half-Mhuruuks, as it turned out – were born with.

She knew she was making herself an irresistible target, but it would take the Mindless Ones a few moments to track her movements and realize she was no longer on the ground. She had to make those moments count.

Clea scanned the area beyond the rock- and tree-dotted plain. She couldn't see past the shimmering wall, but she didn't want to go there, anyway. Not yet. That was Umar's territory, arguably more perilous than that of the Mindless Ones, where Clea's rebels were only ever caught dead.

There. Farther to the left, beyond the outcropping Holly and Elizabeth were limping toward as fast as they could, the lumbering Mindless Ones closing in quickly. The trees began to grow more closely together in that area, some even coming within mere feet of the wall. There were only a few places in the Mindless Ones' territory where the trees had begun to reclaim the ground lost to the often-fluctuating magic of the wall. And one of those places was near a safe haven.

As safe as it got in the Mindless Ones' territory, anyway.

Below her, Margali swung her staff out in a wide shimmering arc, shouting an incantation.

"From the bitter blazing land,
May the Faltine raise their hand.
May their flames now leap and hiss,

And open wide a great abyss!"

At her words, a wide trench filled with fire opened at the feet of the leading Mindless Ones, who ran headlong toward it, ignorant of the danger it presented. When they tumbled to the burning floor, the others behind them followed, until the entire ditch was being refilled, not with dirt, but with the smoking bodies of Mindless Ones. And as soon as it was close to level, they would advance again.

But not all the Mindless Ones were sacrificing themselves to become stepping stones for their fellows. A few of them had finally noticed Clea.

As red optic beams cut through the air toward her, Clea finally found what she was looking for. Near the farthest cluster of trees were the ruins of a crimson dome. Her old rebel hideout, where she and her fellow insurgents had hidden from both the Mindless Ones and Umar while plotting the despot's overthrow. She'd been successful that time and had wrested the Flames of Regency away from her mother. But that was then.

Things were very different now.

Starting with the fact that she was currently doing her best imitation of a laser pointer in front of a mob of cats who all, unfortunately, had lasers of their own. As more and more of the Mindless Ones began to take notice of her purple form flitting to and fro above them, dodging the crisscrossing blasts of their brethren, Clea realized that they were losing interest in her companions. Though a few of them hadn't noticed her and still pursued the other sorceresses, Clea was confident that Margali could take care of them easily with her staff.

In the meantime, Clea herself would play the decoy, allowing the others to find refuge. But not at the dubious and short-lived shelter the rock outcropping would offer.

At the dome.

She didn't have time to explain her plan to the others, as she was trying to evade the ever-increasing number of optic blasts that blanketed the sky around her, turning it more red than pink now. And she didn't have time to argue with them, three strong-willed women who would likely have differing opinions on what the best course of action was, or at least on her methods of following said course.

But she had to make sure her friends understood what needed to happen. It was the only way she could ensure their safety.

So, she did something she had vowed never to do to any ally except in times of greatest need, for it violated their free will, a serious breach of trust between friends that she was loath to commit.

But if this situation didn't qualify as "greatest need", she wasn't sure what would.

So, concentrating, she placed a careful telepathic suggestion in each of their minds, along with a counter to any cloaking spells they might encounter once they neared the safety of the dome.

Margali, do not stop at the rock outcropping.

Elizabeth, run past it, toward the clustered trees, until you see the ruins of a crimson dome.

Holly, hide yourself within it. There you will find sanctuary.

As Clea watched the women to make sure they were doing what she had instructed them to do, she ducked and swerved around optic blasts instinctively, like the star of some aerial ballet. When she saw that they had not stopped at the outcropping, she was satisfied that they would find their way to the dome. That they would be safe.

Now she could focus on her own safety.

She had just turned her full attention back to the Mindless Ones as she zigged when she should have zagged and one of their rays finally hit home, catching her in the side and sending her tumbling out of the sky.

CHAPTER SEVENTEEN

Clea hit the ground hard, and for a moment, the world dissolved into an endless universe of sparkling stars. Then she gritted her teeth, blinked the Dark Dimension back into focus, and took quick inventory of her injuries. The Mindless One's optic blast had scored her left side, right above her hip bone. Enough to stun her for a few moments and knock her out of the sky, but not enough to do any irreparable harm.

At least not yet.

She'd come down on the dome side of Margali's fiery trench, which by now was overflowing with the bodies of Mindless Ones. The ones on the bottom that hadn't been reduced to a smoking ash were slowly being crushed by the weight of the ones above them, while the ones above were ensnared by the grasping hands of those below. Still bent on their single-minded task of destruction, it did not matter to the Mindless Ones if the objects of that destruction were intruders or their own kind. What mattered was that those objects were still moving, their destruction not yet complete.

As before, it would take the Mindless Ones some time to reacquire her as a target, which would give her more than enough time to teleport to the dome ruins.

Except when she started to cast the spell, Clea felt the same familiar electric shock she'd experienced back at Whisper Hill. Then, she'd been trying to teleport herself, Margali, and Holly into the Dark Dimension and been roundly rebuffed by the barrier spell Umar had used to seal off the Archipelago of Anguish and Redemption. Now it seemed Umar must have cut off all teleportation within the Dark Dimension at the same time. Or at least made it impossible to do so without her knowledge.

Clea quickly ended her spell before it could be completed, afraid that it would draw her mother's attention and alert the tyrant to her presence before she was ready.

So. Teleportation wasn't going to be an option for her and her team. That was going to complicate things, both her current situation and the plans she had devised for getting the four sorceresses to the Azure Throne undetected.

First things first. She needed to escape from the Mindless Ones, and her friends couldn't help her. Even if they had seen her fall, the psychic suggestions she had planted in their minds had instructed them to run, not look back.

She was on her own.

Well, it would hardly be the first time.

Flying was also not currently an option, because the sky was still a tight net of interlacing optic blasts that she couldn't hope to pass through unscathed. So Clea quickly ran through a list of incantations that might get her out of this mess.

Illusions rarely worked on Mindless Ones, because it was impossible to trick a mind that couldn't reason into seeing something that wasn't there, or not seeing something that was. And the more frenzied such a mind might be, the less able to reason, and the less able to perceive. A Mindless One lumbering aimlessly around looking for something to destroy might discern an illusory army, but the ones pursuing her now were governed by bloodlust and would simply walk right through such an army's ghostly ranks, never even noticing they were there.

There were binding spells, of course, but none that would work on so many foes at once. Likewise, the myriad offensive spells she knew – there were too many Mindless Ones, and new ones would just keep coming to replace their fallen brethren no matter how quickly she knocked them down.

Clea briefly considered transforming herself into the shape of a Mindless One, but discarded the idea almost immediately. Mindless Ones were like Earth lemmings; Margali's overflowing trench was ample proof of that. If one of their number broke off, striking out on its own, the others would stop what they were doing and follow, perhaps thinking their fellow had discovered something new to attack or destroy. Or, more likely, not thinking anything at all, just obeying some base instinct. Regardless, casting the spell on herself and trying to escape that way would only serve to lead the Mindless Ones straight to her friends, the very thing she was trying to avoid. So that was out.

Then she hit on the perfect solution. Invisibility.

It was a spell she rarely used, preferring to astral project if she needed to skulk about unseen. But leaving her body here would defeat her entire purpose, and it was hardly a viable option in any case. Making herself invisible would be the next best thing.

Invisibility differed from illusion in that it didn't distort perception, it distorted reality. There was a science to it, according to Stephen, having to do with things like wavelengths of light and refraction and other physical laws that applied on

Earth. Whether or not they applied in the Dark Dimension was a matter open to debate, but invisibility spells worked here too, and that was all she cared about right now.

As the first of the Mindless Ones who'd been aiming their beams at the sky began aiming toward her, Clea started her spell.

"By the Vapors of Valtorr whom all things doth conceal,
Obscure my form now from sight, my position unrevealed."

She watched in fascination as her body faded from view, beginning with her hands and feet, then her arms and legs, then her torso, and finally, she presumed, her head. She waved her hand in front of her face. She could feel the wind the motion made and knew instinctively where her hand was in relation to her head, but could see nothing except for the Mindless Ones still shambling toward her.

She could examine her handiwork later. It was time to get moving.

Clea took to the air, the skies having finally cleared enough that she could do so without risking being hit by another optic blast.

She flew over the tree-dotted plain, past the large outcropping, making sure to follow the path her companions should have taken, to make sure they hadn't become sidetracked or accosted somewhere along the way, but she seemed to be the only thing moving besides the breeze.

She reached the ruins of the crimson dome in no time, scanning them for her friends, but seeing no one. She landed lightly on the ground, dropping her invisibility spell as she took a few steps into what had been the great structure's central command room, but was now just heaps of rubble.

The ruins were still partially cloaked from both the Mindless

Ones' and Umar's detection by a powerful spell that compelled the observer to look away, regardless of that observer's intellect or lack thereof. Stephen had once called it her "Nothing to See Here" spell, though she herself had never given the glamour a name and it bore little resemblance to the similar spells used to obscure portals in the Crossroads.

Clea frowned. As the creator of the spell, it should not keep her from seeing inside the ruins and everything they held, but as she gazed around her, turning in a perfect circle, she could detect no one.

Her friends weren't here.

But someone was.

She heard the tiniest of sounds behind her, and began to whirl, a shielding spell on the tip of her tongue.

Too late.

She stiffened as she felt the cold bite of steel at her neck. Strong arms confined her, though she could see no attacker.

"Name and business, or I give you a permanent grin."

Clea laughed in relief, tension seeping from her body.

"By the Vishanti, Margali! That's gruesome! And you already know both my name and far more of my business than I'd like, so if you'd kindly remove your knife from my throat…?"

The grip on her loosened and Clea shrugged Margali's hands off her, stepping away from the green-skinned sorceress who had likewise dropped her own invisibility spell. She had not yet sheathed her weapon, however.

"There is that little matter of psychic manipulation," Margali said in a cool, even voice. Her eyes were banked yellow fires that could blaze up at any moment. "Not very polite of you. Rather rude, actually. Reminiscent of Agatha, if I'm being honest. Or Umar."

Ouch. Clea probably deserved that.

"I understand and I apologize. You were in imminent danger, and it was the only way I could see to get you to safety in time. I didn't have the luxury of time to explain myself, so I chose the most expedient path. I realize it wasn't the most… agreeable."

Though Clea had stilled her face to betray no reaction, inwardly she grimaced, displeased with how much like Stephen she sounded right now. His was very much an "ends justify the means" personality. Clea, though, tried very hard to be something different. It galled her to know how badly she'd failed in this instance.

But she reminded herself that her friends were safe. That had to count for something.

Didn't it?

"Disagreeable? Interesting choice of words to describe treating your companions like pawns."

Clea didn't have a response to that, because Margali wasn't wrong, so she just held the other woman's gaze, prepared to take whatever punishment she and Clea's other friends deemed appropriate.

If they *were* still her friends.

Finally, Margali just harrumphed and secreted her dagger somewhere underneath her dress. "Well, you can hardly blame us for being cautious. Your wards are ancient; how were we to know how well they still worked, or if they even did?"

Clea heard weak laughter from behind a chunk of wall that still stood off to her left. Elizabeth and Holly came out of hiding, their own invisibility dispelled along with Margali's. Clea couldn't tell which of the women was leaning on which for strength.

"We'd be in trouble if they didn't, with the amount of noise Clea was making," Elizabeth said. "No offense, but you walk like a girl who's spent too much time in the big city. Even Margali moves more quietly than you–"

"Sorceress by day, assassin by night," Holly interjected.

"I don't practice witchcraft like Holly or follow the Winding Way like Margali," Elizabeth continued, responding to the young witch's words by reaching up to ruffle her hair affectionately. "Even so, all our disparate sources of magic require us to open ourselves up to the greater world in some way. But sorcery requires more in the way of discipline than connection.

"So, it doesn't surprise me that you couldn't sneak up on your own shadow, except maybe in astral form. But when this is all over, you might think about expanding your horizons."

"I'm sure Agatha would love to have you as a student," Margali added with a wicked smile, and all four women – even Clea – snickered at the idea.

Still, Elizabeth's words had stung a little. Of course, she was speaking from her own area of expertise, not having studied sorcery herself. But to suggest that the mystic arts might somehow be inferior to other forms of magic simply because they didn't require a personal connection to the power used seemed both pretentious and uninformed.

And Clea recognized Stephen in that thought, and that stung even more, since his superior attitude was one of the chief things that had led to the deterioration of their relationship. She didn't like to see seeds of it within herself.

Perhaps she would take Elizabeth's suggestion, though if she did, she would obviously search out a more scrupulous teacher than Agatha Harkness. One who was alive would also be a plus.

Perhaps she should return to Gaea and sit at the goddess's feet. Surely there was no better way to become "connected" than to learn from the font of all creation Herself.

Concerns for another day. For now, there were more important matters to attend to. Like stopping Umar, without which, that future date might well never come.

"How are you?" she asked, a general question to both Elizabeth and Holly, unsure if either of them had been able to heal or receive healing before she'd arrived. "Can you travel?"

Holly nodded first.

"Elizabeth's pouch poultices are the bomb. I told her she should totally package them up and maybe sell them on one of those home shopping networks." Holly paused for a heartbeat. "Then she slugged me."

Elizabeth shrugged with a small smile, as if to say that any rational person would have done the same, and Clea wasn't sure she could argue the point.

"How about you?" she asked the Tsuut'ina woman.

Elizabeth shrugged again, not so insouciant this time.

"My 'pouch poultices', as Holly calls them, are of limited value when I use them on myself, and they require time to work – the worse the injury, the more time needed – so Holly isn't as well off as she'd like you to believe. And most of her healing spells call for the use of components that I doubt very much grow here. Unless you know where we can find some Job's tears or goat's rue?" At Clea's headshake, Elizabeth continued, "I didn't think so. And Holly couldn't just conjure them here, because apparently Umar's barrier spell doesn't just keep people out."

Clea nodded. "I discovered that as well. All teleportation into, out of, and possibly even within the Dark Dimension seems to be prohibited."

"Looks like I'm stuck with you jokers for the time being then," Elizabeth remarked, though the Tsuut'ina woman didn't actually seem all that upset by the notion.

"Powerful spell," Margali remarked with a frown.

Clea nodded again.

"She'd never be able to do it without drawing on Ardina's connection to the Power Cosmic," Clea answered. There was that word again. Apparently even the golden woman used power in a way Clea had seldom considered, given her own training in the mystic arts by their aloof and often arrogant master.

"So, yes, to answer your question," Elizabeth said, "I can travel. Just not terribly quickly."

Clea didn't bother to ask about Margali's healing spells. She had no doubt the Roma woman had known some once – she was a mother, after all – but her life had not been about healing things for a very long time, and Clea didn't think she would have anything meaningful to add to the discussion. Margali's silence on the matter only seemed to confirm that belief.

"Good. My original plan had been for us to meet up with my rebels in our new headquarters, but they are some distance from here. I had hoped to teleport there from wherever we entered the dimension, but that obviously won't work now. We could try flying…?"

Elizabeth made a face. "If you're talking commuter flights instead of nonstop, maybe. Even then…"

"Flying comes with its own dangers in the Mindless Ones' territory, anyway, especially if any of them happen to catch sight of you," Clea replied, pointing to the burn mark along her side. "It can make you a pretty tempting target."

"Probably more visible to anyone watching for rebels, as well," Holly observed astutely.

"You talk too much," Margali said impatiently, bringing the end of her staff down on the rocky ground with a clatter that made the other women start. It wasn't clear which of the sorceresses she was addressing. Possibly all of them. "No teleporting, no flying. So what is the plan?"

"Invisibility seems to work fairly well," Holly opined.

"That was my feeling as well," Clea said.

"I have an invisibility bubble spell," Holly offered eagerly, interrupting her.

"The Coronet of Enchantment can also conceal us," Elizabeth added. "But its powers are often tied to my own state of wellbeing, so… I'm not sure how many of us it could hide at a time, or for how long."

Clea had been afraid that the two women's injuries would make traveling in secrecy difficult for the whole group, especially if some of them needed to be free to cast offensive spells while the others cast cloaking ones. Elizabeth's and Holly's words only confirmed that fear.

"I do think concealment spells are probably the best choice. But each of us holding such a spell for the distance we must travel would be draining and leave us less able to fend off any threats. So that really only leaves us with one option."

Margali brought the butt of her staff down again, whatever small store of patience she had found after her last outburst now depleted. "Words. Too many."

"CliffsNotes," Elizabeth agreed.

Clea took a deep breath. She was pretty sure none of them were going to like her proposal, but she wasn't sure there was a viable alternative.

"We need to split up."

PART TWO

CHAPTER EIGHTEEN
The Dark Dimension

"You want to split the party?" Holly asked, her tone incredulous. Clea could only describe the look on the pink-haired witch's face as horrified. "You *never* split the party! Nothing good ever comes of it. Like, ever."

Clea blinked, tilting her head to one side as she tried unsuccessfully to unravel Holly's meaning.

"I know you are speaking English, and yet somehow I still have no idea what you are saying," she said, in frank amazement. Even though she and Holly both looked human, it was moments like this that reminded Clea that she was something far different, the bastard daughter of a Mhuruuk and a Faltine.

"She's saying splitting up is a bad idea. And for once I think I agree with her," Margali said, her perpetual frown deepening. "There is strength in numbers."

"There's also more chance of getting caught," Elizabeth replied. "More people are harder to conceal, and they make more noise." Clea wondered if that last was directed at her, but finally decided it wasn't. Elizabeth wasn't one to soften her insults with subtlety.

"It looks like a stalemate, then," Margali said, lifting her chin as she tried to stare Clea down. "Two in favor, two opposed."

"Pretty sure the Sorceress Supreme of the home dimension gets more than one vote," Elizabeth observed, giving Margali a falsely sweet smile when the green-skinned woman shot a glare her way.

Clea knew dividing the group physically would also divide its loyalties, which had never been on particularly stable ground to begin with. Margali was here out of self-interest, primarily to keep Umar from hijacking her own source of magic and only secondarily to ensure the safety of her daughter. Elizabeth was here because Clea had guilted her into coming, by playing on the unresolved and complicated emotions surrounding her relationship with her father and what she did or didn't owe him, or her people. Holly was here because Agatha wanted her to be, and probably also because she felt she had something to prove.

None of them shared her cause, not truly. They were companions of convenience who had begun, she thought, to form tentative bonds of friendship.

She wondered if she was about to destroy those fledgling friendships in the nest before they ever had a chance to take wing.

"We have to split up. I can't see any way around it." She held up her hand to forestall any argument when both Margali and Elizabeth opened their mouths. Holly, surprisingly, said nothing.

"Neither Elizabeth nor Holly are operating at full power, while Margali and I are," Clea said, and it was mostly true. She was closer to capacity than the other two women, at any rate. "It only makes sense for one of us who is healthier right now to pair with one who is still recovering her strength. The healthier woman will lead and deal with any encounters, while the recovering woman will use what power is available to her to cloak them from both mundane and magical sight, thereby limiting the number of said encounters."

Clea had almost used the word "stronger", but had substituted "healthier" at the last moment, not wanting to give Margali any ideas about who might best whom in a test of power.

"You mean you're going to split me and Liz up?" Holly asked. While Clea raised a brow at her use of the diminutive for Elizabeth, Holly's face crumpled with obvious disappointment. The girl was guileless when it came to her emotions. Clea thought it refreshing, considering how closed off her other companions were.

How closed off she herself had become over the years, her adventures with Stephen having both opened and hardened her heart in equal measure. Or perhaps not so equal.

"Yes. You will go with Margali, and Elizabeth will come with me," Clea replied, falling into her old role of rebellion general with practiced ease, giving orders with every expectation of being obeyed. "Elizabeth and I will make for the main rebel headquarters, while you and Margali will travel to our secondary base and rally the rebels there. Dividing into two smaller groups decreases the likelihood of detection. And it increases the likelihood that one of those groups will actually make it through to the base to secure the aid of the rebels. Splitting up keeps us safer and raises our chances of success. Given our current circumstances, it's the best course of action."

None of the other women said anything for a moment, and the only sound was the lonely wind whispering sadly through the broken ruins around them.

Finally, Margali broke the silence.

"Fine," she said, her tone indicating that it was anything but. "I do have one question, though, if you'll allow it?"

Clea sighed. It would be good to be separated from the green-skinned sorceress for a while. Her constant bristling was exhausting.

"Of course."

Margali turned and pointed a sharp-nailed green finger at Holly. "Why do *I* have to go with *her*?"

Clea just smiled. She had known what the other woman was going to say before she said it. But her favorite Earth cartoonist had once written, from the point of view of a precocious six-year-old mimicking his parents, that 'being miserable built character'. And while that hadn't been the point at all behind the child's assigned chores, sometimes people had to work that out for themselves.

Whether they were six, sixty, or six hundred.

CHAPTER NINETEEN
Liveworld

The Dreamqueen paced in her throne room, waiting, her red cloak flouncing petulantly behind her with every measured step.

She was always waiting. Waiting for her father to let her out of this prison he pretended was a paradise. Waiting for latent dreamseeds to sprout in some foolish human and give her a way back into the deadworld called Earth. Waiting for centuries-old plans to come to fruition.

Waiting for her sanity to finally trickle away like sand in an hourglass, grain by grain by grain…

But she was not actually waiting for any of those outcomes today, much as she might want or dread them. No, today she was waiting for the Talisman to show herself again.

She was waiting for revenge.

When that hated woman and her three witch companions had invaded the Dreamqueen's domain, she had dreamscanned them all. She knew what they wanted most in the world, what they loved, what they hated. What they were most afraid of.

She had already used that knowledge against the Green One,

a probing attack meant to test the woman's susceptibility to the Dreamqueen's dreamseeds. She'd found that one's mind to be very fertile ground indeed, though the Talisman had stepped in before she'd had a chance to do any real damage. Still, she'd planted her seeds, and they would quickly bear fruit.

She knew they were somewhere in the Dark Dimension – that was where the dimensional rift led – but she had to be careful using her gazing pool to spy on the happenings there. When Dormammu ruled, it didn't matter; he was too focused on his own doings to concern himself with anyone else's unless they directly impacted his plans in some unpleasant way. He was really a very basic creature, and she didn't need to dreamscan him to know what he wanted most: dominion, glory, either fear or respect – both were equally satisfying to him – and, of course, Doctor Strange groveling at his feet.

But Umar ruled now, and very little happened in her dimension that she was not aware of. She was a walking machination, intrigue running through her veins and artifice filling her lungs. She might choose not to act against a shadowy observer viewing her realm, for whatever opaque purpose staying her hand suited, but she would certainly know about it.

The Dreamqueen did have a legitimate, defensible reason for looking in on the Dark Dimension, though. The seeds she'd sown in the subconscious of the Green One would sprout soon, and the Dreamqueen had a right to harvest her crops, regardless of where they wound up growing.

Whether the current ruler of the Dark Dimension would choose to recognize that claim was questionable, but the Dreamqueen had something even Umar the Unrelenting would have a hard time turning her patrician nose up at.

Intelligence.

The Dreamqueen could just contact her now, of course. Umar would undoubtedly be interested in knowing that these four women were running around unsupervised in her playground. She'd likely be even more interested to know who they were.

Elizabeth Twoyoungmen, the Talisman, to whom goddesses knelt. Margali Szardos, the Sorceress Supreme of the Winding Way, who wore the Eye of Agamotto before Stephen Strange. Holly LaDonna, a pupil of Agatha Harkness who the old witch believed might one day rival Wanda Maximoff in skill.

And Clea Strange, Sorceress Supreme of Umar's own dimension, flesh of her Faltine flesh and bone of her Mhuruuk lover's bone. Once ruler of the Dark Dimension in her own right, having bested Umar in front of all her people. Now leader of the rebels who continuously harried the self-styled goddess and kept her from accomplishing her grandest plans of conquest.

All of them here, in Umar's backyard. And they hadn't come for a social call.

Umar would be even more interested to learn that they were here to stop her from invading the rest of the Archipelago of Anguish and Redemption and to rescue the friend whom she had kidnapped to fuel that endeavor.

The Dreamqueen smiled her sharp-toothed smile.

Dreamscans gave her so much more information than just a target's phobias and surface weaknesses. Scan deeply enough, and skillfully enough, and you could learn a victim's entire life history in a matter of hours.

She hadn't needed that long to discover who the Talisman's companions were or what they were up to. Their plans were virtually the only thing they thought about.

It was also the only thing they talked about, so she'd learned just as much eavesdropping on them as they traipsed through Liveworld, as she had plundering their thoughts.

But it wouldn't be enough to go to Umar with the mere fact of the group's presence in her realm – which, given the combined magical ability of these women, Umar might very well not have detected yet, despite her seeming omniscience. It wouldn't even be enough to bring her their objective, since the Dreamqueen did not yet know exactly how they hoped to achieve it.

No, the Dreamqueen needed more. She needed to know where they were, and where they were going.

So, she paced, and watched, and waited.

She waited for her seeds to burrow their way out from the darkness of the fear and shame which nourished them best, to the light of the waking world. She waited for them to release their horrors upon their hosts, unfurling like poison leaves opening to the sun. She waited for that moment of peak maturation when they would be ripe for the reaping, and she would be ready with claws like scythes.

She waited for the screaming to start.

CHAPTER TWENTY

Margali Szardos stomped through the dry yellow grass, wondering which deity she had insulted to wind up getting partnered with the garrulous and too-cheerful Holly LaDonna, and what weapon or spell she'd need to find to send that deity into oblivion.

Bad enough the girl wouldn't shut up, but because she was the one controlling their cloaking spell – another of those ridiculous pink bubbles – Margali couldn't even get far enough away from her for her incessant chatter to become just an annoying background drone.

"...don't really need it to cast your spells, right?" the young witch was asking, her voice slightly breathless from trying to keep up with Margali. "It's just a focus? Or, I dunno... maybe a crutch?"

Margali stopped in her tracks so suddenly that Holly narrowly avoided running into her. She turned to glare at the pink-haired witch whose curiosity she sometimes suspected disguised an arrogance every bit as robust as that of her mentor, Agatha Harkness.

"Excuse me?"

Holly's eyes, already perpetually wide, as if she were in either constant awe or fear, widened even further.

"What?" she asked quizzically, and Margali could see her replaying her words in her head to find where she'd gone wrong. It didn't take her long. "Oh. Oh! I'm sorry! It wasn't meant as an insult. I mean, you *are* a Sorceress Supreme twice over and I don't particularly have a death wish.

"It's just, I haven't seen you cast a spell without using your staff, but as far as I can tell, the staff itself isn't magical, so you don't *need* it to work your magic. So I wondered why you bother with it, other than it making a kickass walking stick.

"But then I thought, maybe you *do* need it. Agatha warned me about using items to contain or focus my spells, because she said it was too easy to become dependent on them. Then, if something happened to the item, my ability to cast spells would be diminished and I'd be royally screw– er, in serious trouble."

Holly stopped talking, apparently done with her explanation as to why Margali should not take umbrage at her words and use the item in question to remove her mouth entirely. But as much as the girl got on Margali's nerves, she would have to be blind not to see the concern on Holly's face. She wasn't mentioning the possibility of dependency to accuse Margali. She was doing it because she cared about her fellow sorceress.

Which honestly might be worse. The roads to most hells were, after all, paved with good intentions.

Even so, her concern probably didn't merit being permanently muted, so Margali just gave her a tiny, thin-lipped smile and shrugged.

"Maybe I use it to make people wonder," she replied. "Uncertainty keeps your enemies off balance."

Allies, too, she thought, though she chose not to share that bit with her companion.

Then she turned and continued on her way, though her pace was more stride and less stomp this time around.

"Nice!" Holly said as she came up to walk beside Margali. "'Thus one who is skillful at keeping the enemy on the move maintains deceitful appearances, according to which the enemy will act.' *The Art of War,* Chapter Five. Though you could replace 'on the move' with 'guessing' for our purposes."

"Yes, well, I believe my version was a bit more succinct," Margali replied, side-eyeing the other woman.

"Definitely. That's one of the things I appreciate most about you, Margali," Holly said.

"Oh?"

"You might mince people, but you never mince words."

Margali could only laugh with her at that. After all, it was only the truth.

Holly LaDonna breathed a small sigh of relief after the short burst of shared laughter faded. She'd accomplished a few things with that little exchange, none of which were getting fried by Margali, so it had been a definite win.

First, she had sussed out Margali's relationship with her staff. The Sorceress Supreme used it to make people think she needed it. If it caused an enemy to focus even one attack on the item instead of its wielder, the ploy would yield benefits far beyond its ability to act as a spell focus or walking aid. While she didn't count Margali as an enemy, she wouldn't say they were besties, so some insight into how the sorceress strategized was good information to know.

Second, Holly thought she had wormed her way a little

further past the other woman's defenses, chipping away a tiny portion of the flint that encased Margali's hypothetical heart. Holly had no illusions about her place in the hierarchy of power in their little foursome. She wasn't here because she could compete with them in terms of strength or experience, though her magic was different enough that, given worlds enough and time – and maybe a teacher who wasn't constantly comparing her to past pupils and finding her wanting – Holly liked to think she might someday be on par with them.

And she certainly wasn't here because any of them had actually requested her presence. But with both Wanda and Agatha out of commission, she'd been what they had to settle for.

Given that, it seemed like a good idea to make sure they all liked her, a goal she'd had varying levels of success with so far, Margali being by far the hardest nut to crack. Sun Tzu might well have been writing about Margali when he said, "If your opponent is of choleric temper, seek to irritate him. Pretend to be weak, that he may grow arrogant."

And, of course, the biggest thing quizzing Margali about the nature of her relationship with her staff had gained Holly was freedom from scrutiny. She already knew that the more she talked, the less Margali listened, so keeping up a constant prattle allowed the Sorceress Supreme to tune her out as the other woman focused on surveilling their path for danger. So she wasn't likely to notice that Holly's concealment bubble wasn't quite as consistent as advertised.

Holly didn't actually think it was a problem, as long as she and Margali stayed close together. And even if one or the other might step outside the boundaries of the bubble gum-colored sphere for a moment or two, Umar didn't know they were here, and had no reason to be looking for them. If she were looking for anyone, it would be Clea. Holly and Margali should slip beneath her radar without incident, regardless of Holly's incomplete mastery of her concealment spell.

She hoped so, anyway.

Chapter Twenty-One

The Dreamqueen was back on her throne, slumped and pouting, when the waters of her gazing pool began to stir. She immediately straightened at the sound of the swirling fluid, leaning over the arm of her throne and peering eagerly into the pool's midnight-blue depths.

She was not disappointed to see the Green One appear, walking in what looked like a never-ending prairie of brittle yellow grass.

Or, rather, parts of her appeared. A booted foot, a green-knuckled hand grasping the shaft of a staff, the golden curl of a horn with some wisps of dark green hair. Enough so that the Dreamqueen could both identify her and determine that she was traveling in some sort of cloaking field, but had gotten too close to its edge and stepped out for the briefest of moments.

Brief, but still too long, alas.

For the dreamseeds she had planted while the Green One and her companions were in Liveworld had germinated, and what had been a powerful but as yet unripe hallucination in Limbo was now ready to sprout into a full-fledged horror.

It was a pity that the sorceress wasn't out of her invisible shell long enough for the Dreamqueen to get a fix on her location, the undulating grasslands in that part of the Dark Dimension being indistinguishable from those in a thousand other places. And she had no idea how fast the group might be traveling under the cover of their concealment.

But she didn't need that information for what she had planned, at least not yet. And even if she'd had it, she wouldn't have been foolish enough to share it. Not until she was certain she was getting what she wanted out of the bargain.

The deadworlders liked to call pacts like the one she was about to propose "deals with the devil". She supposed that was fitting enough, though she was only a demoness and the other party was... whatever she was. Worse than any devil, surely.

But that didn't dissuade the Dreamqueen. On the contrary, it was the first thing that had truly excited her in decades, and the rush of anticipation was as sweet as night terrors on her tongue.

She licked her lips at the thought of that toothsome flavor, her smile reflecting back to her in the now-still waters of her gazing pool.

Then she reached out a finger and stirred them to tumult once again, and when the whirlpool thus created settled, it was no longer her visage staring back at her in imperious annoyance.

It was the flame-wreathed face of Umar the Unrelenting.

Umar stood in the Grand Throne Room before the Azure Throne, hands on her shapely hips as she observed her prisoner, the golden woman Ardina. Ardina stood beside the throne like a sculpted statue. She was tightly bound by the Rings of Raggadorr, seven circles of power that hummed and crackled with mystical energy, the gray Mists of Morpheus twining in and about them like living vines. The rings' color oscillated from indigo to black and back again, the constant shifting patterns threatening to mesmerize any who looked upon them too long.

The spells needed to be periodically refreshed, because they were confining the embodiment of the Power Cosmic and even the mighty duo of Raggadorr and Morpheus might find themselves in frequent need of the boost invocation brought while constraining such great energy.

"As the Seven Rings of Raggadorr
Bind you now from brow to heel,
Let the Mist of Morpheus
Keep your thoughts likewise still."

It was not an elegant spell, to be sure, but rhyming added power even when the scansion was somewhat problematic. The golden woman would stay put until Umar needed her again. When that time came, Umar would invoke the Sphere of Cyttorak, which would keep Ardina trapped but allow access to her power.

Satisfied, the ruler of the Dark Dimension turned away from her throne and surveyed the cavernous room. Peopled by statues of ex-lovers and works of art by renowned artists from a hundred different worlds, it was empty of anything living aside from her and Ardina.

Still, she'd felt a prickling at the base of her neck, as if she were being watched. She strode over to her dimensional window, the heels of her sandals clicking smartly against the cold stone floor, echoing repeatedly off the throne room's stark, bare walls.

Her thoughts went immediately to Stephen Strange. Her unfortunate son-in-law, the man was Sorcerer Supreme of Earth and a constant thorn in her side. He was one of the few people who might be strong enough to break through her dimensional barrier, though it would surprise her to find he'd been so obvious about it. Announcing himself with a frontal assault against an enemy of Umar's caliber was not Doctor Strange's wont, most probably because the man had no desire to die a long and torturous death.

Neither would her brother Dormammu be so conspicuous in any attempt to overthrow her, though she would not have to worry about that for quite some time after the defeat she'd handed her bumbling sibling. Perhaps, with Ardina's power at her disposal, Umar would never have to concern herself with the Dread One again. She could not help but smile with cruel pleasure at the thought.

The only other person who might be able to breach Umar's blockade around the Archipelago of Anguish and Redemption was her daughter, Clea. She'd claimed the title of Sorceress Supreme of the Dark Dimension, and Umar was content to let her have it. What was a sorceress in the face of a goddess?

But, like her estranged husband, Clea would not be foolish enough to let her presence be known if she were trying to enter – or leave – the Dark Dimension. Indeed, Clea had made a career of hiding from her mother as she and her rebels harried Umar's forces at every opportunity.

No, it wasn't Clea, either.

So, who *would* be so foolish as to try to enter her domain without her permission? Umar was equal parts annoyed and intrigued.

She waved a well-manicured hand in front of the dimensional window and her own trim human form, with its long dark hair and tight green dress, disappeared. A white-faced hag with a matted nest of green hair and primitive red horns replaced it.

Umar remembered her. Nightmare's daughter, the Dreamqueen. She didn't bother to hide her look of contempt.

"You have five seconds to explain why you've dared to disturb me before I reach through this window and rip your heart out through your mouth."

The Dreamqueen laughed. "Oh, I don't think you'll want to do that. Not when you hear the information I have about how your daughter intends to thwart your plans to take over the Archipelago. Or the rescue operation she's put together to free that pretty little statue you've got on display over there," the demoness said, indicating the golden woman visible over Umar's shoulder with a quick jerk of her pointed chin and a squinch of her nose.

"I'm listening," Umar said, cocking an eyebrow and crossing her arms in front of her chest. The idea that this inconsequential spawn of Nightmare's would dare come to her, the Unrelenting One, with a lie was… preposterous. Even imprisoned alone in a forsaken pocket dimension, the Dreamqueen still valued her miserable life. And freeing Ardina was exactly the sort of misguided stunt Umar would expect the oh-so-noble Clea to attempt.

"You'll listen after we agree on a price," the Dreamqueen countered, smiling, showing her sharp teeth.

Umar frowned. She could just pull the little chit through the window and strip the information from her mind, but that would take both time and energy. Time she might not have depending on what Clea's plans were, and energy she would need to keep Ardina under control.

"Fine. What do you want?"

"My father's realm, after you conquer it."

Umar shrugged. Nightmare's domain was a gloomy, miserable hellhole that held nothing of value to her. Having a governor oversee it in her stead was not a bad idea.

"Done."

The Dreamqueen's smile widened.

"I wasn't. I meant I want my father's realm… for starters."

CHAPTER TWENTY-TWO

Margali sat high in the crook of a red-barked tree, glad for the chance to relax her vigilance for a while. Having offensive spells constantly at the ready had been nearly as exhausting as if she'd actually been casting them. Now that they were stationary, Holly could likewise attach her concealing bubble to the tree where they rested, lessening her own magical burden.

"You look tired," Holly said from her spot a few branches above Margali. Margali had only gone as far up in the tree as she absolutely had to in order to be out of range of the great horned beasts that roamed these grasslands. She had not imagined there would be any wildlife that would challenge the supremacy of the Mindless Ones, but these armored herbivores traveled in herds large enough that even the Mindless Ones might think twice before crossing their paths, if those shambling brutes were capable of thought.

"You should sleep," Holly continued. "I can take the first watch."

Margali *felt* tired, which was a bad sign. It meant the Teresing Boost spells she'd been covertly casting to revitalize herself during this journey were wearing off early and beginning to lose their effectiveness. And if her spells were becoming less potent, there was only one reason for that.

The power of the Winding Way was beginning to wane, and at a most inopportune time. Not that there was ever a good time for the source of Margali's magic to absent itself, but it was particularly ill-timed now, considering she was in the middle of a mission that would likely end in an arcane battle.

It was truly the bane of her existence, that the very thing she so prized – magical might – was also the most unreliable, waxing and waning like some fickle, unfettered moon, with no rhyme or reason to its patterns that Margali had ever been able to detect.

She thought about what she'd given up to claim that power and become the Sorceress Supreme of the Winding Way. The lies she'd told, the trusts betrayed, the people killed. When the power waned, all those things seemed for naught.

The worst, of course, was her relationship with her children, Amanda and Kurt. She'd used and betrayed them both in different but equally lamentable ways to ascend to the position she held now. Neither of them had truly forgiven her for it, though they had achieved a sort of peaceful accord. She didn't expect forgiveness – the things she had done to the child of her flesh and the child of her heart in the name of power were unconscionable, and she did not deserve absolution. She knew that and accepted it.

But she was still their mother, and she still had a role to play in their lives, regardless of whether any or all of them might like it to be otherwise.

It was still her job to protect them from every harm she didn't cause herself. But there was always a purpose to the pain she brought her children. The world, however, was not so rational, and its ills not so easily predicted or defended against.

The waning of the Winding Way only made that task more difficult, both by draining her power to protect them and by making her question why she had sought to hitch herself to such a capricious wagon.

Margali frowned. Ruminating over past mistakes – if they were mistakes – was not something she did. All actions, right or wrong, had consequences. She measured those consequences carefully before she ever chose to act, and thus had few regrets.

She gave her head a quick shake, green curls stinging her eyes and lips as she tried to dislodge the foreign thoughts. It must be because she was so exhausted. She wasn't thinking clearly.

Maybe she *should* rest. Just for a bit, to give her mind time to settle. Any longer might betray weakness that she couldn't afford to display, even just to Holly. Allies could become enemies so quickly in the magical world. The blink of an eye, the wave of a hand, the whisper of a spell. Better safe than sorry.

Yes, she would sleep. Just rest her eyes. Only for a moment.

Margali's heavy eyelids drooped and closed, perhaps of their own accord.

And then she slept.

Margali woke in the small bed behind the beaded curtain in her wagon. She blinked several times against the ray of sunlight beaming across her face, wondering briefly why the fading golden color seemed somehow wrong and out of place to her. But she blinked the odd worry away with the sleep still crusting her eyes, stretched and yawned, then sat up.

She could hear the circus coming to life around her as evening fell, and that seemed wrong, too. She had a fleeting vision of another wagon superimposed over this one, much older and more rundown, sparsely furnished, and standing alone in a secluded meadow. The laughter of two passing acrobats chased the image away.

She was back at Herr Getmann's Traveling Menagerie.

Back? When had she left?

Margali shook her dream-addled head, dark green curls bouncing about her face like springing vines.

Green? Shouldn't it be brown? And why was she wearing a helmet?

Shhh, now.

Margali knew the voice, or would know it, and she did not think it was one that should be obeyed. She did not, however, seem to have much choice in the matter.

But… now her skin was green, too?

Be still.

Margali's concerns faded. She was at the circus, and she was taking the night off from bilking locals out of their hard-earned coin, lying to them about rosy futures, so that she could watch her daughter Jimaine perform on the trapeze. She needed to hurry. She didn't want to miss what she knew would be a special performance.

Margali stood and grabbed her staff, her white dress swirling about her legs. She pushed her way through the beaded curtain, the argent barrier clicking and clacking behind her like bones thrown to reveal her fate.

She exited her wagon, turned her "The Fortune Teller Is In" sign to the "Away" side and strode quickly to the main tent. She could already hear Herr Getmann beginning Jimaine's introduction.

"Damen! Herren! Ladies! Gentlemen! Look skywards! Look," he was saying as Margali entered the striped tent between two packed stands of onlookers, "and be amazed by the death-defying feats of Jimaine Szardos, the Flying Maiden of the Swing Trapeze!"

Margali's gaze followed everyone else's up to a small wooden platform near the top of the tent, where she could see Jimaine standing in her red and black leotard, her blonde hair pulled back into a tight ponytail. She had the slim trapeze bar clutched in one hand as she waved with the other.

As Margali and the rest of the crowd watched, Jimaine launched herself off the platform. Her body knifed through the air, knees bending just as her swing reached its apex and she released the bar, using her momentum to somersault through the air and grab the bar of the other swing which had just reached its own apex at the exact moment her hands reached for it. It was truly a marvel of both science and art, as well as a celebration of what the human body could accomplish, given the right training.

Not that being a trapeze artist was the right training for Jimaine. No, she would follow the path of sorcery, just as Margali and the women in her line had done for centuries. But Margali clapped and cheered for this interim success of her daughter's, all the same. She was not a complete churl.

The cheering stopped abruptly, replaced with horrified shouts.

"Oh God, the girl!"

"The ropes! They've snapped!"

And from Jimaine herself, the most chilling cry of all, as she flailed helplessly in the air and began to plummet toward the ground, with no net to break her fall.

"Heeeelp–!"

Margali spoke a quick levitation spell, slamming the butt of her staff hard on the ground.

"May the Vapors of Valtorr,

"Wherever they be found,

"Form a cushion 'round my daughter,

"That she may float to the ground!"

But there was no accompanying rush of power, the gem in her staff's cage stayed dull, and, most importantly, Jimaine's descent was not halted.

No. This couldn't be happening. Not now.

The Winding Way had deserted her. Again.

A small part of Margali's mind argued that she had not been walking the Winding Way in earnest when she and the children had been in Herr Getmann's circus, and she could not have lost what she did not yet have. Nor had she been there the night Jimaine fell from the trapeze, and Kurt rescued her, revealing himself as a teleporting blue devil to the townspeople.

But the voice she shouldn't be listening to shushed her, and Margali could only watch in despair as Jimaine tumbled from the heights, and every spell she tried to save her daughter failed.

The Winds of Watoomb would not blow. The Moons of Munnopor would not shine. No Hand of Hoggoth appeared to catch Jimaine or cushion her fall.

Margali could not even do so much as slow her daughter's descent. She was powerless. Helpless.

Then Kurt appeared in the air beside Jimaine and tried to grab her so he could teleport her safely to the ground, his fingers clutching at the smooth fabric of her leotard as she fell past him.

He missed.

The entire tent was transfixed in mute horror as Jimaine's body hit the dirt with a wet thud, like a sack of spoiled potatoes tossed from the truck on the way to market. She reached up a slow, trembling hand, as if trying to find Kurt's. He teleported down beside her, sobbing as he shook his head in denial, but her arm fell limply back to the ground before he could grasp her hand. She didn't move again, and Margali did not have to be standing at her side to know that Jimaine was dead.

She threw her head back and screamed in impotent rage. If she had had access to her power, the echoes of her grief would have carried on currents of tormenting fire and set the tent ablaze, incinerating everyone in it who had watched Margali's daughter die and done nothing.

Including her.

The crowd took her cry as a signal to release the hounds, surging forward in an angry, violent mass, grabbing the distraught Kurt before he could think clearly enough to teleport away.

Margali sent bolts of bedevilment and worse at them, tried to bind them with rings and bands, anything to keep them away from her foster-son, but nothing worked. The magic simply would not respond to her. The power of the Winding Way had not just waned, it had disappeared completely, and she knew in her bones that it would never be back.

She tried to force her way through the crowd to get to Kurt, shoving, punching, biting, clawing, but no matter what she did, she couldn't seem to get any closer to him. She watched helplessly as they took out their fear and anger on her foster-son's blue flesh, not even bothering to cart him off to a stake for burning as would be the case for most warlocks and devils. Their bloodlust finally sated, the crowd trickled out of the tent, parting around her where she stood. Soon, she was alone in the cavernous canvas tomb with the bodies of her two children, one lying over the other, as if they had been enacting the death scene from *Romeo and Juliet*. But while this was an equally stupid tragedy, these actors were truly dead, and there would be no curtain calls for them.

Margali walked numbly over to where her children lay and fell to her knees beside them. She brushed Kurt's dark hair out of Jimaine's face and gently turned his head toward Jimaine. She tried to wipe as much blood from their faces as she could with the hem of her dress. She couldn't tell whose was whose, and she supposed it didn't matter. She knew the two had been in love with each other before they even knew it themselves. That they should at least be together in death was the only shred of comfort she could find in what had become the worst day in a lifetime full of worst days.

But it was finally too much. Her dress was stained scarlet, and she still couldn't get all the blood from their faces, something she had convinced herself was necessary for them to be able to rest in peace and be together in whatever afterlife heroes got to have. She couldn't even give them that much.

Margali felt drained, empty of fury, empty of lament. That was as it should be, she supposed. What right had she to those emotions? She had failed her children when they needed her most.

The magic had failed *her* when she needed it most, and what was she without it?

Nothing. Worthless.

Not a Sorceress Supreme. Not even a sorceress.

Just the powerless mother of two dead children whose blood she could never wash from her hands.

Margali lowered her head, rare tears coursing down her cheeks as she began to weep.

CHAPTER TWENTY-THREE

Elizabeth Twoyoungmen followed Clea as she led the way through terrain that gave the phrase "rolling hills" a whole new meaning. The silver-haired sorceress had told her that they were traveling through the Never Hills, so called because the ever-shifting landscape never looked the same way twice.

"If they're moving, why do we have to?" Elizabeth had asked. "Why can't we just stand still and let the hills take us where we want to go, like some kind of nausea-inducing moving sidewalk?"

Clea had launched into a detailed explanation that Elizabeth tuned out after about ten yards, but she got the gist of it. The Never Hills didn't just move, they phased in and out of physical reality, so that a hill might be in front of them one moment and hundreds of kilometers away the next. And if you were on that hill when it disappeared, there was no guarantee you'd still be on it when – or if – it reappeared. And if you weren't ... well, no one was really sure where you'd wind up, but the consensus was "no place good".

And if the citizens of the Dark Dimension thought a place was bad ... considering what they lived with daily and deemed normal, Elizabeth was certain she didn't want to find out where that place might be.

It wasn't exactly teleportation as Clea understood it; rather, it appeared to be a phenomenon thankfully unique to the Never Hills. Which was why few people dared to trek across them and why she had chosen to locate her rebel base behind the formidable barrier they presented.

When questioned as to why people didn't just fly over them if they were so dangerous, Clea had grabbed a fist-sized rock and chucked it into the air. She had a decent throwing arm, and the stone flew in a high arc until it suddenly just disappeared. Apparently, the strange anomaly that surrounded the Never Hills extended upward in some places, making the airspace above the restless ground the unfriendliest of skies.

And so they walked, close together, Elizabeth's eyes glowing as she concentrated as well as she could manage on maintaining the Coronet of Power's concealment spell, while Clea navigated, threading the needle between disappearing hills with the precision of a surgeon. Though, given the way the other sorceress frowned whenever she heard Doctor Strange's name mentioned, Elizabeth doubted she would appreciate the comparison.

Elizabeth still wasn't sure exactly what the couple's dynamics were at the moment. She'd been away from the magical moccasin telegraph for quite some time, but even before that, she hadn't cared much about what her peers around the world might be up to unless it impacted her in some way. She'd been very angry and self-absorbed back then, she knew. In her defense, she'd been a college student when the role of the Talisman had been forced on her. She could hardly have been expected to take her life being completely upended gracefully.

Despite her eschewing the bulk of the sorcerous community, Doctor Strange was one of the few magic-users whose exploits she had kept up with in any fashion. He had saved her Canadian bacon once – well, hers and the whole world's – so she felt a sense of obligation to him, and she was always on the lookout for a chance to return the favor.

So she knew he and Clea had had some rocky patches, due in large part to living in separate dimensions, and perhaps in larger part to Strange himself, who, while a master of the mystic arts, still had a lot to learn when it came to those of the heart.

It seemed to Elizabeth that they cared about each other very much, but theirs was a truly star-crossed love, in that they each had responsibilities they could not put aside that would always ultimately conspire to pull them apart. Clea, at least, seemed to understand that on some level, though whether she let that subconscious understanding inform the conscious decisions she made to both nourish and protect her vulnerable heart, Elizabeth couldn't say.

Elizabeth bit her lip hard to bring her wandering thoughts back to the task at hand, the pain and the taste of blood reminding her why she was here. It wasn't to play Dear Abby and offer up relationship advice, even if it was only in her own head.

Still not as alert to her surroundings as she should have been, and perhaps a bit feverish from a wound that wasn't healing as well as it ought, Elizabeth didn't notice when Clea stopped in front of her. She walked right into her companion, nearly knocking the other woman over.

"Ouch!" she exclaimed, the sudden unexpected movement jarring the wound on her back. "What is it? Why have we stopped?"

Clea turned to look at her, her expression one of mingled confusion and surprise. "I'm not sure. It seems to be... an oasis?"

It was indeed an oasis, not one offering water in the desert, but one providing stability amidst chaos. The Never Hills seemed to part around it, like a river around an island, and Elizabeth had never been so happy to see a bunch of scraggly-looking trees and a few boulders. It would have been nice if the oasis had also boasted a pool of water, considering the women had been having to conjure it up for themselves for the bulk of their journey; Umar's blight spell had triggered a drought that was already making once-mighty rivers run dry. The woman was a walking climate crisis, and the sooner she was overthrown, the better.

Once they had settled in, Elizabeth anchored the coronet's cloaking spell to stable ground and began probing the wound the Mindless One's optic blast had left in the small of her back to determine the extent of the damage.

It wasn't good. Far worse than she'd let on to the others. Her healing poultice, a mix of traditional First Nations medicine and magical components, would heal the injury eventually, but she needed time and rest, two things that were currently in short supply.

Or had been, until Clea had found this little pocket of immobility. Here, the only thing that would disrupt her healing, aside from Clea's occasional attempts at conversation, were the hills that still insisted on undulating around them. Elizabeth had to keep her eyes firmly on the ground as she leaned up against a tree, her head and shoulder pressing firmly enough into the bark that she knew it would leave marks on her cheeks. She didn't care. She just wanted to sleep.

Her eyes fluttered shut, for just a moment, it seemed.

Which was why she didn't see the group of Mindless Ones until they had already surrounded the oasis.

Elizabeth jolted upright, her movement startling Clea, who had likewise let her guard down in the ersatz safety of their resting place and been in a light meditative state.

Elizabeth didn't know which was stranger: that the Mindless Ones knew she and Clea were there, despite her concealment spell, or that they were just standing there, doing nothing. Whatever the reason, she knew enough not to look a gift horse in the mouth. Clea was right there with her, her hands forming the Karana Mundra in preparation for attack.

But no sooner had Elizabeth begun drawing a spell from the thousands the coronet gave her access to than a voice rang out, all around them, coming from everywhere and nowhere at once.

"Well, well, well. What delights have you found for me to play with today, my pets?"

CHAPTER TWENTY-FOUR

Holly scanned the horizon, her eyes squinted against the monotonous sea of yellow grass that stretched out from their tree in every direction. It was like looking directly into the sun, if the sun were all around you and only a little dimmer than usual.

There were dark spots that could be trees, or rocks, or Mindless Ones, or something worse. If Holly stared too long, she couldn't tell if they were moving or not, and if she looked away and back again, she couldn't tell if their positions had changed. It was giving her a massive headache.

Margali made a small moaning sound below her, and Holly glanced over at the other woman, wondering if she were having a nightmare. She wondered what that might mean here in the Dark Dimension, where they were just a hop, skip, and a jump away from that hell lord's domain.

She was astounded to see tears slipping out from underneath Margali's closed eyelids and sliding down her cheeks to drip from her chin onto her dress.

Holly had not thought the woman capable of crying.

And if she was crying in her sleep, that could hardly be a good thing.

Abandoning her fruitless lookout duties, Holly shimmied

down to the branch Margali rested on and took the green-skinned sorceress by the shoulders, shaking her gently.

"Margali! Margali, wake up! You're having a nightmare."

Margali moaned again, but her eyes remained stubbornly closed. Holly shook her harder and raised her voice, to no effect.

Well, there was nothing for it. Hopefully Margali wouldn't blast her into oblivion for the affront.

Holly took a deep breath, let it out, and then slapped Margali across the face. Maybe a tad harder than she really needed to.

Margali's yellow eyes snapped open, already blazing, and her hand shot out to grab Holly's wrist. There was no recognition in her face, only fury. Holly braced herself, readying a shielding bubble, but then Margali blinked several times and shook her head as if coming out of a trance, letting go of Holly's arm.

"Where… where are we?" she asked, looking around in confusion. Then she gasped and her head snapped back around, her face filled with sudden panic as she stared at Holly.

"My children! Amanda! Kurt! Where…?"

She trailed off, the panic replaced by grief as she answered her own question.

"Dead," she whispered, head lowering. "Dead. My fault. I couldn't stop it. The Winding Way has abandoned me, left me bereft of both power and children. What am I without them?"

Holly had been trying to follow Margali's mercurial mood shifts and her disjointed words. She had assumed the green-skinned woman had been in the grip of a particularly nasty nightmare. But now she wondered if it was something more.

The Dreamqueen had assaulted Margali with hallucinations involving her children in Limbo. Was this more of the same?

Whatever the cause, it needed to be dealt with. Holly needed

Blast First, Ask Questions Later Margali, not Huddled in a Corner Sobbing Margali.

It was times like this where she really missed Agatha, brusque and unpleasant as the old woman could be. She took no crap from anyone, and there was no crisis she could not handle with aplomb. Except maybe the one where Wanda had killed her. Wanda, another grieving mother, though she faced the actual deaths of fictional children, whereas Margali appeared to be coping with the fictional deaths of her actual children.

On second thought, Agatha might not be that much help in this situation, after all.

Holly was on her own with this one.

Wits, don't fail me now.

Holly mouthed a quick spell, her words soundless, though their effect was not.

"Margali," she said in a calm, measured voice, as Agatha had taught her. "Margali, look at me." Compulsion underlay her words, but it was subtle enough to be confused with free will. Not a spell she enjoyed using, especially on a fellow sorceress. Women like them had enough to endure, being misunderstood and persecuted since time immemorial. Infighting was silly and self-defeating.

Margali raised her head, and Holly saw fresh tears sparkling in her eyes and rolling down her cheeks.

"Listen to me," Holly continued. "Your children are *not* dead. You are their mother. You would *know*. The bond between mother and child is a magic more ancient and potent than any sorcery you could ever learn or gain from an outside source. And it's not something that can be taken from you. Ever."

You could give it up, Holly supposed, but she didn't think now would be a good time for that particular discussion.

Margali blinked the tears out of her eyes and wiped the ones on her cheeks away with her fists, but said nothing. Holly thought that was a good sign.

Probably.

She resumed her arguments, like some occult attorney trying to gently lead her witness without getting reprimanded by whoever – or whatever – might be the judge.

"And the Winding Way isn't gone. Can you imagine?" Holly laughed a little. "The destruction of an entire dimension? What the reaction of the magical community would be? Umar is far too intelligent to court that sort of attention.

"The Winding Way hasn't gone anywhere, and it hasn't left you. I can still feel its power in you right now, swirling and eager, as always. It's there. All you have to do is reach out and take it. And you don't need me to show you how to do that."

Not that she could. Witchcraft was based on understanding the energies inherent in all things, including oneself, and learning to manipulate them to achieve desired results. Sorcery was similar, though it focused more on the mastery of self and appeals to higher beings. What the Winding Way was, Holly couldn't really say. Margali used many of the same spells that Clea did, so Holly assumed it shared properties with that practice, but it also included channeling the power of an entire magical dimension through a mortal vessel. It was no wonder Margali had worn the Eye of Agamotto before Doctor Strange. The only real surprise was that she didn't wear it still.

Margali closed her eyes. Though she had not been moving, a stillness came over her. Her breathing was slow and even. Holly could almost believe she was meditating or sleeping peacefully. But this was Margali Szardos. She could just as easily be plotting Holly's imminent demise.

Holly kept her defense spell at the ready, even though she knew casting it would disrupt her concealment bubble. Her death would also have that effect, so it wasn't a difficult choice.

Finally, Margali took in a deep breath through her nose, nostrils flaring, then she let it out slowly through her mouth a few long heartbeats later. She opened her eyes and looked up at Holly, seemingly herself again.

"Thank you for that," she said. "Your timely intervention saved me from that assault when I was… temporarily unable to do so myself."

Holly had a pretty good idea of how hard it was for the other sorceress to admit that. Like Agatha, Margali was proud to a fault, and arrogant to boot. Gratitude and remorse were not feelings the sorceress was particularly conversant with.

Though there were a hundred flippant responses on the tip of Holly's tongue, her amusement wasn't worth losing Margali's trust, so she simply said, "You're welcome."

But, of course, her curiosity prevented her from leaving it at that.

"You said, 'assault'?"

Margali nodded wearily. For the first time, Holly noticed wrinkles around the other woman's eyes. Had they been there before? They didn't make her look old so much as defeated.

"I believe it was another of the Dreamqueen's damnable hallucinations," she replied. "But now I have her scent. She won't be able to attack me that way again."

Then Margali smiled a demented Mona Lisa smile.

"And if she's stupid enough to try, I'll be ready."

Chapter Twenty-Five

Clea turned to see a smug white theater mask floating above what looked like a portal into Earth's universe, blackness dotted with stars and colorful globes and hunks of rock with blazing tails. She groaned inwardly. She knew who this impossible entity was, though she had never had the displeasure of encountering him before – Plokta.

A powerful duke of hell, he had created the Mindless Ones and was the only being in the Dark Dimension who could fully control them. Which made him a dangerous adversary to whomever sat on the Azure Throne at any given time... or would have, if he'd ever been able to overcome the magic of the shimmering wall that separated the Mindless Ones' territory from the dimension's populated regions. Or torture the trick out of the rare few who knew it.

It also made him one of the most hated beings in the whole of the Splinter Realms. No family here had escaped the terror of the Mindless Ones when they first poured into the Dark Dimension, and many others throughout the Archipelago had been impacted when Plokta had loosed his lumbering horrors upon his rivals in their home dimensions. The Mindless Ones were indiscriminate in their destruction, so it was rarely just

Plokta's antagonists who suffered. Often, those individuals didn't suffer at all beyond momentary inconvenience, which made the affected families hate them only slightly less than they detested Plokta.

Clea had never lost a close friend to the Mindless Ones, and of course her only family here were powerful individuals well beyond the reach of such creatures. She wasn't sure how she would feel if she did somehow lose one of them to Plokta's creations. She doubted she would mourn overmuch.

But she *had* seen innocent citizens die when Dormammu's wall had weakened or when Umar had banished them to the wrong side of the barrier. They'd been battered by the things' fists and scorched by their optic blasts until there was nothing left of them, and Clea could do nothing to stop it.

So, it was fair to say she hated Plokta, too. But unlike most of the families whose lives his creations had devastated, she had the power to do something about it. But unfortunately, she couldn't use it.

Clea was careful about using her powers in the Dark Dimension outside of a rebel base or during an attack on Umar's forces. She knew her mother watched for signs of her magical signature, ready to pounce like a cat on a hapless mouse should Clea reveal her location long enough for Umar to bring her considerable power to bear. Even if her mother was unwilling to kill Clea, imprisonment, permanent banishment, and even enslavement were all still viable options. Umar would like nothing better than to get rid of the last nagging contender to what she perceived as her rightful throne now that Dormammu was no longer in the picture.

Clea could only imagine the situation had worsened now that Umar had Ardina's power to draw from. Her mother had to know she would come for her friend sooner or later, so she was likely on high alert for any trace of Clea's magic. And if she found Clea and her friends now, everything they had endured thus far would be for naught. Worse, in addition to Ardina and the Power Cosmic, Umar would then potentially have access to everything from Elizabeth's coronet to Margali's staff.

As much as Clea would love to unleash the Crystals of Cyndriarr or some other equally deadly spell on Plokta, she couldn't risk it.

So, she would have to find some other way to get her and Elizabeth out of the duke's clutches. She supposed it wouldn't hurt to start with a bluff.

"We are no one's playthings, hellspawn," she said imperiously, channeling her inner Margali as she lifted her chin and fixed the floating white mask with a menacing glare. "I would suggest that you remove yourself from our presence posthaste if you don't want to learn exactly what sort of things we *are*, and how roughly we can play." At her side, her hand pressed against her thigh, her fingers surreptitiously forming the Karana Mundra once more. Lesser spells like bolts of bedevilment were generic enough that they were not likely to catch Umar's attention.

Of course, they also weren't likely to do much damage to Plokta, but there was a chance they might occupy him and his Mindless Ones long enough that she and Elizabeth could make their escape. A slim chance, to be sure, but with her choice of spells limited and Elizabeth not at full strength, Clea wasn't sure what other choice she had.

Plokta laughed at her words.

"As much as I would love to test the truth of that threat, my dear, I must regretfully decline. Umar is expecting more Mindless Ones from me, and the magical fuel I require for their creation has become quite scarce in the Dark Dimension since she and her brother decided to dally here. I'd begun to worry that I might disappoint her, but the multiverse has shown its favor by leading the two of you to my very doorstep." Plokta's mask did not move, but Clea was sure he was smiling smugly.

"A duke of hell, reduced to being Umar's errand boy?" Elizabeth chimed in, her tone condescending, dripping with disdain. Like Clea, she realized their best chance of getting out of this situation was to throw Plokta off kilter, so he was too frustrated to think clearly or plan effectively. Clea had chosen intimidation as her means of accomplishing that goal; Elizabeth was clearly going for his pride. "How very... pitiful."

Plokta did not take their bait. He laughed again, his carved mouth never moving.

"Temporary servitude is the better part of survival," he replied.

Seeing that their plan to rattle him was not going to work, Clea decided to change tactics and pump him for information instead. The more she and Elizabeth knew about him, the better their chances of prevailing against him in a fight. Or so she hoped.

"What did you mean by 'magical fuel'?" she asked.

The dimensional portal that formed Plokta's body shifted slightly, and it took Clea a moment to realize that he was shrugging.

"There are certain laws that govern science and magic both. One is that energy is not created or destroyed, but simply changes form."

"The First Law of Thermodynamics," Elizabeth said, and when Clea looked at her in surprise, she added, somewhat defensively, "I did go to college, you know."

"Quite," Plokta responded, ignoring her aside to Clea. "In this case, the energy to 'make' Mindless Ones, which are magical creatures, can only come from 'destroying' other magical creatures. Unicorns, dragons, or…"

The blood drained from Clea's face as she realized what his final word was going to be a split second before it came out of his unmoving mouth.

"…sorceresses."

CHAPTER TWENTY-SIX

The Dreamqueen was pacing again. She had lost track of the interlopers since the last time she'd caught a glimpse of the Green One, a fact she chose not to share with her new partner, Umar. The Unrelenting One had agreed to the Dreamqueen's bargain, but both parties knew betrayal was inevitable. Duplicity was in their natures, as instinctive to them as breathing. Their alliance would last only so long as one had value to the other. And knowing the location of Umar's daughter was the source of the Dreamqueen's value to Umar. Which made not knowing it a very dangerous proposition.

She knew where the Green One had last stepped out of the concealment sphere that surrounded the group. And it seemed obvious that sooner or later they would wind up at Umar's palace to confront her. But with no idea of how they intended to get from one place to the other, that knowledge was useless to her.

So, she paced back and forth, circling her gazing pool and willing it to show her one of the women. Or a part of one, at least.

Something glinted on the surface of the pool. The Dreamqueen whipped her horned head around and leaned eagerly over the still water, waiting.

And waiting. Long enough that she began to wonder if what she'd seen had merely been a reflection from the high, thin, stained-glass windows that rose up behind her throne, though she knew that was not how the gazing pool worked. It was not a mirror; it was a window.

Even if she did catch another glimpse of one of the women, it wouldn't necessarily be helpful information to share with Umar. Every interminable swath of yellow grass looked like every other. Without landmarks, it was impossible to pin the sorceresses down to a specific location.

But it would still be helpful for the Dreamqueen's purposes. She didn't really care where they were; finding them for the sake of saving Umar was not her purpose. On the contrary, dangling that knowledge had simply been an effective ploy to get Umar's attention, since the Unrelenting One most certainly *did* care about the whereabouts of her daughter. The information was a bargaining chip, nothing more.

The Dreamqueen wanted to find the women for another reason entirely.

She wanted to plant more dreamseeds that would bear nightmarish fruit, harvest those already planted and newly ripened, and revel in the blooming anguish. Seeds planted deep enough might not even sprout until the sorceresses returned to Earth, affording the Dreamqueen her long-desired entry to that world.

There. A flash of pink.

The Dreamqueen grinned. Time to tend her ghastly garden.

Chapter Twenty-Seven

Margali didn't say much as the two women continued their journey to Clea's secondary rebel base. She was hardly one to make small talk under normal circumstances, and even though her life often involved traveling to odd places with even odder people, this situation was far from the usual. Not because of where she was or who she was with, but because of the blow she'd just taken to her self-confidence.

Her bravado to Holly notwithstanding, Margali had been deeply shaken by how easily she'd been taken in by the Dreamqueen's hallucination. By how completely she'd believed it and how devastated she still felt at the remembered loss of her powers and her children, even now, hours after Holly had slapped her awake.

It didn't help that her magic was, in fact, beginning to wane. She had followed the path of the Winding Way long enough to know when the tide of power was starting to ebb, though she could never predict it beforehand, or tell how long it might last, or how severe it might be. Some cycles lasted a day, and she could not even conjure a glamour to hide dark circles under her eyes during that time, let alone protect herself or anyone else. Some lasted weeks, but only stripped her of her most potent spells, barely affecting her. It was, as Kurt liked to say, a crapshoot.

The monotonous landscape was no help either, the sheer boredom it imbued practically forcing one to look within for mental stimulation of any kind. But there did, finally, seem to be something different about the prairieland through which they trudged.

Though everything had looked the same for kilometers, the terrain was beginning to change, golden grass giving way to rust-colored dirt and more of the rock outcroppings that had protruded randomly from the plains as they walked. The ubiquitous grain-laden smell reminiscent of a far-off brewery was replaced by that of dirt and dust. Hardly a fair trade in Margali's estimation.

The ground seemed to be rising, too, which Margali took to be a good sign, since Clea had told them that the base was located in a large cavern hidden in the hills. The silver-haired sorceress had – with the group's permission this time – implanted a mental map in each of their minds, so they would head unerringly toward their objective. But the exact destination itself had not been part of the psychic path laid out for them, to thwart any potential captors. An unnecessary precaution in Margali's opinion, but no one else had voiced any opposition, so the Sorceress Supreme of the Winding Way had likewise taken the unfamiliar step of keeping her opinion to herself.

Even though Margali was in the lead – a measure that limited the amount she had to converse with Holly, if not how much the girl actually talked – it was the pink-haired witch who spotted the cave opening first. Hidden behind a patch of crimson scrub brush and a precisely placed outcropping, the entrance was only visible from one particular angle.

"Are we there yet?" she asked, somewhat rhetorically, pointing out the opening to Margali.

Margali realized that the guideline that Clea had placed in her head, a blazing trail that had floated in the air before her whenever she closed her eyes and concentrated on it, was no longer there. This must indeed be the place, though she didn't bother to answer Holly's question. She had finally realized that the other woman wasn't looking for a reply.

But when they tried to enter the mouth of the cavern, moving aside some of the brush and shimmying around the stone outcropping, they found that they could not. Some force pushed back against Holly's concealment bubble and would not let them through.

"I think it's dueling cloaking spells," Holly said after a moment. "Clea did say the place was both physically and magically hidden from Umar and her minions. I'm going to have to drop my spell so we can pass through."

Margali nodded. She didn't particularly care what the issue was or how Holly opted to fix it. She just wanted to get inside and find Clea's rebels. Along with a warm meal, a bath, and a bed, preferably in that order.

She did think it odd that they hadn't encountered any lookouts or guards up to this point, but when manpower was short, it was deceptively easy to rely on magic to make up the difference.

It was also usually a bad idea. No matter the intricacy of the spell, magic could only do so much, and it was no substitute for someone who could observe, weigh, and make split second decisions.

But perhaps Clea's rebels were just better concealed than she expected. After all, they had survived this long against both Dormammu and Umar, so they must be doing something right.

Still, she could not dismiss the feeling that something was amiss. She was about to say as much to Holly when the other woman whispered something behind her back, then pushed her through the opening, following right on her heels. Together they stumbled into a vast, cold, echoing cavern, the roof and back walls of which stretched nearly out of sight.

It was empty.

"Where are they?" Holly asked, turning to Margali with a frown. She hugged herself, shivering beneath her sweatshirt. "It should be a lot warmer in here if it's housing a large military force." She paused to consider. "Well, largeish."

Margali tapped the bottom of her staff against the stone floor and the caged gem flared to life, bathing their immediate vicinity in yellow-white light and brightening the cave for a long distance beyond that.

Not only was it empty of people, it was barren of anything that might conceivably furnish a military installation or rebel headquarters. There were no tables topped with maps or foodstuffs, no beds, no weapon racks. Nothing to indicate other sentient beings besides the two of them had ever been here, except for the concealment spell. And a gaping hole in the rear of the cavern that might have been the opening to a cistern, or a well. Or just a natural feature that meant nothing.

"Do you suppose Umar found them before we got here?" Holly asked. "Wiped them out?"

Margali shook her head.

"We would see signs of a struggle – scorch marks, melted or pitted rock, blood. Overturned or demolished furniture.

Except there is no furniture, and Umar's forces would hardly be inclined to take it with them if they had overrun the place.

"No. I think it's pretty clear there was never a rebel base here to begin with. And that can only mean one thing."

Holly's doe eyes filled with dread. She wasn't a stupid girl. She knew where Margali was headed, and she didn't want to go there.

"This place is a decoy. *We* are a decoy, meant to keep Umar's attention away from Clea and Elizabeth while they... do whatever it is they're doing without us." Margali could feel her eyes blazing yellow with barely contained rage. She'd been played for a fool, and by someone she had actually begun to think she could trust. She didn't know who she was angrier with – herself, or Clea.

Holly was still staring at her, refusing to connect the dots.

"Don't you get it?" Margali snapped. "We've been duped."

The Dreamqueen watched as the Pink One dropped her concealment spell just before she and the Green One entered a cave that was otherwise cloaked from the gazing pool's sight.

There were only the two of them. The Purple One – Umar's daughter – and the Talisman were nowhere to be found.

The Dreamqueen screamed in rage, slamming a fist down into the basin of water, the image of the Dark Dimension obliterated by its sloshing waves.

She had been duped.

Someone was going to pay.

Chapter Twenty-Eight

Elizabeth watched Clea, waiting for the sorceress to make a move before making her own. She knew Clea was afraid to use her powers out in the open now that they were in the Dark Dimension, and Elizabeth wasn't sure how well she would be able to continue concealing them if the other woman chose to go on the offensive against the floating theater mask. Elizabeth's back injury was healing, and the small bit of rest she'd gotten before being so rudely interrupted had helped immensely, but she was not operating at capacity, and she wasn't sure she could wrangle the coronet's power to both conceal Clea and join in any attack she might launch. Not effectively, anyway. And any break in her concentration could be an opening for Umar, whom they weren't yet ready to face.

And though no one had come out and said it, there was a big elephant taking up most of the space in the room. If Umar conquered the entirety of the Archipelago of Anguish and Redemption, it was unlikely she'd stop there. Clea had told the group that Umar had sworn off attacking Earth some time back, but power had a way of making people forget their limits, self-imposed or otherwise. They couldn't rely on the promise of an avowed liar, made under different circumstances when she didn't have a little golden bunny to energize her.

It was just too risky.

As Clea opened her mouth to speak, Elizabeth stepped forward.

"I have something that will generate a potentially limitless supply of Mindless Ones. You don't need a sorceress. You need me."

Clea's jaw dropped, whatever words she might have been going to utter now lost to the ether, her mouth working silently as she tried and failed to come up with some sort of fitting response. The look of shock on her face might have been comical if the situation itself weren't so dire.

But Elizabeth had to ignore her for now and keep Plokta busy. He hadn't yet recognized Clea as Umar's daughter, and the more Elizabeth talked, the less likely he was to do so. It was a tactic Holly used masterfully.

"Indeed? And what might that be?" the duke of hell asked, feigning interest. He didn't believe her, but was clearly willing to play along. Elizabeth supposed he didn't get much opportunity for conversation out here among the Mindless Ones. She was pretty sure they didn't even have mouths.

"Elizabeth, you don't have to–" Clea began, but the Tsuut'ina woman ignored her.

She concentrated on the coronet, making it glow brighter, her eyes mirroring its magical radiance. Plokta's own eyes were carved onto his mask face, lids closed, but somehow Elizabeth could still sense his gaze sharpening hungrily. She wondered idly if he actually couldn't move his facial features, or just chose not to, as some sort of infernal ducal affectation.

"And what might that pretty little trinket be?" Plokta asked, and while his face might be able to disguise his greed, his voice could not.

"Oh, this old thing?" Elizabeth replied, flipping her long dark hair haughtily over her shoulder, doing her best imitation of the wealthy teenaged mean girls she'd gone to school with. "It's nothing, really. Just the Coronet of Enchantment. I think some people also call it the Coronet of Power. Nothing that would interest you, I'm sure."

Were angry hairline furrows beginning to crack that clay forehead? Had the carven eyes narrowed just the tiniest bit? Did Plokta's face look, just for a moment, like Margali before a temper tantrum?

Probably not, but imagining it to be so amused Elizabeth, and anything that dialed back the desperation of this moment in her mind was welcome. Because she had the beginnings of a very bad plan, which had every likelihood of failing catastrophically, with more than just her own life or even her own dimension's freedom riding on it.

But she couldn't think of anything else to do. Clea had to be free. Of all four members of their sorcerous rescue squad, she was the only one who had ever faced – and bested – Umar. And she had created Ardina; if anyone could figure out a way to free the golden woman, it was her. And if Ardina couldn't be freed… well, that was another elephant, a smaller one that she imagined only she and Clea had yet realized was also crowding the room. If the golden woman could not be freed from Umar's hold, then she might well have to be killed. Presumably, only her creator could do that.

"I find human games tiresome, girl," Plokta said, interrupting Elizabeth's racing thoughts. "Your coronet does indeed possess amazing power; give it to me, and I will let you both go free."

"Well, you see, that's where we hit a little wrinkle. I *can't* actually give you the coronet, because it can't be removed. And only I can use its power, so..."

Elizabeth had no idea if the duke of hell could detect lies or not, but seeing as this was a half-truth, perhaps it would not trip any alarms, even if he was a demonic polygraph. While it was true that she could not remove the coronet herself, others had managed to remove it from her for brief periods of time, when she was a younger, more foolish, less powerful Talisman. And she had always gotten it back. But she didn't think those were details that really needed sharing right now.

"So, I'll be torturing your little silver-haired friend until you agree to channel your trinket's energy for me?" Plokta asked, his tone somehow managing to convey both boredom and impatience. "Or are we skipping over that step to the one where my Mindless Ones hold her captive as insurance to guarantee that you don't decide to channel that energy in some way less... beneficial to me while my guard is down?"

"No, we're jumping all the way to step three, where you let my friend go," Elizabeth replied, widening her feet to stand with her hands resting on her hips. The ironic similarity to a western gunfighter's dueling stance was not lost on her, but what she was planning on grabbing for was far more powerful than a gun. "Or the only way you'll feel the coronet's power is when I use it to destroy your pets and blast you into oblivion."

She was almost certain cracks appeared around Plokta's sculpted mouth as he laughed derisively.

"Somehow I believe that if you could have managed that particular feat, you would have done so already, and we would not be having this tedious conversation."

He was right. But the coronet wasn't the only weapon at her disposal.

"Fine. Let me lay it out for you. You need to make more Mindless Ones for Umar, but you have run out of fuel. When she finds that out, she's probably going to kill you or barbeque you or, if you're lucky, turn you into a statue for the Grand Throne Room. So, you are in a bit of a pickle.

"I just happen to have access to an unlimited supply of fuel. But I'm the only one who can access it. You can't get to it – or use it – without my willing consent.

"And you won't get that consent until you let my friend go free." Elizabeth shrugged. "As you have pointed out so pleasantly, I don't have the wherewithal to double-cross you once she is free, so you risk nothing and gain everything by agreeing to my terms. Frankly, you'd have to be a moron not to take this deal."

Plokta regarded her without comment for several long moments, and Clea looked on with anger and appreciation warring across her delicate features. Elizabeth liked to think the appreciation was winning. But finally, the silence outlasted her patience, and she added one last chip to the pot.

"Oh, and this offer expires in five minutes, so you'd best decide soon, or the deal's off, and we'll just fight our way out of here. And then you lose no matter what, because if we make it out, your fuel source disappears. And if we don't, you might still have the source, but you'll have no way to access it. I'll make sure of that."

She almost hoped Plokta could tell when people were being

honest or not. Because she was not making a threat. She was making a promise.

"Very well," he said at last, his mask pristine once more. "You have a deal."

CHAPTER TWENTY-NINE

Margali's words sent Holly reeling.

… decoy… Clea and Elizabeth… without us… duped.

A part of her had always known she couldn't completely trust Agatha. There was no denying that the old witch was loyal and followed a code of morals, but Holly had never managed to uncover the Rosetta Stone for deciphering the exact details of that codex. She knew that the depth of Agatha's affection for her had a limit, even if she didn't know what that cutoff point might be. And without that knowledge, she could never wholly relax around the old woman, never truly feel safe, because she knew Agatha would have her back only up to a certain point, but no further. The needs of the many would always outweigh the needs of the few with Agatha Harkness, but figuring out which group was which could get tricky.

Holly hadn't felt those inhibitions with Clea, or Liz (the less said about Margali, the better). She had felt, almost immediately, that she could trust either woman with her life, and not have to worry that there might be hidden agendas or strings attached.

Especially Liz. Holly felt like she had started to bond with the Tsuut'ina woman over the course of their time together.

Her training with Agatha hadn't left much room for friendships, and Holly hoped to have the chance to nurture this one with Liz, when everything was over and they were back on Earth, unencumbered by tyrant toppling or dimension saving.

Or rather, she *had* hoped for that. Before finding out that Liz had betrayed her and Margali without a second thought, abandoning them in a cold, drafty cave to figure out their own way home, as if either one of them could make it through Umar's dimensional barrier or the Crossroads without her.

In her anguish, Holly had no sooner thought of the Crossroads than she found herself standing there once more, next to the impossible tree with its impossible pointing hands. Margali was nowhere to be seen, and when Holly shouted her name, not even echoes of her own voice answered her.

She was utterly alone, with no idea how she'd gotten there.

And no idea how to get out.

Holly chose a path at random and began walking. It didn't really matter which way she went. Clea had said entering the Crossroads without knowing how to navigate them was a death sentence. Without Liz to guide her, the chances of her finding a doorway back to her own dimension were just a hair's breadth shy of nonexistent.

It was just one more thing she couldn't do, in a long litany of failures and disappointments.

Off to her left, she caught a glimpse of a yellow sun and blue sky through one of the Crossroads' innumerable doorways. Heart beating faster, she began to hurry toward it. Could it really be this easy?

She faltered for a moment when she saw the outline of a figure standing in the doorway. Someone was barring her entry.

And then she saw who that someone was.

Agatha.

Not the spirit Holly had become used to dealing with of late, but Agatha in physical form, white hair falling about her shoulders in orderly waves, cameo at her throat, spindly hands splayed out on her purple-skirted hips, the tips of her pointy black boots peeking out from beneath the voluminous amaranthine fabric.

"Agatha?" she asked timidly as she approached, her pace slowing while her heartbeat quickened. Something was off.

"Holly. Failed already, I see. I don't know why I bothered to send you. I should have known you weren't clever enough to be of any use to anyone on this mission. *You* should have known. No doubt they are well rid of you."

Holly stopped in her tracks, stricken.

"A-Agatha?" she asked again, her voice small against the tomb-like quiet of the Crossroads. "Is that you?"

"I only took you on as a student out of pity, you know. I felt bad for you after the way Wanda deserted you, but I see now that she was right to do so. You aren't smart enough to progress any further in your studies; you haven't made any real advancements in years. This mission was your final test, Holly, to see whether you were worth keeping on as a student." Agatha's icy blue eyes narrowed, and she sniffed in disdain. "You're not."

Agatha's words echoed the vicious little voice that lived in the back of Holly's mind. It was always there, lurking, always waiting to castigate her for any mistake, big or small, real or imagined. And it sounded an awful lot like Agatha.

Holly couldn't bear to hear anymore. She turned and fled from the doorway, tears obscuring her vision, only some inner guide managing to keep her on the path as she ran and wept.

When her sobs had quieted and her tears dried, she found herself back at the tree of hands. There, her thoughts cleared, and she realized what had seemed off about Agatha, aside from the glaring fact of her being corporeal.

She had never once seen Agatha wear her hair long.

So, it wasn't *her* Agatha, but Holly wasn't sure that mattered. She was *some* Holly's Agatha, and, perhaps more importantly, everything she had said was true.

Holly wasn't particularly smart, not really. Oh, sure, she'd graduated near the top of her class, but that was more about having a decent memory and being a good test-taker than due to any inherent genius on her part. There were definitely concepts and spells she still struggled with, and some she hadn't even yet attempted to master because she doubted her ability to do so.

With good reason, apparently.

Despondent, Holly set out down another random pathway, not particularly hopeful that she'd find a doorway she could use, but not knowing what else to do with herself.

Soon, she thought she heard crashing waves. Curious despite herself, she drew near the doorway from which the surf sounds emanated. It probably wasn't Earth, but a beachfront world might not be so bad. Provided there were no giant cephalopods.

As she walked closer, a figure materialized in the doorway, startling Holly. She froze in place, her heart in her throat.

It was Agatha.

Well, another Agatha. This one differed from Holly's tutor in that she dressed in shades of sapphire and cornflower rather than amethyst and lilac, but otherwise she looked much the same. Holly steeled herself for this version's criticism.

"They finally realized how lazy and undisciplined you are and sent you away, I see," Blue Agatha said without preamble.

"Maybe if you'd worked harder, you'd know spells that made you more useful and worth keeping around."

"Love you, too, Agatha," Holly muttered, starting to turn around and head back to the main branch. This Agatha had nothing to say that Holly hadn't already heard from her own insecure brain a million times over. Still, their familiarity didn't take away their sting.

"Doubtful, of course," Blue Agatha continued. "I can't think of anything that would make you worth keeping around."

Holly winced, but kept walking. That one had hurt. Mostly because Holly agreed with it.

The same scenario played itself out several more times, with an Agatha draped in black cats telling Holly she was a talentless hack, a bald Agatha hissing at her that everything she set her hand to soured to rot, and finally, a younger, blonde Agatha in a military uniform laughing at her for thinking she'd ever be the witch Wanda was, or ever be able to replace her as Agatha's favorite.

Each time, Holly wound up back at the hand tree, and each time, she set out again in what she hoped was a new direction, not knowing what else to do, her psyche and heart a little more battered and frayed than the last.

And then she detected the sounds of gunfire through one of the portals and felt a gust of cold wind that tasted of snow. Holly would have just kept walking, but then she was sure she heard Clea yelling at Margali not to hurt the soldiers, and she realized that this doorway led both back to her Earth and back in time.

As she hurried forward, she was once more crestfallen to see another shape appear as she neared the doorway. But this time it wasn't some not-quite-right version of Agatha.

It was Liz.

"Elizabeth!" Holly called joyfully, letting out a relieved laugh as she began to run toward the Tsuut'ina woman. "I'm so happy to see you!"

Only to be stopped in her tracks by the expression of pure hatred on Liz's face.

"I don't know why, because I wish I had *never* seen you, never met you. Don't come any closer, Holly. Look at yourself. Why would anyone want to be around you? I can't stand you and I don't want you anywhere near me."

Holly stumbled to a stop, unable to believe what she was hearing.

No. *No.*

This couldn't be right, could it? This couldn't be happening. Not with Liz, of all people. A woman Holly had trusted, and thought was her friend.

But it was.

Liz looked at her with utter contempt and spit on the path in front of Holly's feet.

"You are dead to me."

Holly felt like she had been sucker punched. All the breath went out of her, all the fire.

All the strength.

She could stand no more. She turned and ran again, blindly this time, though her feet knew the path she had chosen. A doorway she'd passed right before this one. It had opened into a frozen universe, where the Big Freeze was well underway. Dead suns, barren planets, iced-over moons. Nothing had lived beyond that portal for millennia. It was a realm of eternal repose and blessed silence.

There would be no Agathas there to berate her, no Elizabeths there to shun her.

No one there to disappoint or anger.

No one there to live up to.

No one there at all.

A perfect place for her, because once she passed through this portal, all the pain and heartache, the failure and disappointment, would fade away. There would be only peace. She could finally rest.

Holly stood at the threshold of the doorway, feeling the chill emanating from beyond. A single tear escaped from the corner of her eye, crystallizing to frost before it had cleared her lash line. Holly wiped it away.

And then she stepped forward.

CHAPTER THIRTY

Clea tried to argue, but Elizabeth was having none of it. If her plan worked, she'd be rejoining her teammate soon enough. If it didn't, at least the mission itself wouldn't be jeopardized.

She watched as Clea called up her own concealment spell while Plokta ordered his Mindless Ones to make a path for her out of the oasis. Once she was out of the confines of Elizabeth's own spell, she disappeared, so Elizabeth had to trust that she was continuing with their original objective. Clea had ruled this dimension and its people; she had to know that their safety, and that of the entire Archipelago, mattered more than that of any one individual, even if that person had become a friend.

Elizabeth turned her attention back to Plokta, who was speaking again, though his mouth stubbornly continued refusing to move. She had a brief fantasy of herself ripping his mask off its amorphous portal-body and dashing it to the ground, stomping it into white dust. But even that probably wouldn't stop him from talking.

"I have upheld my end of the bargain. Now it is time for you to do the same."

"Of course. But you must come closer. Is there a way we can

touch? I will have to act as a channel between the coronet and you in order for you to make use of its power."

For once, Elizabeth was glad Plokta's expression couldn't change, because she had no doubt it would be full of suspicion. Rightly so. But, as with Clea, Elizabeth had not left him much choice.

As he neared, the circle of Mindless Ones tightened around the oasis, no doubt at his mental bidding. Which meant that on some level these particular creatures could receive and follow commands, so were possibly not quite as mindless as most of their peers. That might complicate things.

Elizabeth's hands had been resting lightly on her hips, her stance loose and easy, trying to convey that she presented no danger to the hell duke as he approached. And while it was a pose that seemed docile enough, Elizabeth had chosen it because it allowed one hand to be placed almost on top of her father's medicine bag.

Her father, Michael Twoyoungmen, had been the super hero known as Shaman long before she herself became the Talisman. He had carried the same bag she now wore, the Pouch of the Void, which had once belonged to Talks-To-Spirits of the ancient Tribe of the Moon. Like most things associated with her father, it was an item Elizabeth had a fraught history with, to say the least. It was said to contain infinite worlds, but for her it had contained mostly infinite pain.

Her first real encounter with the pouch's void had been when her father had sent her inside its pocket dimension to rescue her Alphan teammates who'd been drawn into the pouch during a battle with Omega Flight. While Elizabeth was able to extract her friends from the void within the medicine bag, she could not rescue herself, relying on her father to pull her out.

But as Agatha had so scathingly reminded her, he had chosen to save Narya instead, and the inverted pouch had collapsed in upon itself, with her inside. Elizabeth had all but died, nearly consumed by the mystical powers raging within the void. Her father was unable to free her, because nothing could be drawn from the medicine pouch that was bigger than its mouth. Only the timely intervention of the Beyonder had saved her.

Her other too-close encounter with the pouch's void gave her the beginnings of a migraine just thinking about it. She and her father and several of the other Alphans had been overwhelmed by the Master's Remnant Men, innocent pawns in that egomaniac's machinations that did not deserve to die. Elizabeth had determined that they wouldn't. She knew that the spell to return them to their natural human forms and release them from the Master's thrall existed inside the Pouch of the Void. She also knew it would take far too long to find it using conventional means, resulting in many of their deaths. And possibly in the deaths of some Alphans.

Never one to bow to convention, Elizabeth had chosen the more expedient and far more dangerous route of placing the medicine bag on her head. Her mind became a filter for its vast mystic energies, defining, collating, and absorbing an incalculable number of spells and artifacts to find the exact one she needed, the Spell of Bionatural Equilibrium.

She barely remembered anything after pulling the pouch over her head. A kaleidoscope of light, a cacophony of silence, endless vertigo as she spun through space and time forever, and then she was waking up months later in a hospital bed in Ottawa, having basically given herself a magical lobotomy. It had taken months of intense physical therapy before she could speak, walk, or feed herself, and even this many years later, she still experienced occasional brain fog and blinding headaches if she overdid things, especially in the Talisman department.

Which was another reason she hadn't particularly wanted to take up the super hero mantle again, but that was floodwater under a washed-out bridge at this point. And why she avoided using the medicine bag as much as possible. But desperate times...

When Plokta's mask was floating within arm's reach, the forward movement of his star-spangled blob ceased.

"You may touch me now," he said imperiously. It was then that Elizabeth became aware of the red glow beginning to emanate from the Mindless Ones. They were powering up their optic blasts, just in case. She was only going to get one shot at this.

"You asked for it," she replied as she whipped the Pouch of the Void off her hip with one hand and grabbed Plokta's mask with her other, bringing the tanned leather bag down over the sculpted white face, its expression finally changing as it disappeared behind a veil of brown fringe, the carved mouth now forming a horrified "O".

"*Youuuu–*"

"Yup. Me," Elizabeth said, tightening the bag's drawstring to cut the scream off and returning the pouch to its place on her hip. She had no illusions that the pouch would imprison the infernal duke permanently, but as the shapeless dimensional portal that had served as Plokta's body shrank and disappeared, she figured it would keep him out of her hair for a good long time.

Of course, that now left the problem of his Mindless Ones, all charged up with no one to blast. Elizabeth figured she had, oh... about thirty seconds before they just released all that lethal energy indiscriminately now that they were no longer under Plokta's control, with her on the receiving end of at least some of it. Probably most of it.

Fight? Or run?

Decisions, decisions.

But then the choice was taken from her when Clea materialized in front of her, grabbing her hand.

"Come on!" the silver and violet vision urged. "Let's get out of here!"

They'd taken all of three steps when the Mindless Ones erupted around them.

Chapter Thirty-One

Margali's anger quickly morphed to bewilderment as Holly, whom she had expected to react to the news of their betrayal with the same righteous fury that she had, instead turned and began walking aimlessly around the cavern, unresponsive to Margali's prodding.

"Holly? What are you doing?" she asked, following the young witch, trying to determine what she was up to. Was this some sort of spell?

Margali was no stranger to witchcraft. She had once been part of a coven herself; the most powerful one in Europe, in fact. She and two members of that coven, Maria Russoff and Lilia Calderu, had even attempted to recruit the Scarlet Witch into their ranks when she was still a child, though they quickly gave that up as a job better suited to the talents and temperament of Agatha Harkness.

But no spell Margali was aware of involved the caster wandering around aimlessly with their eyes glazed over. Her bizarre behavior seemed more apropos to the effect of a spell than to its casting, though if Holly was under the influence of some sort of enchantment, Margali couldn't detect it.

But then, she hadn't been able to detect the Dreamqueen's hallucinations, either.

Her lips in a grim line, Margali hastened her steps until she was keeping pace with her pink-haired peer, then jabbed a pointed finger sharply in her ribs.

Holly didn't flinch.

Margali frowned. Holly had been able to slap her back to her senses when she had been under the Dreamqueen's influence – if this was truly another hallucination, why hadn't Margali's poke had the same effect?

"What is *wrong* with you?" Margali demanded, her curiosity and patience both spent. They didn't have time for... whatever this was. They needed to figure out the extent of Clea and Elizabeth's betrayal and the form of their own retribution.

Holly didn't respond to Margali's query, but she did stop suddenly and turn to run in the opposite direction, toward the back of the cave. Margali wasn't sure of the girl's destination, or if she even had one, until Holly had almost reached it.

The well.

Margali hadn't realized the size of the thing until she got closer. It wasn't so much a well as a cistern, though that wasn't exactly right either, because it had the depth of the former while sporting the diameter of the latter.

And Holly had stopped right on its lip.

Margali had seen enough people driven to despair – had been there herself not so long ago – that she knew how this scenario was likely to play out if she didn't intervene. She slammed the tip of her staff down into the rocky floor of the cavern just as Holly stepped off the edge and plummeted out of sight.

Instantly, a stark yellow-white radiance shone from inside the well, and Holly reappeared seconds later, borne upward in a sphere that shone like a miniature, transparent sun. Margali pointed her staff and the sphere floated over to a spot well away from the cistern's edge. Then she abruptly dismissed the spell, and Holly fell about a yard to the ground. It wasn't enough to hurt her, but it was enough to jar her out of the trance she'd been in.

"Where… what happened…?" Holly began blearily, rubbing her eyes and blinking as if she'd just woken from a too-long afternoon nap that left her more groggy than rested. Then her eyes suddenly cleared and narrowed. "The Dreamqueen."

Whatever hallucination the demoness had sent Holly must have been worse even than the one she'd sent Margali. She should have poked harder.

The next words out of the green-skinned sorceress's mouth surprised even her. "Oh. I see. Do… do you want to talk about it?"

She wasn't the kind of person who chose to be a confidante for others or who tended to inspire others to confide in her. And her own hallucination had been horrific enough that it wasn't something she wanted to think about again, let alone dissect in front of a person she barely knew, so she would just as soon not hear about someone else's.

And, if Margali were being perfectly honest, under normal circumstances, she wouldn't have asked, because she just wouldn't have cared.

She tried to tell herself that any appropriate retribution would require a fully functioning Holly, but she knew that was only a fraction of the truth.

Holly had tried to walk into a well. Whether her intent had been to harm herself or not, the act itself spoke volumes.

Holly LaDonna had not let Agatha's dourness corrupt her

natural spunk and cheer. She was always ready with a quick joke or smile and seemed to genuinely care about every member of this team, despite having only known them for half a heartbeat. If the Dreamqueen had assaulted her with visions so bleak that she had considered extinguishing that bright light, even for a moment, Margali could only imagine the psychic sludge left behind. Talking, especially for someone like Holly, might be the only way to clear that filth out of her brain.

Holly actually laughed, and try as she might, Margali couldn't detect any trace of darkness in her mirth. "Who are you, and what have you done with Margali?"

Margali frowned, which only made Holly laugh harder. But she quieted quickly, growing serious.

"I can't believe Clea would betray us. Or Elizabeth, for that matter. I'm sure there is a perfectly logical explanation for why we're here and Clea's rebels aren't." Holly held up her hand when Margali opened her mouth to argue. "An explanation I'm not interested in hearing.

"Clearly, we're not needed. I say we blow this pop stand and go home."

Margali scowled. "There are at least two problems with that idea. First, Umar's closed off the entire Archipelago to both incoming *and* outgoing traffic," she said, though, now that she thought about it, they only had Clea's word for it that they couldn't teleport back home. "And second, even if they didn't technically betray us, they used us as decoys. And *no* one makes a shill out of Margali of the–"

"What's that?" Holly interrupted, destroying the rhythm of Margali's indignation.

"What's what?" she snapped, irritated.

Holly was looking behind Margali, back at the well. Margali turned to see what all the excitement was about.

"There. Do you see? On the far side?" Holly asked, pointing. "Don't those look like... ladder rungs?"

"They do indeed," Margali replied, her curiosity piqued. Without consulting Holly, she tapped her staff against the stone floor once more and recalled the bright translucent sphere that had saved Holly, though this time it encircled them both. Then they descended into the cistern, which turned out to be much deeper than either of them had expected.

Once they had reached the bottom, Margali released her spell while Holly called will-o'-the-wisps into being to light their way.

They appeared to be in a vast underground network of caves, far larger than anything hinted at by the aboveground cavern.

"Are we there yet?" Holly quipped.

Margali assumed "there" meant the actual rebel base. The words were barely out of Holly's mouth when armed figures appeared out of the darkness, surrounding them in a silent, hostile ring. Margali eyed them, wondering if she and Holly could take them out before they had a chance to alert more soldiers. The odds weren't in the women's favor.

"Well, if we're not," she replied, readying her staff, "we're in serious trouble."

CHAPTER THIRTY-TWO

Clea called up a seraphic shield while Elizabeth used the power of the coronet to uproot trees and rocks from the oasis and hurl them at the Mindless Ones as the women tried to break through the creatures' circled ranks. Red optic blasts hit the shield and bounced off in a shower of sparks, while others tracked and destroyed Elizabeth's projectiles midair, burned harmless scars into the landscape, or found targets in other Mindless Ones. Without Plokta to control them, the Mindless Ones quickly descended into chaos, attacking each other when they could no longer see Clea and Elizabeth through the Tsuut'ina woman's cloaking spell. Apparently, their ability to do so earlier had been another consequence of the hell lord's control, and now that he was gone, they were as blind to the fleeing women as they had always been.

While Elizabeth and Plokta had bargained, Clea had kept a close eye on the shifting landscape around them, noting that the mountains that were her objective were gradually nearing, even while the women themselves remained in the same place. Such was the nature of the Never Hills and part of the reason she'd chosen to come this way. It was a risk, but if the Hills cooperated, it could shave days off their travel time.

The Hills, miraculously, did indeed seem inclined to do their part. Now she and Elizabeth just had to take advantage of their gift.

Clea pointed toward the mountains, yelling to be heard over the tumult around them.

"That's where we're headed!"

Elizabeth followed her finger, then shook her head in disbelief. "No way! We'll never make it! Not unless you know a way to make the hills move at Mach five or something."

As they spoke, the two women wove their way through the thicket of hulking bodies, trying to avoid bouncing off the creatures or tumbling into the pits and holes their errant red beams were creating. They were only partially successful, as Clea stumbled over the still-smoking limb of an eye-blasted tree and nearly went down, taking the shield with her. She recovered her balance at the last moment, and the Shield of the Seraphim never wavered.

Elizabeth was not so fortunate.

Her eyes on the mountainous prize, she didn't see the rut caused by a blast gone wide, her foot catching the edge of it and sliding down to get stuck in the bottom. The rut refused to give the foot back without a fight, a struggle which resulted in a hard yank and a pained yelp from Elizabeth.

"Just a sprain," Elizabeth panted, and Clea hoped she was right. But it was the least of their worries.

The Talisman might be nigh omnipotent, but Elizabeth Twoyoungmen was not. Overtaxed by her previous wound, holding the concealment spell, tapping into and weaponizing the power of the earth against the Mindless Ones, and now this latest injury, something had to give.

It was the cloaking spell.

It had barely been able to conceal the two of them before, given Elizabeth's condition. Now it failed completely.

For anyone watching, where there had been only hillside a moment before, a silver-haired, purple-clad woman appeared alongside a dark-haired woman in a fur-trimmed robe who was limping badly.

The Mindless Ones were watching. Clea could only pray Umar wasn't.

But as a renewed barrage of red optic beams sliced into the hill around them, Clea knew that she had to act. Her mother might have blocked ingress to and egress from the Dark Dimension, she might currently be ruling it, she might even have helped create it. But she was not, and never had been, its Sorceress Supreme.

Clea was.

Blocking out everything else, she closed her eyes and conjured up the faces of the Vishanti.

Though the Vishanti – Agamotto, Hoggoth, and Oshtur – often chose to reveal themselves to mortals in different forms over the centuries, Clea had come to know them via her studies on Earth, and so had Earthly associations for each of them.

For her, the Omnipotent Oshtur took on the form of Ma'at, the Egyptian goddess of truth, justice, balance, and order. In her mind's eye, Clea saw the goddess in a long, sleeveless white tunic with a golden collar, gold-strapped sandals, and a serpent headdress with a brightly colored plume. When an image of Margali tried to superimpose itself over the goddess's form, Clea shoved it aside roughly and continued her visualization. Oshtur held her rainbow-winged arms out wide, bearing balanced scales in each hand. She wore a hint of a smile, and her eyes were kind.

Hoggoth she saw as an immense tiger whose eyes burned and smoked with an unknowable fire. Despite this, his was a cold and distant presence, and not her favorite.

Agamotto, the child of Oshtur, had taken on for Clea the appearance of the caterpillar from the book *Alice's Adventures in Wonderland* ever since Stephen had regaled her with his tale of encountering the being in that whimsical guise. Visualizing him thus always calmed Clea, which was exactly what she needed for this to work.

The Teleportation Spell of the Vishanti.

It required years of meditative practice to master, tranquility to cast, and it allowed the caster to directly channel the power of the Vishanti to instantly go from one place in the lower realms to another. The path could not be traced, magically or otherwise, and the spell could transport multiple subjects without requiring the expenditure of extra energy or time.

And, because it utilized a power even Umar could not contest with, her barrier shouldn't be able to stop it.

"Shouldn't" being the operative word, of course.

It would also immediately inform Umar of Clea's whereabouts, though she would only know where her daughter had been, not where she was going. It couldn't be helped at this point. She and Elizabeth couldn't hold off the Mindless Ones indefinitely, and the longer they fought, the more they risked exposing themselves to Umar's watchful gaze. The time for hiding was almost past, and the sooner they got to their endgame, the better.

With her eyes closed and her heart and mind calm, Clea reached out her hand silently to Elizabeth, knowing the other sorceress would take it. As she did, the world lurched, then stilled.

Clea opened her eyes.

She and Elizabeth were in a cavern lit by intermittent floating globes. A man with heart-stopping dark hair graying at the temples was hurrying toward her. His expression was hostile at first, but changed swiftly when he realized who she was. He began to run toward her.

"Clea!" he shouted, then surprised her by grabbing her up in his arms and swinging her around, holding her tightly before releasing her.

"Rahl!" she exclaimed, her delight almost equaling his when she realized he was not who she'd at first feared him to be. She pulled him back into her arms for another, longer embrace, making a face at Elizabeth's raised eyebrow. Then she took a deep breath and stepped back. "It's so good to see you!"

And it was. Rahl had been part of the rebellion from the beginning, since before she had overthrown Umar the first time, fighting by her side. Unbeknownst to her, he and several of her other followers from that time had spent many long years imprisoned in a secret dungeon while she fought on with newer, younger recruits. She had thought them dead, and their discovery in an overlooked outpost still held by Dormammu loyalists had been one of her happiest days in recent memory.

Rahl had never made a secret of his feelings for her, but always stood back respectfully. Except when he thought Stephen wasn't treating her as well as she deserved. Which was often, as it turned out. Especially of late.

He was a devoted general, and a good friend. And he was ready to be something more – with Stephen's blessing (though there were probably times when the Sorcerer Supreme wished he could take that back).

Clea often thought the day she'd be ready to let Rahl be that something more was creeping ever nearer, whether she wanted it to or not.

Of course, those thoughts couldn't help but stir memories of Nobel, another of her rebels who had dreamed of something more with her. When he'd died in her arms in the mountains above the Sarebbe Wastelands, he had even told her he'd secretly been building a home for the two of them. Which was actually rather presumptuous. Bordering on creepy, even. Sweet, but creepy.

Still, she couldn't help but wonder what it was about her that inspired such steadfast devotion in these men, yet couldn't keep Stephen's from flagging over time and distance.

Perhaps it was simply that – time, and distance. Or perhaps it wasn't his devotion that was the problem, but the nature of their separate duties. One day soon she and Stephen would need to sit down and have a long talk.

But it wasn't today. Today was not a day for talk of relationships, good or bad. Today was a day to plan for war.

"You know it's always good to see you, Clea," Rahl said with a soft smile, the wrinkles about his eyes crinkling. Then he arranged his features into a more neutral configuration as other figures began to approach out of the darkness. Clea's heart soared as she recognized them, releasing a fear she had not realized had been weighing it down.

"Well, it's about damned time," Margali said.

CHAPTER THIRTY-THREE

Clea sat with her three companions in a small room carved out of the mountain rock. Her rebels had not created this complex, merely expanded it to suit their needs with sweat both magical and mundane. They'd enlarged this room enough to fit a mismatched divan and two chairs, one a much-patched lounger and the other a conglomeration of uncarved red wood. Clea, Holly, and Elizabeth sat on the couch while Margali, predictably, sat by herself on the lounger.

The rebels were not the first to have inhabited these caverns and would not be the last. Each successive group had helped shape the intricate complex of caves and tunnels into a veritable rabbit's warren that could resist either invasion or siege, with more escape routes than any one person knew, a precaution which ensured that even infiltration would not snare them all. It was one of the few places left in the Dark Dimension where Clea still felt safe. Where she could take a moment and breathe.

Right now, she was using that moment to reunite with and debrief her friends.

"I'm sorry you thought we had abandoned you," she said contritely to Margali and Holly, reaching out to clasp one of the pink-haired witch's hands in both of her own. "I'm especially sorry for how that thought made you… react." Margali had given her a quick telepathic rundown of what had happened with Holly while the three of them had waited for Clea's healers to finish up with Elizabeth's back and ankle. Clea wasn't exactly sure what Holly had experienced during her brief period of disassociation, but she couldn't help but feel responsible for it. Clea was the team leader, and it was her duty to make sure that everyone came back from this mission alive, and at least relatively whole. So far, she was not doing a "bang-up" job of it, and they hadn't even reached the truly hard part yet.

Even so, she did need to try and understand what had occurred, to ensure that it didn't happen again. A lapse like that while fighting Umar face to face would result in more deaths than just Holly's.

"What *did* happen, Holly?" Elizabeth asked gently. She was sitting on the other side of the young witch and placed a steadying hand on the girl's shoulder. Clea realized belatedly that the two of them were probably only a few years apart in age, while she and Margali were both far older. Her, especially, since both Faltines and Mhuruuks lived longer than humans, which often made it difficult to both connect to and maintain relationships with them. It was hard watching people you had come to care for age and die while you remained the same.

Clea pushed aside the well of loneliness that thought threatened to open up and focused her attention back on the two young women. Elizabeth was still speaking. "Whatever it was, you're safe now. You can tell us."

Holly's gaze remained firmly fixed on some very interesting portion of the cave floor. When she spoke, her voice was soft and small.

"It was… one of the Dreamqueen's hallucinations, I think. That's the only thing that makes any sense. She'd already gotten to Margali." She looked up then to search Elizabeth's face. "She didn't attack you? Or Clea?"

When Elizabeth shook her head, Holly's face fell, and her gaze returned to the ground.

"Figures she'd go after the weakest," Holly muttered. When Margali, indignant, opened her mouth to protest, Clea silenced her with a glare.

Not helpful, she sent to the other woman telepathically. Margali didn't answer, silently or otherwise.

Elizabeth reached out one hand to lift Holly's chin so that the other woman had to look at her. She took the other off Holly's shoulder to wipe at the tear that was trickling down her cheek, threatening to drip off her chin onto her sweatshirt.

"Hey. You are *not* weak. You are one of the strongest people I've ever had the honor of knowing. And the Dreamqueen doesn't prey on weakness. She preys on fear. And being afraid doesn't make you weak. Everybody gets scared sometimes. People who aren't afraid of anything aren't brave or strong. They're either liars or sociopaths; nothing anyone should want to emulate."

Holly sniffed loudly. "If you say so."

"I do," Elizabeth replied, her tone gentle but firm. "Please tell me what you were so scared of, Holly. Maybe I can help."

Clea realized that Elizabeth and Holly were so intent on their conversation that they had all but forgotten her and Margali, so she very carefully released Holly's hand and stood, motioning Margali toward the entryway.

We're leaving them alone? Margali asked as she rose from the lounger. From both her expression and the flavor of her thoughts, she wasn't particularly happy about having to give up her comfortable seat.

Holly deserves some privacy, Clea sent back chidingly.

Margali gave a mental snort. *Fine. I don't really want to be subjected to all that cloying positivity, anyway.*

Clea stopped just outside the cave entry, earning her a surprised look from Margali.

"What happened to privacy?"

"I'm giving her as much as I can, under the circumstances," Clea replied quietly, tamping down the guilt she felt for eavesdropping. She did not want to be privy to this exchange, knew it wasn't her right or her place, but she saw no other alternative. "I need to know what happened to her. Even if she swears Elizabeth to secrecy. So I can make sure it doesn't happen again."

"So there are a lot of wells in Umar's throne room? How very peculiar," Margali said sarcastically.

"No," Clea answered. "But there are a lot of other ways to die."

Though her focus was on Holly, Elizabeth knew when Clea and Margali left the room, and she appreciated the gesture, even though she knew they were hovering just outside. She understood Clea's motivation, so didn't begrudge her the intrusion. Much.

"…and then there was another Agatha, and another one, and another, and even though none of them were *my* Agatha, they *all* were, you know? All spouting some way I wasn't good enough, some way I didn't measure up. Not just to Wanda – who, let's face it, is Agatha's favorite *still*, even though she *murdered* Agatha. How is that fair?"

Elizabeth didn't respond, not wanting to interrupt the flow of

Holly's words now that she was talking about her hallucination, though hearing the things she'd endured made Elizabeth sad and angry. She should have punched the Dreamqueen a helluva lot harder.

Elizabeth had released Holly's chin and taken her hand when the other woman had begun to hesitantly speak. Now she gently stroked the back of Holly's hand, hoping the young witch would take some comfort from the contact.

"And it was awful, because that's all I've wanted, you know. To be good enough. To someone. And I guess part of me has always been worried that someone was never going to be Agatha, no matter how hard I tried. But then when she wasn't the only one... anyway, it just got to be too much. I needed to get away. So, I picked a door where I knew I could be at peace for a while and... you know the rest."

Holly put her other hand on top of Elizabeth's, stilling it as she looked up earnestly into the Tsuut'ina woman's eyes.

"But Margali is wrong, Liz. I wasn't trying to hurt myself, no matter what it looked like on the outside of my head." When Elizabeth didn't immediately reply, she continued, "Wanting to check out for a while is not the same as wanting to die."

"Isn't it?" Elizabeth asked, her voice sharper than she intended. "That's splitting some pretty fine hairs, there."

"No, it's not," Holly insisted. "One is intended to be permanent. The other is not."

Now tears were beginning to form in Elizabeth's eyes as well, though she blinked them back with effort.

"Oh, you little idiot," she said, not unkindly. "How did you think you were going to get out of that extinct universe once you were ready to come back?"

Holly's face paled and her sparkling brown eyes, always

so big and full of whatever emotion was in her heart, grew cartoonishly wide.

"I... hadn't thought that far ahead."

Elizabeth heaved a sigh that was equal parts affection and exasperation, then pulled Holly into her arms as the young witch began to tremble in realization and then to sob.

"It's OK," Elizabeth murmured. "You're safe now."

As she held Holly, she sensed when Clea and Margali moved away, apparently having satisfied themselves that the pink-haired witch was truly out of danger.

When Holly had finally quieted and was just resting in Elizabeth's embrace, she thought she could dare to ask the other witch one last question.

"You said there was someone else besides Agatha in the Crossroads with you. Who was it?"

Holly stiffened and went utterly still, like a fawn scenting a predator. Then, slowly, she relaxed back into Elizabeth's arms. "It was... not-you."

Elizabeth had guessed as much. Holly was no good at hiding her feelings.

"What did not-me say to you?"

More sniffling.

"You... you said you hated me, couldn't stand me, wanted me out of your life. Forever." The tears had started again.

Elizabeth leaned back so she could see Holly's tear-streaked features and Holly could see her own earnest ones.

"I could never hate you."

"Are... are you sure?" Holly whispered, hope and fear mingling desperately on her face.

"*Positive*," Elizabeth replied firmly, tousling Holly's fuchsia hair.

"Wait. You didn't... like, put gum in there, or anything, did you?" Holly asked, reaching up to pat her head gingerly. In reply to Elizabeth's confused expression, she shrugged. "I mean, that's the kind of thing sisters who don't hate each other do, right?"

Elizabeth laughed in relief.

"Shut up, you dork," she said, shaking her head as she pulled the other woman into a fierce hug.

And Holly, thankfully, did.

PART THREE

CHAPTER THIRTY-FOUR
The Dark Dimension

"Synth, your group will attack from the air. Rahl will oversee the ground assault. Meanwhile, I and my sorcerous sisters here will teleport to the castle gate, neutralize the Guardian, and engage Umar."

Clea and her companions stood around the map table, along with Rahl, Synth, Buhrn, and several other of her generals and lieutenants. The roughhewn surface bore a map of Umar's palace and the surrounding environs, an exact magical duplicate in miniature, complete with tiny evil minions and heroic rebels that Clea could move to and fro with just a thought. It might actually be fun if it weren't so serious.

And so exhausting. It seemed like she had done nothing but fight one despot or another for the Dark Dimension's freedom for years now. She felt like the Earth titan, Prometheus, doomed to eternal punishment for wanting to free her people, just as he had wanted to aid mankind. Like him, she was chained to this place, winning it back from tyranny only to lose it again, constantly restarting the cycle, just as the eagle had plucked out Prometheus's liver every day only to have it grow back overnight so the eagle could do it again the next day. And the next, and the next.

In one version of Prometheus's story, he'd been rescued by Hercules. Clea wondered what hero was going to come break her chains, and if she would even let one try. It wasn't the chains that were the problem; Clea loved her people and her home. It was the eagle tearing out her liver that needed to be caught, caged, and put down.

Only it was her heart, not her liver, and it didn't grow back every time it was broken. And it was her mother, not an eagle, and while Umar – and Dormammu – had been caught and caged many times, they had never been put down. Not for good.

And therein lay the problem. Clea could no more kill her mother than she could a child of her own. And Umar had shown a similar surprising reticence to slay her daughter when she'd had the chance. Which meant this cycle was going to continue to play out until one of them could put their morality – or, in Umar's case, guilt – aside and do what was necessary.

Or until an outside source did it for them. Clea would be lying if she didn't admit that a part of her hoped her three companions would be able to do just that.

But first they had to get to Umar. And Ardina.

"Once we teleport to the gate, Umar will know exactly where we are. Why would she even bother with Synth's or Rahl's forces when she could bring all her own to bear against the true threat – you? Or just come herself, with Ardina in tow?" Elizabeth asked. She looked askance at Clea's two generals, then added, "No offense."

Rahl smiled and Synth frowned. Clea swallowed down a

sudden burst of panic because she knew the Tsuut'ina woman was right.

In the past, a flanking tactic like this would have worked. Had worked many times, in fact. But that was when Clea and Umar had been equally matched in personal power, if not in manpower. Umar would not be foolish enough to challenge her under such circumstances, preferring to let her minions take the brunt of any assault and only deal with Clea if her daughter managed to make it to the Azure Throne.

But with Ardina boosting her power to unknown heights, Umar might well feel she had the upper hand, even with Clea's companions factored into the mix. If so, she would likely not be content to wait for Clea to come to her. The wolf would pounce the moment the rabbits poked their heads out of the warren.

"But what if she can't tell where Clea really is?" Holly asked suddenly, a gleam in her eye.

"What do you mean?" Clea asked, but Margali groaned.

"She's going to quote Sun Tzu again," the green-skinned sorceress complained. Clea thought she might be rolling her eyes, but it was impossible to really tell when they were completely yellow, with no irises or pupils to speak of. Still, she gave that impression.

"I'm going to quote Sun Tzu again," Holly agreed. And then she did. "Chapter Six, Weak Points and Strong: 'Hence that general is skillful in attack whose opponent does not know what to defend; *and* he is skillful in defense whose opponent does not know what to attack.' Emphasis mine. Also, 'O divine art of subtlety and secrecy! Through you we learn to be invisible, through you inaudible; and hence we can hold the enemy's fate in our hands.'"

Holly looked very pleased with herself when she was finished, but Clea saw her own confusion reflected in many faces.

"Translation, please," Margali said impatiently. Clea noted that the tenor of that impatience seemed to have changed somehow, though. Could one be affectionately irritable?

"We make sure she doesn't know where to attack or what to defend because she doesn't know where Clea really is." Holly looked expectantly around the table, but when no one responded, she sighed. "It's simple. We give her more than one Clea."

"She won't be fooled by image projection," Clea replied doubtfully. "Or even Images of Ikonn."

"I'm not talking about an illusion," Holly said.

"Then what?" asked Margali. "Doppelgangers?"

She looked at Clea as she said it, her lips pursed. It took Clea a moment to realize she was trying not to smile. She was probably remembering when Clea had called Agatha an elderly doppelganger of herself. Thinking about it now, Clea pressed her own lips together to hold in an answering chuckle. Now was not the time for mirth. Holly probably wouldn't appreciate the joke, anyway.

"Well, sort of. We wouldn't be creating actual physical replicas of Clea. Those wouldn't fool Umar any more than illusory ones once she saw that they couldn't work magic."

"So what are you proposing?" Elizabeth asked.

"We need Clea's magical essence to be in more than one place. Someone else can be casting the spells to sell the illusion that it's Clea, but it only really works if Umar can sense Clea's mystical signature at the spells' points of origin."

"How would we go about doing that, exactly?" Clea asked the pink-haired witch, whose enthusiasm was beginning to infect her generals. Synth was nodding her head, and Rahl was leaning forward to catch the girl's next words. She couldn't blame them; she was intrigued herself.

Holly's smile was somehow both mischievous and smug. "Ever heard of a poppet?"

"You mean… like a voodoo doll?" Clea asked, frowning. "I am *not* comfortable with that." There were many religions that incorporated magic on Earth. Learning about them had been part of her studies when she had been Stephen's disciple, but she had not explored any of those paths herself. That magic was reserved for those traditions, and it was considered impolite to cast spells out of school. Since Holly was not a practitioner of voodoo herself, Clea wasn't sure it was appropriate for her to be borrowing that tradition's trappings.

But she had another, much more personal reason for wanting nothing to do with voodoo or its tools. She and Stephen had once tangled with Marie Laveau, the Voodoo Queen of New Orleans. Laveau had been after Stephen's brother Vic and the Darkhold, the dark magic counterpart to the Book of the Vishanti. During one such clash, Laveau had shot Clea with a shaft of iron, spelled to make her hate the first person she saw… none other than her own newlywed husband, Stephen Strange. Clea had eventually recovered, of course, but the memory of that time still left a taste both sour and rotten in her mouth, and she wanted no reminders of it. Not even if they would help her beat Umar. She would just have to find another way.

Holly scoffed.

"First off, voodoo is hardly a monolithic tradition, and what you think of as 'voodoo,'" she said, doing exaggerated air quotes, "probably holds no resemblance at all to what actual practitioners believe. Second, voodoo doesn't have a monopoly on poppets. Practical witchcraft has incorporated them, and other types of sympathetic magic, for centuries. Poppets are usually used for healing, but they can be very versatile. They're a staple of any smart witch's larder, because they're fast, easy, and effective. You fashion a likeness of the person in question, imbed something of theirs in that likeness, say a little rhyme, and presto – multiple Cleas!

"It *is* true that it's not encouraged to make poppets of other people without their express permission. But I'd have yours, so that wouldn't be a problem." Holly peered at her, suddenly uncertain. "I *would* have your permission, right?"

Before Clea could answer, Synth spoke up. "Just how do you plan on embedding Clea's magical essence into these poppets?"

Holly shrugged nonchalantly. "Easy. We bleed her."

"'It will have blood, they say,'" Elizabeth quoted as the others at the table expressed varying degrees of shock, dismay, and disapproval. Clea recognized the line from Macbeth.

"I think you've been spending too much time around Holly," she said, smiling.

"Entirely possible," Elizabeth agreed with a grin of her own, "but don't blame the Shakespeare on her." She shrugged at Clea's questioning look. "It took me a while to decide on a course of study before choosing archaeology."

"I don't suppose any of those studies happened to involve the proper application of leeches?"

Holly interrupted them, talking over the complaints of Clea's generals and Margali's snickering.

"Who said anything about leeches? Seriously, do you people still live in the Dark Ages here, or what?" Her frustration was obvious.

"Well, we are in a cave," Margali pointed out.

"Not helping," Elizabeth and Clea said in tandem, but Margali just smirked. Clea couldn't quite blame her. It *was* a little funny.

"Look," Holly continued, her words carefully measured as she visibly tried to control her temper, "we need something that holds Clea's magical essence. Since Clea doesn't just practice the mystic arts, but is actually literally a magical being – the daughter of a race made of pure magic and one born with an innate command of it – her blood contains that essence. And sympathetic magic works best with blood. So we need it for the poppets, to imbue them with her magic and sell the lie to Umar.

"But we don't have to do anything more barbaric than give her a paper cut to get it. We collect a few drops of blood for each poppet, and we're done. Easy peasy, like I said." She paused for a moment, and Clea waited for the inevitable caveat she had come to expect from the young witch. "Although, I will admit that paper cuts can sting like hell."

CHAPTER THIRTY-FIVE

Clea's "bleeding" was as simple as Holly had promised, and soon the rebels had several Clea poppets, which Holly had crafted from red tree roots Elizabeth had painstakingly harvested to her exact specifications. The carven figures were very basic, Holly never having learned to whittle, and the pocketknife Elizabeth loaned her not well suited to the purpose. They were not even recognizably male or female, but Holly had fashioned little purple shirts for each of them and even found some white fringe to use for hair. And of course, each contained a few drops of Clea's blood in a tiny little vial in its chest cavity.

Rahl and Synth were each given one and the magical word needed to activate it, then dispatched to their hiding spots with their troops, awaiting Clea's signal. Margali and Holly divvied up the rest, while Clea passed out color-shifting hooded cloaks to each of them to wear over their more recognizable clothing. Clea had psychically implanted a map of the palace in the other sorceresses' minds, and they planned to take two different routes to Umar's throne room, in hopes of further confusing the tyrant. Clea would take Holly – at Margali's insistence – in one direction, while Margali and Elizabeth went in the other. They planned to plant the poppets in strategic spots throughout the palace, then activate them all at the same time, just before assaulting the Grand Throne Room from opposite sides, giving Umar the impression that Clea was everywhere at once.

The trick wouldn't work for long; Umar surely knew Clea was going to come for the Azure Throne sooner or later. She might send troops out to investigate every Clea sighting, or she might just marshal her defenses in the throne room and wait for her daughter there, regardless of where Clea's magical signature popped up around the palace. Clea couldn't say for sure which option her mother might choose. Umar was just as likely to wait years for a carefully crafted plan's pieces to fall into place as she was to abruptly decide those plans were taking too long and just take what she wanted by force. Clea had been told many times that giving birth to her had made it so that Umar could not revert to her Faltine form, and that inability had made her mother a little unstable over the years. She was called Umar the Unrelenting, but Unpredictable was just as apt a moniker.

Nevertheless, the tactic would buy them some time. And if Umar chose to pursue both options, it might allow them to pick off some of her heavy hitters, as Holly had put it, since no amount of impatience would make Umar stoop to investigating the sightings herself.

Clea wasn't sure who Holly's "heavy hitters" might be, though, aside from Ardina, who she knew Umar wouldn't let out of her sight. Umar was not one to allow her underlings to gain power, for today's minion is tomorrow's rival. But the gambit might serve to thin out Umar's forces and make their final confrontation with the tyrant that much easier, so as far as Clea was concerned, it was still a solid plan.

Of course, it all hinged on the four of them getting past the

G'uranthic Guardian while Rahl and Synth kept the bulk of Umar's military might occupied.

Constructed in ages past by G'uran the Great to defend the Azure Throne, the Guardian was an immense statue shaped from hard, titian rock. It had six enormous arms and sat poised above the gate to the palace, the arms positioned as if to come smashing down on would-be intruders. Normally immobile, it could come to life either when commanded to by whomever was currently ensconced on the throne, or when someone trespassed beneath its single will- and power-draining eye.

Clea had felt the power of that eye once, before she had risen up against Umar the first time, or even known the raven-haired goddess was her mother. Umar had captured Stephen and placed him under the Guardian's gaze to sap his will and magical knowledge, intending to steal it "for the benefit of the Dark Dimension". By which she had meant, of course, for herself.

Stephen had managed to free himself, but not before the Guardian had absorbed all his mystical power and the knowledge to use it. Clea knew that Stephen could not hope to face Umar without his magic, so she had faced down the Guardian herself, the blind devotion and love she had felt for him at the time helping her find the will to best the creature. She took back Stephen's power and returned it to him in short order.

The entire process had nearly killed her.

Looking back, it had also been a turning point for her. Holding that much power inside her while just a disciple, feeling it course through her as she cast spells she had not yet learned, made Clea more determined than ever to excel at her studies. That singular experience, perhaps more than anything else, had led to her eventual ascension as Sorceress Supreme of the Dark Dimension. Here, she was as powerful as Stephen. Maybe more so.

Here, she didn't need him, and hadn't for some time, if she was being honest with herself.

But needing and wanting weren't the same things, were they?

Perhaps, in this way, she was like Margali. Not a particularly comforting thought. But where the Sorceress Supreme of the Winding Way had sought her title because she wanted power, Clea had sought her own because she wanted to be unconstrained by anyone else's power. She had wanted freedom.

But it hadn't gotten her that. Instead, it had become her only way of ensuring her people's liberty. She had never wanted to rule the Dark Dimension, only to free it from Dormammu and Umar's yoke. But once that yoke was removed, and she herself was not on the throne to ensure it stayed that way, the dimension had fallen back into tyranny. Again and again. Only when she wore the Flames of Regency were its people free. And only as Sorceress Supreme could she keep those flames burning.

She had wanted to be their liberator, not their sovereign, but in her desire for freedom, she had found only more responsibility.

So maybe she was more like Elizabeth than Margali, after all.

Clea sighed and shook her head to clear her mind. She needed to focus on the task at hand. Once Umar had been stopped and Ardina rescued, there would be time enough for pondering the ironies of great power and great responsibility.

"Is everyone ready?" she asked the other sorceresses. "Everyone knows what they need to do?"

The others nodded. Clea freed her mind of thoughts of poppets and people, her mother and Stephen, and focused once more on the faces of the Vishanti. Once she could see them clearly, she held out her hands. Holly grabbed one, Elizabeth the other, and Margali took Elizabeth's other hand, holding her staff in her free hand. Together, they formed a line of linked sorcerous might.

As before, the world hiccuped, then quieted.

The four sorceresses stood in front of Umar's palace, below the massive G'uranthic Guardian. It was even bigger than Clea remembered.

There was a moment of silence, wherein Clea sent the telepathic attack signal to Rahl and Synth. Then Holly, unsurprisingly, spoke up.

"Are we there yet?"

As if in reply, the Guardian opened its eye.

Chapter Thirty-Six

"Now!" Clea yelled.

In response, several things happened at once.

A sickly yellow shaft of energy burst forth from the Guardian's eye. At the same time, Margali slammed her staff into the ground and a ray of pure golden light shot out from its gem to meet the Guardian's beam. Elizabeth's eyes began to glow brightly as a ruby red lance of light sprang from her coronet to join Margali's ray, turning it carnelian. Purple nimbuses formed around Clea's hands, and then amethyst bolts joined the red-orange beam, deepening it to more garnet tones. Finally, a stream of improbable hot pink bubbles exploded from Holly's free hand to mix with the magical energies of the other women, forming a swirling, shining, pulsing stream the color of blood.

"I guess we're crossing the streams," Holly muttered, but no one had any energy left to respond even if they did know what she was talking about.

Sallow ray battled scarlet for preeminence, one beating the other back, then being beaten back itself in turn. Long moments passed, and it seemed like the sorceresses could do no better than a stalemate with the gargantuan Guardian, though each of them was showing signs of strain. Holly's teeth were bared,

Elizabeth's brow was furrowed in deep lines, and Margali was sweating. Even Clea was struggling, a less-than-unstoppable force meeting an immovable object. They needed something more.

This isn't working, and we're running out of time! Clea sent to them all telepathically. *It's not enough for us to combine our magics. Our magics must be as one if we are to defeat the Guardian. Open your minds to me, your power.* She could sense the hesitancy, the distrust, especially from Margali. *As you open to me, so I open to you.*

It was the most she could offer, to let them into her mind and heart in exchange for access to theirs. Because, ultimately, no matter the source of their magic, their tradition, or their training, its use all came down to what was inside them. Their desire and their will.

Clea wasn't at all sure they would do it, but she did as she said she would, opening herself to them. She let them see her uncertainty, her fear. Fear that she wasn't up to this task, or the larger tasks of leading the rebellion and ruling the Dark Dimension, no matter that she had done both handily before. That was then. This was now. Fear that even if they did triumph, she wasn't worthy to lead her people. After all, she had failed them in the past, hadn't she? And more than once.

She let them see the conflicting wants and needs that drove her. Freedom for her people, and for herself. Freedom *from* her people. Love for her people, and for Stephen. Wanting a relationship with Stephen but not sure it would ever really work, with her swamped with responsibility in one dimension and he likewise drowning in duty in another. Wanting an end to all the hurt his broken promises had caused.

She even let them see the parts she often tried to keep

hidden from herself. The longing for someone who could love her without reservation. Rahl's face flashed in her mind, and Nobel's. The longing for the parents she'd never truly had. Her father Orini had been a disciple first of Dormammu, and then of Umar. His loyalty had ultimately gotten him blasted into bits by the Dread One whose favor he had so curried. And then there was Umar, who was just... Umar. That was a tangle of emotions she couldn't unravel for the others, because she had never yet been able to unsnarl it for herself.

As Clea endured the touch of the other women's minds upon hers, some rougher than others, she also caught glimpses of theirs, though she tried to go no deeper than necessary to access their power for this one specific thing.

Still, she couldn't escape Elizabeth's resentment and guilt when she thought of her father. Her feeling of being unmoored, caught between the magical world and the mundane, the Indigenous world and the settler one. Her longing to find her place in those worlds – one she chose for herself, not one thrust upon her.

And as Clea accepted these parts of Elizabeth without judgment, she felt the red thread of the Talisman's power connect to her own. A surge of strength and resolution washed through her.

Clea could likewise not avoid the complicated love-hate pull Holly felt when she thought of Agatha, her mentor and her judge. Her resentment of Agatha's favoritism toward Wanda, and of Wanda's abandonment of her in favor of her own children, especially considering all the trouble those so-called children had wound up causing. Her desire to learn, and know, and uncover all the mysteries there were, all warring with her deep-seated fears that she was not smart, talented, or dedicated enough to do so. Her regret at how her chosen lifestyle had isolated her from her family and friends, and her longing to connect with others who could understand and accept the magic in her life. Not only accept it, but add to it. Elizabeth's image was large in her mind, along with Clea's, and even Margali's.

Clea caught hold of the thread of Holly's power, which was, surprisingly, a bright, shining blue instead of pink. But its color was only a construct and of no consequence. Only the power mattered. It pulsed with creativity, passion, and hope.

And then there were Margali's thoughts. Guarded, surface thoughts, they let Clea in just deep enough to access what she needed, and no further. Even so, Clea still got a taste of Margali's need for power, not just for power's sake, but because she had given up so much in pursuit of it. The sunk cost of her relationships with her children, and maybe even her own humanity. If she didn't become the most powerful, the Sorceress Supreme of the Winding Way and who knew what after that, then of what worth were those most painful of sacrifices? The question haunted the green-skinned sorceress, and she could not keep it from her mind now, regardless of how much she might want to.

But Clea thought she sensed an undercurrent of relief, too. Margali had likely never shared her fears with anyone before now. Being forced to open herself up in this manner allowed her to do so while maintaining the pretense of not wanting to.

And then she had hold of the fiery emerald thread of Margali's power, a flaming pillar of arrogance and envy that burned Clea when she touched it, construct or not. But she did not waver.

Braiding their threads together with the soft lavender strand of her own was harder than she expected, the colored lines twisting and bucking, pushing away from each other like magnets of the same polarity. None of them had ever worked together this way, ever let anyone touch their power, let alone manipulate it, and none of them truly trusted the process, deep down.

Clea understood. The vulnerability made her uncomfortable, as well. But she didn't have time to coax each thread gently into place. Instead, she reached out and grabbed them, yanking them into line through sheer force of will. For a moment, they fought her, but she gritted her teeth and pulled harder. She could feel sweat beading on her forehead and trickling down her back, taste the salt of it on her upper lip. Her muscles strained with the effort of her concentration. Still, she pulled.

Suddenly, like dominoes tapped with the lightest of touches, the colored threads fell into line. First blue, then red, and finally green. Clea heaved a sigh of relief.

Then, not stopping to celebrate this small victory, she gathered their combined might into herself until she felt as if she might burst into a galaxy of rainbow stars. And when she could not hold even a breath more of power, she released it, channeling all that energy into the single, stronger cord of braided magic the sorceresses had already created.

Prismatic fire raced up through the blood-colored ray that had been their combined but separate magics, hit the interface with the pale yellow light of the Guardian's beam, and then kept going. Clea thought it might travel all the way back into the creature's cyclopean eye.

But G'uran the Great, like all ancient Mhuruuks, had been a powerful sorcerer in his own right, one of the mightiest the Dark Dimension had ever seen. And he had imbued his guardian with much of that power.

The jaundiced beam from the G'uranthic Guardian's eye began repulsing their polychromatic ray, pushing it back toward the sorceresses. In her mind, Clea could see it pushing back against each of the individual-colored strands, looking for a weakness.

It found one.

Surprisingly, it was the green thread that snapped, and Margali staggered from the backlash. The abrupt separation of mind and power left Clea momentarily bereft and paralyzed, as if a part of her soul had been forcibly excised, but the other women redoubled their efforts to make up for Margali's absence, and the feeling faded as quickly as it had appeared.

If Clea had been a betting woman, she would have put money on Holly's strand going first, for while the girl had both innate power and top-notch training, she simply lacked the experience of using magic in combat or in a team environment. Then again, Margali was perhaps the strongest willed among them, and the least likely to play well with others. If there was going to be a weak thread in their braid of synergy, she was the obvious candidate.

But Clea had anticipated that one or even more of the sorceresses' strands might fray under the pressure of the Guardian's gaze. There was a fifth thread she had not yet woven into their braid. Like all who wore the Flames of Regency, Clea was able to draw strength from the very essence of the Dark Dimension itself. She did so now, calling up a sparkling black strand of energy from the ground at their feet to join and bolster the others. As it wound itself over and through the existing-colored threads, they, too, began to sparkle. And when the newly braided beam of power reached the interface with the sallow light of the Guardian's ray, this time it was not push it back, as the women's combined power had been before.

It absorbed and transformed it, traveling all the way back to the Guardian's eye, until what was once a lemony light, the last pale remnants of G'uran the Great's power, became the same sparkling sable essence that marked the rest of the Dark Dimension.

The G'uranthic Guardian blinked.

And then its now-black eye exploded in a violent shower of ebon sparks, and Clea released her hold on the other sorceresses' power as the Guardian's gaze went dead. Her desire to collapse with relief and fatigue was eclipsed by a rush of triumph.

The way into the palace was open. This was it. They had done it.

Clea looked at her companions and smiled wolfishly.

"Showtime."

Chapter Thirty-Seven

Once inside, the women lost no time in splitting up. They all had the map to the Grand Throne Room firmly ensconced in their minds and knew their assigned routes. Clea and Holly's path would take them via servant halls and little-used galleries to the Azure Throne, while Margali and Elizabeth had been given the direct course which would take them past more populous areas of the palace. The idea was, again, to confuse Umar and her forces, though none of them really knew if it would work or not.

Umar had wards set throughout the palace that would detect both cloaking spells and teleportation, so they were eschewing the former and planned to only use the latter as a last resort. Hence the cloaks Clea had given them. She hoped the camouflaging garments would help them blend in if anyone should spy them from afar or happen to glance their way. Anyone who got closer or looked longer, of course, would have to be dealt with.

There were no quippy farewells or serious speeches when they separated. When Clea had linked with them to combine their magic with hers, some residual thoughts and emotions from each of them had inadvertently wound up being sensed by the others. So it was a quiet, subdued group of sorceresses who now embarked on this last stage of the mission, most of them avoiding each other's eyes.

Clea was surprised to see that, of them all, Margali was the only one who met her gaze and gave her a brief nod before leading Elizabeth down a side hallway. Or perhaps it wasn't so surprising. Margali's fleeting thoughts hadn't revealed anything that anyone didn't already know or suspect about her. And, despite her appearance, Margali was old enough to have reached what some women on Earth liked to call their "crone phase", where age and life experience made the opinions of others seem inconsequential, and they finally started living for themselves instead of for the families they'd raised. Then again, if those were the criteria, Margali may well have been born a crone, the births of two children and adoption of another notwithstanding.

Agatha had talked about women becoming invisible as they aged, and while she hadn't used the word "crone", that was certainly the phase she'd been referring to. She'd seen it as an advantage, because being underestimated meant your blows would be unforeseen, and unexpected wounds always cut the deepest.

But she hadn't addressed the fact that women also became more powerful as they shook off the confines of youth and propriety. On Earth, older women were often compared to wine aged in casks, but the crone years weren't about fermenting in a dark barrel until someone else deemed you ready for consumption by the world. They were about the wine shattering those barrels and flowing free.

Clea wondered what phase she herself was in, but quickly realized that she had been in her crone years for even longer than Margali. Her Faltine blood kept her looking like a young woman, but she had lived for centuries, and on days like today, she felt every one of those years. Unlike Margali, though, she had gone straight from maiden to crone, skipping right over the mother part.

She spent the briefest of moments pondering if it were possible to experience the phases out of order, then immediately chided herself for such ill-timed, wandering thoughts, pushing them firmly away. She recognized them for what they truly were – manifestations of her own anxiety about the soundness of this scheme and her ability to pull it off. Some of the very thoughts she had shared with her companions when they pooled their power. So maybe there was more than one reason the others hadn't wanted to meet her gaze.

If she failed, it wasn't just her own life on the line. It was Ardina's. Margali's. Elizabeth's and Holly's. The lives of her people in the Dark Dimension. The lives of every denizen of the entire Archipelago of Anguish and Redemption. Maybe even more beyond that. Not Earth, surely, as Umar had sworn never to contest with Stephen for that realm again. But anywhere else was fair game. Umar had never been one to be satisfied with anything or anyone for long.

Sometimes Clea wondered if she had inherited that trait, and that was why she didn't want to rule the Dark Dimension, or why it was often so hard with her and Stephen.

She frowned at the thought. She didn't need Umar's capriciousness. She needed her mother's fierceness.

Something of her thoughts must have shown in her expression, for Holly stopped her as they passed through an empty, dusty hallway, a look of concern on her face.

"Are you OK?"

"I'm fine," Clea replied, whispering as Holly had done and forcing a smile.

"Whoa, boy," Holly said, eyes widening. "I am a woman, Clea. I know what it means when a woman says she's 'fine'. Hopefully we get to the throne room soon, so you can direct all that 'fineness' toward a fitting target."

Clea's smile was real this time, though she didn't quite laugh. The halls were too quiet for that.

"Oh, I intend to."

They walked along in silence after that, Clea taking point, alert for any actual servants or others using these deserted back ways for their own purposes. When she had worn the Flames of Regency, these halls had been bustling with happy servants who were treated fairly and paid well. Working at the palace had been a coveted position. But with Umar in charge, those servants had quickly found employment elsewhere – those that hadn't been imprisoned or killed outright for their suspected loyalty to Clea and her rebels. The few servants who remained were mostly magical constructs or demons of some variety; Umar despised Mhuruuks, and had done since Clea's birth. She did not allow them in her palace, save for a few loyal guards who had pledged their fealty when she and Dormammu first took power. Clea's own father had been one of those few, for all the good it had done him.

Clea tried to push these distracting thoughts from her mind, as well, but it was more difficult now, as they were nearing the quarters where she and Orini had lived when she was growing up here, a child of shackled privilege, a princess among slaves. She and Holly had already gone to the kitchens, sneaking in unnoticed by the stressed and shouting cooks to deposit one of the poppets in an unused cauldron. Then they had backtracked here, where they would leave another, before placing the third in Umar's private baths, which should be vacant, as even Umar wasn't vain enough to fret about her appearance in the middle of an all-out attack and infiltration.

At least, Clea hoped Umar's common sense would outweigh her conceit. It was by no means a given.

Then it was on to the Azure Throne and their confrontation with Umar. Clea's stomach was a clenched knot of dread and anticipation.

As they rounded the corner to the dead-end hallway which housed the old family quarters, Clea was surprised to see someone exiting the door opposite the one to her rooms. She was about to duck back around the corner and safely out of sight, but there was something familiar about the broad-shouldered shape and its quick, assured stride. As the figure passed into the halo of light from one of the hall's scattered torches, Clea could not suppress a gasp of recognition.

"Father?!"

Chapter Thirty-Eight

Elizabeth and Margali headed down a hallway opposite the one Clea and Holly had taken. They had agreed that, if accosted by humans or reasonable facsimiles thereof, like the Mhuruuks, Elizabeth would take the lead, while Margali remained hidden beneath her cowl. If they encountered non-humans, Elizabeth would stand back while Margali spearheaded their invasion force of two, her green-skinned and horned appearance being less likely to cause a furor here in the Dark Dimension than it would in other places.

Clea had given them three locations for hiding their poppets: an old gallery that had once contained paintings of Mhuruuk heroes and now contained only portraits of Umar (some of which, she had cautioned, were rather lewd), a smaller throne room in which Umar occasionally entertained petitioners she did not want dirtying up the Azure Throne, and a barracks for the palace guard that Clea did not think would be in use.

The duo didn't pass many others on their way to the gallery. Most of those, like the sorceresses, kept their heads and eyes down. No one seemed to know what their fellow servants might be up to, and as long as it didn't interfere with the timely discharge of their own duties, they also didn't seem to care. Which Elizabeth supposed was understandable. The magical constructs would be focused on their many and varied instructions, following them to the last letter, and the rest of the world might as well not exist to them. The Mhuruuks, few as they were, would not want to attract Umar's attention by failing to perform their assigned tasks or keeping anyone else from doing the same. Even those who, Elizabeth suspected, were rebel spies. Maybe them most of all.

As for the demons… well, they were a cowardly lot, but the stronger ones might step out of line if they could do it without getting caught. They would bear watching.

The two women reached the gallery without incident. It was, as Clea had warned, a bit like walking through a boudoir photographer's portfolio where all the pictures had the same subject. Elizabeth stopped to admire some of the more tasteful paintings of Umar. In one, she was bathing beneath a cascading fall of water, her sleek black hair just reaching the curve of her buttocks while she glanced playfully over her shoulder. In another, she sat upon her throne, legs crossed, her trademark green dress falling so that her knee-high sandals and most of her well-muscled thighs were on display. She was leaning forward with the Flames of Regency cavorting about her raven-haired head, eyebrows arched as she stroked the scales of some sort of demon dog who slavered at her feet.

Pet choices aside, Elizabeth had to concede that Clea's mother was an astoundingly beautiful woman. Or goddess. Faltine. Whatever. And if she wanted to own and celebrate her beauty, then more power to her.

More feminist power, of course. Umar did not need any more of the mystical kind. That was sort of what they were here to put an end to. With prejudice.

Margali placed one of the poppets behind a dusty burgundy curtain that hid a blank spot on the wall where another painting had once hung. As she did, Elizabeth couldn't help but wonder who the missing painting was of, and why Umar had seen fit to remove it. As if the narcissistic despot needed a reason beyond its subject being someone other than her.

They passed a pair of demons on their way to the secondary throne room – Clea had called it "the Less Grand Throne Room" – but the creatures took one look at the scowl on Margali's chartreuse face and hastily scurried on by, which earned a miffed "harrumph" from the sorceress, though Elizabeth wasn't quite sure why. Had the Sorceress Supreme expected them to perform obeisance? Or maybe she was just itching for a fight and had hoped to be challenged. If so, Elizabeth could certainly understand that desire. She was tired of all the hiding and skulking about herself. Subtlety really wasn't her thing, though she could engage in subterfuge when necessary. It just always left a taste like unripe gooseberries in her mouth, unpleasantly tart and often bilious when consumed in large quantities, as lies tended to be.

They backtracked to the smaller throne room without incident. It, too, was empty, which Clea had assured them would be the case. Margali placed the second poppet dead center on the throne, grinning wickedly as she did so. Clea had wanted the dolls hidden, but Elizabeth understood and approved of the statement Margali's placement would make to whomever found the poppet. It was only a matter of time before the real Clea sat on the real throne again.

Their last stop before arriving at that throne was the barracks for the palace guard. Since that guard now consisted largely of constructs and demons, Clea had told them to expect the barracks to be empty. Magical constructs did not need a place to rest or store personal belongings, and while demons might, they'd be far more likely to do so in an uninhabited tower room or some dank corner of the dungeon.

Demons were not social creatures, although there were exceptions to every generality, of course. But even those demons who did live and work together usually did so out of necessity, not desire, their cohabitation marked by constant squabbling. Umar wouldn't tolerate that level of disorder amongst her guard. Soldiers who couldn't work together off the field of battle would be the first to die on the field. Umar didn't give a fig for their lives, but she *did* care about winning, and that was much easier when your living – or at least animated – troops outnumbered your opponent's. It was simple math, not a desire for unity, or even discipline, among her troops. Elizabeth supposed it wasn't a bad approach when you could simply create or summon more soldiers to replace any that perished.

When they entered the barracks, the long room was only sporadically lit with guttering torches. The flickering flames revealed soot-stained walls lined with dusty wooden cots, small trunks at their feet. Most of those trunks were open, and empty. A few toward the farthest wall, where the room was darkest, were not. Elizabeth squinted and realized there were tables at the back of the narrow room.

Then she realized there were figures seated at those tables. Figures who had all turned and were now looking at her and Margali.

Oops.

In the pregnant silence that followed, Elizabeth heard the distinctive clinking of coins on the table's wooden surface, followed by the scraping of wooden chair legs across the stone floor. And then, like clockwork, a voice growled from out of the darkness.

"Get 'em, boys."

Chapter Thirty-Nine

Holly looked from Clea to the man approaching them and back again in confusion. Wasn't Clea's father dead? Holly distinctly remembered Elizabeth telling her that Clea had tried to bond with her over the fact that they both had dead dads, to get her to join their little interdimensional adventure. And by "bond", she had meant "manipulate", à la Agatha Harkness, which Holly had found profoundly disappointing.

The man was bald, but wore a full gray beard and mustache. He was shirtless, and his pecs, abs, and biceps belied everything above his neck, everything below it seemingly belonging to a much younger man. A man who went to the gym regularly and wanted everyone to know it.

He must look like Clea's father – what was his name? Olini? Orini? – but Clea had said that Dormammu had vaporized her dad right in front of her, so this couldn't really be him. Could it?

Holly wondered for a moment if this was another of the Dreamqueen's hallucinations, but dismissed the idea almost as quickly as she thought it. She didn't know if the Dreamqueen did nightmare packages for two, but even if the demoness did, Orini meant nothing to Holly, so why include her? There was no shock value in it for her, so why waste the energy?

No, whoever this Orini clone was, he was real. Which was worse, because Holly was pretty sure she could have talked Clea out of accepting a hallucinatory miraculously resurrected father. But a living, breathing lookalike that Clea could actually touch, actually hug? Holly had a feeling that was going to be a lot harder.

A premonition borne out when the Orini clone spoke.

"Daughter?"

Clea rushed forward, throwing her arms around the man she believed was Orini. And maybe he was. There were more things in heaven and earth than were dreamt of in Horatio's philosophy, or hers. Holly's own mentor was a ghost. Who was she to judge?

"Oh, Father!" Clea exclaimed, embracing Maybe-Orini, who, after a moment of apparent shock, returned the hug stiffly.

Clea released her resurrected father and stepped back to study him, while Holly hovered anxiously behind her. Something seemed off, but the pink-haired witch couldn't put her finger on what exactly was bothering her. Aside from the whole Clea's-father-might-be-a-zombie thing, that was. Holly quietly prepared a repulsion spell, just in case he started to look bitey.

"You're looking surprisingly well, all things considered," Clea said, her words careful and measured. From her tone, Holly could tell her friend now had some suspicions of her own.

That realization wasn't particularly helpful, however, as Holly had no idea what the sorceress's play was. She wondered if she should have a defensive or offensive spell at the ready instead of the repulsion one, but then decided her repelling spell would suffice. Basically the cartoon physics version of the target touching a high-voltage electric fence and being blown back an improbable distance, sans sound effects, it combined the best aspects of both spell types.

"As are you," Probably-Not-Orini replied, his tone mirroring Clea's. That was when Holly realized that this was not, in fact, a living person in front of them, but a magical construct that someone had fashioned to look like Clea's father and programmed to do little more than parrot back what was said to it.

Holly didn't need a full hand of fingers to guess who that someone was.

But why? According to Clea, there was no love lost between her parents. In fact, Umar had given Orini the one-night-stand treatment, sweet-talking him until she got what she wanted, then kicking him to the curb after she realized the experience wasn't all it was cracked up to be. And she'd allowed Dormammu to exile him and ultimately kill him. So why would she want constructs walking around that looked like him? Surely she didn't… miss him?

Holly almost laughed out loud at the sheer ridiculousness of that idea.

It was far more likely that Umar got some perverse kick out of torturing the man who had saddled her with Clea and the human form she could not escape. Or maybe she'd made him on the off chance Clea would run into him and be fooled. Or maybe not even to fool her. To hurt her. Maybe there were dozens of Not-Orinis wandering around the palace at this very moment, their continued existence predicated on a random encounter with a silver-haired sorceress.

"You're not really my father, are you?" Clea asked the construct, her voice betraying only the tiniest bit of the sadness those words must cost her.

"Are you truly my daughter?" the construct countered. "Does it matter?"

That was when Holly saw the knife stuck in the false Orini's waistband, at the small of his well-muscled back. She opened her mouth to warn Clea, but she never got the chance.

"I'm afraid it does," Clea said, lifting one hand and making a gesture in the air too swift for Holly to follow. "Goodbye," she whispered, before raising her voice in chant.

"By the light of Agamotto and in the name of the Vishanti,
Return this creature to its substance true. Begone now; you
* are free."*

The construct had been in mid-movement as Clea started to speak, but now it seized up and began to melt away into a soft, formless clay and then sink in between the floor's flagstones and disappear. But before its face could dissolve completely, Holly thought she saw a look of gratitude cross its features. She was probably just imagining it, though.

She released her repulsion spell and then laid a comforting hand on Clea's shoulder.

"I can't even fathom how hard that must have been for you," Holly said. She paused, then added, a little guiltily, "I only hope you casting that spell hasn't alerted Umar to our presence."

Clea didn't respond for a moment, and Holly didn't press, giving the other woman time to compose herself.

"It won't have registered. She doesn't pay attention to low-level magic. If she did, she'd be sending guards to the kitchens every time they burned something and tried to hide the fact. Burnt offerings can be a death sentence here, depending on Umar's mood." Clea turned to her with a hard smile. She looked pale. Paler than usual, at any rate, which Holly supposed wasn't saying much for someone who had grown up in the literal Dark Dimension. "My mother has a lot to answer for."

"No arguments there," Holly replied, though secretly she thought Clea might be giving her mother too much credit. If she understood the story correctly, Umar hadn't actually made Orini disown his daughter. The deadbeat had done that all on his own.

But Clea didn't need to be reminded of that. She'd no doubt been hurt enough by what had just happened.

A thought which turned out to be truer than Holly knew.

Clea had been holding her hand against her stomach since banishing the construct. Holly hadn't thought anything of it. Family tended to tie your guts in knots, in good ways and bad.

But when Clea removed her hand, Holly was horrified to see it was covered with blood. The construct had knifed the silver-haired sorceress right before she banished him, and he'd done a good job of it, too. If the amount of red staining Clea's bodysuit was any indication, he'd at least nicked something vital.

Holly looked from the wound to Clea's ashen face, panicked. She didn't know what to do.

"So much for being Daddy's little girl," Clea quipped weakly.

And then she collapsed.

CHAPTER FORTY

"How very gauche," Margali complained. Somehow, she'd expected better of Umar than demon guards playing cards in the barracks, although she wasn't exactly sure why. She'd seen the portraits the goddess had had commissioned of herself, after all. She might be nigh omnipotent, but Umar the Unrelenting was sorely lacking in taste.

"This could get noisy," Elizabeth said, as three overlarge demons stood and began stalking their way. They reminded Margali of Haus from the circus Freak Show – too big, and hopefully not too bright. One broke the chair it had been sitting on to use its frame as a misshapen club. Another grabbed a torch out of a wall sconce. The third didn't bother with a weapon. As it approached and Margali got a good look at its long, serrated claws, she realized it didn't need one.

"Well, we can't have that," Margali muttered, and slammed the butt of her staff into the stone floor, the impact ringing through the long room, which earned her a sidelong look from Elizabeth. It *had* been a bit louder than intended.

Banishment would be unlikely to work; there were as many different spells for doing that as there were types of demons to dispel. And if the demon was already in its home dimension, the question became where to banish it to? Too many uncontrollable variables for Margali's taste.

She preferred to just turn them into jelly.

"O Mighty Oshtur, Tower of Towers,
Without limit are thy powers!
To these fiends, now reveal them,
And as one mass, now congeal them!"

Elizabeth wrinkled her nose in distaste.

"That is just gross. Both the spell *and* the rhyme."

Margali ignored her, instead focusing on sending out a triple beam from her staff, one prong to gelatinize each demon.

Only a single beam shot out from the staff's gem, striking the clawed demon and reducing it instantly into quivering goo. The other two just waded through the pulp of their former companion, their progress not impeded in the slightest.

Margali quickly schooled her features to betray no alarm, but her pulse began pounding in her ears. What she had thought she'd sensed earlier before the Dreamqueen's mental assault was now beginning in truth.

The gifts of the Winding Way were failing, its pendulum swinging back from the pinnacles of power to the depths of impotence.

She couldn't let the others know.

"I guess the next one's mine, then," Elizabeth said, seeming not to have noticed that Margali's spell had been far less puissant than she'd intended it to be.

The Talisman's eyes began to glow, and a knot of electric blue vipers suddenly appeared around the torch-wielder's ankles, wrists, and neck. They appeared to be disintegrating whatever they slithered over.

The vipers that had materialized at the demon's neck were propagating quickly, and one of the first ones had gone for the guard's mouth, so he, like the demon Margali had congealed, had no opportunity to sound an alarm. It was difficult to cry out for aid when your vocal cords ceased to exist.

The other snakes completed their tasks just as quickly, disappearing when they had consumed all there was to consume, and soon all that was left of the demon was his torch, guttering on the floor.

"Guess you should have folded, 'boys'," Elizabeth said, smirking.

The third demon, a squat thing with fangs like a sabertooth and mottled brown and black fur, was no fool. Seeming to understand that discretion was the better part of valor, he dropped his makeshift club and held up his hands, hairy palms outward.

"I got no beef with you," the creature said. "You just handed me the pot."

Margali frowned, not following him. Elizabeth, seeing her expression, clarified.

"We got rid of the other card players, so this one wins the game, by default. And all the money."

"Ah," Margali replied. Money *was* often an excellent incentive to ensure someone's silence.

As if reading her mind, the demon said, "Let me go with the winnings, and as far as I'm concerned, those two went AWOL and you were never here."

The idea possessed some merit. With her power waning, Margali needed to preserve it as much as possible. But they were dealing with a demon here. Trustworthiness wasn't in their DNA.

"A tempting offer," Margali said. "Unfortunately, you won't be walking away a winner today."

"Margali–" Elizabeth began warningly, but Margali cut her off with another tap of her staff on the flagstone floor.

"Demon of darkness, in the name of Satannish,
By the Flames of the Faltine, your mind shall now vanish!"

The demon's face went slack, arms dropping to land limply at his sides.

"What have you done?" Elizabeth asked. She looked appalled, which Margali thought was a bit hypocritical, considering the Talisman had just dissolved a demon using flashy neon blue serpents. Pot, meet kettle.

"Relax. It's only temporary," Margali replied shortly as she strode past the inert demon. "He'll wake up in an hour or two with a massive headache and no memory of what happened here." She refrained from mentioning that he likely wouldn't remember anything from the past few days, possibly weeks. Maybe more. Margali wasn't actually sure. The last person she had cast this spell on was still comatose, but she had been at the peak of her abilities then. With her power waning, it was hard to say how lasting the effects of the spell would be.

But surely a bit of memory loss was preferable to nonexistence? Of course, depending on the memories lost, it might wind up being essentially the same thing, but there was nothing she could do about that.

"What are you doing now?" Elizabeth asked from behind her as Margali made her way to the back of the room and the table where the demons had been playing cards.

"Placing the poppet," she replied, setting the doll on the scarred wooden surface, then quietly scooping up the coins the demons had been using for stakes and depositing them in a pouch inside her dress. No sense letting it go to waste. The exchange rate for gold back on Earth was on the rise, after all.

She returned to Elizabeth's side. The other woman was, unsurprisingly, frowning.

"We're just going to leave him standing there?"

Margali shrugged. "You can move him if it matters that much to you. I personally think it's a waste of energy."

Elizabeth harrumphed, but didn't make any effort to rectify the situation.

"If that's all, we should move on. There's no telling when the guards change shifts. When they do, it's probably better if we aren't still in the vicinity."

"Well, *that* at least I can't argue with," Elizabeth muttered, her tone best described as petulant. Margali just smiled serenely in reply.

A smile that turned to a look of horror when her trusty staff suddenly shuddered in her grasp and then broke in two.

Margali could only stare at the pieces in her hands, aghast. The staff was only a focus, but it was still a vital tool in her magical arsenal, and its ruin would make some spells harder to direct. It was just one more sign that her power was failing.

One that everyone could see.

"What the–?" Elizabeth began, her eyes widening to Holly proportions. But before she could finish, as if to add insult to injury, somewhere deep within the palace, a claxon began to blare. "Oh, you have *got* to be kidding me."

"Would that it were so," Margali murmured, still looking at her broken staff in disbelief. She wondered idly if it had been Clea and Holly who had alerted the guards, or if the card-playing trio had been overdue for a shift change after all. Or it might have been something completely unrelated to either of their situations, though that seemed unlikely. In the end, the who and why were irrelevant. Now all that mattered was the where.

Then she tossed her dark green hair, squared her shoulders, and took one piece of her staff in each hand. She looked over at Elizabeth, her smile returning, a bit forced this time, but still determined.

"I believe that's our cue."

CHAPTER FORTY-ONE

"Clea!" Holly shouted, lunging forward to catch the other sorceress at the last moment so her head didn't slam against the flagstones. As she slowly lowered Clea to the corridor's cold floor, Holly tried to assess the severity of the other woman's wound. She was no doctor, but it didn't seem to have produced much blood, and it wasn't bleeding now. So the Orini construct's knife either hadn't actually hit anything vital, or Clea was bleeding internally, where Holly couldn't see what was happening or gauge how bad it might be. Or the blade could have been poisoned, or otherwise magicked to cause harm in ways not immediately visible to the naked eye.

Whatever the mechanism of injury, Holly had seen Clea take a shot from Amanda Sefton's magic and not go down, so if she had to make a guess about her companion's condition, she would have to go with "pretty bad".

Healing spells were not Holly's forte, and even if they had been, she had none of the components such workings often required in witchcraft. She had no doubt there were plants, stones, and other natural items with equivalent properties here in the Dark Dimension, but she did not have the luxury of time to go search them out.

313

Except it wasn't exactly true that she had none of the trappings needed for a healing spell, was it? She did have a Clea poppet.

Holly had never actually used a poppet for healing purposes, but she did know restoration was both slow and incomplete. Which wasn't going to work for her purposes. She needed an upright and functioning Clea immediately, if not sooner.

So, she was just going to have to MacGyver the doll.

First, she tore some of Clea's shirt from where the construct had knifed her and tied it around the doll. Then she plucked a few strands of Clea's silvery hair from her head and braided them into the white fringe already on the poppet's head. Finally, she opened the chest cavity and removed the tiny vial with its precious drops of the Sorceress Supreme's blood.

Then she took Elizabeth's knife – the Tsuut'ina woman had insisted Holly keep it after making the poppets – and dug the tip of the blade into the doll's abdomen, roughly in the same place Clea's wound was.

If she'd been back on Earth, she might have gone through the process of casting a sacred circle and calling the corners. It was a Wiccan practice Agatha frowned on, calling it cheap reconstructionist theatrics and unnecessary for spellcasting, and the old witch might be right. She usually was. But not always, as Holly was beginning to learn.

Even though Holly didn't follow that particular path, she still found the ritual calming, and considering she was about to make up a sympathetic magic spell from whole cloth, without knowing what it might do to the friend she was casting it on, she could have used a little peace of mind. But there wasn't time, and she had no idea which direction was which here, anyway. Gravity was more of a suggestion than a law in the

Dark Dimension, if the orientation of the floating islands she'd seen in the sky were any indication.

Holly took a few moments to formulate a quick rhyme. Then, taking a deep breath, she removed the miniature stopper from the top of the vial.

"Here goes nothing," she said to the empty hallway. Except, of course, it was actually everything. If she couldn't heal Clea, the Sorceress Supreme could very well die, and her plot to save Ardina and the Dark Dimension would die along with her. And they didn't really have a plan B.

"Image of woman, echo of wound,
Through the kindred bond attuned.
As done to image, so too real,
And with Clea's blood, now heal."

As she spoke, Holly poured the scant scarlet drops of Clea's lifeblood onto the gash in the poppet's stomach she had just made. Then, figuring it couldn't hurt, she added, "And as I will, so mote it be."

Then she sat back on her heels and held her breath, waiting. She hadn't actually practiced this type of magic in a very long time, having moved on to more complex workings that required neither couplets nor components, and sometimes not even words. A desire and a focused will were all that were truly necessary, but it could take decades, even centuries, to reach that level of mastery. She still had a lot to learn, but she definitely had the need and intent part down for this spell, if nothing else.

After a few heart-stopping moments, Clea took a hitching breath and sat up so suddenly that Holly, who'd been squatting beside her, was knocked on her rear.

"Wh-what happened?" Clea asked, looking around in

momentary confusion before focusing on Holly. "And what are you doing on the floor?" She paused. "What am *I* doing on the floor?"

Holly could hardly believe the spell had worked. She felt a thrill of satisfaction.

Take that, Agatha!

"Would you believe we slipped?" Holly replied lightly, focusing on her friend. If the silver-haired sorceress did not remember being stabbed by her father's lookalike, Holly wasn't going to be the one to remind her.

Clea looked at her oddly, one slim white eyebrow raised. Then she seemed to notice her wound, or what remained of it – a thin white line that cut diagonally across Amanda's fading sigil, like an interdictory symbol without the circle. But just as she opened her mouth to ask Holly about it, a deep clanging noise began to reverberate through the hallway.

"That's the breach alert," Clea said, scrambling to her feet. "Either Rahl and Synth have made much better headway than we could ever have hoped for, or Umar knows we're here."

"I'd like door number one, please, Bob," Holly quipped, even though she knew the second option was far more likely. Hopefully her poppet spell had been "low-level" enough not to catch Umar's attention, but worrying about it now was like trying to close the barn door after the horse had already bolted – pointless. Instead, Holly grabbed the doll that they had intended to place in Umar's baths and chucked it as far back down the hall as she could. "Sorry, poppet. Change of plans."

The other doll was no longer usable for its intended purpose, so she left it where it was. It no longer had any connection to Clea, so would pose no danger to her. It was just a poorly carved figure in badly made clothing. Perhaps a servant child would find it and take it home to play with. Or wrinkle their nose and throw it in the trash. Both choices seemed equally likely.

"So," she said to Clea, "time to turn these puppies on and head for the throne room?"

Clea nodded, the corner of her mouth quirking upward.

"I'd intended to wait until we rendezvoused with the others before activating the poppets, but that decision seems to have been made for us. Go ahead. Say the word. I know you've been dying to, though I still don't understand why."

While Holly thought that was a poor choice of words, all things considered, she had indeed been looking forward to this part. Facing the back of the corridor where she had thrown the poppet and trying to suppress her fangirl glee, Holly drew herself up haughtily and jabbed the pointer finger of her right hand out into the air in front of her with authority.

"Engage!"

CHAPTER FORTY-TWO

Umar sat on the Azure Throne, pulling a steady stream of golden power from the woman trapped in the Sphere of Cyttorak rotating slowly in the air beside her. She was using the siphoned Power Cosmic to both maintain the sphere and to test out the effects of different offensive spells when amplified by its energy. So far, she had been delightfully pleased with the results of the experiment.

She was simultaneously projecting two images in the air in front of her through mystic gemstones, one for each of the rebels' attacking forces. Clea's spell signature had been detected with each group, as well as at the G'uranthic Guardian, but Umar had yet to catch sight of her. She suspected her daughter was not actually at any of these places, but somewhere inside the palace with her group of witches, making their slow way toward Umar via stealth and trickery. She was almost impressed by the deviousness thus displayed, except that she suspected it wasn't actually Clea's. Her daughter tended to be revoltingly forthright and would no doubt have preferred a frontal assault, given her druthers.

Umar wrinkled her nose in distaste. The fact that she even had a daughter still made her squeamish at times. She had done her best to block out the memory of the birth, but it had driven her to the brink. The unrelenting pain that she could not stop, her body beyond her control, obeying some instinct deeper than magic as it fought to eject the child it had incubated. Clea deserved to die for putting her through that alone, never mind all the trouble she'd caused since.

But when she'd had the chance to kill her, Umar had refrained, choosing to save her daughter and her daughter's lover, the most irritating Doctor Strange, instead. And she couldn't say for certain why she had done that. It wasn't as if she hadn't killed family before. She and Dormammu together had destroyed their Faltine progenitor, Sinifer. And she'd certainly *tried* to kill Dormammu many times, though he always came back.

Umar didn't like not knowing things, their whos and hows and whys. You had to know a thing to manipulate it. You had to know *yourself* to keep from being manipulated. That this "why" question existed in her mind and remained unanswered was a source of both perpetual disquiet and annoyance.

Which made her all the more determined to get rid of Clea for good this time. Umar couldn't afford softness, whatever its source. She would do away with Clea and crush her petty little rebellion here and now, and then there would be nothing standing in the way of her conquest, external or internal.

Umar turned her focus back to the images of the rebels that moved in the air before her. She had already sent spells that opened the earth up in front of the ground troops and sent their front ranks plunging deep into the abyss, as well as drained the power from their ranged weapons and swapped out the forms of about half a dozen of the rebels with the bodies of Mindless Ones. She could not help but laugh as she watched the remaining rebels turn on the lumbering cyclopes, not realizing that the minds inside of those creatures were those of their friends. By the time they figured it out – if they ever did – it would be too late. The Mindless Ones outside the shimmering wall would have destroyed the swapped rebel bodies on sight, so even if the rebels did realize their mistake and cease trying to murder their hapless companions, those companions would have no bodies to return to. It was all just too delicious.

As for the aerial assault, she had already buffeted them with super-powered Winds of Watoomb and made the clouds congeal around them so they couldn't see to avoid the attacks of her warriors or mount their own reprisals. She particularly liked that last one and thought she would add it to her campaign repertoire, though she would need to modify it for dimensions without clouds, or even skies.

She was contemplating which spell to send against the hapless rebels next when an alarm began to blare throughout the palace. One of the two constructs she'd created to look like Orini – the younger version – hurried up to her. She'd made an older one as well, but he reminded her too much of Clea, so she had sent him away to another part of the palace.

"The castle has been breached, mistress," the Young Orini construct reported.

"Obviously, you dolt," Umar snapped. Why this one was even in the throne room, she wasn't sure. Still, if he knew something she didn't, that intolerable situation needed to be rectified. Now. "Where? By whom? More rebels? And why hasn't my guard been summoned here yet?"

"I don't know about your other questions, but I can answer the first two," said another voice behind her. "Second one first: your daughter, Clea."

Umar turned to see the Dreamqueen, her own throne room visible through the dimensional window. Umar considered pulling her through the window and freeing her from her pocket dimension, because having the demoness here in the Dark Dimension would make it easier to kill her once their alliance had ended. Which Umar fervently hoped was soon; the demoness was just as annoyingly obsessed with Earth as Dormammu had ever been. Umar suspected that, while the pasty-skinned wretch had asked for her father's realm, it was, in fact, Doctor Strange's domain that she ultimately wanted for herself.

Not that it mattered. Umar had no intention of handing over Nightmare's realm to the Dreamqueen once she had conquered it. Once the demoness had served her purpose, then her life, pitiful as it was, would be forfeit.

The object of Umar's scorn was currently watching her own gazing pool, which she'd been monitoring for signs of Clea or her friends. The pool, which had been displaying rotating images of the palace interior and its immediate surrounds, now showed an overhead map of the palace.

"I've detected her magical signature in your palace. It's the same as the one with the rebels, and the one that was at the gate," the Dreamqueen said.

"Excellent," Umar replied. The sooner her brat of a daughter got here, the sooner Umar could finish this unpleasant business and get on with conquering the Archipelago of Anguish and Redemption. And then, who knew? Now that she had an endless power source, the universe was the limit. "Where is she?"

The Dreamqueen looked at her, her bright red lips twisted into a scowl that stood out starkly against the white landscape of her face. Umar found it a bit disconcerting.

"Apparently," the Dreamqueen said, gesturing at the map, which suddenly sported a multitude of glowing purple dots, "she's everywhere."

CHAPTER FORTY-THREE

The Grand Throne Room, wherein sat the illustrious Azure Throne, had three entrances: a wide set of double doors opposite the throne and set apart from it by an intimidating length of sanguine carpet, and two entrances on either side of the throne, leading to separate wings of the palace. The configuration very much resembled that of an old Earth church, with the Azure Throne sitting above all on its raised dais in the sanctuary, its supplicants before it and its sycophants on either side.

Clea had always secretly hated the room and its layout, because it was designed to emphasize the divide between ruler and ruled, not connect them, as it should. She had always preferred to do as much of her day-to-day business as she could in the smaller throne room when she had ruled here, only sitting upon the Azure Throne for state functions or other necessary shows of power. Of which there had been, unfortunately, more than Clea would have liked.

If only the people would accept someone brave and level-headed like Rahl… well, maybe more like Synth… for their leader. But they had come to associate the Flames of Regency with rulership, when in fact, Clea had come to believe, they were nothing more than an indicator of which Faltine was currently ascendant. Only someone with Faltine blood could wear the Flames, and outside of the Faltine dimension, that meant only her, Umar, and Dormammu. Two of which were awful choices and one of which would rather be doing anything else.

If the rebellion was successful and she reclaimed the throne from Umar, she had to find a way to convince the people of the Dark Dimension that someone who did not bear the Flames could also be fit to rule. But that, she supposed, was a war for another day. She had to win today's battle first.

She and Holly hid at the left side entrance to the throne room. They could see the Azure Throne, and Umar perched atop it, the Flames of Regency taller and brighter than Clea had ever seen them. Umar herself was limned by a golden light coming from the other side of the dais, where Clea assumed Ardina must be. They could see the projections from Umar's mystical gems currently showing Clea's rebels being decimated. And they could see Umar's dimensional window, and the green-haired, red-horned woman who moved about within it.

"She teamed up with the psychopathic Christmas elf?" Holly whispered, affronted. "That's just rude. And that construct… is that another…?"

But Clea wasn't really listening. She had overheard the Dreamqueen telling Umar that her magical signature had appeared in the palace, and when the demoness called up the overhead map in her gazing pool to show her mother where, Clea decided to add a little more chaos into the mix.

"As my magic's trace shines with purple light,

"Images of Ikonn, now confound their sight!"

As she spoke, what should have been only a handful of dots on the Dreamqueen's map suddenly became three times that many, some of which appeared well within the confines of the Grand Throne Room.

Umar howled in rage, jumping up from the throne and whipping her head this way and that, her dark hair snapping behind her as she scanned the room for any sign of her daughter. She seemed to relax slightly when Clea did not immediately appear out of nowhere and attack.

"Invisibility, perhaps?" the Dreamqueen suggested, her expression betraying some confusion. Which was only natural; Clea's spell couldn't reach through the dimensional window to affect the gazing pool, so where Umar saw dozens of potential Cleas, the Dreamqueen still only saw the handful of signatures left by the poppets. And by Clea herself, of course.

"Impossible!" Umar hissed in reply. "The entire palace is spelled against such subterfuges."

Elaborate spells against magical cloaking that could be foiled, as it turned out, by using simple peasant cloaks. Probably because Umar would never have seen those she considered so far beneath her as anything resembling true threats, so would never have thought to guard against them and their simple, mundane tactics. Clea would have to remember that.

Just then, the other two members of her team made contact.

Clea, are you there? Margali's thought came through sharp and loud. Clea winced at the volume.

We are, Clea responded, her mental voice pointedly softer. *Are you and Elizabeth in place and ready?*

We are. It was Elizabeth who replied this time, and Clea didn't have to look to feel some heretofore unrealized tension leaving Holly's body beside her.

Liz, you should know– Holly began, but she never got to finish.

Well, then, Margali interrupted, *let's end this.*

It was the last thing Clea and Holly heard before the fire-works started.

CHAPTER FORTY-FOUR

From their vantage point at the right side of the room, Elizabeth could see Umar on the Azure Throne, the pitched battle against the rebels in the air, and a crackling crimson sphere from which a steady stream of golden energy was flowing to Umar, feeding her Flames of Regency. Stoking them, it seemed to Elizabeth, to new and dangerous heights. She could see the outlines of what looked like a dimensional window, but she couldn't tell what it might be displaying, if anything.

"First things first. We need to get Ardina out of that Sphere of Cyttorak," Margali said.

"A spellbreaker?" Elizabeth suggested. She knew there was one in her father's bag; she'd run across it during her quest to save the Remnant Men, and even in her nearly debilitated state, she had memorized its location. If she concentrated and reached into the Pouch of the Void for it now, it would come right to hand – one of the artifact's more convenient features, which helped ensure that only the items you actually wanted to be released could come out of the pouch. Of course, she didn't know exactly what the thing would *do* once she had it, but if it could free Ardina, that's all that really mattered.

Margali looked at her with evident surprise, and perhaps a hint of admiration.

"You have a spellbreaker? That will work on a sphere?"

"In theory," Elizabeth hedged. And then she pretended to glare at Margali. "And why are you so surprised that someone besides a Sorceress Supreme might have access to your so-called higher magics?" It wasn't as if magic was the sole purview of wealthy white – or green – folks, after all. "I'm pretty sure I should be offended."

Margali smiled that wickedly, falsely sweet smile of hers.

"Undoubtedly."

Elizabeth had no idea if the other woman was also teasing or not.

Then Margali's smile disappeared, and she was all business once more.

"I suppose I'm the distraction, then."

"Aren't you always, though?"

The corner of Margali's mouth twitched, but she wasn't going to give Elizabeth the satisfaction of a laugh.

"Touché," she said. "And… good luck."

The green-skinned sorceress held out her hand. Elizabeth took it.

"And to you."

There was an air of finality about the exchange, and Elizabeth couldn't help but wonder if Margali planned on making it back from whatever distraction she had up her sleeve.

Then again, would any of them?

Margali released her grip, gave her a nod, and turned with a whirl of dress and hair. Then she strode out into the Grand Throne Room, where a squadron of demon guards was entering through the double doors opposite the throne.

Margali paid them no heed. Instead, she raised the broken pieces of her staff high into the air and, without warning, let out a one-two combo of white bolts and blue bands of bedevilment, aimed straight at Umar.

Elizabeth didn't have time to see what the uber-goddess's response was, though a howled "You *dare*?!" gave her a pretty good indication. She ran toward the swirling scarlet sphere that confined Ardina, reaching into her father's pouch as she did so.

She stopped behind the throne, out of Umar's sight and that of the guards, and withdrew an unassuming metal cube, its sides devoid of marking or decoration.

Elizabeth had referenced Margali's sorcery, and by inference, the same magic that both Clea and Umar practiced, which often relied on invoking higher powers. But, in truth, the cube was not a tool of invocation. Though there was no real analog in sorcerous terms, if she were forced to make the comparison, she would have to say that the cube itself *was* the higher power.

The metal cube wasn't actually a spellbreaker, per se. It was a nameless magic-devouring entity from another dimension utterly inhospitable to lifeforms like her own. It likewise could not long tolerate this environment.

Long enough, Elizabeth hoped. Enough to destroy the sphere, and only the sphere, and then she could return it to its own dimension. As it consumed the spell's magic, it would grow, and if it grew too much, she wouldn't be able to fit it through the pouch's mouth to send it back. And then Umar would be the least of their problems.

The cube began to vibrate in her palm as it sensed the closest active spell, its chief source of sustenance. Then it rose slowly and floated toward the sphere. When it reached the roiling red surface, it stopped. Nothing seemed to happen for a moment, and then the area around the point of contact started to disappear.

It was working.

Elizabeth stepped up behind the expanding cube and what was quickly becoming a powerless shell, bag ready. As soon as enough of the spell's power had been leached, she would swoop in and trap the cube back in the pouch, much as she had done with Plokta's mask. Hopefully, that would be enough to release Ardina, though she doubted the sphere was the only measure Umar had employed to ensure the golden woman's docility.

There. Only the lower half of the sphere still stood, and it no longer glowed or showed any movement. Ardina stood revealed within it, unmoving, a gold foil-wrapped treat in a child's Easter egg.

As Elizabeth prepared to pounce on the cube, she suddenly felt a hand on her shoulder and she was spun around to face a young man who looked oddly like Clea, but with dark hair.

"What are you doing back here?" he demanded. Then he seemed to recognize her; his eyes widened, and his voice rose. "Mistress! I've found one of the tres–"

But he didn't get a chance to finish his warning, because just then, a metal blur shot over Elizabeth's shoulder, latched onto the man's face, and began to feast.

CHAPTER FORTY-FIVE

Damn it! Clea thought. She rarely cursed, even in her own head, but fireworks had definitely *not* been part of the plan. But then, Margali was never one to stick to plans if more expeditious means of achieving her goal presented themselves. She had a lot in common with Umar in that respect. Clea would just have to trust that Margali's goals continued to align with her own in this instance. She at least genuinely cared for her daughter and was fighting to keep her safe in Limbo, unlike Clea's own mother, who only sought Clea's destruction.

As much as Clea had longed for even as tortured a relationship as Margali and Amanda had, she knew the time for that was long past. If Umar wanted destruction, Clea would give it to her.

Stepping out from hiding, Holly at her heels, Clea readied the Crystals of Cyndriarr spell. She doubted the crystals would kill her mother, but she imagined they would hurt her, allowing them to rescue Ardina with a minimum of interference from the goddess. Which was preferable, considering that the demons streaming in through the double doors coming to aid their mistress would be interference enough.

But I don't want destruction, child.

Umar's voice in Clea's head was so unexpected that she stopped where she was, flat-footed, momentarily losing her spell. She felt Holly bump into her, heard her say something, but somehow the pink-haired witch's words seemed very far away compared to Umar's.

I have never wanted destruction. I only want the same things for our people that you do: Happiness. Prosperity. Peace.

There was something very wrong with that, but Clea's thinking was suddenly slow and foggy, and she couldn't work out what the problem was. After a moment, she began to doubt there was a problem at all. Umar wanted the same things for the people of the Dark Dimension that Clea did, and why shouldn't she? She was their ruler, after all.

"That's right," Umar said, smiling down at her from where she sat on the Azure Throne. She gestured to a second throne on the dais beside her, this one at the same height as hers, only done in shades of plum and eggplant instead of hues of blue. "And I only wish to rule with wisdom and benevolence, with my daughter here at my side."

Clea frowned. Umar had never wanted to share anything. Had she?

"Oh, child, you've allowed the lies of others to cloud your thoughts. People who hate me, like my brother, and your husband. People who would see both of us diminished and weak, the better to perceive themselves powerful."

That… sounded right, actually.

"If you don't believe me, why not listen to the friends you brought with you to celebrate your coronation?"

Holly startled her by putting a hand on her shoulder. Clea had forgotten that the pink-haired witch was behind her.

"It's true, Clea," she gushed, her big doe eyes as wide as

her smile. "Your mother is amazing! I'm honestly jealous of your relationship. I only wish Agatha treated me with half the respect and kindness that Umar treats you with. What an amazing opportunity, to share rule of the Dark Dimension with her, equal in all things. Think of all the good you will be able to accomplish by working together!"

"I envy you, Clea," Margali said from the other side of her, and Clea turned to face the green-skinned sorceress. She, too, was smiling, an earnest expression that Clea for some reason thought should include fangs. "You have this incredible chance to reconcile with your mother, after all these years. Would that I were offered the same opportunity with Amanda, or Kurt. What wouldn't I give for it?

"And think of all the time you've already wasted! And for what? So some man could come along and snatch the Flames of Regency from you when you were too weak from battling each other to stop them? Don't you see? That was their plan all along! Dormammu's. Stephen's. To keep both you and Umar under their thumbs, too busy fighting each other to see how you were being manipulated! *They* are the ones who have kept you apart. The ones who have stolen all these years away from you. They're the ones who stole your mother from you, Clea. Don't let them get away with it!"

Before she could even start to process that, Elizabeth was spinning her around and grabbing her by both shoulders, giving her a firm shake.

"Margali is right, Clea. You can have the loving, nurturing relationship with your mother that you've always wanted. You can have what the rest of us have messed up or lost or never even got the chance to try for. It's yours for the taking." She took one hand off Clea's shoulder to point up toward Umar, who was now standing on the dais beside the twin thrones, arms outstretched. "All you have to do is join her. Just sit beside her and finally give your people what they need. Give your heart what it needs. Be happy, Clea."

Clea took a few halting steps toward her mother and the dais, the other sorceresses encouraging her from behind.

"You're making the right choice, Clea," Elizabeth cooed.

Clea took a few more steps. She was nearly at the bottom of the dais now.

"I'm so happy for you!" Holly added, barely able to contain her excitement.

Clea's foot was on the bottom step, and she only had eyes for her mother, waiting with open arms above her.

"Finally," Margali sighed, her voice somehow sounding as if it were right in her ear. "You're finally going to have what you've always wanted. You will rule the Dark Dimension hand in hand with Umar, your beloved mother."

Clea stopped where she stood, alarms bells ringing in her mind.

Wait. That wasn't right.

"But I… I don't want to rule the Dark Dimension," Clea said slowly, shaking her head as if to throw off something unpleasant that clung stubbornly to her hair. "By myself *or* with anyone else."

She looked up at the top of the dais, eyes narrowed. Umar sat on the Azure Throne, which no longer had a purple counterpart, looking back down at her and smirking. In between them, wicked-looking spears at the ready, were a trio of very large, very drooly demons.

"I only ever wanted…" she said, making several quick hand movements and recalling the Crystals of Cyndriarr. Instantly, a swirling maelstrom of sharp, thin rectangles of crystal began to churn before her, each glowing with an infernal yellow light. "…to free it."

And then she let the deadly crystals fly.

CHAPTER FORTY-SIX

Holly's first clue that there was something wrong was when Clea stopped walking abruptly and Holly ran into her. Well, not the first one, she amended. That had come way back when Clea's teleportation spell to get them to the Dark Dimension hadn't worked, and she'd frankly lost count since then. She couldn't even go with "first one since entering the Grand Throne Room", because the Dreamqueen video-teleconferencing in on their confrontation with Umar had already taken that honor.

Still, something was obviously amiss. Clea wasn't moving, she wasn't casting a spell, and she most definitely wasn't responding to Holly's own less-than-gentle poking at her ribcage.

It didn't take a genius to realize she was under a spell of some sort herself. Or, given that the walking punchline to "What's green and white and red all over?" was currently leering at them through Umar's dimensional window, one of the Dreamqueen's hallucinations.

She needed to think. She'd slapped Margali back to her senses. Maybe the same thing would work with Clea?

Except now Umar, who had been toying with Margali, had finally caught sight of Clea. A fleeting look of pure, murderous hatred crossed the raven-haired goddess's features as she stared down her nose at her daughter, quickly replaced with one of cold calculation. She waved a shapely hand and a trio of demons detached from the group harrying Margali and began heading toward Holly and Clea.

At the same time, Liz came tumbling out from behind the dais upon which the Azure Throne sat, limbs tangled with those of a bloody, headless body. She seemed to be fighting to get her father's medicine bag around the corpse's stump of a neck, where something metallic and quick-moving flashed.

Holly spied her a split second before the Dreamqueen did. She, however, did not howl with rage at the sight.

"You!"

And as if that weren't enough, Margali, whose blue and white bands and bolts had been coming at a much slower frequency for several minutes now, seemed to finally be succumbing to the sheer force of numbers. As Holly watched, the green-skinned sorceress, who'd been focusing spells through the gem-topped half of her broken staff and beating the snot out of demons with the other half, gestured once, twice, three times with the jewel, with no evident reaction. A look of terror washed over her face, followed quickly by despair. Then she started using that half of her staff as a second club until she disappeared beneath a mountain of demonflesh. Holly waited for some eruption of power to blow the infernal creatures sky high for their affront, like a mini Margali Vesuvius, but the seconds ticked past and it didn't come.

Holly knew what had happened. The thing Margali feared the most – the waning of the Winding Way and the loss of her powers – had finally occurred, and at pretty much the worst time imaginable. And while the sorceress had been holding her own against the demons when she had both magical and mundane weapons at her disposal, Holly did not think relying solely on Margali's unexpected and rather impressive tanbō skills was going to save her now.

Liz finally wrestled the softball-sized silvery thing back into her pouch, but not without cost. Not satisfied with decapitation, the metal creature appeared to have opted for new and unusual body parts and chewed off part of Liz's hand, though there was so much blood, Holly couldn't be sure of anything beyond the fact that someone's vein had been opened.

Chaos was now the true ruler in the throne room, and Holly had no idea where to focus her attention.

But Liz was struggling slowly to her feet, and Clea was blinking, a confused expression on her face. Umar was shouting at her demon trio to move faster. And there was still no sign of Margali.

Holly knew what she had to do, though it about ripped out her heart. Sun Tzu said, "You can be sure of succeeding in your attacks if you only attack places which are undefended." The corollary being that you could be sure of losing places you do not defend. Places, and people.

She was not about to lose Margali.

Meeting Liz's gaze across the throne room floor with an anguished look, she sent a message along Clea's mental connection, which she hoped was still functioning, even if Clea wasn't quite.

Liz, I am so sorry. I'll come back for you as soon as I can. But Margali's in trouble, and I think she might be dying. I have to help her. I'm the only one who can.

Holly knew Liz must think she was doing the exact same thing her father Michael had done, choosing someone else over her. But it wasn't an equal choice; even missing some fingers, Liz was still in better shape than Margali, who was currently playing padding for a demon carpet.

She might not care about the other woman as much as she did Liz, or even admire her like she did Clea, but Holly respected her, and she would never be able to forgive herself if she left Margali to die like that. If the two-time Sorceress Supreme was going out, she deserved to go out the same way she'd spent every other moment of her existence – fighting tooth and nail for what was hers. And Holly was bound and determined to give her that.

She only hoped Liz would be able to forgive her.

Her teeth gritted and her face set in determined lines, Holly drew on the power of the stone used to build the palace, the fire that fueled so much of it, the water that ran below and through it, and the air that ghosted through its halls. Then, powered and fortified by this dimension's version of the elements and limned in pink light, she marched over to the demon dogpile. Wading in, she began flinging bodies left and right like offal as she dug for her nemesis, ignoring the screaming and sounds of snapping bone as the demons landed on the stone floor, and stayed there.

She found Margali's broken and bruised body at the bottom of the pile, a short, pointed shard attached to the caged gem all that remained of her two half-staffs. She was barely conscious.

"Are we there yet?" the green-skinned sorceress asked, her voice barely above a whisper, but still managing a sardonic tone.

Holly laughed, glad to see Margali wasn't quite as close to death as she had feared when she'd uncovered the first bits of chartreuse skin and pine-colored hair. She didn't bother to answer as she helped Margali climb to her feet and began transferring some of her elemental protections over to the other woman.

"Stone and sky, flood and flame,
As I have called you each by name,
And you have answered me this day,
So too, now Margali of the Winding Way."

As Holly felt power draining from her into Margali, she saw the color returning to the other woman's cheeks, changing it from vomit green to lime, which she assumed was an improvement. But the transference of power was causing a sharp pain in Holly's upper back, making it hard to breathe.

And then she saw the horrified look on Margali's face, and realized it wasn't just a pulled muscle, or even just one too many fast-food tacos. A glance down revealed the truth of the matter – the tip of spear protruding out through her chest, now slick with Holly's heart's blood.

The spell she'd cast earlier had not siphoned off all her elemental fortifications to Margali, which was probably why she wasn't dead yet, let alone in much pain. But this was definitely not an ideal development.

Margali, as angry as Holly had ever seen her, let out a little screech of fury. She took the sharp end of her staff and aimed it over Holly's left shoulder, an easy enough feat considering she probably had six inches on Holly. Holly heard the squelch of the wood piercing something, the sucking sound of it being withdrawn, and the thump of something heavy hitting the ground. She assumed Margali had just dispatched whatever horror movie extra had skewered her, but she didn't turn to look. She was suddenly very tired.

Margali walked behind her, and she felt a tug, but the spear didn't budge. Instead, there was the snap of breaking wood, and as Margali reappeared, Holly realized the sorceress had broken off the weapon's shaft. Then she put her arm solicitously around Holly, who sagged against the taller woman in relief.

"I think it's time," Margali said gently.

Holly was confused.

"Time for what?"

"To call Agatha."

CHAPTER FORTY-SEVEN

Elizabeth hadn't been able to save the man from the magic-eater. She had realized too late that the only reason the metal cube had gone for him first instead of her was because he was a construct, made entirely of magic and powered by an ongoing spell, whereas she was just a conduit for it, via the Coronet of Power. He made the tastier meal.

Still, construct screams sounded the same as human ones, and Elizabeth couldn't help feeling guilty that she hadn't gotten the cube back into her father's pouch fast enough. Even then the thing had taken a decent chunk out of her hand before she could push it all the way through, though the bite admittedly looked worse than it was. But she was losing more blood than she'd like, and the world spun a bit as she clambered slowly back up to her feet, looking for her companions as she simultaneously called upon the powers of the coronet to cauterize the wound. It wouldn't take away the pain or make it any easier to use her hand, but it would at least stop the flow of blood for now, so she could focus on completing their mission.

As a wisp of smoke rose from her palm and she tried to swallow her rising gorge at the acrid smell of cooking flesh, Elizabeth quickly assessed the situation in the throne room.

No one else was following the plan. She saw Clea just standing there, as if lost in thought, oblivious to the chaos raging around her. She saw Umar rise from the Azure Throne, and gesture to her demon threesome.

She saw the dimensional window and the Dreamqueen's face framed within it and realized what must be happening to Clea. She saw the Dreamqueen see *her*, saw the uncontrollable hatred twisting the demoness's features, heard her scream of rage. Elizabeth would be curious to know if that was a shadow on the Dreamqueen's face, or if her earlier haymaker had left a bruise. She hoped it had.

She saw Margali go down under the pile of demons that she'd been keeping away from everyone else. Go down, and not get back up again.

And she saw Holly, cycling through these same images as she was doing. Heard her mental apology.

Watched her walk away, leaving Elizabeth alone to finish what the four of them had started while she ran off to play hero. Just like Elizabeth's father, the Shaman, had done. Choosing someone else over her. And not just anyone else – Margali, of all people! Margali, who had only ever treated Holly with irritation and derision.

Because when push came to shove, someone or something else always seemed to matter more to the people who claimed to care about her than she did. She never measured up. She never would.

Elizabeth shook herself angrily. She would have liked to have blamed this sudden bout of self-pity on the Dreamqueen, but she knew the demoness's perception-altering abilities wouldn't work on her while she wore her coronet.

She knew in her heart Holly had made the right choice, and

she didn't fault the young witch. Somehow that just made it hurt worse.

But the pity party with pjs and ice cream would have to wait for later. Right now, people were counting on her.

In the space of that thought, she saw several more things happen. Demons were suddenly flying off Margali like popping corn out of a pan. Umar's trio of demons was stalking toward Clea, Umar enchanting their weapons as they approached. Clea was finally moving, her hands fluttering in front of her, birds in some deadly dance. A spinning tunnel of crystals appeared before her.

Holly was helping Margali up, then casting some sort of spell to strengthen the other sorceress. Neither they nor Elizabeth saw the spear-wielding demon coming up behind them until it was too late.

Everything was happening so fast. Elizabeth saw Clea release her spell, the churning crystals slicing through the demons like buzzsaws, heading for Umar. She saw the spear-tip exploding through Holly's chest. She saw Margali's swift retaliation. She saw another squadron of demons heading in through the double doors to replace the ones already slain. She saw the Dreamqueen start to laugh.

What she did *not* see was Ardina, released from her prison but still under Umar's control, coming up behind her and tearing the Coronet of Enchantment painfully from her head. As agony washed over Elizabeth in waves from the coronet's forced removal, she staggered and turned, and saw one thing more: the top of the golden woman's head connecting with her face.

CHAPTER FORTY-EIGHT

The Crystals of Cyndriarr cut through the demons in front of Clea like sparkling amber scythes held by a multitude of tiny, invisible Deaths. They left a scarlet sheen on the floor and little else to show that the demons had ever existed, let alone threatened her. The whirling crystals, more orange than yellow now, continued along their deadly path, straight at Umar.

Clea saw her mother's eyes narrow, and then she threw back her head and laughed. As she did so, she waved her arms in a swirl of green fabric, and the crystals dissolved into nothingness.

"Is that the best you have to offer, 'Sorceress Supreme'?" Umar taunted, her arched brows pulling down into an ugly sneer. "Why don't you let a true sorceress show you how it's done?"

She raised her arms up high on either side, the long emerald sleeves of her gown fluttering about her with every arcane motion.

"By the blackness of space,
And its lack of all form,

345

May the Maelstrom of Madness,
Engulf you now in its storm!"

At her words, a rotating blue and gray whorl appeared in front of her, hovering there for a moment. Then she made a shoving motion, and the spinning mass shot toward Clea.

The spell as her mother used it was a glorified version of the Maze of Madness, and Clea knew if the spiraling colors touched her, she would be trapped in a web of distortion that stretched her body out in painful and impossible ways. Stephen had told her the maze spell would eventually reduce its target into a "nameless, shapeless nihility". The maelstrom version would do the same, but it would take longer and hurt more. Its effects were also, unlike those of the lesser spell, irreversible.

Clea summoned the Winds of Watoomb about herself like a shield, although she knew they would not hold the maelstrom at bay for long. But she had just seen Ardina, apparently acting as Umar's puppet, headbutt Elizabeth hard in the face and send the Tsuut'ina woman flying. If she hadn't been the Talisman and imbued with magical power even without her coronet, the blow might well have broken her neck. As it was, Elizabeth had fetched up against a pillar and wasn't moving. Clea could only hope she was alright, because she had no way of helping the other sorceress at the moment.

Even worse than any potential injury was the fact that Elizabeth no longer wore the Coronet of Power. Instead, Ardina held it in her hands and was even now bearing it like a gift up the dais stairs to Clea's mother, who stood waiting before the Azure Throne.

Clea could only assume that the Dreamqueen had told Umar about the coronet and its mystical powers. If her mother had command of both the coronet's power and Ardina's, there might well be no force in the multiverse that could oppose her.

They couldn't let Ardina give Umar the coronet. They had to stop her. But Elizabeth was only just now beginning to stir after her impact with both the stone pillar and Ardina's head. And Margali and Holly were leaning heavily on each other as they prepared for a new onslaught of demon guards, covered in so much blood that Clea couldn't tell what was theirs and what wasn't.

That left her. But she was too far away and too busy fending off Umar's storm to do anything herself – which was no doubt exactly what Umar had intended when she'd sent the maelstrom spell against her.

Correction.

She couldn't do anything *physically*. But one trick Stephen had ensured that she mastered as his disciple was astral projection. And since it was often more a question of mental discipline than magical ability, leaving one's body via ectoplasmic form was not a skill Umar had ever cared to study herself. So she might not be expecting it from someone else.

It wasn't the best plan Clea had ever devised, nor one with a particularly high chance of success. Plus, she risked having Umar's spell break through her own and ravage her physical body before she could get back to it. But Ardina had only a few more steps to go before placing the coronet in Umar's outstretched hand, so there was no time to come up with something better.

It was this, or nothing, and it was now, or never.

Clea closed her eyes and centered herself. She tried not to think about the winds losing strength around her as she withdrew her focus from them. They would hold long enough. They had to.

"In the name of the All-Seeing, in the name of the All-Spawning,
In the name of the All-Freeing, let my astral self be borning."

Clea felt an immediate lightness as she emerged from the bondage of her physical form and rose above it. Floating over the chaos of battle both magic and mundane, and momentarily removed from it, Clea had to suppress the fleeting urge to do loop-the-loops to revel in the feeling of pure freedom.

But it would be a short-lived freedom and one that no one else would enjoy again if she didn't do what she'd come here to do and stop her mother. With that goal firmly in mind, her astral form darted over to hover above Ardina. Then, with a mental apology to the golden woman, Clea dove into her body and mind and took possession of her.

Ardina fought her at first, of course; Clea had expected her to. But Ardina's mind was not controlled by Umar, merely muzzled, and once she recognized Clea, she willingly relinquished dominion of her physical form. Clea settled into her shining skin and fully inhabited the other woman's body.

Just in time to snatch the Coronet of Power away from her mother's grasping fingers and quickly twist to hurl it, frisbee-like, toward Elizabeth with a shouted, "Catch!"

Then she turned back to Umar and smiled. And as recognition dawned on Umar's face, Clea took a page from Elizabeth's book and used all Ardina's strength to punch her mother full in the face.

The force of Clea-Ardina's blow was so strong that Umar reeled backward into the Azure Throne, overbalancing it. Both goddess and throne tumbled backward off the dais to land with an echoing crash against the flagstones below.

Clea spoke into the shocked silence that followed as Umar's spells failed and her soldiers hesitated.

"No, Mother. *That* is how it's done."

CHAPTER FORTY-NINE

Clea turned and surveyed the throne room. Her mother wouldn't be down for long, so whatever she was going to do to get Ardina and the rest of her team out of here, she had to do now.

To her surprise, the translucent spirit of Agatha Harkness suddenly appeared beside Holly and Margali, her dimension-hopping strength seemingly restored. Clea wondered how the shade had managed to regain her power so quickly. Or did Umar's barrier spell not affect the dead and how they traveled between dimensions?

Or was Agatha simply far more powerful and cunning than she let on? That was a truly unsettling thought, given the old woman's temperament.

With a dismissive gesture, Agatha raised a wall of arcane blue fire between the women and the demons harrying them. Clea understood immediately that the blood that had covered both her companions must have been mostly Holly's. Agatha had told Holly she would come if the young witch were in dire need, but she wouldn't have appeared for anything less than a grievous wound.

But now that there were five witches here, Clea realized how she could rescue Ardina and the others.

Still in Ardina's body, she hurried down the dais stairs. She couldn't break Umar's hold on Ardina's mind, but she was able to make the golden woman kneel and cast a quick binding spell on her before exiting her form and re-entering her own. The spell would only last until Umar noticed and dispelled it, but Clea hoped that would be long enough.

Once back in her own body, Clea wasted no time summoning the others.

Gather around Ardina! We need Agatha, too. Hurry! We don't have much time.

She did not have a mental link with Agatha, but she trusted Margali to pass on her message. She rushed over to Elizabeth, who was still leaning heavily against the pillar, though the Coronet of Power was about her brow once more.

"Remind me never to make Goldilocks mad again," Elizabeth said weakly, as Clea approached.

"I'd start by never calling her 'Goldilocks' again," Clea replied, putting her arm around Elizabeth's shoulders to help bear some of the Tsuut'ina woman's weight. "Come on. It's time to go home."

As she did so, Elizabeth looked around quickly and saw Agatha hovering behind Holly and Margali as they limped toward Ardina's spellbound form. She froze.

"Why is *she* here?" she demanded. Then, as she came to the same realization Clea had about what Agatha's appearance must mean for Holly, her shoulders slumped and she added angrily, "And why didn't she come sooner?"

Clea didn't know, and she didn't even try to answer. She imagined Elizabeth didn't really expect her to.

The other three sorceresses reached Ardina before she and Elizabeth did. Agatha had called up more walls of arcane fire to cut off attacks from the demons who were now streaming in through the Grand Throne Room's two side entrances. Judging from how pale Holly was and how annoyed Margali looked, Agatha was the only one of the trio currently capable of casting spells. It was only as she and Elizabeth reached the others that she saw the gravity of Holly's wound.

There was more than one reason to hurry now.

"Everyone, place one hand on Ardina's head." The woman formed of the Power Cosmic normally towered over all of them, her height topping six feet, which was why Clea had taken recourse to having her kneel before binding her. "Our hands need to be touching each other's, as well."

She placed her right hand on Ardina's head, and Elizabeth followed suit. Clea saw that her hand had been maimed and burned at some point in between when they defeated the G'uranthic Guardian and now. That small victory already seemed like it had happened several lifetimes ago.

Margali was next, her green skin crusted red and black with blood. She shoved what was left of her staff through her belt and used her other hand to raise one of Holly's and hold it in place; the pink-haired witch was conscious, but too weak and tired to follow Clea's instructions on her own.

Agatha was last, her ghostly hand placed atop all the rest. Her touch would have been imperceptible if not for its bone-chilling cold.

The old witch looked at Clea, raising an eyebrow. "The Pentagram of Farallah? Interesting choice."

Clea didn't respond. She was actually modifying that spell, which was, at its core, a simple mass teleportation incantation. By itself, it wouldn't be enough to break through Umar's barrier. So she was going to have to give it a little oomph.

A little bit of each witch's lifeforce. In Holly's case, a *very* little bit.

She wasn't sure how well the spell would work with Agatha being dead, but obviously there was some sort of force keeping her around, so Clea hoped the spell would tap into that.

There was, of course, only one way to find out.

"By all who were, who are, who will ever be,
Those of life and those of love, I say unto thee... "

As she spoke, a stream of silver flashed out from her forehead to Margali's, then from hers to Agatha's, from Agatha's to Elizabeth's, and from Elizabeth's to Holly's before returning to Clea's, leaving an argent pentagram flaming in the air between them.

Thus connected to each of the others, Clea felt their lifeforces, their essences. She gathered them for the second part of the spell.

And then Umar appeared above the dais, fury blazing so hot in her eyes that Clea could feel it from where she stood. Her mother raised her arms, a spell on her lips. No doubt a fatal one.

Clea realized in that fraught instant that, by channeling the combined might of the other witches, and with Umar unable to take advantage of Ardina's extra power boost for at least a few more moments, she could do the one thing she'd never been able to accomplish before.

She could destroy Umar and free the Dark Dimension from her tyranny forever. Free its people.

Perhaps even free herself.

Holly groaned softly, and the sound brought Clea back to reality. If she did what she imagined doing, she would be no better than Umar, no matter how much good she wrought. Good ends could never justify evil means, and hijacking her sisters in sorcery like that, using their lifeforces without their permission for a goal they had not agreed upon, would be nothing short of betrayal. And betrayal was one of the worst sorts of evil, as she had good cause to know.

No, she would complete this mission, get her friends back home, and cede the Dark Dimension to Umar.

For now.

But she would be back. She and her rebels would regroup and continue their fight. They may not have won today, but they had dealt Umar a serious blow – to her ego, if nothing else. That had to count for something.

"By the Fangs of Farallah, we do implore,
Ye grant us passage through thy door!"

Instantly, they were elsewhere. Warm sun kissed their skin while a soft breeze caressed it. Waves lapped soft sand nearby.

The Parringtons' private beach.

"Cheese and crackers!" exclaimed a familiar voice in surprise. "Talk about making an entrance!"

EPILOGUE
The Dark Dimension

The Dreamqueen watched it all unfold through Umar's dimensional window. Though she had initially used her gazing pool to communicate with Umar, the goddess had quickly established a link that allowed the two to confer through the window while freeing up the Dreamqueen's pool for more important things, like tracking Clea and her companions.

She saw the Golden One, Ardina, climbing the stairs to hand Umar the Talisman's Coronet of Power – something demoness and goddess had *not* agreed upon – when suddenly the living statue threw the coronet back to Elizabeth and then punched Umar in the face, so hard that both goddess and throne toppled. When the Golden One ran back down the steps and knelt there, unmoving, the Dreamqueen realized she must have been controlled by one of the others, most likely Clea, who had remained immobile during Ardina's revolt.

She watched with interest as a spirit appeared and moved to protect the Pink and Green Ones. The Dreamqueen recognized her from the Pink One's dreamscans – Agatha Harkness. Or, rather, her ghost. Still more powerful in death than most practitioners ever became in life.

The Dreamqueen didn't recognize the spell Umar's daughter cast with the five witches linked over the Golden One's head, but she saw Umar appear above the dais as the Purple One was completing the incantation and watched intently as the goddess unleashed a powerful bolt at the women just as they disappeared. She thought the spell might have struck the Pink One at the very last instant, but she couldn't be sure.

Then Umar was screaming in rage, the Flames of Regency flaring so brightly they obscured her demonic expression as she laid waste to her throne room and everyone who had been stupid enough not to have fled already.

At that point, the Dreamqueen broke the connection to the Dark Dimension and Umar's dimensional window disappeared. She didn't need to watch the goddess's tantrum. She'd had enough of them herself to know the destruction that would ensue, and she would just as soon not be a target for it.

Besides, as frustrating as this setback was, the witches still bore her dreamseeds, not all of which had bloomed. Her own plans for reaching Earth might yet come to fruition.

With a sigh, the Dreamqueen sat back in her throne to wait.

The Parringtons' Private Beach

"She's not breathing!" Elizabeth yelled as she knelt in the sand beside Holly's body. She turned to Agatha, accusation plain to read in every line of her face. "*Do* something!"

For a moment, it seemed like Agatha might argue. Then she sighed, closed her eyes, and murmured an incantation none of the others could quite make out. As Clea watched in amazement, the spear head protruding from Holly's chest retracted and the wound that it had caused knit itself back together, organs, muscle, tissue, and all, almost as if the old witch had reversed time. And maybe she had; she was clearly one of the most powerful practitioners on Earth. If she could do this as a spirit, what had she been capable of while alive?

Elizabeth quickly laid her head against Holly's chest, so she missed the way that Agatha deflated. Powerful or no, the spell had taken a great deal out of her. Clea wondered how long the woman's spirit could possibly continue to manifest after such an energy drain.

Then Elizabeth moved her head frantically to Holly's, and Clea realized she was checking for Holly's breath. She must not have detected a heartbeat.

"She's still not breathing!" Elizabeth snapped angrily, not even bothering to look at Agatha as she placed her hands on Holly's chest and began doing compressions, counting under her breath. After thirty compressions, she stopped and opened Holly's mouth, sweeping it with her finger to clear it of obstructions. Then she tilted the other woman's head back and breathed into her mouth twice, allowing Holly's chest to rise and fall between breaths. And then she started compressions again. From her huge eyes, clenched jaw, and corpse-white face, it was clear that she was trying hard not to panic, and not doing a very good job.

Sorrow and guilt warred in Clea's heart as she watched the Tsuut'ina woman try to revive the young witch. Holly would never have gotten hurt if she hadn't so freely agreed to help Clea, not because she shared Clea's cause, but simply because Clea needed her. If Holly died, it would be Clea's fault. She might as well have stabbed the young woman herself.

"I think Umar might have hit her with whatever that spell was, right as we teleported away," Margali said pensively, her face drawn with worry. "Healing the physical wound might not be enough."

"You think there was some magical backlash?" Clea asked.

"Hard to say."

As Elizabeth had been performing CPR on Holly, Agatha's spirit had floated down into the ground beside them so that she was only visible from the waist up. Clea supposed it was more palatable to the prim and proper witch than either kneeling or hovering cross-legged above the sand.

"Holly, I know you can still hear me, child. You need to fight to return to us," Agatha urged. Elizabeth's hands spasmed on Holly's chest and Clea thought that if she hadn't been in the middle of chest compressions, she might have launched herself at the ghost. "You are strong, capable, and brave. You always have been, and you never needed my affirmation to prove it. I wish you had understood that. I wish I had said it before now, so that you might have."

Elizabeth had just blown a second mouthful of air into Holly's lungs when the pink-haired witch suddenly drew in a deep, hitching breath.

"Holly! Oh, thank Creator!" Elizabeth said, placing her hand gently on the other woman's cheek.

Holly opened her eyes. She looked at Elizabeth, then at Agatha. There was no recognition in her face.

Alarmed, Elizabeth leaned close.

"Holly? Do you know who I am?" She gestured sharply with her chin over at Agatha. "Or her?"

Holly just stared at her, uncomprehending. Then her eyes fluttered closed, and her body relaxed. Her breathing became slow and even, and there was no movement behind her eyelids. Clea knew that lack of eye movement meant that Holly slept, but did not dream.

Elizabeth sat back on her heels, looking up in anguish at Clea. Her eyes glistened with tears she refused to shed.

"Magical brain death – the same thing that happened to me after putting the Pouch of the Void on my head. She may never walk or talk again, let alone be able to use magic."

Elizabeth closed her eyes against the pain of her next whispered words.

"Never know I don't blame her for her choice."

Then she opened her eyes again and looked over at Agatha.

"You should let me take care of her. I've been through this. I know what it takes to recover. When she wakes up, she'll be like a child, but given the proper treatment and enough time–"

"That won't be necessary," Agatha replied briskly, floating back up out of the sand so that she stood above Elizabeth, stiff and proud. "Holly is my charge, and I will see to her care. I do know how to take care of children."

Elizabeth stood so that she was face to face with Agatha, laughing scornfully.

"Really?" she scoffed. "Is that why your own son wants to kill you? Why Wanda *did*? As far as I can tell, your idea of childcare involves instilling them with crippling self-doubt.

"Holly wouldn't even be in this condition if it weren't for her toxic need for your approval, and her willingness to get herself killed to show you that she is just as worthy as your precious Scarlet Witch. Maybe if you hadn't waited until she was literally *dead* to tell her she already was, she would still–"

A quiet hiccup from Holly silenced her tirade. Everyone looked at the young witch, whose eyes were open again, but still cloudy with confusion. Her gaze met Clea's.

"Are we there yet?" she asked, her words slurred and slow. Then her eyes drifted shut again and she fell into the deeper sleep of coma.

Surprisingly, it was Agatha who answered, her voice as choked and full of emotion as Clea had ever heard it.

"Not yet, my child. But we will be. We will be."

And then she and Holly disappeared.

Elizabeth didn't stay much longer after that. She said goodbye to Margali, then walked over to where Clea stood talking quietly with Patsy Walker and Ardina. After introducing Patsy, Clea thanked Elizabeth for all her help and asked her what her plans were now.

"Go back home, continue serving my people as their spiritual leader, probably get in some good trouble. But not like my father did. I'll be doing it as just plain old Elizabeth Twoyoungmen, not as the Talisman. The Coronet of Power has caused me nothing but pain, and even though I may never be able to remove it, I don't have to use it. Besides, there's no good I can do as the Talisman that I can't do just as well as Elizabeth. Holly taught me that.

"Oh, and I'll probably spend some time plotting how to get her away from Agatha, or at least how to make the old witch let me see her. Want in?"

"Of course," Clea replied, her heart aching for her friend.

They hugged for a long time before Elizabeth finally stepped back, breaking the embrace.

"Stay well, Clea," Elizabeth said, and then, eyes glowing, she, too, disappeared.

Then it was Margali's turn to say goodbye. With her power beginning to wax again, she wasn't planning on returning home immediately. Now that Umar's connection to Ardina had been severed, and without the golden woman to energize it, her barrier spell had collapsed. So Margali was going back to the Winding Way to recharge. But first she was making a pit stop.

"I think I should look in on Amanda," the green-skinned sorceress said with a sheepish smile, and Clea no longer expected fangs when she saw the small, desultory upward curve. "And perhaps discuss certain shortcomings I may or may not have heretofore demonstrated as a mentor." She paused, and the smile turned regretful. "And as a mother."

The two Sorceresses Supreme embraced briefly, and then Clea's arms were suddenly empty. She turned to Ardina and Patsy.

"I will depart as well," Ardina said. "I believe I need a vacation from this vacation."

And with that, the golden woman flew up into the air, buoyed by the Power Cosmic. Then she waved once, and was gone.

And then there were two.

"You think she's OK? What's to stop Umar from going after her again?" Patsy asked. "I mean, aside from crippling embarrassment?"

Clea flashed her a tired smile.

"Before I gave up possession of Ardina's body, I put a 'Nothing to See Here' spell on her, with her permission," she replied. "One that would only affect Umar. I also apologized for unwittingly making her a target, but she's still basically a newborn and amazingly just views it all as a 'learning experience.'"

"Possession, huh? Wanna come up to the beach house for lemonade and fresh cookies and tell me about it?" Patsy ventured. "You look like you could use them."

Clea shook her head.

"Thank you, but no. I must return to my rebels. Who knows what vengeance my mother may try to take on them in her anger over losing Ardina?"

Patsy nodded.

"I totally get it." She hesitated for a moment, then abruptly flung her arms around Clea and gave her a quick, hard squeeze. "I don't know how to thank you for rescuing Ardina. I wouldn't have been able to live with myself if Umar had done something terrible to her." She hesitated. "Well, more terrible."

"You're welcome," Clea replied. There didn't seem to be anything else to say. Or else there was just too much. Because terrible things hadn't just happened to Ardina, but to all the women who had helped Clea, and that was something *she* had to live with.

But Clea knew that was part of what it meant to be a leader. Of rebellions, and sometimes, of families.

She was about to cast the teleportation spell that would take her back to rebel headquarters to rendezvous with whatever was left of her rebellion when she paused.

"Oh, and Patsy?" she said lightly.

"Yeah?" Patsy asked, her tone suddenly guarded. Clea was rarely flippant.

"Remember how you and the Defenders owed me that big favor before?"

"Yeah?" Patsy repeated. Clea hadn't known it was possible to pack that much trepidation into a single word.

"Now you owe me two."

Acknowledgments

First and foremost, I want to thank all the folks at Aconyte Books and Marvel Entertainment for giving me the opportunity to play in this sandbox with such kickass characters; it has been a dream come true. I especially want to thank Lottie, who is hands down one of the best editors I have ever worked with. Everything in this book that is good, she made better.

I also want to thank all the Marvel fans who love these characters as much as I do, both for their support and for their invaluable wikis (of which I made liberal use), as well as my fellow Aconyte authors who welcomed me into the fold, especially Carrie Harris, who is the bomb diggidiest.

Finally, I want to thank Catherine and Sir Speedy, because I said I would. And my family, always, for their unflagging support and patience while I worked on this book, especially my amazing husband Jeff, who picks up all my slack. Love you most!

About the Author

MARSHEILA (Marcy) ROCKWELL is an award-nominated tie-in writer and poet. Her novels include SF/H thriller *7 Sykos*, as well as The Shard Axe series, set in the world of *Dungeons & Dragons Online*. She has published two collections, and has written dozens of short stories, poems, and comic book scripts. She lives in the desert with her family, buried under books.

marsheilarockwell.com

MIGHTY HEROES
NOTORIOUS VILLAINS

POWERFUL STORIES
ICONIC HEROINES

MARVEL HEROINES